The Mansion of Mirrors

PER JACOBSEN

HUMBLEBOOKS

THE MANSION OF MIRRORS

Copyright © 2020
Per Jacobsen & HumbleBooks
1st US edition, 2025

Cover art: Per Jacobsen

ISBN (paperback): 978-87-94319-35-5
ISBN (hardback): 978-87-94319-36-2

All rights reserved.

This book is dedicated to **Stefan Grave**, *whose untimely death sent me on my first journey through the Wastelands of Urari. Back then, my search for the Mansion of Mirrors ended blindly. Only now, more than twenty years later, have I been able to gather the courage to return.*

—Per Jacobsen

FOREWORD

Dear Reader,

Before we start, I'd like to tell you a bit about the book you're about to read—because there's a fair chance that you and I have met before through one of my other stories. And if that's the case, you may have certain expectations of this one.

Now, for the most part, your expectations will be met, as *The Mansion of Mirrors* fits my usual M.O. The themes are dark, no one is safe, and there's no guarantee of a happy ending.

However, this book is also a bit different from the others. The reason is pretty simple, though: although it's being released as my eighth book on the international market, *The Mansion of Mirrors* is actually the first novel I ever published. It was originally released by a Danish publishing house in 2020, and I only recently got the rights back, allowing me to translate it and bring it to my international readers.

So, this is my first novel—and not only that, it's also the first story I ever wrote. You see, it wasn't really in the cards for me to become a writer. I didn't grow up dreaming of publishing novels, nor do I have a drawer full of unpublished stories that I just had to get out. I only discovered—relatively late in life and mostly by accident—that I had stories to tell.

And since *Mansion* is my first written work, it's also the story that taught me all the basics of the craft. I must admit that, at times, I was speeding down the highway with my eyes closed. But I learned a lot from this book, and if you look for it, I'm pretty sure you'll be able to spot a development in my writing style throughout the novel—especially if you've read some of my other stories.

Another difference is the genre. *The Mansion of Mirrors* has an element of fantasy that you won't find in my other books. That shouldn't matter too much, though, as I rarely stick to one genre anyway. I like to mix and match. Besides, my regular readers will know my opinion on genre: it's just the wrapping around the real story. Most good stories could work in any genre.

Okay, I've said what I needed to say. Let's see what's on the other side of that mirror, shall we?

PER JACOBSEN

*"Hell isn't fire.
Hell is a hall full of mirrors."*
—TOM CERVEAU

PART ONE
GIVEN YOUR SITUATION

PROLOGUE 1

For some artists, it starts with the blank canvas. For others—arguably the best—it starts with the final motif. The best don't see the glossy surface of the canvas. They see the picture.

This is also the case for the boy who now sits in the warm lamplight in front of a blank canvas. He doesn't see the frame, nor the white fabric stretched across it. He sees only the image that has called him up from his sleep and drawn him to the desk and the blank canvas.

For now, the picture is clear, but experience has taught him that it won't necessarily stay that way. Like dreams, the images are fleeting, and if you don't know how to grab ahold of them, they can crumble and disappear right in front of you. Therefore, he doesn't hesitate to reach for the tools that will help him immortalize it.

He starts by making the outline of the central motif; A girl sitting on her knees, hunched over. As more details are added, it becomes clear that the girl's hands are resting on her own shoulders, clinging to them as if she is trying to embrace herself. She sits with her back turned, so her face is hidden from the viewer. Never-

theless, the young artist manages to make the lines that his brush leaves on the fabric come together into an unambiguous message: The girl is grieving.

I

Jean Cocteau was right, he thinks, as he stands there in front of the mirror in his bathroom. *Mirrors should reflect a little more on what they show us.*

Michael Bendixen is only thirty-three years old, yet the man staring back at him seems much older. The deep, marine-blue eyes, which during his teen years were his strongest weapon in the battle for the favor of the opposite sex, have taken on a grayish hue and appear expressionless. Underneath them lies a network of furrowed wrinkles that he has never noticed before.

As if expecting to be able to wipe away the wrinkles, he raises his hand and runs a finger beneath his eye. When that doesn't work, he leans over the sink, turns on the tap, and lets the cold water flow freely over his hands for a moment before shaping them into a bowl and bringing them up to his face.

A stinging sensation spreads through his skin when the water splashes against his cheeks, but it doesn't have the desired effect. The uneasiness in his body that drew him out to the mirror in the first place still lingers. In fact, it increases, and while he closes his eyes and feels his way over the tiles to the towel on the wall, it grows into an absurd thought:

The bathroom will be gone. When he opens his eyes, it simply won't be there anymore, and he will find himself isolated in some godforsaken place. A desert, maybe.

On the rational level, he is obviously aware that this idea is completely insane. Still, it seems so real that he can almost hear the wind pushing tumbleweeds over the sandbanks and crows violating the calm of twilight with their shrieks.

Slowly, he lowers the towel and opens his eyes. Meeting his own gaze behind the glass this time, he is relieved to find that the anxiety attack—if that is the explanation—has passed. The bathroom is still there, the sound of screeching crows has been replaced by a lawnmower engine at one of the neighbors' houses, and the man in the mirror is once again Michael Bendixen, a thirty-three-year-old high school teacher.

He starts to turn away from the mirror but hesitates as his gaze catches something on the sink next to the tap. Something small and light brown. He picks it up by pressing the tip of his finger down on it—and feels a chill run down his spine when realizing what it is.

Three tiny grains of sand. Were they there a moment ago?

As if to emphasize the question, his cell phone starts to vibrate with a soft:

Hmm ... hmm ... hmm ...

The phone lies on the kitchen table alongside a stack of flyers that somehow made it past the *No Junk Mail* sign they put up the year before. His wife, Ann, has—after a lot of campaigning—convinced him that advertising flyers are the root of all evil when you have a ten-year-old son.

Poverty guarantee with glossy toy illustrations was the main slogan of her campaign, and, as with so many other debates, Michael had to concede she was right.

That was nothing new, though. The fact that Ann usually has the better arguments and the deeper insight is the rule rather than the exception—even though he is the one who teaches psychology.

He'd never dream of complaining about it, though. After all, Ann's intelligence, along with her ability to always bring out the best in others, is the main reason he chose to share his life with her.

He picks up the phone from the table and taps the green icon.

"Hello, Michael speaking."

"Oh? Yes, hello," says a man's voice on the other end, its tone suggesting that its owner wasn't expecting the call to be answered. However, it doesn't take many seconds before its brought down to a calm and thoughtful pitch. "You're speaking to Erik Starck. I'm calling from the County Library regarding . . . is this a bad time?"

"No, it's fine. How can I help you?"

"It's about a problem that we've had with your profile here at the library in connection with the implementation of our new system. There have been a number of teething problems, and unfortunately, your profile has been hit pretty badly. We don't know why, but the system keeps registering new loans in your name."

"I see. And I'm guessing that also means a bunch of fines?"

"Well, sadly yes. One of the consequences is that the circulation fees are piling up on your profile."

"But I haven't received any reminders," Michael says as he roams through the flyers on the kitchen table with his free hand to check if there is a letter from the library hidden somewhere. "I should have gotten a bunch of them, right?"

For a moment, there is silence at the other end of the line, as though the question has rendered the librarian speechless. Then he clears his throat and says:

"Well, you would have, but we turned off all automatic emails and letters in the system as soon as we became aware of the problem. So that part is under control. Unfortunately, we have not been successful in stopping it from adding new loans to your profile. Hence, you will probably have to create a new profile and delete the old one."

"Aha," Michael says. "I'm guessing I can do that online?"

"Well, if it's not too much of a hassle, it'd be best if you could come in person," the librarian says. "You see, I'll need your signature to set up a new library account. Technically, you *could* do it from home, but with all the issues we've had, I'd much rather handle it the old-fashioned way. Would that be a big problem?"

"Not at all," Michael says. Although he isn't overly enthusiastic about the solution, he can easily follow the librarian's way of thinking. Being employed in the public sector himself, he knows all too well the challenges of IT systems on public budgets. "I work at Oakwood High, which is close by, so I'm happy to swing by. I'm just impressed that you actually called me in person to inform me. You should be commended for that."

"Of course. That's the least we can do . . . given your situation."

Something about the way the librarian hesitated before the last three words bothers Michael. He can't quite put his finger on it, but it's as if that slight pause makes the words sound awfully solemn. As though the librarian knows something he doesn't—and that the situation he's referring to is something completely different.

"Um, yeah . . . why don't we say that I swing by after work tomorrow? I'm off at a little past four."

"It's up to you," the librarian says. "You just come by whenever you're able."

Whenever you're able. There's nothing inherently wrong with this phrasing, but coming right after the other words, it sends an unsettling prickle down Michael's neck. Therefore, he is relieved when the man on the other end of the line takes the initiative to end the conversation with the words:

"Well, I'd better get on with today's work."

"Huh? Oh yeah, of course. Thank you again, and I'll make sure to swing by the library as soon as possible."

"You're welcome. Goodbye."

"Goodbye."

After the conversation, Michael pulls a small yellow note from his work bag, writes *Library issue* on it, and places it loosely between the pages of his calendar.

Before returning the calendar to his bag, he adjusts the position of the photo that he has placed behind the plastic of its cover.

The picture is one he took on a cold and cloudy December day three years ago, yet it always fills him with warmth. On it, a seven-year-old version of his son, Benjamin, sits with one hand outstretched. Between two of his fingers crawls a small lizard, and under the hood of the raincoat, the winter-red nose and the blue eyes on the boy's face are drawn together in an expression of unreserved wonder. Maybe even a stronger feeling. Because Benjamin loves animals, he always has, and whether they have four or eight legs, fur, skin, or scales doesn't really matter.

Once the calendar is back in place in his work bag, Michael glances out the window and then up at the clock above the bulletin board.

Quarter past four . . . and the driveway is still empty. It shouldn't be. They should be home by now. It's Wednesday, so he knows Ann gets off work at 2:30. He can't remember if Benjamin finishes at the same time, but usually, the boy spends the waiting time doing homework on the days he goes shopping with his mom before they head home.

Michael reassures himself that it's probably just the usual traffic jam on the Haywood Bridge and then picks up a flyer from the top of the stack. With FullCart's best offers in hand, he then walks into the living room and takes a seat in his favorite chair; a classic Chesterfield in dark brown leather.

Sitting there in the autumn sun's rays from the window, slowly surrendering to the enticing siren song of sleep, Michael hears the sound of a car parking in the driveway and breathes a sigh of relief. His relief is short-lived, though, as the sound he is waiting for next—Ann and Benjamin yelling that they're home—never comes. What he gets instead are three short knocks, followed by a sharp, metallic ringing from the doorbell.

As he gets up from the armchair and walks out into the hallway, he considers if Ann could have somehow left her keys at home. That thought can quickly be dismissed, though, since she and Benjamin took the car today. Besides, the silhouette waiting behind the frosted glass of the door is at least a head taller than Ann could ever hope to be, even with the highest stiletto heels on the market.

With that thought in his head, Michael straightens his shirt collar and puts on his most welcoming smile, after which he opens the door . . . and freezes.

The person on the other side of the frosted glass indeed isn't his wife. It's a police officer.

"Are you Michael Bendixen?"

The sight of the police uniform has Michael's heart beating

so hard that the man's words are muffled behind the sound of his own pulse. But he doesn't need to hear them clearly, because he has a deeply disturbing premonition at this moment. A sense of what's about to happen, so strong that it feels like an indisputable knowledge.

"I, yeah . . . yes, that's me."

The pale man in the police uniform nods and pulls the corners of his mouth up in the hint of a smile that makes the hairs on Michael's neck stand up. Undoubtedly, it's just a service smile —a rehearsed expression the officer keeps in reserve for easing the tension in uncomfortable situations where some tragic news needs to be delivered. But accompanied by the large and shiny pupils in the man's eyes, that smile seems eerily real.

"Married to Ann Bendixen?"

Michael replies with a hesitant nod, and the officer's face takes on a different, far more compassionate expression, putting to shame the idea that he should have found the situation amusing.

"And the father of Benjamin Bendixen?"

Without him even noticing, Michael's one hand slides over and grabs the doorframe. Hooks onto it. He tries to answer, tries to force the words over his lips, but they refuse to come out, and he has to settle for another nod.

The officer stares down at his folded hands for a long, nerve-wracking moment. Then he takes a deep breath and nods.

"There really is no easy way to say this," he says.

Three weeks after the day when Michael Bendixen opened the door to a police officer and watched his world crumble, he is still far from ready to go back to work. He decides to do so anyway.

Not because he has studied psychology for five years and understands the importance of everyday routines for processing grief. By now, he has realized that one doesn't necessarily understand what grief truly entails, just because one has read what Cullberg has to say on the subject.

No, Michael decides to return because every single night since the terrible car accident that claimed the lives of both his wife and his son, he has been haunted by different variations of the same nightmare—and because this night's version has been the worst so far. He is, quite simply, starting to fear that the demons of the night will eventually drive him insane if he lets them.

The nightmare takes place in a huge, dark hall, in which the only source of light is a dusty column of moonlight streaming in through a skylight. Below it, he finds himself wandering among endless rows of sheet-covered mirrors, arranged with such meticulous precision that they resemble pieces in a massive domino run.

What in the dream enables him to determine that it's mirrors hiding under the dusty, burgundy red sheets, he doesn't know. Nevertheless, he doesn't doubt it for a second.

In the same way, he instinctively knows that the low, jarring chorus of voices that all of a sudden rises from the darkness belongs to them. It's the voices of the mirrors, and it's *him* they're calling out to. There is something in this large, dark hall that they want him to see.

With hesitant steps, he moves in the direction of the sound, and as row upon row of burgundy shadows glide by at the edges of his field of vision, Michael notices an unsettling detail about the mirrors. Like tombstones in a graveyard, they all bear names. They're engraved on small bronze plaques hanging from chains draped between the twisted, ornate legs jutting out from beneath the sheets.

This realization fills him with an unpleasant suspicion, and shortly afterward, upon entering the passage where the mysterious voices seem to come from, it's confirmed.

The mirror is one among hundreds of others, all covered by the same dusty sheets, and if it weren't for the bronze plaque, it would have been impossible to distinguish this one from the others.

But the plaque is there, and although Michael at some level of his consciousness is prepared for it to carry his son's name, he still feels a fierce, suffocating panic seeing it on the inscription.

With his heart pounding against his ribs, he runs to the mirror and grabs the sheet. As he pulls, a cloud of white dust swirls up in the cold glow of the moonlight. For a moment, they linger there, like a glittering, blue-white winter fog, before slowly falling to the floor.

Michael is numb, frozen like a statue. What he is staring at *is* a mirror, but it's not the reflection of his own face that he sees on the other side of its glass. It's a door. A door that he recognizes with devastating terror.

Behind the glass, a hand—*his* hand—reaches out and grabs the handle. The door opens, leaving Michael to once again stare into the pale face of the man tasked with blowing his life to atoms.

However, one detail has changed this time around. The officer isn't standing in Michael's driveway. It has been replaced by a barren desert landscape with charred trees casting long, unsettling shadows toward him.

"Are you Michael Bendixen?" the officer asks in a shrill, almost unreal voice. His eyes are like polished black marbles in his pale face.

Michael wants to look away, escape them, yet something keeps him fixated on those pitch-black pupils.

"Are you Michael Bendixen?" the officer repeats. Behind him, the red sun creeps down, hiding behind the horizon line, as if afraid he should turn around and look at it.

"ARE YOU, MICHAEL? ARE YOU?" This time the officer shouts, and it seems like he is getting closer, even though he isn't moving at all.

"ARE YOU MICHAEL BENDIXEN?" Behind the maggoty-white skin of his face, a network of faint blue veins pulsates. A smile grows on his chapped lips.

"MARRIED TO ANN BENDIXEN?" He pauses, and the smile turns into a wide, hysterical grin.

"FATHER OF . . ." He reaches to pull something out from behind the left side of the frame. ". . . *THIS GUY?*"

At 7:45 a.m. Michael wakes up with the image of his screaming son, trapped in the officer's arms, burned onto his retinas. It's this image that motivates him to pick up his phone and call his workplace to let them know that he would like to return as soon as possible.

2

In the yard outside Oakwood High School, a massive oak tree stands as a majestic centerpiece. On a bench in front of this tree, Lisa Swann sits in the autumn sunlight, spending a free period pondering if things will ever change. If there will ever come a day when people around her see her as more than the weird girl with the blonde hair and the colorful bracelets, who always keeps to herself. A day when they'll no longer look down and seem engrossed in their own thoughts the moment they catch sight of her.

She had hoped things would change when she transferred to the new school. That she would get the fresh start that her mom promised her. But Helena Swann was horribly mistaken, and her daughter came to realize that rumors respect neither school changes nor municipal borders.

It's been more than a year since it happened, but for Lisa, it seems like no more than a week. Apparently, this goes for everyone else too. They'll make sure to recap her story every chance they get—especially if her back is turned.

Above her, a gray cloud covers the autumn sun while she leans forward and stubs out her cigarette on the pavement.

You heard what happened to her sister, right? I've heard that . . . shh, here she comes.

They're so damned busy. Still, in a way, it's the teachers who are the worst. Lisa hates the teachers who always scan the room at the beginning of class to check if she's there. It's as if they cannot possibly start without giving her the obligatory look of pity first.

On the other hand, she could be imagining it. She could just be paranoid, like her mom says. Maybe all of it is in her head.

But so what? she thinks to herself. *You're still sitting here, alone on a bench. In the end, it's the same result.*

She puts her hands against the cracked surface of the wooden bench and pushes herself up. The wood creaks ominously beneath her, despite her measly 114 pounds.

Lisa has always been a slim girl, but the past year has been tough, and that word isn't really adequate anymore. She has become *scrawny*.

Behind her, a window creaks open with a sharp, metallic screech. Lisa pulls her phone out of her pocket to check the time. Still five minutes until class starts. Time enough for one more cigarette—and one more round in the ring with the question that torments her.

What if she asked for microphone time at a Friday assembly and served it to them, no filter? What would happen if she just walked up on the podium and tapped the microphone the way they always do in movies?

Yeah, hi. My name is Lisa Swann. I've noticed all of you are afraid to look me in the eye. I'm guessing it's because of the tragedy that struck my family last year.

She lights a fresh cigarette and discovers that her hands have started shaking, causing the row of purple and yellow bracelets around her left wrist to dance like a little, multicolored caterpillar.

You probably have a load of questions about the incident, but I only caught the final part. So, I can only tell you what it felt like to see my little sister sitting with . . .

In Lisa's head, a new voice breaks in. She knows it well, actually assumes that most people have their own variation of it. It's the voice that tells you to stop before entering areas of the mind where red *DO NOT ENTER* lights are flashing. In Lisa's version, it's usually a distorted version of her mom's voice that tries its best to keep her away from the dark places that the tragedy has opened the doors into.

This time, however, the voice's efforts are unnecessary, because from the open window behind her, Lisa hears the students starting to fill the classrooms again. That's her cue.

While she mentally prepares for another game of *Dodge My Gaze* and goes inside, the autumn wind behind Lisa struggles to pull leaves off the oak tree in the center of the schoolyard. The vast majority have withered already. Only a few hopeful green leaves are still holding on. But it will only be a matter of time before they, too, must give in to the strong wind.

While her history teacher struggles to keep the attention of the class during the second-to-last period of the day, Lisa sits in her chair at the back of the room, doodling in the corners of her notebook. The teacher, Bridget, is a hunched woman with white hair and a lined face, revealing that her retirement isn't far off. Even so, she has somehow managed to keep her passion for teaching alive. But even the best have their off days—and today,

Bridget is having what Lisa's grandpa would've called a *lukewarm coffee kind of day*.

Lisa smiles at the memory of her granddad, always trudging around in the cornfield in blue overalls and rubber boots. She adored that man. He was the most sincere and good-natured person she has known in her life, and it was a colossal shock when cancer stole him from her. It was the first time she really understood what it means when a person dies.

Now, she knows all too well.

"Pass on to Rose."

Lisa looks up. The soft whisper came from the student sitting next to her, a girl called Kitty, who is now making a *come-on* gesture while sliding a folded piece of paper toward her.

Lisa puts her hand on the paper, discreetly rolling her eyes as she slides it farther. Still, deep inside, she feels a sting of nostalgia. It's been a long time since she was the one waiting to see if a private message from a friend would make it under the teacher's radar and reach her.

On the whiteboard, Bridget has just written: *William Penn—Visionary or Opportunist?* in her curvy, hurried handwriting, and she now proceeds to explain how groundbreaking Penn's ideas about religious freedom and peaceful relations with the natives were. She is fighting valiantly, although it has hardly escaped her attention that the entire room is buzzing with rocking chairs and drumming fingers—and that even the most tireless students have begun to look for shapes in the clouds of the autumn sky outside the window.

Meanwhile, Lisa closes her eyes and travels back to a better time. In her mind's eye, she sees herself at five years old, sitting next to her sister, Emma, on the couch in her childhood home. On the table in front of them is a glass bowl filled with popcorn, shining enticingly in the glow of the TV. On the screen, they're watching Timon and Pumbaa burst into song to introduce Simba to their *problem-free philosophy*. In the kitchen behind them, their mom is rattling with plates while she cheerfully hums along to the chorus.

It's a good memory. Lisa often uses it when she needs to get away from all the people who are *oh-so-busy* looking away when they see her. Or worse yet, sending her pity-looks. When she hides in that memory, it's as if her sister and her dad are still with her, and that they're still just a normal family. As if she is still that little, innocent girl who isn't constantly on the verge of a breakdown because she hears voices and sees scary stuff in mirrors. Stuff that isn't even real.

Her own thought catches her off guard, and to her horror, the mental photograph of her childhood memory starts to crack.

She needs to focus now, because she has a nasty hunch about what's hiding behind it. That she occasionally gets a glimpse of that damned desert in the mirrors at home is plenty. She has no desire to be tormented by the creepy landscape during school hours as well.

Breathe, she commands herself. *Just take a deep breath and relax.*

In her head, she describes the details of her childhood memory to herself: the wooden coffee table with the popcorn bowl, the two cushions on the couch that shared a cloudy, brown smudge from the time her dad was surprised by the cat and spilled his coffee.

That memory brings a gentle smile to her lips. Her otherwise masculine father, a man with a capital M—emphasized by him earning his living as a lumberjack—had screamed like a little girl back then. He was completely absorbed in his TV show when the cat's tail stroked the back of his neck and sent him flying with a squeal.

Must have been the only time she ever heard her dad scream, she thinks, but then a new, unpleasant thought crashes into her mind.

It wasn't the only time. There was one more time, and at that moment, he was *really* scared. With good reason too, because that was the night when it happened. The night when life changed forever for Lisa and her mom.

Upset by yet another unforeseen sidetrack, Lisa puts one hand over the other and squeezes it, attempting to drown out the thoughts with pain. She keeps pressing until her knuckles turn chalky white, and it's throbbing all the way up her arm.

Get a grip. Find the image again. The popcorn was always salted, with lots of hot butter. They crunched when we chewed on them—and sometimes the seeds got stuck, so it looked like we had black holes in our teeth. That always made us laugh.

She concentrates on remembering what her sister looked like when she gave her a wide smile with those black holes in her teeth. She draws every detail she can think of: Emma's smooth, dark hair, which started in a middle parting and ended slightly below the chin, where the tips met and made her face look like a small, white heart. The cat-like, green eyes that both of them got from their mom. Emma's red *Winnie the Pooh* T-shirt, which was perfectly oversized, allowing her to tug her bare legs in under it if she was cold.

As Lisa's knuckles slowly regain their rosy glow, her focus drifts back to the classroom. The hands on the clock above the door read 1:54 p.m. One more minute until the next break. Just one more class after that and then a quick trip to the library to return *Walk it Off* before she can head home and unwind. Maybe snack on some popcorn—if there's any left in the cupboard.

3

All things considered, Michael's first lesson is going well. Although most, if not all, of the students by now must have heard what happened, he started the class with a brief account of his situation. He also gave them the opportunity to ask questions, but no one did. Presumably, it's not because they aren't curious about it or don't feel sorry for him, but talking about death, which can be difficult for adults, can be extremely overwhelming for teenagers.

At the moment, though, this suits Michael just fine. After a full hour in the teacher's lounge with colleagues hesitantly forcing themselves to approach him to ask the same questions and utter the same words of compassion, it's liberating just having to focus on teaching.

Today's topic is a summary of the basic principles of behaviorism, and Michael is happy to discover that whoever substituted during his absence has done an excellent job. Many of the students seem genuinely interested and eagerly raise their hands. The vast majority are also able to answer his questions—

even the difficult ones about the difference between Ivan Pavlov's concepts of punishment and negative reinforcement.

At first, Michael wondered if the high level of participation was an attempt to keep the conversation going, thus keeping it from circling back to his loss. He dismissed that idea pretty quickly, though, since everyone came prepared with detailed notes and no one seems worried about him bringing up his situation again.

That's the least we can do . . . given your situation.

The memory of those words—and the uncanny feeling he got when the man from the library said them—makes Michael stiffen. He tries to recall what time of day the librarian called. Could he have known? Is that even . . .

"Um, Michael?" It's Marcus, one of his favorite students, who is now staring at the whiteboard, obviously both confused and worried. "I think there's something missing. Don't you mean *operant*?"

Michael follows the boy's gaze and discovers that he has indeed stopped halfway through a word. What should have been *Operant Conditioning* never got further than *Opera*.

As he turns back around, Michael clearly feels the students observing his face, *analyzing* it. He fends off their concern with an easygoing smile and shrugs.

"Alright, we need to get some group work going. No more than five in each, and you're welcome to work outside the classroom—as long as you come up here first and tell me where you're hiding."

Only one group chooses to leave the classroom. The rest sit in scattered clusters, quietly debating among themselves, while Michael searches for the small yellow note he tucked into his planner after talking to the man from the library.

It seems high time he went over there.

∽

As always, when the bell signals the end of the last class, the school's main hallway is invaded by a chaotic swarm of young people. They weave in and out of each other's paths, and joining them, Michael can't help but think that they look like fish in an aquarium right after the food pellets have hit the water's surface. A few move calmly, absorbed in their own thoughts, but the vast majority charges ahead, determined not to miss their buses and trains.

To the untrained eye, the crowd may seem overwhelming, but Michael knows that there is a structure behind the madness. At this time of day, everyone has the same destination, and just like migratory birds, they can easily zip around, greeting other members of the flock, without forgetting that the goal—*freedom*—lies just outside the glass doors of the main entrance. For them, the sound of the bell is a signal that the worst part of the day is over.

For him, it's a signal that it has only just begun.

"DAD!"

The high-pitched scream comes out of nowhere, startling Michael so badly that he barely manages to keep the stack of textbooks in his hands from falling to the floor.

He looks around, first in the direction of the door to the bathroom, where the voice seemingly came from, then at the faces of the nearest migratory birds. None of the kids in his immediate vicinity seem to have registered the sound or his reaction to it.

His gaze falls back on the door to the bathroom. It's ajar, a narrow beam of bluish light flickering restlessly on the floor in front of it every time one of the students walks past. The sound *did* come from in there, he's certain of it. Despite its unnatural, muddy sound, he's also sure who the voice belonged to.

And had he felt any doubt, that one deeply unsettling word the voice—a boy's voice, mind you—chose to shout would have settled the matter. The word *Dad*.

Michael is sure of all these things, but above all he is sure of something else. The voice isn't real. His reasoning? He appears to be the only one who heard it, and it's not the first time something like this has happened. Because on top of the terrible nightmares, there has been another unsettling side effect over the past few weeks, namely that he often thinks he recognizes his wife and his son in the faces of strangers on the street.

As a psychology teacher, he knows that it's not uncommon for people in grief to see and hear their lost loved ones in all kinds of places. Consequently, he has tried his best to ignore it when it happens to him. He sees it for what it is: hallucinations brought on by grief, nothing more.

Yet, at this moment, something in his body insists on disregarding the protests from the rational part of his brain and pulls his feet in the direction of the door to the bathroom.

You're a psychology teacher, damn it, he says to himself as his hand grabs the door handle. *You spend hours and hours explaining to students that, according to Piaget, magical thinking ceases around the age of seven. So, what exactly are you hoping to achieve here, dumbass?*

The door slides open, exposing a room that looks exactly like what you'd expect from a high school restroom; crumpled toilet paper on the floor, dried-out water stains on the mirror, and doodles on the wall next to the paper dispenser . . . and, of course, no panic-stricken ten-year-old boys calling for their dad.

He stays in the doorway for a while, his brain racing at full speed to find a plausible, psychological explanation for his behavior. He settles on a psychoanalytic temporary regression to an age where magical thinking still holds sway.

That would make sense, he concludes, nodding to himself. *The grief activates a defense mechanism, which pushes my mind back to . . . what? The age of five? Yeah, that must be it.*

With a strange mixture of rational relief and emotional disappointment in his body, he reaches over to the wall and turns off the light switch. Next, he turns his back on the empty restroom and steps out to reclaim his spot among the migratory birds whizzing across the white-speckled floor of Oakwood High's main hallway.

4

Beneath the gray canopy covering the bicycle racks outside the school, Lisa Swann stands, sighing loudly. Her otherwise faithful steed—a worn, light blue women's bike—has a flat tire. It won't have major consequences for her plan to return the book, since the library is only a few hundred yards away, within walking distance of the school. The real challenge is the walk home afterward.

"It's gonna be one hell of a hike," she mumbles, annoyed at the prospect of having to climb the steep hill between the school and her home on foot.

Shortly after her sister and dad died, Lisa and her mom moved to the city. The country house they used to live in was far too big for a single mom and her daughter, so they found a small apartment in Newcrest instead. Of course, this means that they are no longer able to enjoy the benefits of a life in the countryside—such as cranking up the stereo and running around in the backyard hurling water balloons at each other. But in the time following the loss, the desire for those kinds of games faded anyway.

To make sure that the trip to the library won't be a waste of time, Lisa checks her bag one more time before she starts walking. The book is where it's supposed to be, and seeing it, the irony makes her smile. She is on her way to the library to return *Walk it Off*... on the very day her bike gets a flat, so she's forced to walk home.

Lisa loves that book. She must have read it five or six times over the past three years, not to mention the interdisciplinary paper in psychology and English she has just turned in. Randall Morgan, more than any other author she knows, has a way of capturing the essence of human behavior under extreme conditions. That was the conclusion of her paper, and she feels pretty good about it.

Lisa has always been an *above-average* student, never really having to struggle with schoolwork. Of course, there was a rough patch after what happened with her dad and sister. *The incident.* That's how she usually refers to it. Using a word like that makes it feel more clinical, more detached. As though she's just observing something that happened to someone else. It helps her forget how Emma's piercing scream woke her up that evening. And how, even now, it lingers faintly in the shadows when she is lying in bed at night.

Something in her brain links that thought to what happened a few minutes earlier in the hallway. Passing the bathroom on the way out, she heard a boy's voice cut through the noise. It didn't belong to any of the students, she's sure of that. It was far too bright. Besides, it had a muddy tone that made it sound strange, almost dreamlike.

That fact that she heard a voice—which may well have been something she imagined—isn't really what bothers her. By now, she has accepted that her mind sometimes plays vicious tricks on her. Still, something was different this time. Firstly, it wasn't her sister's voice, which it usually is, and secondly, someone else apparently heard it too. One of the teachers.

At first, she thought that was another trick of her mind, but the more she thinks about it, the more convinced she is that he did, in fact, react to the sound. Not only did he raise his head and look around, she could swear that he, like her, decided that the sound of the shrill voice came from the half-open door to the bathroom.

You could go back and try to find him, she says to herself, but something in her immediately objects. She has been burned by that kind of thing before, and it wasn't exactly a fun lesson to learn.

In the first few months after the tragedy in their family, both Lisa and her mom started seeing a psychologist, and when the voices and visions started to appear, Lisa told the psychologist about it, hoping to get help. What she got wasn't help and support, though. Quite the contrary, actually. First of all, it quickly became clear that the psychologist interpreted confidentiality—specifically Lisa's wish that the content of their conversations weren't to be shared with her mom—quite freely. Secondly, the highly educated adult counselor's proposed solution could be boiled down to three simple, yet rather unhelpful pieces of advice: *Pull yourself together. Stop your craving for attention. Focus on daily routines.*

So no, while Lisa wishes she had someone to share her inner struggles with, the idea of going back isn't particularly appealing. Moreover, it feels risky; like opening a Pandora's box and letting out the repressed pain of the last thirteen months. Because whether she is right or not, seeking out the man from the hallway would force her to confront something she fears. If he didn't hear the voice, she'd have to face the possibility that she has finally lost it—*gone swimming in the loony lagoon*, as her granddad would have put it. And if he *did* hear it . . .

This last thought is very disturbing, so it's a welcome surprise when she looks up and discovers that she has already made it all the way to the library—and as the sliding glass doors pull aside, it's like they take her worries about her mental state with them.

5

The elderly gentleman behind the reference desk stares at Michael for a moment, then adjusts his glasses and squeezes his chin with the thumb and forefinger of his hand, feigning a heartfelt and sincere disbelief.

"As far as I know, we haven't had any problems with the IT system," he says, turning toward his colleague. "Alice, do you know anything about that? Apparently, this young man received a call from us. Something about a breakdown in our—"

He doesn't get any further before he is interrupted by another elderly gentleman stepping out from an open door next to the counter.

"I'll take this one, Carl," he says, upon which he makes eye contact with Michael across a box full of books that he is holding in his arms. "You must be Michael Bendixen, right?"

"Yeah, that . . . that's me."

The elderly gentleman nods, first to Michael, then to his colleague at the counter, who shrugs and moves on to the next patron in line.

"This way," the elderly gentleman with the box says, leading

Michael in the direction of the reading room—and once they've put some distance between themselves and the counter, he whispers: "Don't mind Carl. I'd bet fifty bucks that old geezer doesn't even know how to log into our IT system."

That old geezer? Michael finds this description somewhat ironic, since the man in front of him doesn't seem to be a day younger than his colleague. He does, however, have a far more charismatic presence.

"My name is Erik Starck," the man says. "I'd shake your hand, but . . ." He glances down at the box of books he is holding in his arms and shrugs. "I was the one who called you that day. The two of us have a couple of things we need to talk about. I'll probably have to put these books down in the basement first, though. Would it be too much trouble to ask you to wait for me in there?"

He nods in the direction of an open door that seems weirdly small compared to the two bookshelves flanking it. The room behind it looks like a small office.

"It'll only take five minutes. Ten, tops."

Before he has a chance to respond, Starck is already walking away, leaving Michael standing there, feeling a mixture of confusion and disappointment. Prior to the meeting, he had planned to figure out whether the man on the phone had actually expressed sympathy for his impending loss that day—something he couldn't possibly have known about at the time. That was the whole reason for visiting the library. Yet now, standing there, that idea seems completely nuts.

You need to get a handle on yourself, he says to himself. *Otherwise, you'll go mad.*

Deep down, though, he can't deny that there is something liberating in the idea of just letting go and going insane. Then he could spend his days in some institution blabbering about psychic librarians and little boys coming back to haunt him, all while the nurses try to lower the hallucination count with morphine-fermented mashed potatoes.

This image, equally ridiculous and frightening, puts everything back into perspective, and he shakes his head at his own paranoia.

He's gonna get a handle on the problem with the fines, and then it's straight home to relax on the couch and watch some mindless Netflix show. No more self-destructive ghost hunts—and certainly no more attempts to involve others in them.

Heading over to the bookshelves, planning to pass the wait with a little reading, it's this thought that fills Michael's head. At least until a nagging feeling creeps in, slowly but surely stealing his focus.

The feeling that he is being watched.

6

Standing there between the bookshelves, he doesn't attract much attention, and if Lisa hadn't happened to turn her head at exactly that moment, she probably wouldn't even have noticed the dark-haired man studying the blurb of one of the library's books.

But Lisa *did* glance to the side at that moment, and her gaze did land on him. The teacher from the hallway at the school. The one who also heard the voice.

You knock that stupid idea right out of your head, she hears her mom say in her mind. *You just walk on and get out of here before you make a fool of yourself.*

Although basically agreeing, Lisa only follows the advice to some extent. She does walk on, but just the seven feet it takes to bring her over to one of the library's public computers where she sits down. Behind its screen, she is out of the man's field of view —while still being able to watch him secretly by leaning to the side.

For good measure, she also places her school bag on the table, making sure it's upright. That way, she has it *and* the computer screen to hide behind if he should look in her direction. It does happen a couple of times, but she's not too concerned about it, as it, on both occasions, coincides perfectly with the group of teenage boys farther down the table bursting into laughter over some YouTube video. Besides, he seems very caught up in the book he is holding. He has turned it around now so she can see the front. It's a paperback edition of Andrew Van Wey's *Forsaken*, and it strikes her that it matches him eerily well. He definitely looks pretty forsaken as he stands there between two tall shelves.

Maybe she should take the chance and talk to him after all. What's the worst that could happen?

Even though that ball practically would be a guaranteed homerun, the inner version of her mom's voice refrains from batting. It's of no matter, though, because Lisa knows all too well what the worst would be. The things she is struggling with could be brought out into the light. Be presented to the outside world for everyone to analyze and assess—which might bring them to the conclusion that she fears the most. That she is mentally ill. Just like Emma.

Erasing this image requires a moment with her eyes shut, and when Lisa opens them again and directs her gaze to the man, she feels her stomach tighten.

He has put the book back on the shelf and now stands with his eyes squinted, staring in her direction.

No, not just in her direction. At her. Straight at her.

She locks her gaze on the computer, tries to fake a profound interest in the subject on the screen, while droplets of sweat trickle out in her temples.

His gaze doesn't wander. Neither does he. He just stays there, arms crossed, his blue eyes fixed on her. There is no anger or hostility in them, but there *is* curiosity, and for some reason that scares her just as much. If there was a moment earlier when she seriously considered approaching him, it's definitely gone now.

You just stay cool and get up, she says to herself. *If you walk out of here, not making a big deal of it, he'll lose interest.*

Despite the simplicity of the plan, its execution turns out to be tricky. She does get up and she does put the chair neatly back into place before leaving the table, but she is so nervous that every movement becomes clumsy and awkward.

In her eagerness to get away, she also completely forgets about her school bag. Only after having zigzagged through several aisles between the bookshelves, trying to ensure that she's out of sight, does it dawn on her that she left it on the table next to the computer.

Annoyed with herself, she changes direction and starts to walk back. She doesn't get very far, though, before stopping abruptly.

The man has followed her. He is standing at the end of the aisle she is in. Right in front of her.

The shock of getting caught in the act like this causes her to gasp and take a step backward.

"I'm sorry," the man says. "I didn't mean to startle you."

Lisa tries to say that it's okay, but the budding panic has closed her throat, and she has to content herself with shaking her head dismissively.

The man smiles. A friendly but also vigilant smile.

"You were in a bit of a hurry," he says. "And I think you forgot your school bag. It's still at the computer back there."

"Oh, um . . . yeah, I guess I did," Lisa stammers. "Thanks."

She smiles and nods at the man while trying to use her body language to signal that she'd like to move past him. He returns the smile but makes no effort to step aside.

"Also, I wanted to ask if there was anything I could help you with," he says. "I had this weird feeling that you were . . . keeping an eye on me back there. So, I thought maybe there was something you wanted to ask or . . .?"

Don't even think about it!

The warning comes promptly and in a very shrill version of her mom's voice. There is no doubt that her inner version of Helena Swann wishes to close this conversation as soon as possible.

And if Lisa had spent the next few seconds differently, she would undoubtedly have followed that advice. Had she kept her eyes fixed on the floor and spent a moment thinking it through, rather than meeting the man's gaze, the next words would never have crossed her lips.

Lisa doesn't, though. Instead, she looks up at the man and recognizes in his face the same exhaustion and loneliness that meets her every night in front of the mirror at home. And it's this recognition that makes the words spill from her mouth before she is able to stop them.

"You heard it too," she says. "Didn't you?"

7

"I'm not entirely sure I'm following you," Michael stammers. "What is it I'm supposed to have heard?"

Why he feels the need to play dumb and lie to the girl, he doesn't quite know. Maybe it's because the only explanation he can find is that she's talking about the voice he heard over in the hallway. And that, obviously, makes no sense.

"But I . . . I saw you," the girl says, the expression in her green eyes shifting. Up until this moment, they've had an anticipating, almost pleading expression, but now, it's turning into a sort of tormented embarrassment. "You *are* a teacher over at Oakwood, aren't you?"

"That I am," Michael confirms while he crosses his arms without thinking about it.

"It's just, um . . . I'm a student there," the girl continues. "And I heard a . . . a voice in the hallway today. I mean, not a *real* voice, but . . ."

A chill seeps down Michael's spine, and his throat goes bone dry. Is this some kind of sick joke?

"A voice?" he says, pulling up his lips in a hesitant smile that hopefully will conceal the budding panic inside him. "And that's the one I'm supposed to have heard?"

"Yeah, I, um . . ." The girl hesitates and looks from side to side, after which she lowers her voice to a whisper. "I *saw* you. You looked around right when it happened."

Michael's panic grows stronger. So does the urge to get away from this conversation—and since maintaining the lie seems like the quickest way out of the corner he's in, he decides to do just that.

"I'm very sorry," he says, "but I think you've mistaken me for someone else."

"So . . . it wasn't you I saw back there?"

The disappointment in her voice sounds sincere. If it *is* a joke, she's a fabulous actress. However, he doesn't think it is. The girl seems convinced that both of them heard that voice, and him denying it clearly hurts. The problem is that he has no idea what to do with that fact. Because even though he hasn't been able to figure it out yet, there must be a logical explanation to all of this.

"I really am sorry," he repeats. "I have no idea who you saw over at the school, but I assure you that I didn't hear any weird voices coming from the bathroom. So, whoever you saw in the hallway wasn't me."

Realizing he has made a mistake, Michael's facade falls for a split second, and although he immediately tries to rebuild it, it's too late. The girl caught it, and now, a new, skeptical look flickers across her face.

"The bathroom?" she says. "I never said the voice came from the bathroom."

Michael opens his mouth, hoping that the answer his brain seems incapable of producing will come on its own. He's immediately interrupted, though, when an elderly woman abruptly parks a book cart behind the girl.

"You're in a library," she whispers, emphasizing the obvious by gesturing toward the bookshelves. "I'll have to ask you to be quiet or to continue your conversation outside."

Michael glances at the girl, who is staring at him with the same anticipating look she had at first. Except it's more defiant now.

A part of him is tempted to use the interruption as an excuse to escape the awkward situation. On the other hand, the girl has just caught him in a lie, and he knows himself well enough to realize that he will have a hard time looking himself in the mirror if he bails on her now.

"We'll keep it down," he says to the lady with the trolley, who shrugs her shoulders and nods, after which she grabs the handle of the cart and pushes it on. Meanwhile, Michael turns back to the girl.

"Maybe we should go in there so we don't disturb anyone," he says, gesturing toward the door to the room that Starck had directed him to.

The girl follows the line from his finger with her gaze, hesitates for a moment, and then nods.

Starck's office isn't very big and contains nothing more than the bare essentials: a bookshelf, a cluttered bulletin board, a couple of half-wilted plants, and a leather chair paired with a small oak desk at the center of the room.

At the moment, the girl is leaning against that very desk, her arms crossed as she nervously rubs her shoulders like she's freezing. Her gaze is fixed on the floor as if maintaining eye contact would be too much of a challenge. Knowing that his awkward handling of the situation is the cause of this behavior doesn't exactly make Michael proud. There's no changing that now, though. All he can do is try to salvage what's left of the shipwreck.

"I'm sorry I lied to you," he says. "Because, yes, it was me you saw, and I know what you mean by that strange voice. I . . . I heard it too."

"Why didn't you just say that?"

"Because . . ." Michael shrugs his shoulders and sighs. "Because it doesn't make any sense that you heard it too."

"What do you mean?"

"I'm saying you shouldn't have been able to hear it." He rubs his temple and shakes his head. "It wasn't a *real* voice, okay? It was a hallucination. Something I heard in my head, nothing more."

Saying it out loud like that—laying it out in the open for another person to hear—makes him feel incredibly vulnerable. He has allowed a fragment of his inner self to come out into the light. Something over which he has no control . . . and something that stands in stark contrast to his own self-image as a rational person.

"That makes no sense," the girl mumbles. "I heard it too, so it must be—"

"It *can't* be real," Michael says. "It can't. Because the voice I heard in the hallway belonged to my son, who . . . who isn't alive anymore."

The words make the girl twitch. She lifts her head, locking her gaze in his. Her eyes are watery, and something in them has Michael paralyzed.

It's like staring into a mirror. One that mercilessly reflects his own confusion and rising panic.

But it's more than just that. He feels *sick*. As if making eye contact with the girl has triggered some dormant virus inside him, sending his body into a state of fever.

She knows what it's like.

In the reading room outside the office, one of the young men at the library's computers has apparently found another hilarious video to make his friends roar with laughter. Michael tries to focus on the sound but finds that it's causing him trouble. It's like trying to pick up voices coming from the bottom of a deep well.

"I don't feel so good," he hears the girl mumble. "I'm dizzy. I'd like to get out of here now."

Yet she doesn't move an inch.

The movement of her lips suggests that she is saying something more, but despite there being less than six feet's distance between them, the words vanish before they reach Michael. They fade out, he thinks, in the same way that the sounds from the TV always seem to fade right before he falls asleep on the couch. To his surprise, he discovers that the light in the lamp above them also dims in time with the sounds.

Am I passing out?

It doesn't feel like he is about to faint, though. It's more like he's... waking up?

In a small bowl on the desk, a pile of paperclips slowly begins to spin, like water going down the drain of a sink. It should've alarmed him, but it's something he merely perceives without feeling any fear or astonishment.

He looks up at the girl. She shows no signs of surprise either. Not even when a pen to the left of the bowl suddenly rolls—pushed by an invisible hand—across the tabletop and over the edge.

The sound that follows when it hits the floor is almost inaudible, but it's as if it gives a starting signal to the bookshelf, which begins to tremble gently. Shortly after, the office chair chimes in with a low rattle—and then the rest of the furniture follows. Before long, the entire office is buzzing like a swarm of angry wasps trapped under a plastic bucket.

The girl is gesturing something, but Michael has a hard time deciphering what it is because, by now, the light has almost completely disappeared from the lamp above them. Only a single flickering glow remains, barely holding its ground—and the light it provides is only just enough to outline the room's contours, while the girl has been reduced to a blurry silhouette.

Except for her eyes. They're still there, clear and distinct. Like lights on a runway at nighttime, just before the plane hits the ground.

Something in him protests:

No, not before landing. Before taking off.

And that's exactly what it feels like. Sitting on a plane headed for a foreign country, quivering with a cocktail of excitement and fear of the unknown.

Somehow, he knows that the same thought is hidden behind those sparkling green eyes. That the girl in front of him shares the same feeling of being reduced to a passenger in her own body.

The tremors grow stronger, making one of the books on the shelf pull free of the others and tumble over the edge. It hits the floor with a thump far louder than it should be.

That was the kickoff signal, Michael thinks. *Press your feet against the floor and hold on. It's happening now.*

And it is. Just as the thought passes through him, a white flash of light spreads from the center of the girl's pupils, expanding out into the room like the burst of a camera flash.

Instinctively, Michael closes his eyes and reaches out for the girl's hands, which, in this moment, feel like the last fragile lifeline tethering him to reality.

For a couple of nerve-wracking seconds, the light lingers, leaving violet imprints on the inside of his eyelids and wrapping his face in a blanket of warmth.

And then, all of a sudden, it's over. The wasp-like hum of the furniture vanishes, and darkness returns behind his eyelids. The heat on his cheeks also subsides, getting replaced by a damp prickling. The same tickling feeling that comes when the dew falls in late summer after a long and hot barbecue.

I . . . smell the coal? he thinks, while something that feels like fingernails gently brushes against his left ankle between his pant leg and his shoe. *Why do I smell charcoal?*

"NO! NOT THIS PLACE! WHAT IS HAPPENING?"

The girl's desperate outburst tears him back into the present. He opens his eyes and freezes.

Above him, a crow caws, breaking the silence of twilight, and on the ground next to him, the wind pushes the tumbleweed that brushed against his ankle farther across the sand.

PART TWO
THE DESERT

PROLOGUE 2

Sometimes an unfinished image can carry its own powerful expression, and as she sits there, crouched and enveloped in her own pain, the same applies to the girl in the painting. The white emptiness that surrounds her, because the young artist hasn't yet directed his focus and his skilled hand toward this part of the canvas, takes on a life of its own, telling its own story. A story about a girl who is alone, surrounded by white nothingness.

And although the hope that this interpretation is wrong is allowed to live for a moment while the boy with his next brushstrokes marks the silhouette of another person, it soon becomes clear that the blank canvas was telling the truth.

For the other person, the girl in the nightgown, now emerging from the chalk-white emptiness, isn't really there. Her wide-open, expressionless eyes and her hands resting limply on the floor speak for themselves. This second girl, the center of the first girl's attention, the focal point of her grief, has left the world of the living.

And should a hopeful observer, despite the revelation of the obvious, still insist on letting doubt prevail, it's doomed to be a short-lived affair. Because now, the young artist grabs a fresh brush, chooses a new color from the table in front of him, and begins to fill in the details of the girl in the nightgown.

The new brush is wider than the previous one, and the color is crimson red.

He starts at the girl's wrist.

8

Michael Bendixen widens his eyes and spins around for the eighth time while his brain desperately searches for something—anything—rational to cling to. However, there is nothing, and every single spin leads him to the same terrifying conclusion:

The office is gone, the library is gone, and wherever he looks, the moonlight reveals the same thing. A gray, rolling desert landscape, broken only by a few black trees casting long, unsettling shadows across the sand.

It wasn't charcoal.

The origin of this thought—the smell he initially associated with charcoal from a barbeque—apparently comes from behind one of the sandbanks ahead, where a column of smoke rises, dividing the sky in two. Behind the column, he can glimpse the full moon. The heat haze from whatever is burning behind the hill makes it dance like a restless spirit in the night sky.

It wasn't charcoal I smelled.

To his horror, he realizes that this thought has latched onto him, looping in his mind like some senseless mantra. He breaks it off by shaking his head.

Now he spots the girl. She is marching back and forth in a straight line about twenty yards from him, her hands covering her ears while she mumbles to herself. Behind her, sand swirls up with every step, rising like a dusty, translucent wall along the path she treads.

He shapes his lips to call her name, then realizes that he never got it.

"Hey!" becomes the alternative. "Hey, hello!"

No reaction.

With a nagging feeling that the sand could vanish beneath his feet at any moment, he starts walking toward her.

"Hey," he shouts again, then a bit louder: "Hey, um . . . girl! Are you okay?"

The distressed teenager—who has seemingly abandoned the idea of marching her way out of the situation and is now examining whether better results might be achieved through hyperventilation—doesn't seem to register his presence at all. It doesn't really matter, though. He is just grateful to have something other than his own breakdown—and the question of how it's possible to close one's eyes and end up in a completely different place—to focus his attention on. Besides, she needs help as she appears to be in shock. Hell, given the circumstances, anything else would be strange. After all, they're in . . . what? A desert? Did they teleport to some other place? Some other world?

Oh, would you just stop already? You're hallucinating, probably because you're stressed.

Yeah, that's all very fine and dandy, but what about her? How does he explain her being here with him? Some kind of collective psychosis?

He shakes his head. It has to be about the girl now. First, he needs to focus on helping her. He can worry about his own state of mind later.

With a calmer voice, he makes another attempt to break through her wall of hysteria—and this time he appears to succeed. The girl pauses mid-breath and stares at him with a hazy expression.

"Are you okay?"

The instant the words cross his lips, he catches the irony. It's the exact same question his colleagues bombarded him with in the teachers' lounge. And of course, she's not okay—just like he wasn't when they asked.

"Nope, sorry," he says, shaking his head. "I just want to know your name."

The girl stares at him and presses a hand to her forehead as though even recalling her own name is a challenge. The other hand is at the side of her head, squeezing her left earlobe—presumably her version of the *pinch the arm* trick.

"Lisa," she says at last. "I'm . . . my name is Lisa."

"Nice to meet you, Lisa. I'm Michael."

"Okay," she says. "And, um, this . . . this is a dream, right?"

There is an almost pleading tone in her voice, and he can hear her holding her breath as she waits for the answer. Another panic attack might not be far off, so he had better try to rein in his own distress so as not to push her in the wrong direction.

This is easier said than done, though, because on the inside he is shaken by what she just said. Especially since he's pretty sure that adding a sunset to the desolate desert landscape around them would make it a dead ringer for what he saw behind the officer in the nightmare that drove him back to work. That it was those same charred trees that stood in the background when the pale policeman behind the mirror asked if he was Benjamin's father—right before pulling out the boy like he was some kind of hunting trophy.

"I honestly don't know," he answers. "But if it *is* a dream, then I'm glad to at least have company."

Lisa's lips curl into the faintest hint of a smile. It's not much, but far better than the pale, horrified expression she had before.

"What's happening?" she asks. "Where are we?"

Chances are that she is better equipped to answer that question than him, given that he heard her screaming *No! Not this place!* while he stood with his eyes closed in the office. Still, Michael decides that it's probably best not to stress her more than he has to right now.

"I don't know *where* we are," he says, scanning the barren landscape surrounding them. "But I think I've seen it before. It's gonna sound nuts, but I think I've . . . dreamed about this desert."

He opens his mouth to say something more but closes it again when he sees the girl nodding to herself. As if she knows exactly what he's talking about.

"Those burnt trees," she murmurs.

"You know what?" Michael hastens to say. "That's not important right now. What matters is figuring out where we are so we can get the hell out of here. How about we head over there?"

He nods toward the large pillar of smoke behind the dunes up ahead, and then waits for Lisa to get her eyes, still moving in a kind of foggy slow-motion, adjusted in the same direction.

"Where there is smoke, there are probably people," he continues. "And if there are, they'll be able to tell us where we are. And how we get back home."

Lisa stares at the column of smoke for a while, then swallows and gives him a half-hearted nod.

"Yeah . . . I guess that's true."

With that sentence, the decision has evidently been made,

and without uttering another word, she starts walking toward the large sand dunes behind which the pillar of smoke hides.

Before joining her, Michael stands still for a moment, watching the long shadow that the girl is dragging behind her. It's surprisingly clear in the moonlight, stretching all the way from her feet back to the place where their footprints have appeared in the sand out of nowhere.

9

"What the heck? It's . . . empty?"

This outburst comes from Starck's colleague, Carl—the elderly librarian who wasn't able to help Michael at the desk earlier.

The reason for Carl's disbelief is the sight of the empty office whose door he and Starck have just ripped open because a couple of guests at the library complained about a noise coming from inside.

"It looks that way," Starck confirms, making an effort to sound just as surprised as his colleague. "They must have slipped out."

"But they . . . I *heard* them," Carl stammers, running a hand through the sparse cluster of hair still rooted in his head. "I mean, you heard them, right?"

Starck lets his gaze wander around the office, which—aside from a book and a pen lying in the middle of the floor—looks exactly as it usually does.

"To be honest, Carl, I'm not sure what I heard."

That's not true. Starck has a pretty good idea of what the noise, the sudden silence, and the empty office might mean. And while it also worries him, it's for entirely different reasons.

Around the two librarians, a small crowd of people has gathered. At first, they were loud and eager to get involved, but once the noises from inside the office died out, so did their voices.

That part is understandable, though. To them, the silence could mean anything. It could mean someone got hurt—or worse. And Starck is pretty sure the revelation of the empty office hasn't exactly improved the situation.

He leans close to Carl and whispers: "Are we a hundred percent sure that they couldn't have snuck out while you were calling for me to come?"

"I mean . . ." Carl raises a bushy eyebrow. Clearly, he is sure, yet the lack of perpetrators forces him to say the opposite. "I suppose they could have."

"I don't really see any other explanation," Starck says, still in that confidential, whispering voice. "So, maybe we should send the paparazzi home?"

Carl nods and immediately grabs the chance to deliver what might be the biggest crime-movie cliché of all time.

"Show's over, folks!" he roars into the faces of three young men in the front row, startling them so badly that the phones in their hands nearly end up on the floor. "Nothing more to see here. We'll take it from here, so go ahead, turn off the cameras and get back to your internet videos."

"Take it easy, dude," one of the three young men hisses. "We were just trying to help."

"And we appreciate that," Starck interjects. "But it looks like it was a false alarm, and the situation is under control now, so . . ."

The young man glances over at his friends—maybe to gauge if holding on to the rebellious attitude might earn him some extra respect. Then his gaze shifts to the rest of the dwindling crowd, now reduced to a middle-aged couple, a chubby man in his early thirties, and a young girl noisily chewing gum. Finding no support from either group, he shrugs and starts heading toward the computer desks, motioning for his friends to follow.

Moments later, the rest of the crowd disperses. Once they're gone, Starck places a hand on his colleague's shoulder.

"You head on back to the counter, Carl. I'll stay here for a bit. I have some paperwork I need to finish."

After a moment of reflection, Carl nods and starts walking toward the reference desk, muttering to himself that this must be the craziest thing he has experienced in his time at the library.

Starck waits until his colleague is out of sight, then he steps into the office and closes the door behind him.

Two for the price of one, he thinks as he bends down to pick the things up from the floor. *You got your work cut out for you, old man.*

He returns the book to the shelf and runs his hand along the spines of the other books, pushing them back into place. Next, he puts the pen in the breast pocket of his checkered shirt and takes a seat in the chair. Beneath him, air seeps out between the seams of the leather with the sound of a long, tired sigh.

What are you sighing for? You're not the one having to deal with a stowaway.

He opens the bottom drawer of the desk, pulls something out, and places it on the table in front of him. It's a rectangular object, roughly the size of a deck of playing cards, wrapped in light brown suede. On the front, a thin strip is zigzagged through a series of holes in the edges of the leather, ending in a bow at the top.

After casting a final glance over his shoulder toward the door, he grabs the bow and tugs on it. The ends slide apart, revealing the upper edge of a small mirror, which he eases out of the casing. He handles it with such delicacy that you would think he was defusing a bomb. The leather lets go, and he holds the mirror up in front of him.

Shortly after, a discreet, metallic rattle emerges from the bowl on the desk, where the paperclips have begun to move again.

10

"I've changed my mind," Lisa moans as they reach the top of the hill and see where the column of smoke is coming from. "I don't feel like going down there after all."

The town is about five hundred yards farther on. A small, gray-black oasis in the middle of the desolate landscape.

It doesn't feel like finding an oasis, though, given that the buildings—which perhaps just days ago were proud symbols of a small community—have been reduced to crumbling ruins. Between them runs a narrow road that must have served as the town's main street, and a bit farther ahead, where it takes a sharp turn, is the source of the smoke. They're still too far away to tell what's burning, but judging by the height of the flames, it certainly isn't a cozy campfire like the ones you would find at a summer camp. In fact, Michael is positive he can feel the heat against his face, despite the considerable distance.

"I'm afraid we don't have a choice," he says—and at that exact moment, almost as a dramatic underlining of his words, the fire grabs hold of something new and flares up, momentarily bathing the landscape between them and the town in a dark, orange glow. "It seems to be the only town out here."

Out of the corner of his eye, he sees Lisa nodding, but at the same time, she doesn't move an inch. Can't really blame her, though. This crap is scaring the shit out of him too. And no, he's not keen on going down there either, but there really is no real alternative. Moreover, he's the adult here, and that means that he has to put his own fear into the background.

"Ready to move on?"

Lisa flinches and stares at him for a moment, confused, as if his question pulled her out of some deep trance. Then she takes a breath and shrugs.

"Yeah, um . . . yeah, I guess so."

As they approach the outskirts of the city, the temperature increases dramatically, and by the time they set foot on the asphalt of the main road, the pressure from the heat is so massive that it stings when they breathe.

"I don't think we're gonna find much help here," Lisa says. Her voice is calm, but her fingers have again found their way up to her earlobe. "It looks pretty abandoned, and it's so quiet."

"Yeah," Michael replies. "It is pretty quiet . . . not counting the fire, of course."

Frankly, he is amazed at the amount of noise coming from the fire. As a kid, he once found a conch on the beach, and his dad told him that he would be able to hear the roar of the sea in it if he held it up to his ear. And he could. What he heard back then was roughly the same hissing sound coming from the burning buildings now. Except that this is ten times louder and far more unpleasant.

"What now?" Lisa asks. "What do we do next?"

Michael closes his eyes and shakes his head. He'd love to be able to give the right answer, to say the comforting words that would explain everything and help them out of their predicament.

He's got nothing. There is nothing rational about this. No good explanation of how they disappeared from the library and ended up in the middle of a desert.

Nevertheless, he has to at least *try* to look like he's holding it together. Thus, he nods toward a building that could very well have served as the town hall. At any rate, it's too large to be a private residence. Whether that's a good thing or not, he can't quite decide, though.

"I think that one is our best bet," he says.

"Why?"

He shrugs.

"It's the one that looks the cleanest, I guess. The only one where the facade hasn't gone completely dark with soot. That's gotta be a good sign, right?"

The cleanest, maybe. Still, this house, as well as the rest of them, has a strange . . . *foggy* quality. As if he's looking at the town through a grimy pane of glass.

In the end, it probably doesn't matter which house they pick. Maybe Lisa comes to the same conclusion. At least, she doesn't spend long comparing the house to the others on the street before nodding. And when Michael starts walking toward it, she follows without protesting.

"What do you think it is?" she asks as she catches up to him. "Like, a school or something?"

"Not a school," Michael says, pointing to a wooden sign hanging from the railing of the covered staircase leading up to the building's door. Several of the letters are too worn to read, but the part of the word that's still visible is enough to answer the question about the building's purpose. "It's a community house."

Reaching the stairs and stepping onto it, they both instinctively pause and look at each other. Maybe it's the creaking sound of the wobbly boards below them, or maybe it's the sight of the door to the large, dark building that suddenly seems quite intimidating. Whatever the reason, it takes a while for Michael to gather the courage to close his fingers around the door's handle and press it down.

The door squeaks open, revealing a long, gray corridor. It's empty except for a bulletin board on the wall to their left. On it, an old piece of paper flutters slightly in the breeze they've let in. At the end of the hallway, a metal staircase leads up to the first floor. The sparse light entering through the doorway behind them is reflected in its railing, revealing two more doors hiding in the shadows—one on each side of the stairs.

You're kidding yourself, he thinks as he feels his way across the old wallpaper and finds the light switch. *It's not gonna work.*

At first, it seems like he might be right, but after a moment, a fluorescent tube above them starts to hum. It flickers a few times before filling the hallway with a cold, bluish light—eerily reminiscent of the lighting you always see in morgues in the movies.

He glances at Lisa, who immediately starts shaking her head.

"Forget it! I'm *not* staying out here alone. You're stuck with me!"

Michael nods. Truth be told, the idea of heading in there alone doesn't exactly thrill him either. Because even though it makes no sense, there is a part of him—a small and irrational, but not insignificant part—that fears that the girl could disappear without warning, just like the rest of the world did, if he lets her out of his sight.

Before moving on, he considers calling into the room. In the end, though, he decides not to and instead heads for the door to the right of the stairs.

Above the door hangs a sign with elegant lettering, telling

him he's about to enter the community house's *Kitchen*. Hesitantly, he presses the handle down and pushes inward, but the door only opens a few inches before it bumps against something on the other side.

He leans forward, pressing his head against the frame to look through the narrow crack. For a second he is convinced that something will fly out from the darkness and leap up toward his face, but the terrifying opponent turns out to be a harmless chair. It's lying on the floor just behind the door, its back wedged between the floor and the bottom edge of the door.

He breathes a sigh of relief, puts his shoulder against the door, and pushes harder.

The chair gives way with a scraping sound, and the thin beam of light that came in through the gap between the door and the frame unfolds like a fan on the tiled floor.

A couple of inches to the left of the doorframe, his fingers find the switch for the overhead light. To his relief, this lamp turns on without a dramatic pause.

The room is still pretty creepy, though. Various utensils are scattered across the floor around a prep table in the center, and despite the wind having free passage through the shattered window above the sink, the air carries a repulsive blend of disinfectants and rotting meat.

He lifts his foot and steps over the overturned chair—but as soon as the sole of his shoe meets the floor, it slips due to a puddle of something greasy on the tiles.

Attempting to regain his balance, he blindly reaches out. However, this only makes the situation worse, given that it's the door to the fridge he gets hold of. It swings open with a resounding pop, throwing him off balance, so he crashes to the floor, the back of his head banging against the edge of the prep table.

The impact is jarring, yet he barely registers it as the stench of decay pouring out of the open fridge drowns out everything, including the pain.

"Oh, gross! That's so disgusting! Are you okay?"

The words come from Lisa, who stands in the doorway with the top of her shirt pulled up so it covers her nose and mouth.

Michael responds with a nod, then reaches for the back of his head. His hair feels soft and spongy—like touching wet seaweed. When he looks at his hand again, two of his fingers are stained red.

"It really . . . smells bad in here," Lisa says, her voice revealing that she is on the verge of throwing up. "Maybe we should try one of the other rooms?"

"It's the fridge," Michael says. "I opened it by accident when I slipped."

He gets up on his knees, points toward the open fridge—and regrets it immediately. On the shelves are various food items, all covered in a grayish layer of mold, along with a bottle of a milky liquid full of yellow, yolk-like clumps.

"I'm sorry. This is really . . . I . . . can't . . ." Lisa stutters between pursed lips, and before Michael can react, she spins around and storms back out into the hallway.

Michael stares at the empty doorway, and for a moment, he is incapable of grasping what just happened. Then he hears the girl fall to her knees and make a guttural sound that can only mean one thing. She is about to puke.

Moving carefully, so the dizziness triggered by the corner of the table colliding with the back of his head doesn't overwhelm him, he struggles the rest of the way to his feet and follows after her.

He finds her crouching on all fours, staring down at the remnants of her lunch lying in a puddle on the hallway floor.

"You okay?" he asks, gently placing his hand on her back.

She lifts her head and gives a small nod, causing the thin strand of saliva hanging from her chin to sway back and forth.

"Here, take this." He hands her a tissue, and when she looks at him as if to ask where he found it, he shrugs, saying: "I've been a little under the weather lately."

In truth, he hasn't had a cold in a long time, and it's definitely not why he's been carrying a pack of Kleenex in his pocket every day for the past couple of weeks. However, the thought of having to explain the real reason makes *his* stomach churn.

Lisa wipes her chin with the tissue and flashes him a smile that looks weirdly creepy because her eye makeup has been smeared out, creating two large stains that contrast sharply with her pale face. In many ways, it makes her look like a character from a Tim Burton movie.

When she's done with the tissue, she crumples it into a ball and then makes a *can you help me up?* gesture.

Michael takes her hand and pulls her to her feet, but when he loosens his grip to let go, she does the opposite. She tightens her hold.

And then, without saying a word, she presses her face against his shoulder and starts to cry.

Michael opens his mouth to comfort her but lacks the words and instead puts his arms around her.

It's a long while before Lisa lifts her head again, yet when she does, there is a clear change in her expression. Her face has turned solemn, and in her green eyes burns a raw determination that almost scares Michael.

I don't think you should underestimate this one, he thinks. *She's tougher than she looks.*

"I'm better now . . . thanks."

"You're welcome. Ready to try the next one?"

Lisa brushes her bangs away from her face and nods, then walks straight toward the door on the left side of the staircase.

Behind the door is a large hall that looks just as messy as the kitchen. Overturned tables and chairs lie scattered across the wooden floor, most of them with at least one broken leg. Only one table remains upright, but its top is broken in half, making it look like a clumsy sculpture of the letter *M*.

"It can't have been that long since this happened," Lisa whispers as she runs her finger along the edge of the *M*-shaped table. "There's hardly any dust on it."

As if to check if she's right, Michael copies the motion. No dust sticks to his fingers either, but the nearly dried blood on his index finger leaves a small, dark red mark on the wood. He had almost forgotten about his fall in the kitchen, but the sight of the blood seems to bring the pain back.

"Does it hurt a lot?" Lisa asks, seeing him touch the back of his head.

"No, it's okay. I've had worse."

Lisa gives him a *I know you're downplaying it to make me feel better* smile and then starts moving toward the back wall, which has a small stage built into it about five feet above the floor.

Reaching it, she places both hands on the edge of the stage floor and climbs up. Then she goes over to the left side where there is an old, worn piano.

"I've always wanted to play the piano," she says, gently pressing down a few of the high keys. "Do you play?"

"Not really. I fiddled a bit with the guitar when I was your age, but it's my, um . . . my wife who is the artist in our family. She plays the piano. *Played* the piano. I keep forgetting."

"Oh, I'm sorry," Lisa says. "I didn't know that . . ."

She falls silent, her eyes locking onto something high up on the wall facing the street.

Michael follows her gaze upward, toward the row of glassless windows sitting just below where the ceiling meets the wall. Though the moonlight and the glow of the fire outside illuminate the hall reasonably well, it's dark near the ceiling. Therefore, his eyes initially slide right past the black shadow on the wall.

It's only when it starts to move that he spots it.

"Get down here . . . and hurry."

Why he feels the need to whisper, Michael isn't entirely sure. It's as though he's afraid the thing on the wall might be listening. Hell, maybe it is. It doesn't matter, though, because Lisa is already making her way down from the stage. She moves quickly, but her gaze never strays from the hairy creature.

This can't be real, he thinks. *It's the size of a fucking dinner plate.*

As if to emphasize this idea, the being stretches out the front two of its numerous legs, making it appear even larger. Simultaneously, a quiver runs through its furry body—and despite it being at least thirty feet away from him, Michael is sure he can hear its bristles scraping against the wallpaper.

With careful steps, he starts backing across the floor toward Lisa, who is edging her way past some of the overturned furniture.

"Alright," he whispers as he gets close enough to grab her hand. "We're gonna head back to the door, nice and calmly."

"Is it . . . a spider?" Lisa whispers, her breathing so rapid that the words come out in uneven bursts.

Michael shakes his head and gestures that this is a conversation for later. Right now, getting out is what matters.

As they continue sideways across the floor, the spider-like creature creeps farther down the wall. This time, Michael has no doubt he can hear it moving. It's the sound of impatient fingers drumming on a tabletop.

"Wait," Lisa whispers, tugging on his arm. He stops, and she slowly crouches down without letting go of him while she picks up a broken table leg with her free hand. "Just in case."

Michael nods, then looks around and breathes a sigh of relief. They're almost at the door. Only one obstacle left, and the furry monstrosity is still on the wall. Farther down, sure, but still on the wall.

Technically, they could go around the pile of tables and chairs between them and the door, but that would mean getting closer to the creature—which neither of them wants. So instead, they let go of each other's hands and start moving the furniture to clear a path . . . still with the sound of drumming fingers looming in the background.

As they remove the last chair, the spider is just three feet away from reaching the floor. There, it pauses for a moment, legs tucked beneath its abdomen, before suddenly pushing off and leaping down to the ground. It lands out of sight behind an overturned table.

Shortly after, it reappears, but to Michael's surprise, it's not heading toward them. Instead, it scuttles sideways—first in the direction of the corner, then toward the door, as if it's planning to cut off their only escape route. All the while, its legs clack up and down with a speed that reminds him of a sewing machine needle.

"LET'S GO!" he roars, shoving Lisa toward the door. "WE HAVE TO GET OUT OF HERE!"

Lisa runs a few steps forward, then stops and looks around.

"WHAT ARE YOU DOING?"

"THE LEG!" she screams. "THE TABLE LEG!"

It takes Michael a moment to realize she's talking about her improvised weapon. She put it on the floor when they were moving the chairs—and now she's heading back for it. Meanwhile, the drumming legs are getting closer. They're close now. Far too close.

"GOT IT!" she shouts, after which she sprints back toward Michael. She catches up to him just as he yanks the door to the hallway open—and the instant she's through, he slams it shut behind her.

A second later, there's a loud thud when something crashes against it on the other side.

"It doesn't make sense," Lisa moans. "It just doesn't."

Whether she expects an answer to this astute observation, Michael doesn't know, but if so, she'll have to put up with waiting a bit. He needs a moment to process all of this. A moment to *think*.

Ten minutes have passed since they slammed the door to the hall shut. They've also closed the other doors in the hallway. Now, they're both sitting on the floor, knees pulled up under crossed arms.

"I mean . . . it can't be real. We agree on that, right?"

Lisa turns her head and stares at him, but when he still hasn't answered after a while, she resumes her monologue, fiddling with the yellow and purple plastic bracelets on her wrist.

"I mean, it was huge. Freaking huge! And the way it changed direction, like it was trying to cut us off. It was almost like . . ."

Now, Michael lifts his head after all.

"Like it was thinking. That's what you mean, right?"

Lisa bites her lower lip and lets out a sound that was probably meant to be a chuckle but never amounts to more than a hiss.

"It's too much," she sighs, leaning back until her neck rests against the wall. "We're stuck in a desert town . . . a *desert* town! Completely cut off from—"

Suddenly, her eyes widen. She almost jumps up on her knees, then leans her torso sideways to squeeze her hand into the pocket of her jeans. From it, she pulls out an old cell phone whose screen is so full of scratches it looks like a spiderweb has been spun across it. That detail doesn't matter to Michael, though, because in this moment, that phone is nothing short of beautiful.

In her excitement, Lisa drops the electronic miracle on her lap twice before she manages to steady her hands and hold it triumphantly in front of her.

Sitting there, kneeling in the bluish glow of the fluorescent lamps with both hands folded around the phone, she resembles the main figure of a mural that Michael once saw in an Italian cathedral on a holiday.

The Virgin in Prayer it was called.

II

While Michael and Lisa sit on the floor of the community house's hallway, staring anxiously at a phone screen, Erik Starck stands in front of an abandoned warehouse about twelve miles away.

He has only just arrived and, as always, he takes a moment to get accustomed to the place. Even though time is of the essence, experience has taught him it's a moment well spent. This place rarely hesitates, and not being properly prepared can cost dearly.

Once he feels ready, he pulls a bundle of keys out of his pocket, fans them out, and lets his fingers glide across them until they stop at the one that fits the padlock on the gate leading into the building.

In truth, the padlock is more of a symbolic gesture than an actual barrier, a way of marking the area as off-limits. If someone wanted to get in, the thin, corrugated metal of the gate would likely give way without putting up a lot of resistance.

Besides, no one can truly claim ownership of anything here —not along the Perimeter.

Before opening the gate, Starck scrapes away a pile of sand

that has gathered in front of it. Clearly, it's been a long time since he was last here. Longer than it feels.

All the more reason to be careful, he thinks as he turns the key until the shackle on the padlock pops open. *There's no room for mistakes. Not with these two.*

Inside the building, it's dark, but that doesn't prevent him from walking straight over to the workbench on the right side of the room. Nor does it keep him from reaching out and finding the right drawer on the first try. From it, he retrieves a flashlight, which he turns on and places on the table. Then he pauses for a moment, giving his eyes a chance to adjust.

The padlock and the pile of sand suggest there haven't been any unwelcome visitors. Still, he lets his gaze wander along the walls once his eyes have adjusted to the light.

To his relief, everything is where it's supposed to be. The car is parked in front of the gate at the opposite end of the building, the canned food is neatly arranged on the shelving unit alongside bottles of water, and next to the shelves is the metal locker where he keeps backpacks, sleeping bags, tarps, and other general survival gear they'll need once they reach the Wastelands.

On the front of the locker hangs an old postcard. The image shows a tall, snow-covered mountain, and across it, a message is scrawled in capital letters. Over time, some of the letters have gone blurry, but the text is still legible.

I ATE A HAM SANDWICH RIGHT HERE!

Beneath the third word, an arrow is drawn, pointing down toward the mountain's peak. As he follows it with his eyes, a faint smile appears at the corners of Starck's mouth. It fades, though, once his gaze drifts to the right, landing on the rifle leaning against the side of the locker.

A loud, jarring screech fills the room as he pulls open the

doors of the locker. From the top shelves, he grabs two large backpacks, places them on the table, and begins to fill them.

He can't fit as much food and water as he'd like, since he has to use some of the space in one of the backpacks for an extra blanket—a necessary adjustment due to the addition of a stowaway. On the other hand, if the girl's presence means what he believes it does, losing a ration or two of the food is a small price to pay. Also, it shouldn't be a problem before they reach the Wastelands and are no longer able to use the car.

With the backpacks packed to full capacity, Starck double-checks the straps securing the sleeping bags to the top of each one. Afterward, he slings the backpacks over his shoulders and carries them to the vehicle parked in front of the gate.

With deliberate, routine movements, he loads the car. Once finished, he spends a moment studying the packed trunk to make sure he hasn't forgotten anything. Satisfied, he nods to himself, checks that there's fuel in the spare canister, before heading back to grab the final—and perhaps most important—piece of survival gear.

The one that's still leaning against the locker.

12

Lisa's cell phone—the technological lifeline that was supposed to solve all their problems and save them from their predicament—delivers nothing but a shrill, metallic hum. Even so, she keeps pulling it away from her ear, staring at it in despair before hanging up and trying again.

This ritual is repeated several times—and could probably have kept on forever—if she hadn't recognized the expression in Michael's eyes. It's the same pity-look her teachers always give her. The sickening mixture of obligation and sympathy.

"Why do you keep staring at me like that?"

The words come out more sharply than intended, but she genuinely is surprised. She hasn't seen that look in his eyes before. Not even back in the desert when she broke down.

"Sorry," Michael says. If he's offended, he hides it well. "I just don't think it's gonna get us anywhere."

"I'll give it one more shot, okay?"

He nods and then walks over to the bulletin board as though he wants to give her some privacy. Meanwhile, Lisa takes a deep breath, preparing herself for another fruitless attempt, before she locates her mom in the phone's contacts list and presses *Call*.

Come on, let me get through to her, so I can . . .

That's how far Lisa gets before hearing her mom's voice. But it's not coming from the phone. It's the version of it that lives in her own head, more condescending and sarcastic than ever.

So you can do what? Tell me that you're sitting in some godforsaken desert town with one of the teachers from school? Ask if I'd mind swinging by on the way home from work and pick you up? Something like that?

She closes her eyes and lets her head drop forward in defeat, her bangs closing on her face like a stage curtain. More than ever, she needs the darkness behind her eyelids. More than ever, she needs to escape into the memory of Emma on the coffee-stained couch, mouth full of popcorn, knees tucked up under her T-shirt.

When Lisa opens her eyes again, Michael is standing in front of her. She looks up at him, her lips pressed tightly together, and answers his unspoken question with a slight shake of her head.

"What now?" she sighs. "What are we gonna do?"

Michael shrugs his shoulders and glances up at the ceiling, as if hoping to find an answer there.

"I don't know," he says. "But I think maybe it's time we talked about what's going on here. I mean, for real."

Lisa stares at him hesitantly for a moment. Then she puts her phone down on the floor and leans forward, resting her elbows on her knees.

"I know it sounds weird," Michael continues. "But just about every psychological research paper I've ever read underlines how important it is to process extremely stressful situations like this properly—and as soon as possible."

Maybe it's because he has that look in his eyes again, or maybe it's because she has the feeling that the conversation is heading to a place she has already visited—unsuccessfully—with the therapist after Emma's death. Whatever it is, something about his words ignites a flicker of resentment in Lisa.

"So, you're telling me there are theories about stuff like this?" she snaps. "What, like a fucking ten-step guide on what to do if you blink and suddenly find yourself in a desert?"

Her outburst is born out of frustration and anger, and the comment is in no way an attempt to be funny. Still, hearing herself say the words, she realizes how stupid they sound. And when she notices Michael fighting to suppress a smile, his lips twitching despite his best efforts, something inside her gives way, bursting open a dam.

All the confusion, helplessness, and desperation she has felt on this terrible day pour out in a series of gasping, choking outbursts of laughter, each one edged with a hysterical undertone she doesn't like. In fact, the sound is downright scary, but it still takes her a while to kill it.

When she finally manages to stop, she wipes her eyes and looks up at Michael. She expects him to be staring at her with concern—which, in a way, he is—but there's something else in his expression as well. A gravity that makes her instinctively sit up straight.

Without saying anything, he walks over and crouches down next to her. Then he folds his hands and clears his throat.

"There's something that has been bothering me ever since we met at the library," he says. "A question. I think I already know the answer to it . . . but I have to ask it anyway."

13

The man in the dark brown fleece jacket scratches his beard and whistles cheerfully. Jackpot. He had almost given up hope of finding anything edible when he saw that the grocery store had burned down. In fact, he was just about ready to lie down in the middle of the street and wait for starvation to take him. Now, however, standing in the glow of the vending machine in the abandoned theater, those kinds of thoughts are water under the bridge.

"Jeez, yeah, wishy water under the bridge," he mutters, winking at his own reflection in the vending machine's glass.

Except it's not him. Not really.

What he sees is the eerie glare of a scrawny drifter who looks like him and copies his movements down to the tiniest detail, but in many ways it's still a complete stranger. One whose life began only a year and a half ago when he woke up to find himself wandering the Wastelands, alone and abandoned.

In the beginning, it bothered him that the only remnants of the life he must have had before were a series of blurred images that couldn't even be pieced together to form a single meaningful memory. Over time, though, other worries took the wheel—things like where his next meal would come from—and his past got pushed into the background.

He crouches down in front of the vending machine, sliding his arm into the tray where the items land.

Damn it! There's a panel blocking his arm from getting to the chocolate bar he had his sights on. He slams his hand against the underside of the panel in frustration, but it doesn't budge.

"Jeez," he moans and makes another attempt, this time a bit harder. "Come on, you stupid machine!"

Suddenly, his eyes widen, as if he has just remembered something, and he presses his cheek against the glass, whispering in the sweetest tone his voice can muster: "Pretty please?"

As if expecting it to increase his chances of persuading the device, he curls his lips into a smile, which his semi-transparent doppelganger in the glass immediately returns.

The sight of his yellowed, uneven-toothed grin would send a chill down most people's spines. It doesn't faze him, though. He's just as oblivious to his own mental illness as he is to the events in his past that caused it.

The stubborn machine, on the other hand, is blatantly indifferent to both the smile and his pathetic appeal. The only answer he gets is the sleepy hum of the ventilation grate in its lower left corner.

His stomach growls in frustration now—and so does he.

"Well, then it's your own f-fucking fault!" he roars, yanking his arm out of the hole with enough force to have dislocated his shoulder had it been stuck. "Miserable shit! Shit!"

He grabs both sides of the vending machine's door with his hands, then pulls his right leg up high toward his chest and kicks the glass.

"Kriit!"

One single crack. Not good enough. He lifts his leg for the second attempt, tensing every muscle his brain is able to establish a connection to.

"STUPID SHIT-CRAP-PIECE OF JUNK!" he screams as his foot smashes through the door, sending a shower of glass shards flying over the snacks, the floor, and himself.

Reaching in for his prize, he cuts his arm in several places, but it doesn't matter. He doesn't care. Not. One. Bit.

Chuckling, he sits down cross-legged on the floor in front of the vending machine and kicks off a full-blown feast, starring an assortment of chocolate bars and cookies, all washed down with —*oh yes, jackpot alright*—cold cans of soda.

He brushes crumbs from the beard around his mouth and casts another glance at his reflection in one of the glass shards on the floor. What he sees still looks, to him, like a perfectly normal person.

He registers no trace of madness.

14

Michael got the answer he expected. Nothing more, nothing less. Even so, it hurt when Lisa confirmed that the voice she heard in the school's hallway had, in fact, belonged to a boy who (it hurt like hell) was calling for his dad.

And it *was* Benjamin. As outrageous as it sounds, it must have been Benjamin's voice she heard . . . but what does that mean? What the hell does that mean?

He touches the back of his head, the ache from his run-in with the prep table's edge flaring up again. The blood is starting to clot, feeling rough under his fingertips. The healing process has begun. Soon it'll start to itch.

He wonders if the same will be true for the wound in his soul. Will his grief and longing fade over time if he resists the urge to scratch at it? And would he even want that?

"Michael?" Lisa sounds a little worried. "Are you okay?"

"Yeah . . . yeah, I am."

"This is some messed up shit," she says, fiddling with the filter of a cigarette that's long since been smoked down. "I'm really sorry all of this is happening to you."

To his surprise, Michael realizes that this is the first of the many condolences he has gotten that actually means something to him—and that thought leads him to another. The same one he had in the library when their eyes met, just before the world disappeared around them:

She knows what it's like.

"Thanks," he says. "You've been through some stuff too, haven't you?"

"Yeah, I guess I have. I, um . . . I lost my sister and my dad a little over a year ago."

"Damn. That must have hurt. What happened?"

As soon as he asks the question, Michael regrets it. Because it *does* hurt, that much is clear from her tense body language. And if there had been any doubt, Lisa's next words would have erased it.

"I don't mean to be rude," she says, "but if I don't find a bathroom soon, I'm gonna pee my pants."

Michael doesn't need his background in psychology to know that it's just an excuse to shut down the conversation, but he also doesn't see any reason to stress her out by pressing the issue. So instead, he places a hand against the wall and pushes himself to his feet.

"Well, guess we'd better go see if we can find one," he says, pointing to the door above the stairs. "The question is whether we try up there or we drop this house and try another one. What do you think?"

"To be honest, I'd like to get as far away from that . . . thing as possible."

"It's settled then. We'll try another house. With any luck we'll find one with a working toilet and without . . . wildlife."

The last word makes Lisa's eyes dart quickly around the ceiling, scanning each corner, before she leans down and picks up the broken table leg.

"I'm bringing this."

"That's probably a good idea."

Once out of the building, Michael and Lisa decide to brave the heat and head down the main street toward the burning buildings. They do so for two reasons: firstly, they figure there's nothing of relevance to be found in the direction they came from, and secondly, they both need a moment to gather courage before stepping into another house.

As they walk there, Michael repeatedly lets his gaze wander over the buildings surrounding them—and once again, it strikes him how weirdly foggy they seem. Like a photograph left out in the sun for too long.

Along with this observation comes another: The town's houses and shops look like they've been randomly plucked from entirely different time periods. There are half-timbered houses with crooked roofs and tiny windows next to Art Deco buildings with glossy, arched windows and ornate cornices. Alongside them are gray concrete blocks of the kind you'd expect to find in poor parts of Eastern Europe.

The businesses seem just as randomly mixed. A small shop with a curved roof and hand-painted signs sells niche stuff, like antique telescopes and pocketknives. Right next to it is a sleek, minimalistic glass building, where modern office furniture can be glimpsed behind the large windows.

Nothing seems to fit together. Each building bears the traits of its own time and style, but the placement is random, as if someone has pulled in elements from different historical eras and put them together with no regard for the bigger picture.

Their plan of walking to build up courage before venturing into a new building doesn't work too well, because the farther into town they get, the more demotivating elements they encounter.

One of the bad ones is a flower shop, which, judging by the sign above the entrance, was once a charming little business. However, the gold lettering with the clever name, *FLORA'S FLORA*, loses most of its charm when you notice the flowers behind the window and in the pots outside drooping, their leaves carrying a dry, brownish hue conveying their neglect.

Potted death and decay.

An icy chill creeps up Michael's spine at this thought, and for a second, he's almost genuinely worried that a creepy zombie-version of an old lady named Flora is gonna appear in the doorway.

The shop next door doesn't exactly make things better. It's a men's clothing store where the mannequins in the glassless windows have had their faces deformed due to the constant heat. Their noses and cheekbones have taken on a strangely bleached color and have almost sunken inward. It's menacing. Not least because Michael has a childish—but extremely insistent—fear that somewhere in the folds of those macabre faces, a pair of eyes are following them, patiently awaiting the right moment.

The sight of the waning plastic people has clearly also affected Lisa, who discreetly steps down from the sidewalk onto the street and stays there until they're past it.

She does the same a minute later when they pass a butcher shop, where three large pieces of meat—rotten and crawling with tiny, wriggling maggots—hang from hooks behind the store window. She deliberately keeps her gaze fixed in the opposite direction as they walk by. That's what makes her notice the theater—and the faint glow of light behind its sooty glass doors.

"Stop!" she exclaims, grabbing Michael's upper arm. "There's light over there!"

"Huh?"

"Over there!" she says, pointing toward the building, which—given the words *PEOPLE'S THEATER ATTICA* written on the façade—presumably is the town's theater. "Do you think there's someone in there?"

"It looks that way," Michael replies, wiping the sweat from his forehead with the back of his hand. "But, to be sure, we'd have to check."

Lisa nods with her lips pressed tightly together, and he notices the knuckles turning white on the hand that's holding the broken table leg.

From her hand, Michael's gaze wanders back to the theater's facade—and the buildings that surround it. They, too, seem strangely blurred and washed out, as though they're somehow there and not there at the same time.

"Attica," Lisa mumbles, looking like she literally tastes the word and finds it utterly bitter. "Do you think that's the name of the town? Attica?"

Though he does find that word to have an uncanny quality that perfectly matches his view of this abandoned desert town, Michael merely responds with a shrug before crossing the street and heading toward the theater's glowing facade.

PART THREE
THE THEATER

PROLOGUE 3

As the details of the two girls—the blonde girl curled up on the floor at the center of the painting, and the dark-haired girl lying half-slumped, half-sitting lifelessly in front of her—come into focus, the horrifying narrative begins to take shape. The dark-haired girl has bid life a final farewell, and the deep red handprint on the knife lying beside her suggests that the decision was her own.

The relationship between the two girls—what bond ties them together—is something the young artist can only speculate about. The symbolism of the red stains on the floor between them suggests a connection of blood, but he can't be sure. What the boy doesn't doubt, however, is that there is a bond between them, and that it's strong.

That's also the feeling he gets as he slides his brush over to the left side of the canvas and starts to draw the outline of the painting's last character.

The man on the bed.

15

"Whoa!"

The last few hours of Lisa Swann's life have been absolutely terrible. There's no other way to put it. In a very short span of time, she has experienced things that would push most people over the brink into madness, and frankly, she's not confident she'll be able to keep her balance on the edge much longer. But this? This is nothing less than:

"Whoa!"

The theater isn't very big. That's not what impresses her. It's not in overwhelmingly good condition either. Like everything else in town, it's been subjected to its share of destruction. But that's not it either.

No, what makes Lisa widen her eyes and let out a *whoa* is the journey through time. The one that began the moment the dirty glass doors slid apart and now culminates in her cautiously stepping onto the dark red carpet.

It's like walking into an old movie, she thinks, pausing for a moment to take it all in: The warm light from the ceiling spots casting large circles on the floor. The oval glass booth on the left side of the room, where countless tickets must have been pushed through the bronze-framed opening, accompanied by a smile and an *enjoy the show*. The elegant rope stretched between three metal posts with golden finials, marking the entrance to the theater halls.

She closes her eyes and imagines what it must have felt like to be here back when the theater opened. In her mind, she can almost hear the voices of people eagerly chatting about their excitement for the big premiere. She pictures them—women in evening gowns and men in suits—filling the space, swirling around her like ghosts from a bygone era. Finally, she moves on to the unmistakable smell of popcorn.

Salted popcorn, she thinks with a smile. *In big paper tubs, drenched in warm butter. Lots of it. Just like when Mom used to make it for me and Emma.*

"WATCH OUT! GET DOWN!"

In the wake of Michael's warning follows a series of events that Lisa only registers in fragments. First, she opens her eyes, only to have them shut again as something red and shiny hits her hard above her left eye, sending her to the floor. Subsequently, out of the corner of her eye, she catches the outline of two figures who—absurd as it seems—appear to be dancing in a tight embrace. One of them must be Michael, but her vision flickers constantly, making it impossible to determine which one of them he is.

Behind her, a strange hissing sound emerges, like the noise of air escaping from a balloon.

The skin on her cheek feels wet. Blood? No, it's not warm. Sticky but not warm.

The balloon-like hiss fades away, and what little remains of Lisa's awareness shifts back to the two silhouettes. They've abandoned their bizarre waltz and moved to the floor instead, one straddling the other. From them comes a torrent of sounds—an almost animalistic mix of grunts, growls, and roars.

You have to help him, she thinks, but her body doesn't listen, and before she knows it, the scene fades, and the theater goes dark.

16

Michael's perception of the events is far more detailed than Lisa's. What to her was simply a shiny red object, he easily identifies as a soda can—even though it's flying through the air at an alarming speed.

He's also able to see what causes the wet sensation on her cheek as she lies face-down on the floor. It's a question of basic chemistry. Upon hitting her, pressure starts to build up inside the can—and when it lands on the floor, the aluminum seal pops open, releasing a spray of soda into the air, some of which lands on her face.

Michael also perceives the sender of the can—a skinny hobo in a dark brown fleece jacket—who, with an outraged look in his eyes, hurls the improvised weapon at the girl.

Sadly, Michael's warning doesn't reach her in time. He does, however, react quickly and with surprising efficiency in the seconds following her fall, when he breaks into a run and lunges toward the stranger.

The man lets out a roar of pain as Michael's hands slam into his shoulders, shoving him backward. He quickly regains his composure, though, grabbing hold of Michael's shirt sleeve and yanking hard, so Michael tumbles around in a half-circle.

The loss of balance leaves Michael vulnerable, and before he knows it, the frantic vagabond has both hands wrapped around his neck. He squeezes hard while bellowing a muddled jumble of words that are impossible to make sense of.

"Yuwahnam! Yuwhangheme!" is what it sounds like, and while the words flow, the eyes above the man's protruding cheekbones are glowing with madness. Around the corners of his mouth, small patches of frothy spit bubble and gleam.

In an attempt to break free, Michael plants both palms against his attacker's chin and pushes upward while forcing his elbows outward, trying to pry the man's arms apart.

He can't apply enough pressure to get free, but the effort does buy him a deep breath before the hands once again tighten around his neck.

The crazed drifter resumes his incomprehensible mantra. This time, though, his voice keeps cracking, so the noises he produces aren't even close to resembling coherent words. He sounds more like a wild animal than a human being.

Darkness begins to creep in from the edges of Michael's vision, and he realizes it's now or never if he wants to make a final attempt at breaking free. He grabs hold of the man's upper arms and pulls up his left foot, planting it firmly against the drifter's kneecap.

And then he kicks.

The sound is one of the most unsettling things Michael has ever heard. It's the snapping of dry bundles of spaghetti—not a pleasant sound when coming from inside a kneecap.

The result, however, is satisfying. The man releases his grip on Michael's neck and collapses on the floor with a pathetic wail.

And it's at this exact moment that Michael's detailed perception of Lisa's fall becomes crucial. Because during his meticulous observation, he saw the table leg roll out of her hand as she hit the floor. Now, it's lying right there, no more than ten feet away from him.

Without hesitation, Michael slides across the floor and grabs Lisa's improvised weapon. With it in hand, he tries to get on his feet, but he barely makes it halfway up before the hobo attacks him again. Somehow, despite his injured leg, the man manages to throw his full weight onto Michael's back. Now he is straddling him while pummeling his clenched fists down between his shoulder blades.

Once again, he's screaming the mantra from before—except this time the words are separated, allowing Michael to make them out as they burst out, accompanying each painful blow against his spine.

"YOU . . . ARE . . . ONE . . . OF . . . THEM!"

He's gonna kill me, Michael thinks. *That fucking maniac won't stop until I'm not breathing anymore.*

"YOU . . . WON'T . . . GET . . . ME!"

And then he's gonna kill the girl. We're gonna to die here. And then he'll drag us out into that fucking desert and bury us.

"YOU . . . ARE . . . ONE . . . OF . . . THEM!"

In a brief flash, Michael sees it play out in his mind. He sees the madman dragging their lifeless bodies out into the desert the next day, burying them in shallow graves. He sees him standing over two mounds of sand, his hands folded, his mouth letting out a deranged laugh, just like—*oh God*—just like the officer in his nightmare.

This final image hits him harder than the rhythmic blows landing on his back, and in it, Michael finds the strength to twist himself around beneath the weight of the man.

With one last burst of effort, he summons all his willpower—every ounce of energy that lies in the hope that this terrible fate won't become reality—and channels it into the hand still gripping the club.

And then he releases it.

Directly into the man's left temple.

17

"What do we do with him?" Lisa whispers, glancing toward their disturbed prisoner, who now sits on the floor behind them, tied to one of the metal poles with the stylish rope she admired earlier.

How Michael managed to cut the rope free, she doesn't know —that part happened while she was still unconscious—but she assumes that the glass shard sticking out of his shirt pocket played a role.

"I don't know," Michael replies, his voice carrying a little more resignation than she'd hoped for. "I think we have to keep trying to get him to talk. After all, he's the only person we've seen, and he must be able to tell us *something* about this place, even though . . ."

He finishes his sentence by drawing a circle in the air next to his temple with his finger, and Lisa nods. Reaching the same conclusion didn't take her long.

"Yeah, but how?" she asks. "He just sits there with his fucking *jeez*. It's driving me nuts."

"I know, but what else are we supposed to do? Beat the answers out of him?"

He says the last sentence with a tone of voice that emphasizes that it would be an absurd solution, which of course he's right about . . . even though there is a part of Lisa that wouldn't mind letting her anger take the wheel and pay the looney hobo back for hurling a can at her.

"If I get one more *jeez* from him," she snarls, "I'll volunteer to give him a couple of whacks."

"I doubt that," Michael replies, annoyingly calmly. "Besides, I'm not sure we should be too quick to judge him."

"Too quick? He threw a can at my head!"

"I know . . . but who's to say we wouldn't have done the same thing in his shoes? Think about it. What do we know about him? He could've ended up here in the same way that we did and be just as confused. Who says we wouldn't have thrown a can at him if the roles were reversed?"

"You can't be serious."

"Look, I'm just saying that it might be a good idea to take a deep breath and consider whether it's the situation, rather than the man, that's the real problem here."

Lisa casts another glance back at the man, who now sits with his head buried in his hands, rocking back and forth while mumbling to himself. The sight of him still makes her simmer with anger, but it also makes her realize that Michael might be right. After all, they've only been here a short while and are already on the verge of a breakdown, but for all she knows, this man could've been wandering around out here for months.

"Fine, what do you suggest then?"

"First of all, I think we need to get him to calm down," Michael says. "And I also think it may be best if only one of us talks to him. So he doesn't feel attacked."

"Attacked?" Lisa doesn't know whether to laugh, cry, or go ballistic at that remark. "So *he* doesn't feel attacked?"

"Calm down," Michael whispers, placing a hand on her arm. "You know what I mean."

"I *am* calm," Lisa grunts, even though it's bullshit. She's a lot of things right now, but *calm* isn't one of them. "And yes, I know what you mean."

"Good," Michael replies. "And besides, didn't you say you had to go to the bathroom?"

"Yeah . . . yeah, I guess I did."

"Why don't you do that in the meantime, then? When I was looking for something to cut the rope with, I saw a door with a bathroom sign."

He points in the direction of the passage that leads to the theater halls.

"There's a beat-up vending machine in there, it's right after that."

Now, out of the blue, there is a reaction from the man behind them. He yanks hard at the metal pole and kicks his feet frantically across the floor.

"It's mine," he snarls. "My jackpot. Mine!"

Lisa raises her finger and opens her mouth, but Michael stops her.

"What's yours?" he asks calmly.

The man presses his lips together and shoots them both a spiteful glare but says nothing.

"What's yours?" Michael repeats. "Is it the vending machine . . . the candy? Is that what you mean?"

It sounds like a shot in the dark, probably based solely on the fact that the man looks pretty starved. Apparently, though, Michael hits the bullseye, because the rage in the man's eyes vanishes, getting replaced by a pleading expression.

"Please don't take it," he moans. "Please!"

His face, which until now has only awoken disgust in Lisa, twists into a grimace she can't quite define. It could be the precursor to tears. Then again, it could just as well be the lead-up to another outburst of rage.

"You know what?" Michael says. "If you calm down and answer our questions, I promise you that we won't take your . . . *jackpot* from you. Can you do that?"

The man rocks his head back and forth, *Rainman*-style, as he considers the offer. Occasionally, he runs his tongue over his teeth, causing his upper lip to bulge. After sitting like that for a while, he finally lifts his head and nods.

"And what is it you want to know?"

18

There are *a lot of* things that they'd like to know. Nevertheless, Michael chooses to start with a question that doesn't particularly interest him. It's asked for tactical and psychological reasons, with the sole purpose of establishing a better foundation for communicating with the man.

"First of all, I'd like to know your name," he says. "Will you tell me your name?"

The man stares at him with a puzzled expression, as though trying to determine whether the question is some kind of trap. Apparently, he decides that it isn't, because a moment later, he mumbles his response:

"Tom."

"Just Tom?"

"Yeah, just Tom."

"Fair enough. My name is Michael . . . and this is Lisa."

He gives Lisa a gentle nudge on the back, prompting her to nod indifferently to the man. After that, she gives Michael a questioning look.

"Sure, you go ahead and go to the bathroom."

Lisa nods, then walks in the direction of the hallway. Passing their prisoner, she walks so close to him that her knee almost brushes against his elbow. This deliberate provocation surprises Michael a little. There's no doubt that the man on the floor really has her blood boiling.

As Lisa disappears around the corner, he turns to the prisoner again.

"Okay, Tom. Now, I'd like to know where we are and what has happened here."

Tom squints and stares at him in disbelief, shaking his head as if he can't fathom just how stupid the question is.

"We're in Attica," he says. "There's a big, fat sign outside . . . but maybe you guys don't know how to read?"

"Hey now, no need to get snarky," Michael replies, aiming for a calm and measured tone. "That won't do any of us any good. Besides, we know the name of the town—that's not what I'm asking. And I think you know that."

"Uh-huh," Tom exclaims, resuming his *Rainman*-rocking. "Yup, I'm on to you now. You're *not* one of them, and neither is the girl. You're new here, aren't you?"

"Yeah, Tom. We're new here. Just a couple of hours ago, we were standing in a library in Pennsylvania, and now we're stuck in this hell."

For a moment, the defiant look in Tom's eyes wanes, and he stares at Michael in confusion, as if struggling to make sense of the words. However, after shaking his head a few times, the defiance returns at full strength. He adopts a new expression, clearly the darkest and most dramatic in his repertoire.

"Oh, you've got it all wrong," he says, nodding slowly. "You're not in Hell . . . not yet anyway. Don't let the flames fool you. This is just the courtyard. The real Hell isn't some land of fire below ground . . ."

Michael takes a breath, getting ready to ask the raving philosopher to kindly get back on track. He doesn't have time to say anything, though, before Tom finishes his rant. And when he does, his words leave Michael completely speechless.

"Jeez, no," Tom says. "The *real* Hell is a hall full of mirrors."

19

There is a beat-up vending machine in there. That was the way Michael described it, and technically, he's not wrong. Still, Lisa can't help but feel it's quite the understatement.

Beat-up? she thinks, pushing some of the crumpled candy wrappers in front of the machine with her foot. *More like totally demolished.*

Amazingly, the machine still works—at least to the extent that a small light is glowing behind the top edge of the frame, and a lazy hum emanates from a vent in the bottom left corner.

She reaches in through the gaping hole in the glass door, holding her hand still a couple of inches from the middle shelves.

Sure enough—the temperature drops. The beast is still alive.

Behind her, she can hear the voices faintly coming through from the theater's lobby. One of them—probably the psycho on the floor—has just burst into a shrill laugh that makes the hairs on her arms stand on end.

Now, another sound joins in—a deep, guttural growl. It's

coming from her stomach, which has caught the scent of a chocolate bar on the top shelf.

You might wanna rethink that, she says to herself, glancing at the streaks of blood that decorate some of the glass shards still hanging in the frame of the machine. *I don't think the psycho out there is gonna take it too kindly if you grab a chocolate bar.*

Truth be told, her need for a bathroom break isn't nearly as urgent as she made it seem. When she mentioned it the first time, it was just an excuse to stop Michael before he dug too deep into the topic of her father and sister. And when he brought it up again just now, it was the perfect opportunity to get a break from Tom's endless barrage of *jeezes*.

But whatever, now that she's out here, she might as well take advantage of the fact that there is a bathroom. Who knows when she'll see another.

After walking over to the bathroom door, she pushes it open without hesitation, afraid that, otherwise, she might not be able to do it at all.

Applying the same strategy, she continues straight to the middle one of the three stalls inside. She's not exactly comfortable being alone in this cold, tile-covered room, but still, pushing the stall door open, she feels a smile creeping onto her lips.

Who is General Failure and why is he reading my hard drive? Your nose runs and your feet smell—there's something wrong, isn't there? How many egomaniacs does it take to screw in a light bulb? One. He holds the light bulb while the world revolves around him.

The inside of the toilet stall is covered with this kind of witty philosophy. In Lisa's opinion, the level is relatively high. She's especially fond of the comment someone added beneath the bold, black marker inscription, *QUESTION EVERYTHING*, above the paper dispenser. Directly below, in pencil, someone has added three dots, followed by the word *WHY* and a large question mark.

In a way, it's reassuring to read these little scribbles. It shows that at least there was life in the town once—and it also gives her hope that they might find other people.

Normal people, she thinks, shifting slightly to get the loose toilet seat to settle into a stable position. *Not like that psycho out there.*

Lisa really doesn't like Tom—and it's not just because he chose to introduce himself by chucking a can in her face.

No, her aversion toward their new acquaintance runs deeper than that. It stems from the fact that he, obviously, is mentally disturbed and, in many ways, reminds her of her younger sister in the final years. During those years, Emma's mental illness accelerated dramatically, and with each passing day, she became more reserved. That was also when she started having violent fits where she would lash out at others with neither reason nor warning. In the end, her mental decline led to the events of the night when her life ended. The incident.

And *that* is why Lisa doesn't like Tom. The look in his eyes as he sits there, rocking back and forth, is just too familiar. Too much like the one she saw in Emma's eyes, back when . . .

Okay, that's enough. This is where you get off. No need to ride this train all the way to the end of the line.

Once again, the inner version of her mom's voice has come to her rescue, but this time Lisa isn't satisfied with the intervention. Because why shouldn't she just ride that train? Why is it so important for her to suppress those thoughts? After all, Emma did it herself. She was the one who chose to leave *them*—not the other way around. She did it herself, damn it!

Trembling, Lisa pulls the sleeve of her shirt up over her hand and wipes a mix of snot and tears away from her bare thighs. She feels pathetic. Here she sits, pants down around her ankles, in a bathroom in some fucked up desert town, whining about her little sister. Her bloody coward of a sister whom she loves with all her heart, but also despises, because it was her and her disease that caused all the pain that Lisa now has to live with.

You need to shut it down, now, she says to herself. *Otherwise, it's just gonna hurt even more, and you don't have the strength for that right now. There's plenty of other stuff to worry about.*

She places one hand on top of the other and starts scratching the edges of her bracelets, hoping it will take her thoughts away from Emma.

Sitting like that, her gaze once again lands on the encouragement to QUESTION EVERYTHING. It's not so funny anymore.

When she feels better, Lisa reaches out to grab a piece of toilet paper from the roll. Of course, it's one of those stupid metal dispensers where you have to shove your whole forearm inside and fumble around blindly just to find the edge of the paper. The kind that would be just big enough to house a spider the size of a dinner plate.

To her relief, there's no eight-legged crawler in the box, but just the thought of it is more than enough.

Before flushing the toilet, Lisa stands still for a moment, listening. She is trying to make out the voices coming from the foyer, but the relentless humming of the fluorescent light in the ceiling and the water pipes in the walls make it impossible.

It's okay, she reassures herself. *Michael has got it under control.*

Given how the day has progressed so far, there aren't many people Lisa would dare to trust—but her newfound companion in misery is definitely one of them. He is the only reason she is not still trudging around in the sand with her hands over her ears. And even if she had somehow mustered the courage to enter the spooky desert town on her own, her encounter with the eight-legged creature in the community house would likely have ended very differently without him. So yeah, the least she can do is show him some trust.

This is Lisa's last thought before she flushes the toilet and walks over to the sink . . . where she'll have her first encounter with a mirror in this other world.

20

Hell is a hall full of mirrors.

When Michael finally regains his voice after the pause that followed Tom's definition of hell, he hasn't yet reached the point where he's willing to resort to violence. He is, however, at the point where he has to remind himself of the words he said to Lisa earlier. That it's the situation—and not the man—his anger should be directed at.

Clearly, Tom has also sensed the change in his captor's state of mind. He is cowering on the floor, his legs pulled up to his chest as far as the rope allows.

"I'm gonna ask you a question," Michael says, crouching down so he can make eye contact with him. "But before I do that, I want to tell you something."

Tom bites his lower lip and squints his eyes. His pupils are still small and rebellious, but there is also a bit of fear to spot in them.

"The things is, Tom," Michael continues. "I lost my wife and my son three weeks ago, and ever since, I've been feeling like I was losing my mind. I've been seeing things, Tom. Seeing *them*. I actually believed I saw them, all kinds of places. I even heard my son calling out to me a couple of times. And that's fine, completely normal. That kind of stuff often happens to people who lose someone."

He lets out a hollow, half-choked chuckle and grabs his forehead. Meanwhile, Tom keeps staring at him, not saying a word.

"I also had nightmares, Tom. The kind that keeps coming back. That's fine too—normal even. What's *not* so normal, though, is that you've just described the essence of that nightmare very accurately. In few words, that's true, but still very accurately. How did you put it? Hell is a hall full of mirrors . . . was that it?"

Tom nods, still not making a sound. Not even a *jeez*.

"You were spot on," Michael says. "You see, in my nightmares, there are also mirrors. A big-ass hall filled with them, actually. They're covered with sheets, but they *are* mirrors, alright. I know because I pulled one of the sheets off."

Michael pauses again, but this time, it isn't a deliberate, rhetorical choice. The image of Benjamin trapped in the officer's arms behind the glass of the mirror has popped up on the screen inside his mind again. And with it comes the same gut-wrenching feeling of powerlessness he had when he woke up from the nightmare. And the same anger.

"Now, all of this brings me to my question, Tom. This hell that you're talking about—does it exist? Is it a real place . . . in this world?"

21

Tom Cerveau—because that is his full name—is conflicted. A part of him feels bad for the man who has just laid bare his deepest sorrow. It's a strange sensation. Rational people might describe it with a fancy word like *sympathy*, but for Tom, it's more like a gnawing unease in his gut, something he can't quite place.

Come to think of it, he isn't even sure if he's ever had that particular feeling before. Still, there's something familiar in the man's story. Like it's stirring a memory of an experience in Tom's past.

Loss? Losing someone? No, it isn't that . . . is it?

For the first time in a long while, Tom actively tries to break through the hidden barrier that keeps him from accessing his memories. It's strong, and every previous attempt has been futile. Nevertheless, he has to try. Because when the man talked about what happened to his son, it had an effect on that barrier. It didn't open, but it . . . *responded.*

Is it a real place?

He considers lying and just telling the man that he's never

heard of the Mansion of Mirrors. If he were to go with the strange feeling in his gut, that would probably be the right thing to do. It would most likely also save the man's life because the mansion is a dangerous place. That much Tom does remember, although everything else is pretty blurry right now.

He could also just tell the truth, but then there's something else bothering him—his jackpot prize. Because if they find out that the mansion not only exists but is also their ticket home, the man and the girl will probably head for the Wastelands straightaway. And bring the contents of the machine with them as provisions for the journey.

The more Tom dwells on that possibility, the more likely it seems. And the more likely it seems, the more his fury grows.

What a greedy fucker! Jeez! Doesn't he get that it's mine? That I was the one who found it?

Suddenly, the feeling in his stomach takes up much less space. It's actually a relief. Moral dilemmas always exhaust him. It's easier to give in to the anger. Just like he usually does.

Besides, he's only about half an inch away from cutting all the way through the rope with the shard of glass he pulled from his forearm. The crybaby's long monologue has given him plenty of time to saw away at the knots behind his back. If he wants, he can easily stall until his hands are free. Maybe he'll even buy some extra time by giving his captor a bit of insight into the mysteries of the Mansion of Mirrors. After all, he plans to slit the guy's throat anyway—so what harm could it do?

Tom smiles to himself.

Yeah, that's probably the easiest solution.

"Oh yeah, it's a real place," he says, trying to make the words sound dramatic. "They call it the Mansion of Mirrors. But you don't wanna go near that place. Jeez, no. It's dangerous."

"What do you mean?" Michael asks, the timbre of his voice

telling Tom that he is shaken by the information. That's fine with him. The more shaken he is, the more distracted he will be—and that means more time for Tom to get free.

"What do you mean, what do I mean?" Tom snaps back, at the exact moment that the knife gets all the way through the rope. Now, he just needs to get free of the ropes around his upper arms and chest, but they're fairly loose. A few good tugs should do the trick. "I mean what I said. It's a dangerous place."

With his childish behavior, Tom hopes for one particular reaction from his captor—and he gets it. Michael responds by letting out a sigh of frustration and grabbing his head, after which he turns around and walks to the window facing the street. There he stands now, leaning against the glass.

What a gift! The dumb fuck actually turned his back. Time to get a move on—without making too much noise.

Tom stretches his legs and presses his feet against the floor, arching his body into a curve between them and the pole. Next, he tilts his head back and lets his upper body go slack, sliding free of the rope like a snake shedding its skin.

The movement sends a jolt of pain through his injured leg, but he couldn't care less. The only thing on his mind right now is driving that shard of glass as deep as possible into the crybaby's throat—deep enough to prevent him from ever bothering anyone again with his pathetic sob story.

And the plan is working. He's almost over there, and Michael has only just started to turn around. A few more seconds, and his miserable whining will be over for good.

Tom raises his arm high above his head, clasping the shard of glass so hard that thin, warm streaks of blood trickle down his wrist.

This is it, he thinks with an almost euphoric enthusiasm. *If you're lucky, you might get to see your family in a minute.*

All of a sudden, something steals Tom's attention and makes him hesitate. Just outside the entrance doors is a tall, dark silhouette. Behind it, two bright white beams of light shine, spreading out on either side of it, like the wings of an angel. However, as Tom's gaze drifts downward, focusing on the object the man on the other side of the glass is holding, that idea is dismissed.

It's no angel standing out there. Tom Cerveau might never have been strong in the Bible, neither in this world nor the one his mind doesn't allow him to remember, but he knows that much. That is no angel.

Angels don't carry rifles.

No further does Tom get before one of the doors explodes with a deafening blast, sending a shower of glass shards down on him.

22

"That was the warning shot," Michael hears an astonishingly calm voice say somewhere out in the darkness of the street outside the theater's foyer. "I hope I won't have to take proper aim next time. Are we clear?"

For a moment, Michael thinks the message is meant for him, but then, out of the corner of his eye, he notices Tom crouched on the floor, nodding frantically, glass dust drizzling from his greasy hair. His wide, mortified eyes are locked onto the unknown adversary, who now steps through the shattered window of the theater's entrance.

Michael also watches the eerie black silhouette as it transforms into a man of flesh and blood in the encounter with the light inside the theater—the same man he met at the library earlier that day.

There is, however, a noticeable difference. Back then, the elderly gentleman held a box of books in his hands. Now, the books have been replaced with a hunting rifle.

"It's you, from the library . . . Starck?"

The librarian nods and then lets his gaze drift over Michael's forearms. The column to the left of the entrance took the worst of it when the window exploded, but he still got a few cuts.

"I apologize for the dramatic entrance," Starck says, his voice still so bizarrely calm that you'd think he were narrating a nature documentary. "There really wasn't time for anything else. I see you've already made some new acquain—"

He stops mid-sentence, putting on a more sympathetic face.

"My apologies. I forget how overwhelming it can be the first time. Are you okay?"

"Huh? What? Yeah, I'm . . . I'm okay." Michael opens his mouth as if he has more to add but then closes it again.

"Good . . . and the girl?"

Michael narrows his eyes. It takes him a moment to figure out what the question is actually about—and another moment to actually find the answer.

"She's okay too," he says, raising his hand with fingers spread as though to say, *Wait, there's more.* Next, he closes his hand, leaving only his index finger extended, and points it toward the hallway leading to the theater halls. "She's in there. She had to use the restroom."

"Oh Christ, can't catch a break," Starck exclaims, after which he points the rifle at Tom, still cowering on the floor. "You stay right there. Got it?"

Tom remains quiet but nods frantically. Meanwhile, Starck turns to Michael.

"And you're coming with me."

The rifle alone is reason enough to obey, but Michael would probably have followed no matter what. Because there's something troubling in the armed librarian's voice. It sounds like he is genuinely worried that the girl might be in danger.

23

When Starck fired his rifle and shattered the window, the noise was deafening. In fact, the blast was so loud that it made the stage curtain in the theater's back hall tremble. And yet, Lisa didn't register it. Because Lisa is far away. Her physical body is still there, but her mind—perhaps even her soul—has left the present.

She also doesn't hear Starck and Michael as they come running into the hallway, shouting her name. She hears someone calling, but it's not their voices. There is only one voice, and it doesn't come from the hallway of the abandoned theater.

No, the voice she hears comes from the mirror. The oval mirror above the sink, whose glass is speckled with yellowish grease stains, which Lisa is staring straight through.

The room she sees behind the glass is almost completely dark and could have been any other room than her own old one . . . if it weren't for the poster on the door adorned with Garfield's grinning face.

The writing below the world's favorite fat cat has vanished in the dark, but that doesn't matter. The poster was a gift from Emma, and Lisa doesn't need to read the words to know what the Sultan of Sass and Lasagna wants to tell the world.

It's all about the ME-ow!

She squints her eyes, trying to see if that'll help her decipher the letters in the darkness, and without even thinking about it, she takes a step closer to the mirror.

Although well aware of what will follow in the scene that is about to unfold behind the glass, she shivers when she hears her sister calling once again.

In the mirror, she follows her own movements, every step she took that night. Countless nightmares have taken her from start to finish in the scene over the past thirteen months . . . yet something is different this time around. It seems more real. She can feel, with all her senses, the panic and confusion that her younger self felt as she jumped out of bed and pulled on her oversized bathrobe.

Mom's robe, she corrects herself. *It was Mom's robe I had on.*

Behind the glass, she sees herself tearing open the door with enough force to make Garfield's square set of teeth tremble. Afterward she watches herself running down the hallway and up the stairs to her parents' bedroom, her robe fluttering behind her like some kind of superhero cape.

Turn around, she tells the girl in the mirror, who now stumbles on the fourth step of the stairs. *It's too late. You don't have to go in there. You don't have to see it.*

The girl doesn't turn around. She just grabs the railing, pulls herself up, and traverses the last five steps in two big leaps.

Reaching the door to her parents' bedroom, she pauses for a moment. It's quiet in there. Far too quiet. That's what she thought back then, and that's what she thinks now.

In a last-ditch attempt to prevent the inevitable, Lisa closes her eyes, clenches her hand, and sends it with full force into the darkness in front of her.

A bolt of pain shoots up through her forearm as her knuckles hit resistance, but the sound that follows is not that of shattering glass. It's the short, dull thud of flesh, bone, and skin colliding with wood.

In that moment, Lisa realizes she is powerless. In a few seconds, her eyes will be forced open, and her hand will be guided to the doorknob, whether she wants it or not. Some force in this other world has taken control of her now, and the door to the past will be opened—not by some empty replica that she can safely observe from behind a pane of glass, but by herself. *She* will open the door. That's just the way it is.

When the inevitable moment comes, Lisa tries to call for help, but just like the first time, she discovers that she can't. The sight behind the door has her chest rising and falling in such short intervals that it doesn't allow any words to pass.

On her cheek, a cold tear wanders down until it stops in the corner of her mouth. She makes no attempt to wipe it away. She just keeps staring.

Her parents' bedroom has a high ceiling. Because of that they put up a miniature chandelier, claiming it added a 'royal touch' to the room—even though it's just one of the cheap ones with plastic crystals that you'd typically find at a hardware store.

To match this marvel of a light source, they chose to keep all of the room's furniture in dark-stained oak. Aside from an old rocking chair, this includes the bed—where Lisa's father right now lies, his upper body hanging so far over the edge that it almost looks like he's floating in midair—and a wardrobe, against which her little sister is leaning, gasping for breath.

Her hands.

Lisa can't tear her eyes away from the small, pink palms, where Emma's slightly spread fingers twitch in short, rhythmic jerks as if trying to hold on to the thick, red liquid seeping out between them.

Lisa puts her hands over her mouth to stifle a scream that never comes. Around her, the whole world begins to tilt sideways, and for a moment, she thinks she is about to faint. Almost hopes so.

". . . Lisa?"

The half-choked sound of Emma's voice puts the world back on its axis, and Lisa discovers that her sister has raised her head. She sits there, glancing around the room with a feverish expression in her eyes. Her face is so pale that it's almost impossible to distinguish where her neck ends and the collar of the white nightgown begins.

"Lisa, is that you?"

Lisa steps over the threshold. The thick gray carpet feels like cold concrete beneath her bare feet.

"Oh God, Emma, what have you done?"

No reaction, just blank eyes alternately rising and falling without finding anything to focus on.

In an attempt to gain control of her thoughts, Lisa presses her hands against her temples. For some reason, she can't get her brain to link all the sensory impressions together into a comprehensible whole, for while her mind insists that she has experienced it all before, all the cells in her body object and claim the opposite. They tell her that what she is experiencing is nothing less than the harsh, merciless reality.

The pressure on her temples is so intense that small, silvery spots flutter around in her field of vision.

She closes her eyes. It doesn't work. In fact, it only makes it worse. In the dark behind her eyelids, it's as though the rusty smell of blood and the sound of Emma's heavy breathing are amplified.

When she opens her eyes again, her gaze lands on the knife lying on the floor between Emma's legs. It's a large kitchen knife. The light from the plastic chandelier reflects off the steel, making it glint in the few spots where the blade isn't covered in blood. She flinches, noticing a small, red handprint on the wooden handle.

From the handle, her gaze continues up along the blade, past its tip, and across the floor in the direction the knife is pointing. This leads her to the last part of the terrible drama. Her dad on the bed.

Robert Swann is lying on his back with his upper body hanging over the edge. His arms are spread wide so that both hands lie flat against the floor. White sheets cover his lower body and most of his stomach, but his chest is exposed. So are the numerous stab wounds. From them, small streaks of blood run down toward his neck. Some gather into puddles between his collarbones, while others continue all the way to the neck, drawing a macabre necklace.

Slowly, Lisa lowers her hands from her temples, letting them drop limply to her sides. It has dawned on her. The sight of his chest neither rising nor lowering did it.

Her dad is dead. Even though his frightened eyes look like they belong in the kind of portrait paintings where the gaze follows you no matter what angle you watch it from, he is definitively dead and gone. And all signs suggest her sister is on her way to join him.

The blood, Lisa thinks, fumbling to pull the robe's belt free of the straps. *I have to stop the bleeding before—*

She doesn't get any further before Emma lifts her head for the last time. For a brief second, the feverish emptiness is gone from the green eyes, and she looks at Lisa . . . *sees Lisa*. Her lips move, but nothing comes out but a faint, hissing sound. Shortly after, she closes her eyes again and her head drops, the black hair falling down, covering her face. Her fingers twitch one final time before curling into her pink palms, like the legs of a dying insect.

Unable to fathom the evident, Lisa continues to pull on the stubborn fabric belt of the bathrobe, her brain screaming to her that there may still be hope, that Emma may just be unconscious and that the belt can be used to stop the bleeding.

When the straps finally let go, she runs toward her sister. However, two steps away from her, she hesitates, then stops completely.

Something is wrong. Something about Emma isn't right.

She studies the curled-up girl—the black hair sticking to her pale, sweat-dotted forehead, the narrow shoulders visible beneath the white fabric of her nightgown, the blood-soaked hands lying flat against the carpet.

Suddenly, it hits her. Emma's slender wrists are bare. She's not wearing her flashy, yellow and purple bracelets. And Lisa knows that Emma almost never takes off her beloved bracelets. She also knows for a fact that Emma was wearing them the night she died—because ever since the funeral, Lisa has been wearing them herself as a keepsake.

All at once, her inner struggle is over, and a wave of memories crashes over her. Countless moments from the past thirteen months of her life flood her mind—the funeral for Emma and her father, moving to the new apartment, the sessions with the therapist, the loneliness, switching schools, the voice in the hallway, meeting Michael, arriving in Attica—and not least, the giant spider in the community house.

The grief and pain are real, but she now realizes that everything else she has just experienced was an illusion. Even if her body insists that it can still feel the soft fabric of the robe, it wasn't real.

It's this place. She closes her eyes and tries to ignore the rusty smell that still lingers in her nostrils. *It's doing something to you. It wants you to think that it's happening right now, but in reality, it has been a long time since she died—more than a year. Emma isn't here, and you're not in Mom and Dad's bedroom. You're standing by yourself in front of a mirror in the restroom of an old, abandoned theater.*

In the darkness behind her eyelids, she listens for something that will confirm the thought; bubbles in a water pipe, water in a cistern . . . anything to help her prove the claim.

Suddenly, there is something. Someone is calling her name. They're far away, but they're there.

She tries to shut everything else out and focus solely on the sound.

Two voices. One is Michael's, the other she doesn't recognize. For a brief moment, it crosses her mind that Michael might have freed the prisoner, but she quickly dismisses the thought. He is too smart for that.

Carefully, she gropes through the darkness in front of her. If it really is Michael she can hear, that must mean she's back in the bathroom. Nevertheless, she has no intention of opening her eyes until she feels the surface of the sink beneath her hands.

For a few terrifying seconds, the fear hits her that she might be wrong—that her fingertips might meet Emma's face instead. But then, they touch the cold steel of the faucet, and she sighs in relief.

The voices are also clearer now—and it sounds like they are right on the other side of the door.

Hesitantly, she opens her eyes. Sure enough, she's back in the temple of toilet poetry—the restroom at the *People's Theater Attica*.

She spins around in a semicircle and takes a few steps away from the sink before lifting her gaze. And when she does, she keeps her eyes locked on the door.

She has no intention of giving the mirror another chance to finish what it started.

24

When Michael yanks open the bathroom door, he does so without having the faintest idea of what awaits him on the other side. All he knows is that Starck sounded genuinely concerned, and that feeling has rubbed off on him. He is afraid of what might have happened to the young girl that he—despite only having known her for a couple of hours—has formed a strong bond with.

And something did happen to her—because there she is, standing motionless in the middle of the floor. Small, pale, and terrified.

"Lisa?" he says and takes a step into the room.

No reaction. Her gaze is locked on something behind him. When he realizes that it's Starck—and in particular the rifle in his hands—Michael motions to the librarian to put it away.

Starck raises his hand in a silent apology before setting the rifle down. Meanwhile, Michael continues walking toward Lisa with careful, measured steps. He still doesn't understand what's going on, but it's clear that the librarian's alarm wasn't unfounded. Whatever happened in here was bad. Her eyes reveal that much.

Once close enough, he places his hand on her shoulder. She puts her hand on top of his and pulls it to her cheek.

"I'd like to go home now," she mutters. "I wanna see my mom."

Michael doesn't answer. Instead, he looks back over his shoulder and silently passes the request on to Starck.

The librarian's answer isn't articulated either, but it's still clearly written in the eyes behind his glasses.

It won't be quite that easy, I'm afraid.

"Let's get you out of here," Michael says, after which he wraps his arm around Lisa's shoulders and guides her out of the bathroom.

Returning to the foyer, it's no surprise for Michael to find that Tom has seized the opportunity to take off while they were gone. The only thing left of him is the rope, lying in a crumpled pile at the base of the metal pole he was tied to.

Lisa looks at the rope and from there up at the window that Starck shattered into a thousand pieces with his rifle. Then she turns to Michael, her eyes filled with concern.

"I don't think we'll see him again anytime soon," Michael reassures her.

"For his own sake, I hope he stays gone," Starck adds, nodding toward the rifle now resting in his hands again.

"We've got questions," Michael says. "A ton of questions. You know that, right?"

"And I'll be happy to answer them as best I can," Starck replies, gesturing toward the two large beams of light outside. "Right now, however, we need to get a move on. Cars are scarce around here, as is fuel, and mine is still running."

Those words pull Lisa out of her state of shock, turning the unease in her facial expression into a kind of confounded indignation.

"You expect us to jump into a car with you?" she exclaims. "I don't even know who you are!"

Starck rubs the back of his neck and glances toward the vehicle again, as though weighing whether it's even worth the trouble to argue or he should just give up and leave them to fend for themselves.

"I don't *expect* anything," he says. "I'm *offering* you a ride. I'm here to help . . . and to be quite frank, it looks like you could use it."

Lisa looks at Michael, her eyes glowing with anxiety and frustration. He turns around, positioning himself with his back to Starck, and motions for her to do the same.

"Listen," he whispers. "I'm not loving it either, but he's right. We haven't exactly been on top of things so far, and it seems like he knows this place. Besides, he did save my life a minute ago. Tom got free of the rope, and it could have ended really badly for me—but he stopped him."

"Okay, but . . . you do know that he was in the library before we, um . . . disappeared, right? I saw him over there."

Michael glances back toward the entrance where the librarian stands, his rifle resting so casually on one shoulder that it could just as well have been a folded umbrella. It's an absurd sight, and the thought he had when they first arrived in the desert resurfaces: Is this even real, or are Lisa and him stuck in some kind of shared psychosis? Is the armed librarian just another element of their collective hallucination?

"I realize that he was in the library," he whispers. "And I plan on getting an explanation for that too. Right now, I just don't see any other option besides going with him. That said, if you'd rather say no and stay here, I'm with you. I'm not about to leave you alone out here."

"I'm . . . no," Lisa says, shaking her head. "We'll go with him."

"You sure?"

"Yeah, I'm sure. I've had enough of this crappy town anyway."

Michael gives her a solemn nod, then turns back to face Starck.

"We'll go with you."

"Glad to hear it. Now, let's get going while we still have fuel in the tank."

With that, the librarian gestures for them to follow his lead, after which he steps through the broken window, out into the night.

PART FOUR
URARI

PROLOGUE 4

The man on the bed is, in many ways, an ambiguous element in the young artist's painting. On one hand, he appears overwhelmingly dominant. His sheer size, broad shoulders, and the sinewy muscles of his arms make him seem imposing, even threatening. This impression is reinforced by the crouched girl at the center of the canvas—her withdrawn posture amplifies his presence, making him seem even larger.

On the other hand, he appears to be the weakest of the painting's three figures, as any observer will quickly notice that all the most threatening aspects of his presence have been systematically neutralized using the knife on the floor as the tool. His muscular chest is riddled with deep stab wounds, and his huge arms hang limply over the edges of the bed. As was true for the girl in the white nightgown, this man is no longer among the living.

Unlike her, however, it's not a choice he has made himself.

25

Their dirty, rusty, but otherwise decent vehicle is a dark blue station wagon that on the inside smells like oil and dust. It's a brand Michael has never heard of before—*Revor*—and like many of the buildings in Attica, it feels like something from an entirely different era. There's nothing wrong with its seats, though, and while they may not be able to compete with the cushions of the Chesterfield in his living room back home, it's still nice to feel the soft foam against his back and his butt.

After settling into the passenger seat, he glances over his shoulder and smiles when he sees Lisa pull her legs up and lean her head against the headrest. She's clearly also thrilled to be sitting on something other than sand and hard tiles.

"You okay back there?"

She responds with a shrug and returns his smile—which he can't deny impresses him a bit. Whatever she experienced in that bathroom wasn't nice, and yet she manages to find a smile for him now. He's not sure many people would be able to do the same in her shoes.

Lisa raises an eyebrow, as if to ask what he's thinking about, but before he can answer, the librarian switches on the windshield wipers, causing them both to jolt.

Considering how old and worn the car looks, the engine is surprisingly quiet as Starck shifts into gear and releases the clutch. Normally, that would be a good thing. Right now, though, it only enhances the eerie, scraping sound of sand grains being hurled against the window by the rising wind. Grains that it brings in from the desert that surrounds the town—that part Michael is still struggling to wrap his head around.

As the car starts pulling them forward, slowly making the light behind the shattered windows of the theater's foyer fade into the distance, the librarian turns his face toward Michael.

"It would be a good idea for you to get some rest during the drive," he says. "Maybe even sleep a bit."

Michael doesn't say anything, but in the back seat, Lisa lets out a loud snort.

"I think what Lisa is trying to say is that we probably won't sleep much until you've explained some of this," Michael says.

"Yeah, well," Starck says, sighing. "Then let's get on with it. Where would you like to start?"

Michael meets the gaze in the brown eyes behind the librarian's glasses and suddenly feels overwhelmed. The past few hours of his life have been filled with so many things he doesn't understand that sorting through the pile of questions seems impossible. In the end, he decides to start with what led him to seek out Starck at the library in the first place.

"I think we should start at the beginning," he says. "At least where it all started for me. That day, three weeks ago, when I lost my wife and my son—you called me that day, and you, um . . . somehow, you knew before I did. Didn't you?"

Starck nods, slowly and thoughtfully.

"In a way, I did," he says. "But it's more complicated than that.

Up until this moment, I didn't know it was your wife and your son. It doesn't work that way."

"But you knew something had happened?"

"I knew that you would need to come here and that it would be my job to help you. When people end up here, it's often because they've lost someone they care about. So, in that sense, I knew you had suffered a loss, but the details of it are new to me."

Now Lisa's head appears between the front seats. She says nothing but listens carefully as Starck continues.

"However, I want you to know that it affects me and that I feel for you. In a just world, no parent would outlive their child."

"Thanks," Michael says, turning his face toward the side window. Outside, Attica's gray buildings still flicker past, now at a faster pace. Empty, sad, and lifeless. The will to live seems to have completely abandoned this lonely desert town—just as it's close to abandoning him.

"What do you mean he *needed* to come here?" Lisa interjects from the back seat. "And what even is this place?"

Starck sighs loudly as if to emphasize that it's complicated to answer.

"Do you know what I mean if I say that you're no longer in Kansas?"

Michael nods—and when he sees Lisa squint her eyes, he explains:

"It's a quote from *The Wizard of Oz*. It's what Dorothy says to her dog after a tornado carries them to Oz . . . to a fairy-tale world."

"Exactly," Starck says, nodding. "And just like Dorothy in that story, you've ended up in a different world. A parallel universe, you could say."

Michael exchanges a glance with Lisa . . . and as crazy as it seems, he sees in her green eyes that she—like himself—is neither particularly surprised nor in doubt that the librarian is telling the truth. Heck, part of him has known ever since he opened his eyes to that desert landscape.

"But like . . . what world?" Lisa stammers. "Where are we, exactly?"

"It's difficult to give a definitive answer," Starck says, adjusting his glasses. "Over time, this world has been given many names. Some are gloomy, and more than once, the place has even been mistaken for Hell. But that's not really a fair description as there are also things here of great beauty—and it has been given positive names as well. In fact, there is reason to believe that many of the worlds we know and love from books and movies were inspired by this one. But all those names came from people who only got a brief glimpse of this place. Those who live here permanently have a different name for it. They call it *Urari*."

"Urari?" Lisa repeats. "That's . . . kind of weird."

"We can agree on that," Starck says. "I've wondered about it too—especially after doing some research and discovering that the word also exists in our world. It's a Swahili word that means *balance*, which actually isn't a bad description of Urari."

Perhaps Starck's job at the library is just a cover for his real work as a tour guide in an alternate dimension, but the excitement in his brown eyes reveals to Michael that his interest in words and their origins is very real.

"Interestingly, this particular name has never found its way into our literature," Starck continues. "However, this detail is probably due to the strange phenomenon that everyone seems to understand and speak the same language while they're here."

"Not following," Lisa says.

"Like the sign by the community house," Michael says, half

questioning, half stating. "We shouldn't have been able to read it."

"Exactly," Starck says. "You'll read things here as though it were your native tongue, and so would a Frenchman or a Chinese person."

Lisa holds her hands up in front of her face, then lets them drop to her sides as if to say that she is giving up trying to understand any of it.

"But if we've been pulled into some kind of fantasy world," Michael says, "what should we expect? I mean, how, um . . . different is this place gonna be?"

While considering his answer, Starck takes a deep breath and stares down at his hands—for a long time and with more concern in his eyes than Michael likes.

"As long as we're close to the Perimeter, this world won't feel that different from the one you know," he says. "Urari is divided into different interdependent societies, just like your own world. There is structure in the form of rules and laws, and the residents live, work, and . . . have an everyday life, although it's often a simpler way of life, which to you may seem old-fashioned and primitive."

Now he lets go of the steering wheel with one hand, so he is able to turn around and make eye contact with both of them.

"Having said that, there are also significant differences between the two worlds. And the deeper we venture into Urari, the more . . . unnatural things you'll encounter."

"But I don't *want* to go deeper into this place," Lisa exclaims. "I want to go home. My mom has got to be worried sick by now. She probably already reported me missing."

"I understand your frustration, but if it's of any consolation, your mother likely won't even know that you're gone yet."

"She . . . what?"

"That's another thing you need to realize about this place. Time moves differently here. Faster, much faster. Hours in Urari will be nothing more than minutes in your own world. Besides, if you want to go home, there is no way around it. We will need to travel deeper into Urari, to the very center, in fact, as that's where your exit is located. And, like I said, going there means encountering unnatural things. You need to be prepared for that as well so you don't underestimate how dangerous it can be to navigate this place."

"I don't think you need to worry about that part," Michael says, shuddering at the thought that this world might have worse things to offer than the creature they faced in the community house. "We've had a taste of it."

Starck stares at him in silence for a moment, then nods and turns his gaze to the road. Michael does the same and is surprised to see that they're almost out of town already. All that remains ahead are a few of Attica's burned-out houses and a gas station, proudly proclaiming that fuel prices haven't been this low in fifty years . . . which feels ironic, given that both the building and the sign look like they belong to that exact era.

"What is the Perimeter?" Lisa asks.

"Oh yes, of course," Starck says. "I should've explained that. The Perimeter is kind of a gray area, a merging point, where our world and Urari overlap. It's where the two worlds resemble each other the most—and when you arrive here, you can show up in different locations, but it's always somewhere on the Perimeter. And before you ask, I have no idea why. Smarter people than me have tried to figure it out without any luck. The best theory I've heard is that Urari has some kind of consciousness and gives newcomers a gentle start, so they have a better chance at getting ready for whatever brought them here."

A gentle start? Michael thinks, and looking at Lisa, he sees that this phrasing didn't escape her attention either.

"For whatever brought them here?"

"Yes," Starck says, nodding. "You only come to Urari for a reason. Because you're looking for something. Otherwise, the gate is closed. Most often—like in your case—it's related to pain and grief because you've lost someone. And one could argue that the same probably applies to the artists who have managed to bring elements from this world into their artwork. Even though their connection to Urari is usually intuitive and they rarely end up here physically, there's reason to believe that it's also linked to grief in some form. After all, it's not unheard of for an artist to claim that their inspiration comes from life's agony."

"Because they're looking for something," Lisa repeats in the back seat. "And what do they find, then?"

"What they're looking for," Starck says. "Whether you like it or not, in Urari you always find what you're looking for."

26

Only when he is a hundred percent sure the car is gone does Tom Cerveau stagger out of his hiding spot in a dark alley between two nearby buildings and start making his way back toward the theater. His knee still hurts like hell, so he stays close to walls and lampposts, using them for support.

Every so often, the pain forces him to his knees on the sidewalk, but each time, he stubbornly pushes himself back up. It'll take more than this to stop him. A lot more. He's used to walking for days, maybe even weeks, without food or water.

As if he feels an urge to prove this claim, he speeds up, and before long he is standing in front of the shattered windows of the theater's entrance. Bent over and out of breath, but close to the goal . . . to his jackpot.

He gets ready to step over the finish line and let his efforts be rewarded with the best from the vending machine, but then something makes him hesitate. The feeling of being watched.

He glances around. The street is empty except for a couple of tumbleweeds rolling along in short, jerky movements. The windows in the houses are also dark and empty. There's absolutely nothing suggesting the presence of other people.

It doesn't have to be people, though.

His own thought sends shivers down his spine. Because Tom knows very well what this world has to offer in terms of wildlife. And should he forget, there's always the scar on his hip to remind him. That cursed maulwert left so many of its small, razor-sharp teeth in him that it took him hours to get them out after he had trampled the beast to death.

He looks around one last time before deciding that whatever is out there can come at him or fuck off. Right now, what matters is collecting his jackpot.

With that thought in the back of his mind, Tom steps into the theater's lobby and, from there, heads straight to the hallway where the vending machine is.

After spending a moment scanning the shelves, he's relieved to see that his prizes are still there. In fact, it doesn't look like the crybaby and his buddies took anything at all.

Lucky for them, Tom thinks as he pulls down a handful of snacks from one of the shelves. *Otherwise, I'd find them.*

The thought of all the fabulous cruelties he would put his new friends through in that scenario brings a smile to his lips.

He'd start by tying up the crybaby and the old fart with the rifle, he decides, as the first chocolate bar makes its way to his stomach, quieting the worst of his hunger. Tie them up just like they did to him. Afterward, he'd cut the girl into little bits while they could do nothing but watch helplessly, knowing that they're up next.

Now the feeling returns, and this time Tom is convinced. He is *not* alone. Someone or something is watching him.

"Where are you hiding?" he hums, wiping crumbs and bits of chocolate off his beard with his sleeve.

Immediately, almost as an answer, there's a noise coming from the bathroom farther down the hall. It sounds like a running faucet.

Tom narrows his eyes and takes a few steps toward the door. It's slightly ajar, gaping no more than an inch, but a thin strip of light spills onto the floor, revealing that the light inside is on. That light wasn't there a moment ago. It definitely wasn't.

This realization stops him in his tracks. If someone really is in there, he might need to defend himself.

Oh, well, why not? he thinks, limping back to the vending machine and grabbing a can of soda from one of the shelves. *It worked like a charm on the girl.*

Now another sound arises from the bathroom, this time a short whistle, as if someone is trying to call a dog.

Tom pats his pocket. Yup, he has still got the shard he meant to bury in the crybaby's throat before the old asshole with the rifle showed up. Might also come in handy now.

27

"It's too early to worry about that. It's a waste of energy."

On the surface, Starck sounds calm and collected, so Michael isn't sure what gives him the impression. Still, something tells him that the librarian isn't thrilled about the direction their conversation just took. However, that doesn't mean Michael plans to throw in the towel and let him dodge the topic so easily.

"But it does exist?" he insists. "There *is* a place called the Mansion of Mirrors?"

"Where did you even hear that name?"

"Right before you made your big entrance in the theater, I had a chat with the man that you . . . by the way, did I ever thank you for saving my life?"

The librarian makes a gesture saying that it's unnecessary and that Michael should just continue.

"Well, anyway. I told the guy you saved me from that ever since the accident, I've had a recurring nightmare about a hall full of mirrors. And he told me that it's a real place. Here, in Urari. A place called the Mansion of Mirrors. He also said it was a dangerous place."

For a long while, Starck sits in silence, staring at the road ahead. There are fewer potholes now, making for a smoother ride—not counting the tumbleweeds that occasionally roll into the headlights, causing him to jerk the wheel slightly. Each time that happens, Michael flinches—not because of the driver's reaction, but because his imagination insists on mistaking the damned tumbleweeds for giant spiders.

"Very well," Starck says, straightening his back as his moment of contemplation comes to an end. "I was hoping we could save this conversation until later, but it looks like there's no way around it. I'll tell you about the mansion . . . but it'll be the last thing on today's agenda. We've got a long day ahead of us tomorrow, and it's important that you're well-rested."

"Fair enough," Michael says and nods.

Starck waits for Lisa to do the same and then takes a deep breath.

"Your confused friend is right," he says. "At least when he says that the mansion is a dangerous place—especially because of the properties mirrors have here in Urari. To the locals, they don't pose a threat, at least not directly, but for newcomers like you, mirrors can be rather unpleasant acquaintances."

He turns to Lisa, who is sitting with the seatbelt tucked under her arm, using it as a makeshift armrest.

"Something tells me you already know that."

She nods, and despite the darkness in the car, Michael notices the exhaustion in her eyes shining through the smudges of makeup. It won't be long before she drifts off.

"Mirrors are problematic in Urari because they don't just reflect your physical appearance," Starck continues. "It can be difficult to fully grasp what happens when you look into one, but I've always found it useful to think of them as a kind of door or portal. I think it's fitting—partly because mirrors open doors into the more closed areas of the mind, and partly because they're also the doors through which one can leave Urari."

Those words chase away some of Michael's fatigue. He sits up, listening intently. Lisa, on the other hand, remains slouched against her improvised armrest. In fact, she looks like she has started to doze off already. That's probably for the best.

"So, you're saying that our ticket out of here is a mirror?"

"Well, I'm afraid it's not quite that simple. Your way home does indeed go through the Mansion of Mirrors, and my job as your guide is to lead you there safely . . . but just as importantly, my job is to keep you away from there until you're ready."

Before continuing, Starck grabs the frame of his glasses and pulls them down so he can look at Michael across the lenses.

"The thing is, if you stare into a mirror in Urari before you're ready, it won't work as a portal," he says. "That's one of the reasons I say that *balance* is a fitting word for Urari. Because the mirrors here amplify your mental state—they bring your inner demons to life, so to speak. And if your mind isn't in balance when you face them, the mirrors won't open a door between worlds. Instead, they'll open a door into the deepest, most painful corners of your own mind, where you'll be confronted with— no, you'll *experience*—your biggest fear."

Instinctively, Michael glances back at Lisa and is suddenly filled with a deep, almost fatherly affection for the skinny girl with the light-blonde hair, whose heavy breathing reveals that she has indeed surrendered to her fatigue. Something about her reminds him of Benjamin. It must be the way she slumps in her seatbelt. God only knows how many times he has seen his son sleep in the same position on long car rides.

He shifts his focus back to the driver and engages in a silent conversation made up of questioning glances, slight shrugs, headshakes, and small nods.

Was that what happened to her back there?
Presumably, yes.
It must have been terrible.
If you only knew.

~

Although there is no longer any doubt that Lisa is fast asleep, several silent miles pass before Starck and Michael once again speak aloud about the frightening properties of the mirrors in Urari.

For Michael, it's a surprisingly pleasant break. He still has a lot of unanswered questions, but the calm reigning in the vehicle gives him a chance to digest everything Starck has said.

As such, it shouldn't be that difficult to understand. They've been pulled into a parallel world—one that, throughout literary history, has been given many names because some artists have managed to catch glimpses of it. This idea resembles the Romantic era's notion that artists find their inspiration outside of the ordinary world—and after all, that's not a new concept for Michael. Heck, it regularly serves as the foundation for academic coffee-break discussions among the language teachers at Oakwood.

Except, of course, that's in a *metaphorical* sense. Not as an *actual* alternate world with societal structures, where people live and *have an everyday life* as Starck put it.

An everyday life. Can the same still be said about him? Does what he has led for the last three weeks qualify as *an everyday life*?

There's been some sort of routine, of course. He has gotten up every morning, and he has eaten the food necessary to survive, sure. But the rest of the time he has spent sitting in the armchair, staring blankly at the pages of an old photo album. Or out into the yard, at the basketball hoop Benjamin will never throw a ball into again. And is that enough to call it an everyday life . . . or does having an everyday life require more content? Like meaning? Purpose? Love?

Leaving aside this gloomy sidetrack in his thoughts, there is, of course, also something comforting in the notion that the inhabitants of Urari have lives and daily routines. Especially because it must mean that not everyone in this world is as nuts as the sociopath in the theater.

Still, one comforting element isn't enough to shift his focus from the two biggest and most disturbing differences between Urari and their own world. On the one hand, Starck suggested that the spider in the community house might not be the only frightening creature they'll encounter, and on the other hand, his description of what the mirrors can do here is worrying.

Not least because their way home apparently goes through a mirror.

A hall full of them, Michael thinks, his mind's eye catching a fleeting image of the endless rows of sheet-covered mirrors he has wandered among in his nightmares every night for the past three weeks. *The Mansion of Mirrors.*

He feels a rising nausea and rolls the window down a bit on his side to get some air.

Outside, darkness stretches in every direction. The full moon has slipped unnoticed behind a bank of gray clouds, leaving only the faintest outlines of the endless sandbanks visible on the horizon. The only real source of light are the car's headlights, but even they seem marked by the stillness of the night, casting only just enough light for Starck to steer clear of the worst holes in the road.

You need to keep your head straight, he tells himself. *Other-*

wise, this shit will drive you nuts, and you'll end up like Tom—crazy, alone, and ready to kill for a chocolate bar.*

It's not a pleasant thought. What would it take to push a person that far? Surely, it has to be more than a rough childhood with an absent father and an alcoholic mother—which used to be the go-to thesis whenever they were handed a new case in psychology class.

The more he thinks about it, the more obvious it becomes that there is one, and only one, plausible answer.

Mirrors. Gateways to other worlds. Gateways to the corners of the mind. Gateways to madness.

At once absurd and yet so undeniably true. And didn't he feel it himself? Wasn't that, in fact, where it all began? In front of the mirror in his bathroom?

Up until this moment, he has been convinced that it was the phone call with Starck that set in motion the wheels that keep dragging him deeper and deeper into hopelessness. But now, he knows better. It was the mirrors—the one in his own bathroom, the one behind the restroom door in the school's main hallway —and, above all else, the one hiding beneath the sheet in his nightmare. Every goddamn time something has happened to make him doubt his own sanity, there has been a mirror involved.

Something in him protests:

Not every time. We got here without a mirror, didn't we? There was no mirror inside that office.

He rewinds the situation a couple of times in his head, trying to include as many details as possible—and since he keeps coming to the same conclusion, he decides that the silence has lasted long enough.

"There was no mirror in your office."

Starck jolts, clearly just as lost in thought as his passenger, and for a brief moment, Michael fears he might lose control of the car. However, the librarian quickly regains his composure.

"I'm sorry," he says, rubbing his eye. "What did you say?"

"*I* said that there weren't any mirrors in your office at the library. But *you* said the mirrors are portals. And if mirrors are the doors between Urari and our world, then how did we get here if there wasn't a mirror in your office? Shouldn't there have been one?"

"Actually, there was a mirror in the desk drawer, not that it matters. I don't think it played any role in your . . . crossing. I believe the explanation lies elsewhere. I believe it's found in your minds. For some reason, there's a very strong connection between you and the girl. Am I right in assuming that you made eye contact when you crossed over?"

"Well, yeah," Michael says, giving Starck a puzzled look.

"You're not the only ones," Starck explains. "There have been others who were able to travel across the two worlds that way. What's unusual about the two of you is that neither of you had been here before—or knew each other beforehand, for that matter. And *that* is uncommon."

Starck pauses for a moment, then turns to face Michael, his eyes radiating an unmistakable determination.

"I hope you believe me when I say that I'm here to help you through this, and that I have no intention of letting you down . . . and with that, I'm going to ask you to hold up your end of the deal. You need to sleep. It's just the two of us driving, and at some point, I'll need you to take the wheel so I can rest."

Michael nods but at the same time feels torn. On one hand, there are still far too many unanswered questions for him to blindly trust the old man behind the wheel. On the other hand, that man did save his life—and so far, he's the only living being they've met in this world who hasn't tried to kill them.

Using this as justification to himself, Michael nods once more at Starck before reaching for the handle and reclining his seat. Before lowering it all the way, he glances behind him to make sure Lisa's feet are clear—and once again, a twinge of emotion grips his chest at the sight of the sleeping girl, shifting restlessly in the back seat.

Afterward, leaning his head against the headrest and closing his eyes, he can still see her. She seems so young, so innocent, and he wonders whether the librarian is right. Whether he and Lisa really do have some mysterious connection—and if so, what is the reason for it?

28

Tom doesn't like this one bit. A minute ago, he was full of confidence, ready to punish the sucker who had dared to mock him by whistling at him like he was a fucking dog. He had played the entire scenario out in his mind—how he would burst through the bathroom door, use the element of surprise to overpower his opponent, and then stab the bastard until it wasn't fun anymore.

But then, out of nowhere, it went quiet in there. No sound of running water and no annoying whistling, just the faint sound of Tom's own thumb rubbing against the edge of his glass shard.

The silence worries him, because it could mean that the stranger knows he is coming—and Tom doesn't like prepared opponents.

You could turn around and walk away.

Nah, that's never gonna be more than a half-hearted consideration. After all, he's got his jackpot prize to think about. The wolf in his stomach might be temporarily subdued by chocolate and caramel, but it won't be long before it starts growling again, and then he'd surely regret it if he walked away from the machine. Ergo, the answer is obvious: he has to do it, and he has to do it now—before he loses his nerve.

As quietly as possible, he moves to the wall next to the door, pressing his back against it—just like the special forces always do in the movies before they storm in, take down the bad guys, and shout *Clear!*

He stands like that for a moment, both hands raised to chest level, weighing which of his two deadly weapons should go in which hand. In the end, they stay where they are—the can in his right hand, the glass knife in his left. Finally, he runs through the plan one last time.

a) Kick in the door with a bang and a war cry to intimidate the enemy.

b) Locate the fucker.

c) Toss the can in his face.

d) Stab him with the glass shard until he no longer poses a threat.

With this simple yet brilliant plan, and a manic smile on his lips, Tom lifts his right leg and kicks the bathroom door as hard as he can. Just as planned, it swings open, slamming against the wall with a loud bang . . . but that's as far as his plan holds before falling apart completely.

For what comes over his lips at the sight of the stranger is not an intimidating battle cry, but rather the words he screamed over and over earlier in the evening while slamming his clenched fists down on Michael's back. Then, they came out in a stream of incoherent sounds. This time, however, they're articulated clearly on the first try—and with an undertone of genuine fear.

"You're one of them."

The stranger shrugs, adopting a wounded expression that sharply contrasts the excitement bopping in the pupils of his dark eyes.

"You really shouldn't label people like that," he says. "It can hurt, you know."

"B-but you *are* one of them!" Tom stutters. "One of the mirror men."

Now the excitement in the stranger's eyes spreads across his entire face. He grins, revealing a set of teeth as pearly white as his skin.

"The mirror men?" he repeats cheerfully. "Just when you think you've heard it all. You do know that there is a more correct term for us, don't you, Tom?"

Tom stiffens at the sound of his own name, and the pale man's smile grows even wider.

"That's right," he says. "I know your name, Tom. The mirror man knows your name . . . and I also know what you were planning to do with those things."

He points toward Tom's hands, and Tom immediately opens his mouth as if to explain away the makeshift weapons in them, but all that comes out is a heavy and nervous breath.

The stranger takes a few steps closer. Every time he lifts a foot, he leans slightly forward, and when he sets it down again, he straightens his back. This odd way of moving makes him look like an actor in an old black-and-white silent film—and his colorless appearance only adds to this idea. Nearly everything else is a pitch-black contrast to his ghostly pale skin. His hair. His clothes. His eyes.

"But you can relax, Tom," he says. "I'm not one to hold a grudge. Besides, you're not going to do anything to me with your toys anymore, are you?"

Tom shakes his head. That is the honest answer. His chance has passed, and he knows it. You'd have to be mental to knowingly attack a mirror man.

"That's great, Tom. Now, how about we start over?"

With those words, the mirror man extends his hand. For a moment, Tom is convinced it's a trap—that the man will charge if he returns the polite gesture. But the pale hand simply hovers there, waiting in the air between them. Eventually, Tom shoves the soda can into the pocket of his fleece jacket and shakes the stranger's hand. Naturally, it's cold as ice.

"Daniel Crane," the man says with a smile. "Seems only fair that you know my name too if we're going to help each other out, right?"

Tom tries to decipher the reptilian smile. Another potential trap? No, he doesn't think so.

"Help each other?"

"Exactly," the mirror man says, nodding. "I have this job that needs doing, and I think you're just the guy for it."

"And what, um . . . what's in it for me?"

The moment he hears himself say the words, Tom realizes he may have been a little too bold, and his hand instinctively shoots up, covering his mouth. He stays like that for a moment, anxiously observing the other man's face for any sign of incoming retaliation. But the mirror man looks neither offended nor angry.

"Answers, Tom," he says calmly. "At the end of the day, isn't that the most basic human drive—wanting to find answers to everything? All the big questions. Why are we here? Is there a God? Is there a paradise? All that stuff."

He lowers his voice to a whisper and moves in closer. So close that he could take a bite out of Tom's ear if the urge were to strike him.

"However, in your case," he whispers, "the questions aren't all that complicated, are they? You just want to know who you are . . . or perhaps, rather, who you *were*."

The words slip into Tom's ear canal and travel through his

body until they reach his heart. Once there, they latch on and start gnawing like malicious parasites. The suppressed need to uncover his past—his life before he woke up in Urari's Wastelands—now floods his body, reverberating in every cell. He wants to know, he *has* to know, he *needs* know who he was before and what has been stolen from him.

And so, he nods.

29

It was no exaggeration when Starck said that there are also things of great beauty in Urari—and the breathtaking view that greets Lisa as her freshly opened eyes adjust to the light more than confirms his words.

They're still driving in the desert, but it's no longer the same monotonous landscape of rolling dunes. Now, the endless blanket of sand is broken by scattered rock formations, their veins glistening in the sunlight. At first glance, these rocky outcrops seem placed at random, but after observing them a while, it starts to feel like there's a purpose to their placements. As if they form a hidden pattern—one that can only be fully grasped if seen from above. Everything in and around these small rock islands seems to flicker with an almost ethereal silvery glow. Even the birds hovering in the distance catch the sunlight in a way that makes them shimmer, like crystals suspended in the air.

"Oh, you're awake?" sounds from the driver's seat. "I was starting to worry. I know they say teenagers need more sleep than grown-ups, but you're really going for the gold."

Lisa unbuckles her seatbelt and leans in between the front seats. Michael is the one behind the wheel now. Apparently, he and Starck switched places while she was asleep, and now the librarian is taking a nap in the passenger seat.

Even though she's still wary about his intentions, it's definitely a point in his favor that Starck has handed over the wheel to them. For all he knows, he could wake up in a ditch while they're already halfway to . . .

Yeah, well, that's just it, isn't it, sweetie? her mom's voice begins, but Lisa, who isn't in the mood for clever remarks and snide comments, simply ignores it and asks Michael what time it is.

"No idea."

"How far have we driven?"

"Far."

"You sound like you're in a better mood today."

In the front seat, Michael lets out a peculiar snorting sound. For a moment, Lisa thinks he might be choking on something, but then it dawns on her.

Suppressed laughter. The first laughter she has heard from him since . . . well, ever, actually. After all, they've only known each other for about a day, even though it feels like a lot longer.

"I don't know," he says. "Maybe getting some sleep helped."

"Have we passed any towns?"

Michael shakes his head.

"Not many—and definitely nothing worth stopping for. They were abandoned and wrecked, just like Attica. We did pass a sign about half an hour ago, though. Fifty miles to . . . Baxor or Baxan? It was something with B and X."

"What about fuel?"

"Getting close to the red . . . but we've got a spare can in the trunk, so we should be good."

Lisa stares at the road ahead, hoping he's right. Running out of fuel all the way out here where the gray, cracked asphalt seems to stretch on forever wouldn't be fun.

She pauses for a moment, expecting that the inner version of her mom's voice must have something mocking to add to that thought, but all she hears is a rumble from her stomach.

"Do we have any food?"

"You bet," Michael replies, his voice still carrying a hint of the chipper morning tone. "We've got a fine selection of canned goods in the trunk. I think I saw some cocktail sausages—if that sounds tempting."

"Mmm . . . delicious!" Lisa hadn't thought she'd ever use that word to describe long-shelf-life food and actually mean it, but right now, the idea of sinking her teeth into a cold cocktail sausage sounds amazing.

"I know, right?" Michael says, turning in his seat so he can wink at her. "You don't mind waiting until we find a rest stop, do you? I haven't seen any yet, but I'm sure there's one just around the corner."

Lisa rolls her eyes and makes a gesture with her hand in the air as if she's giving him a smack on the cheek.

"You know what?" she says as he slows down and pulls over to the side of the road. "I'm not sure I like this chippery side of you."

But she does. She really does.

After parking the car on the side of the road, they both get out and walk to the trunk, from which they grab a small stack of cans. They bring these with them to their dining area—a large, gray rock that sticks out of the sand about a hundred feet from where the car is parked.

For lack of a better option, the rock serves as a decent alternative to a classic wooden bench. Granted, its surface is burning hot, and it has got some rough spots that gnaw at Lisa's thighs, but it's the perfect size for the two of them and their small collection of canned goods.

As they sit there, Lisa's gaze keeps drifting toward the car, where the librarian is still sleeping in the passenger seat.

Through the window, she can see the outlines of his wrinkled face and silver hair. He is no spring chicken, but despite him being well on his way to retirement age, he is undoubtedly the most capable of the three. At least as long as they're out here.

"Do you trust him?" she asks when she catches Michael staring in the same direction.

"I haven't decided yet," he replies, picking up a small, rust-colored stone, examining it briefly, before tossing it back into the sand.

Lisa nods and wipes the sweat from her forehead with the back of her hand. Even though she has rolled up the legs of her jeans and is wearing nothing but a thin, pink T-shirt, the intense midday sun is relentless. She has nothing but her intuition—and the fact that her hair and T-shirt cling to her skin like a wetsuit—to back it up, but she's convinced the temperature must be somewhere close to a hundred degrees. It seems completely insane that less than a day ago, she was shivering on a bench outside the school, surrounded by dry autumn leaves.

"How long have you been teaching at the school?" she asks.

"At Oakwood? Come January, it'll be five years." He winks at her and adds, "Imagine that—five whole years dealing with twisted teens."

"Hey, hey. Remember, I'm one of them."

"Present company excluded, of course," Michael says, smiling.

Lisa gives him a *that's more like it* nod and brushes crumbs from her hands. Then, she carefully leans backward until her back rests against the rock's uneven surface.

"But you like it, right? Your job, I mean."

"A lot. Oakwood is a great place to work—good colleagues and, for the most part, good students. What about you? It's your first year, right?"

"Yeah, I changed schools and started at Oakwood right after the summer break. My mom thought it would be good for me to get a fresh start after everything with my dad and Emma. She, um . . . no, *we* hoped it would be a clean slate—new surroundings and new friends who didn't know the story."

"And was it?"

"Nah, I wish it was, but apparently, that kind of thing is pretty hard to shake. Even though it's been a long time, it still feels like people are afraid to talk to me. And if somebody actually tries, I freak out, thinking they just want all the gory details so they can tell it to their friends as soon as I turn my back. You know what I mean?"

"I think so," Michael says. "I got a taste of it when I came back to work and walked into the teachers' lounge."

In the long silence that follows these words, the two of them remain on the rock beneath the blazing sun—Lisa halfway lying down, her upper body resting on one elbow, Michael sitting hunched, his arms dangling loosely between his knees. Both of them with their gazes directed toward the past, the same weary expression in their eyes.

When words finally break the silence between them, it's Lisa who sits up and takes an initiative that in many ways is as unexpected to her as it appears to be to Michael.

"My little sister killed herself," she says. "She, um . . . she killed my dad, and then she took her own life."

While she waits for his reaction to having such a bomb dropped on him, Lisa steals a nervous glance at Michael. A part of her expects that, as a member of the Oakwood High staff, he already knows the story. But from the look on his face, he doesn't.

Perhaps the inner version of her mom's voice has been right all along. Perhaps her past takes up far less space in other people's minds than she thinks.

Another thing that catches her off guard is Michael's reaction once he recovers from the initial shock. Because he doesn't drop his gaze when their eyes meet. He doesn't look away like everyone else has. He's shocked, affected, and probably feels sorry for her . . . but he doesn't look away.

"I . . . I don't know what to say, Lisa. That's really terrible."

"I know," Lisa replies, nodding. "Emma's mind was . . . she wasn't well, and one day, something just snapped. She grabbed a kitchen knife, stabbed him to death with it, and then slit her own wrist afterward. And my mom was on the night shift, so, um . . . so I was the one who found them."

"Fuck."

"Yeah, fuck," Lisa repeats and sighs. "Finding them up in the bedroom was bad . . . but sitting alone in the kitchen afterward, waiting for the police, wasn't much better, I can tell you that much."

"No, I can only imagine."

"She wasn't always like that, though. Before her disease got really bad, she was the most awesome sister anyone could ask for. All my friends who had younger siblings were always complaining about them, but it was never like that with Emma and me. We always had fun together."

"When did it start?"

"Her disease?"

"Yeah."

Lisa thinks for a moment, then shakes her head.

"I'm not really sure, actually. I think she was diagnosed around nine—maybe a little earlier. But it didn't get really bad until she hit puberty. That's when she started shutting herself off and reaching her got harder and harder."

"Even for you?"

"Even for me, yeah. She went from being a happy little kid to being . . . well, completely unpredictable."

"That must have been very lonely for you. With you being so close before, I mean."

Lisa nods and stares into the horizon, thinking that *lonely* is a good word to describe what it felt like to watch helplessly as the person she loved most went from being a fun and caring sister to an emotionally cold ghoul.

"You're pretty good at this."

"What do you mean?"

"This talking thing . . . or well, listening. It's been a long time since I've talked about it with anyone."

Michael shrugs and offers her a cautious smile but says nothing.

"It must be the five years of twisted teenagers you were talking about," she says as she puts her hands on the stone and pushes herself up.

Deep down, though, she doubts that the explanation lies in Michael's background as a psychology teacher. It's more likely rooted in the fact that he has been—and in some ways still is—in the same boat as her.

30

"How was it?" Crane asks, while Tom swallows the last bite with a ferocity that doesn't seem to wane, no matter how much he eats.

"Awesome," Tom replies, pulling his lips up in a smile, the beard around his mouth speckled with soda drops and chocolate crumbs. "I can't remember the last time I was this full."

"Good. So can I count on having your full attention now?"

"Uh-huh," Tom says, letting a burp slip out along with the words. "You've got my attention." He pats his bloated stomach. "My stuffed-full attention."

"Excellent, then it's time for you to answer a couple of questions. Before I arrived, you met some other people here, right?"

"Yup. The crybaby, the girl, and an old fucker with a rifle. They tried to steal my jackpot. My food."

"And they're the ones who gave you that?" Crane asks, poking at the swelling on Tom's temple.

"Hey, ouch!" Tom winces in pain and grabs his head. "Jeez! Yeah, it was them. Why'd you do that?"

Crane ignores the question. He just tilts his head and studies

Tom, perhaps reconsidering his choice, wondering if the scrawny vagabond might actually be pretty useless after all.

"You'd like to get back at them, wouldn't you?" he suddenly says. "Pay them back for humiliating you. For trying to take your food. Wouldn't that feel good?"

"Of course, but they're long gone. The old guy had a car. They'll be far away by now. Even if we had a car, we—"

"You're forgetting something, Tom," Crane says. "You're forgetting who I am. What I'm capable of."

He smiles and waits patiently while Tom's mind races to put the pieces together. A moment later, Tom smiles too.

The mirrors, of course. If Tom knows where the three of them are going—and he thinks he does—Crane will be able to get there first through the mirrors. That way they'll be able to catch the crybaby and his gang with their pants down.

"They drove south," he says.

"On the main?"

"Yeah. I think they're heading for the Mansion of Mirrors. At least one of them is. He has been dreaming about it. He told me when they had me tied up."

Out of nowhere, the gnawing gut feeling pops up again—the same one Tom had when the crybaby told his sad story . . . and for some reason, it makes him doubt that Crane is going to keep his promise.

"And what about our deal?" he exclaims. "You said you'd tell me who I was . . . before Urari."

"Don't worry. I'll fill in the gaps in your memory, but not before we've sorted out the other stuff."

Beneath Crane's voice lurks a barely concealed threat, making it clear that Tom can forget about getting any answers if there's any more trouble—and he waits for Tom's eyes to signal that the message has sunk in before he continues.

"If they really are dumb enough to head straight for the mansion right off the bat, they'll undoubtedly try to stick to the larger cities. On the South Road, that'll be Baixa and Soto. They'll have to stop in both for fuel and food. Once they've passed Soto and begin their hike into the Wasteland, they'll be left to survive with what they can carry, and nothing more."

Crane hesitates, then raises his index finger close to Tom's face—so close that it makes him go cross-eyed.

"However," he says, "*if* they get that far, it also means that there are no more mirrors before they're inside the mansion. That means we only get two good opportunities for taking out the girl and the librarian."

"And the crybaby," Tom interjects, but Crane immediately shakes his head.

"The girl and the helper are yours to do with as you please, but Michael is mine. I've got plans for him."

"But . . ."

"No buts. He wants to go to the Mansion of Mirrors, and we're not getting in the way of that. Touch him and you can forget all about our deal."

Something about the look on Crane's face makes Tom wince and take a step back. Maybe it's the way the black-and-white contrast of his hair and skin is now broken by thick, blue-violet veins pulsing at his neck and temple. Maybe it's the way his black eyes burn with a mixture of excitement and insanity. Whatever it is, it makes Tom swear, loud and clear, that he'll keep his hands off the crybaby.

PART FIVE
BAIXA

PROLOGUE 5

To possess such untainted talent, as the young painter does, is a gift. Undoubtedly, that's how many would see it. The scene in the finished painting has been recreated down to the smallest detail, exactly as he saw it in his dream. The girl at the center of the bloodbath kneels, clutching her own shoulders, just as he saw her. Meanwhile, the painting's two other figures—the girl in the nightgown and the man on the bed, which both have left this world in different ways—cement the depth of her tragedy. Every element is an exact recreation of the image the boy saw in his dream.

A reflection, if you will.

A gift, yes. However, the boy's talent is also—perhaps to a greater extent—a curse. For despite the maturity of the composition and despite the uncompromising depiction of the brutal motif, he is only a boy. A boy who is blessed and cursed with the ability to see things that no child should witness.

Whether or not he wants to.

31

"Jeez!" Tom shouts, spinning around himself with his arms raised above his head. "That was fucking crazy!"

Really, he ought to be confused as he has no clue where he is. Right now, however, the rush from traveling through the mirror drowns out everything else. The trip lasted only a few seconds—but the tingling sensation in his nerves lingers, broadcasting the same message to every part of his body: That traveling through mirrors is freaking *awesome*!

A short distance from him, Crane stands, his back resting against the wall in the narrow hallway. His bluish lips carry a faint smile, but above them his black eyes announce that his patience won't stretch forever.

Slowly, Tom's expression starts changing. His bright eyes squint, darting side to side in confusion.

"Baixa," Crane says dryly.

"Oh, yeah... that's right," Tom mumbles, biting his lower lip.

"The girl, the old librarian, the crybaby," Crane sighs.

"Oh yeah, that's right," Tom repeats—and this time there's actually a bell ringing in the back of his mind.

He looks around again, examining the new environment. His gaze wanders from his new best friend's pale face to the tall mirror that hangs on the wall. Next, he tilts his head back, following the line where the walls meet the ceiling, tracing it all the way around.

The ceiling has the yellowish hue you'd expect to find in the home of a heavy smoker, and Tom is pretty sure his nose picks up something that could be the scent of old tobacco smoke. Beneath it, though, there's another smell hiding—something nauseating he can't quite define. Mold? Mildew, perhaps?

He glances into the room at the end of the narrow hallway, hoping something in there might help him identify the smell. The only thing he can see from this angle is the side of a black leather couch. The leather is tattered, with several cracks where the stuffing pokes out. Like the ceiling, it carries a nicotine-stained yellowish hue.

Some of the stuffing has been pulled completely out of the couch, maybe by rats or other vermin, and now lies scattered across the wooden floor like little yellow foam islands. Based on that, Tom concludes that the place must have been abandoned for quite some time.

"Shall we?" Crane asks, sweeping his arm in an arc toward the open door.

Tom steps into the room and notices that, besides the couch, there is a large dining table. Above it hangs a cast-iron lamp by a chain. The light coming from the room's three windows strikes it from different angles, creating a macabre shadow on the wall. A shadow that, to Tom, looks like a man hanging lifelessly from a gallows.

"How do we do this?" he asks, his hand finding its way back to the pocket in which the glass shard still lays. "How do we get those fuckers?"

"Take a seat," Crane says. "And listen carefully."

Tom does.

32

If Tom had moved to one of the windows in the same room around midday the following day and looked outside, he would most likely have seen a dark blue station wagon rolling down the street. He would probably also have recognized the blonde girl sitting in the back seat with her face pressed against the window.

That girl is Lisa Swann, and what keeps her glued to the window are the streets of Baixa, which she takes in with an almost inhuman appetite. Even though Starck had told them what to expect from the city, Baixa is still a mesmerizing sight. He called it the *City of Columns* and an *architectural masterpiece*, but even such grand words seem to pale when seeing it in real life.

Every building is chalk white and has at least one pair of columns, adding more than just a hint of ancient Greece. Many have far more than a single pair—in fact, Lisa counts fourteen beautifully carved columns on one of the larger buildings, their details so intricate that the figures adorning the columns—humans, animals, angels, and demons—almost seem a natural, living element of the life on the streets.

And that's the best part. There actually *is* life—and there are people. On the road, they only caught fleeting glimpses of others —occasional oncoming cars and trucks hauling goods to smaller towns—but here, there are people all around. And not one of them have hurled soda cans at their car or tried to stab them.

"Welcome to Baixa," Starck says. "Nice, isn't it? Seeing someone other than just yourselves?"

"You have no idea," Lisa exclaims, smiling when she realizes that Michael said the exact same thing at the same time.

"And it's gonna get even better," Starck says. "I have someone I'd like you to meet. Good and welcoming people."

He smiles at them as he turns off the main street onto a smaller road that is also surrounded by houses with beautiful columns. Between them, people sit and chat casually while sipping their coffee.

Five minutes later, he pulls up in front of a charming little watchmaker's shop. The window on the building's facade is freshly polished, and across its glass, the store's name, GILDED GEARS, is written in gold-trimmed letters. On the door beside it, a less pretentious cardboard sign hangs sporting the slogan: *Come on in, we've got time for you!*

Starck is the first one to step out of the car. After stretching his legs and his back for a moment, he walks around to the other side and opens the door for Michael and Lisa. They get out and go through the exact same stretching routine before following him up the small set of stairs to the door.

Before reaching for the door handle, Starck raises his hands to his forehead and peers through the store window. Lisa does the same, but since they're standing in the shadow of a balcony, she can only make out the first two rows of watches and jewelry displayed on the windowsill. Still, her eyes are quickly drawn to a silver bracelet that she instantly falls in love with. It's a delicate silver chain with a pendant shaped like a small clover, its leaves adorned with sparkling stones.

"Well, we better see if anyone is home," Starck says as he puts his hand on the doorknob. "I'm sure that . . . oh?"

He tries again, but the door is apparently locked, so he instead raises his hand and knocks on the window.

Almost immediately, a bright voice sounds from the balcony above them.

"He'll be back in five minutes if it's Elias you're looking for. He's at the market."

"Is that so?" Starck shouts back. "That doesn't prevent his young assistant from getting off his lazy butt and providing some customer service, does it?"

Michael and Lisa stare at the librarian in shock, but he just raises his hand as if to say: *Don't worry, this is gonna be good.*

For a moment, it's quiet up on the balcony. Then, a face appears—a young boy with Asian features. He is leaning so far over the railing that Lisa feels a sudden jolt in her stomach.

"Erik?" the boy shouts. "That you?"

"Hey, Sunni. Yeah, it's me. Be careful up there, don't want you to fall. Can you come down here and unlock the door so we can get in?"

"Just a sec!"

With that, the boy's head disappears behind the railing, and then follows a series of noises that make the three newcomers exchange concerned glances. First comes the sound of hurried footsteps, starting on the balcony and continuing into the upper floor of the house. Next, the sharp creak of a door being flung open. More footsteps follow, this time down a staircase, then a clatter as something topples over downstairs. Finally, there's a click from the lock. Immediately after, the door swings open, and the boy leaps straight into Starck's arms.

"These are my new friends, Michael and Lisa," Starck says when the boy finally releases his grip on his shoulders. "And this is Sung Jung—one of my *old* friends. Even though he's not that old."

He ruffles the boy's ebony-colored hair and gets a headshake and a smile in return.

"You can just call me Sunni. That's what everyone does."

"Nice to meet you, Sunni," Michael says.

"It sure is," Lisa adds.

Sunni narrows his eyes and looks up at Starck—who confirms with a nod.

"You're not from around here, are you?" the boy says.

"No, we're not," Lisa sighs, pulling a stray tuft of her blonde bangs into place behind her ear. "We're pretty far away from home."

"Is Mary in?" Starck asks.

"She's out on the patio, I think. She's gonna go nuts when she sees you."

With those words, Sunni grabs Starck's hand and pulls him inside. Michael follows, and so does Lisa—but only after taking one last look at the street scene.

Inside, Sunni gives his guests a tour of the shop, which turns out to be much larger than its facade suggests. The décor is enchanting, somehow making the room feel both dim and shimmering with golden light at the same time. Glass cabinets line the walls, displaying watches that tick softly, while a beautiful grandfather clock dominates the back wall. On a small workbench, illuminated by an old-fashioned desk lamp, delicate tools and tiny screws lie ready for careful craftsmanship.

Sunni takes them around to the various displays while he proudly explains that Elias and Mary—who aren't his real grandparents but have taken care of him always and therefore are considered as such—have made the majority of the watches and jewelry themselves in the larger workshop out in the back. He even persuades Lisa to try on the silver bracelet from the windowsill she fell in love with.

After putting it on, she turns to Michael and holds her wrist up in front of his face.

"What do you think?"

Michael inspects the pendant and nods in approval.

"Not bad. Definitely a major upgrade compared to those."

He is referring to the row of purple and yellow plastic bracelets that Lisa wears on her other arm. And yeah, the remark lowers her spirits a little, even though she tries to tell herself that Michael has no way of knowing that they were Emma's bracelets and what they mean to her.

It doesn't take long for her mood to lift again, though, because after the tour, Sunni leads them into the kitchen behind the shop—where they'll get to meet some of the kindest people Lisa has ever encountered.

33

"Grandma!"

Nothing.

"Mary!"

Still nothing

"GRANDMAA! WE'VE GOT VISITORS!"

Now something seems to be happening. In any case, Sunni pulls his head back through the doorway to the yard behind the house and nods enthusiastically to Michael and the others.

"She's coming," he says, cupping his hands around his mouth. "I hear her panting and groaning."

From the garden, the reply comes instantly—a woman's voice that tries to sound offended but at the same time is so melodic that no one would believe that it's owner was actually upset.

"I heard that, you little rascal! You have to be nice to the elderly. Didn't we teach you that? You better start running. Once I get my hands on you . . ."

The boy rolls his eyes and walks over to the kitchen counter where he jumps up and takes a seat next to the sink, his legs dangling in front of the cabinet below.

"Don't worry, she's just kidding."

"Kidding, am I?" the voice exclaims, now right outside the door. "Oh, you just wait and see!"

The older woman, to whom the voice belongs, stops in the doorway, frozen in place. She is a sturdy woman with dark gray, curly hair, wearing an apron featuring a drawing of an Italian madame (who, to Michael, looks almost identical to her) holding a steaming pot of spaghetti. Below the drawing, in large, curvy letters, it reads: *Mama Mia!*

"What's all this?" she says, letting her gaze sweep over the unexpected guests until it lands on Starck—and the moment it does, she marches straight over to him, grabs his shoulders, and plants a kiss on his cheek.

"It's great to see you, Mary," he says.

"You too, Erik." She gives him another kiss on the cheek before turning to Lisa. "Now, who do we have here?"

"I'm Lisa," Lisa says, taking a step forward and extending her hand. "It's very nice to meet you."

The lady completely ignores the polite greeting. She just grabs Lisa's shoulders and studies her face. Then she nods approvingly.

"Aren't you just adorable?"

Michael glances over at Lisa and isn't the least bit surprised to see her blush and drop her gaze to the floor. Meanwhile, the woman turns toward the boy sitting on the kitchen counter.

"What do you say, Sunni? Isn't she just gorgeous? A real knockout?"

Her question makes the boy's cheeks turn the same shade of red as Lisa's—and it also makes Starck chuckle.

"Easy now, Mary," he says. "You're embarrassing the boy."

"That'll teach him not to make fun of his poor, old grandmother," she says. "Now get down from my counter and make yourself useful, you little bully. We need to get some water boiling so I can make a cup of tea for our guests."

While Sunni heats the water, Mary greets the last guest. Michael doesn't get kisses on his cheeks or compliments on his good looks. Instead, she says something that warms his heart and instantly makes him like her.

"I don't know what brought you here," she says, "but you should know that here, in our home, there is room for both you and whatever you carry with you."

When Mary's husband, Elias, comes home fifteen minutes later, he finds the guests sitting around the table in his kitchen—and so the whole scene plays out for the third time. He, too, ends his welcome with the same message: that they should consider his home their own.

Much like his wife, Elias has an open and extrovert personality. However, that's about as far as the similarities go, Michael concludes. Because when it comes to physical appearance, finding a more mismatched couple would be a challenge. Elias is tall, his wife is short. Elias is thin, she is . . . well, generously built. Elias has blond hair and blue eyes, she has dark on dark. And Elias is dressed in neutral tones; she wears an explosion of colorful florals.

One could go on. Still, Michael has the feeling that most people, after knowing them for only a short time, would conclude that Elias and Mary are made for each other.

Witnessing such an obvious and deep love isn't entirely easy for Michael, as it serves as a painful reminder of what he has lost. When he gets as old as the watchmaker and his wife, he won't get the chance to look at Ann the way Elias looks at Mary now. Ann is gone, and he'll never again be able to finish another of her sentences or gaze into her eyes and tell her that he still loves her.

As the last drops of tea are finished, Elias starts setting the table while Mary prepares a light meal for their guests.

The conversation that takes place around the table while they eat is also light—which Michael is grateful for. There's no talk of family tragedies, grief, or scary mirrors. Mostly, it's Elias and Mary talking a bit about their business before shifting to the topic of Sunni's special talent.

"I'm telling you, that kid can paint," Elias says in a voice that almost overflows with pride. "Isn't that right, Mary?"

She puts her hand on his and gives it a squeeze.

"Definitely," she says, winking at Starck. "But now you're embarrassing the boy."

"Embarrassing?" Elias exclaims. "Ha! In my experience, it takes a hell of a lot more to embarrass that little runt."

A single glance at Sunni is enough to see that, in fact, no more is needed. Especially not when he's sitting next to Lisa, who seems to have . . . caught his attention.

"Besides," Elias continues, raising a finger, "there's no reason to hide your light under a bushel if you, at just eleven years old, paint like a professional."

"What's a bushel?" Sunni asks.

"A bushel . . ." Mary begins in that instructive tone that people used to dealing with children have ingrained in them, but then she falters. "Well, what actually *is* a bushel?"

"A bushel is a small wooden barrel that people used in the old days to measure their crops," Starck says, sliding his glasses down so they rest on the tip of his nose. "Potatoes and things like that. The expression *to hide one's light under a bushel* actually comes from the Bible. Matthew, if I'm not mistaken."

"So . . . a bucket?"

"Well, yes, Sunni," Starck sighs as he reaches over the table and helps himself to one of Mary's homemade cookies. "One could argue that it stifles a bit of the poetry of the metaphor, but yes. A bucket."

Starck takes a bite of the cookie and chews slowly while staring at the boy.

"Oh, come on! I'm not stupid. I know what a metaphor is," Sunni says, glancing nervously at Lisa. "You use metaphors in painting too."

"You know, I'd really like to see them," Lisa says. "Your paintings, I mean. I'm getting pretty curious."

Sunni looks at Mary, who smiles and nods.

"You go ahead. I'll clear the table today."

"Thanks, Grandma. And the food was delicious."

"No need to butter me up. I already said I'd do it for you."

"He's not lying, Mary. The food was really good."

"Thank you, Lisa. My pleasure."

34

What she actually had expected, Lisa isn't sure. However, it certainly wasn't art of this level that she thought she'd find when stepping through the door to the room behind the workshop, where Sunni has a small studio.

The paintings have a powerful effect on her—overwhelming yet strangely soothing. It feels as though they're calling to her, as if they were created just for her and no one else—and she can't shake the uncanny sensation that the artist somehow knows her story and tells it with his brush more eloquently than she ever could with words.

In fact, the paintings move her so deeply that, in this moment, she has completely forgotten that the artist is just an eleven-year-old boy. The very same boy, mind you, who stands right beside her, watching her reaction with a mix of pride and terror in his eyes.

"Do you like them?"

"Like them? They're freaking *beautiful*, Sunni. Absolutely amazing!"

She walks over to one of the paintings propped up on a chair in the back corner of the room and lets her fingertips glide along its frame, her touch gentle as a lover's caress.

The painting is one of those where a simple everyday object takes center stage. Normally, Lisa isn't particularly drawn to those kinds of paintings. She finds the traditional subjects—fruit bowls, wine bottles, and such—pretty boring. Yet, this painting is anything but boring. It's interesting. Not least because it feels as though some invisible force has sifted through the depths of her memory and handpicked this exact image.

It's an oil painting in a wooden frame, about twenty-five inches wide and thirty-five inches tall. The motif is something as simple as a glass bowl filled with popcorn sitting in the center of an oak tabletop.

In the bowl's glass, there's a faint reflection of something outside of the canvas, a blurry, orange-brown glare. To an uninformed observer, it could be anything. For Lisa, there is no doubt.

"Is that from a movie?" she asks, pointing. "The reflection in the glass. It's from the TV in the background, right? *The Lion King*?"

Sunni looks at her, perplexed and slightly embarrassed.

"I don't really know," he says with a shrug—and something tells Lisa that the boy might not even know what a TV is. "I just paint them."

"You don't know?" she stammers. "But . . . where did you see it?"

"I really don't know," he says, shrugging once more. "Sometimes it's things I dream about, and other times, I just . . . see them. I can't really explain it."

"But if you're the one who painted it, how can you *not* know?"

Sunni takes a step back, and Lisa realizes that she sounded a lot more accusatory than she had intended.

"Oh God, I'm sorry, Sunni. I didn't mean to snap at you. It's just that this painting—well, actually, a lot of your paintings—look like things I've experienced."

She grips the frame of the painting with the bowl of popcorn once again.

"Take this, for instance. It looks like . . . no, it *is* a picture of the coffee table from my childhood home. I know because I sat on the couch with my sister, eating popcorn from that exact bowl while we watched *The Lion King*."

She turns around and walks over to another painting—a watercolor depicting a large oak tree.

"And this one," she says. "This is the tree that stands in the yard outside my school. I sit under it all the time."

As she speaks, she takes care not to snap at the boy again. After all, she isn't angry. She is just confused and a little frightened. Frightened by the way he has been able to put her thoughts, *her*, onto a canvas like that.

"Oh, and this one," she says, moving over to a framed charcoal sketch standing on a shelf between an old clock and a plaster statuette of a winged animal. She opens her mouth to explain why this is yet another example of her life expressed in art, but she realizes that she can't.

It's not that she has any doubt that the picture—which depicts a newspaper boat with the words *EVERYTHING CRUMBLES* written along the edge of its sail—also belongs in the same category as the other two. She just can't explain why.

35

On their first evening in Baixa, Michael spends most of his time in an armchair in the corner of Elias and Mary's living room. Seated on its soft cushions, he can watch the darkness settle over the city of columns beyond the windowpane while also following the events of the peculiar card game that has occupied Mary, Sunni, Starck, and Lisa for most of the evening at the dining table.

The game is *Spindle*, a typical Urari card game that Sunni taught Lisa when they returned after he had shown her his paintings. Michael didn't take part in the lesson, but he has been observing the game for a while now, and he believes he has figured out the rules, even though it's played with a somewhat different deck than what he is used to. The number cards are the same but go all the way up to thirteen—and only in three suits.

The face cards, however, are very different. Instead of the usual jack, queen, and king, there are four animal symbols: a turtle, a wasp, an eagle, and a lion. Weirdly enough, the turtle is the strongest.

"You never play at all, Michael?"

The question comes from Elias, who is sitting across from him in the living room's other armchair. Like Michael, he declined to play, instead spending his time repairing a wristwatch. This now lies in front of him as a small—and to Michael, rather overwhelming—pile of gears and tiny screws on the wooden table between their armchairs.

"Nah," Michael replies. "Card games were never really my thing."

That couldn't be further from the truth. He, Ann, and Benjamin always loved playing cards. In fact, it was a tradition in their family to reserve Friday nights for board games and card games. That's the real reason why he declined when Lisa asked him to play. It felt like a step he's not ready to take yet.

"Spindle! I'm closing . . . again," he hears Sunni shout, and looking over there, he sees Lisa throw her cards down on the table, letting out a theatrical sigh.

"How do you keep doing that?" she says. "Are you cheating? Just admit it. You are, aren't you?"

Sunni laughs and shrugs his shoulders.

"Guess I'm just a natural at this game . . . unlike you."

"Yeah, well, confidence definitely isn't an issue for you," Lisa replies, returning his smile. "But I've gotta hand it to you—you're pretty hardcore at this Spindle thing."

"Alright, who has it?" Starck asks, glancing around at his opponents. "Who is getting plucked?"

"Me," Lisa sighs. "I've got it."

She lifts the Fenris card and turns it so everyone can see. The illustration depicts a wolf-like creature with gray-brown fur, glowing yellow eyes, and a terrifying set of teeth. It's standing in an eerily human-like posture, hunched over a small, indistinct swaddle—and it doesn't take much imagination to guess that whatever is beneath the fabric is deeply unsettling.

From what Michael has gathered, the Fenris card acts as a wild card at certain times and as a losing card at others—like right now, when Lisa is holding it in her hand after the game has ended.

"It's nasty, isn't it?" Elias says, referring to both the wolf's appearance and the consequences of holding the card after the final round. "A real nasty bugger."

"Yeah," Lisa replies, turning the card back to herself to study the beast more closely. "Good thing it's just a game. If those things were real, I'd be . . . oh, come on, you're not serious."

She looks back and forth between Elias, Mary, and Starck. So does Michael. All three have a look in their eyes that he definitely doesn't like.

"Seriously?" Lisa sighs. "Here?"

"In Baixa, no," Starck replies. "In Urari, yes." He puts on a reassuring smile and then adds: "They live in the desolate area where there's no people . . . and, practically speaking, there have been almost no cases of them attacking humans."

"Practically speaking, almost no cases," Lisa repeats sarcastically. "Great. That's practically almost not worrying at all."

Starck grimaces and looks to Elias and Mary for support, but they just shrug.

"Listen," he then says while his gaze flickers back and forth between Michael and Lisa. "In the car, I told you that you'd have to prepare yourselves for unusual things as we venture deeper into Urari. One of those things is the wildlife, and unfortunately, it's inevitable that we will encounter some creatures that will seem strange to you. Especially since our final destination, the Mansion of Mirrors, is located right at the center of a desolate area called the Wastelands."

He takes a sip of his tea, giving them a moment to process the information. During the pause, Michael exchanges a glance with Lisa and feels his heart sink slightly. Her green eyes reveal that this is pushing the limits of what she can handle. Truth be told, he feels the same way, although he does his best to hide it behind a relaxed smile.

"Maybe we should call it a night and get some rest," Elias suggests. "Tomorrow, we can take them to see Scruffy and Felicia. I think it might help if they also got to experience some of Urari's beauty."

"That sounds like a fabulous idea."

With these words, Starck gets up and starts clearing the table. The rest of the party follows his lead, and soon, three flickering candles is all that is left on the dining table. However, when Mary leans in to blow these out, Elias stops her.

"Just let them burn, Mary. Erik and I are gonna stay up and talk for a bit. We've got some catching up to do."

Mary slowly lets her hand drop and stares—for quite a while—at her husband, with eyes that contain love and concern in equal measure, before shifting her attention to Michael and Lisa.

"Let me show you where you'll be sleeping," she says, motioning for them to follow. Before leaving the living room herself, however, she casts one last glance back at the two old men and whispers, "Don't let it get too late."

36

"Well, go ahead and lay it on me. How bad is it?"

"It's definitely not good, Erik. Not good at all."

Starck watches his old friend's fingers as they fiddle with the label of the whisky bottle he has retrieved from the bar cabinet in the corner. Over the years, they've had plenty of these kinds of quiet evening conversations, and the golden liquid floating around inside the bottle has been a constant in all of them.

"Yeah, that was the impression I got as well," Starck says. "We arrived near Attica, and it wasn't a pretty sight. Same pattern as before—completely deserted, everything burned down and destroyed."

"At least some managed to get away," Elias says. "We've taken in a good number of refugees from there. They say they had to walk all the way here because there was no help to be found in the towns along the main road—that they were just like Attica. You must have come that way. Is it true? Has Crane really gained that much power?"

"Sadly, it would seem so. We saw the same thing—empty, destroyed towns all along the main road. No signs of life."

Starck takes a sip of his whisky and stares into the glass. He doesn't recall it being this bitter.

"He needs to be stopped," Elias says. "If he keeps gaining followers, he'll soon be strong enough to attack Baixa. Hell, maybe even Soto."

"Stopping him won't be easy. Crane has an obvious upper hand."

"You're thinking about the mirrors?"

"Exactly. As long as they don't hesitate to use them for traveling within Urari, they'll always be one step ahead of us."

Starck studies Elias' face, trying to gauge whether he's following his train of thought. Elias is—but judging by the way he shakes his head, he doesn't like where it's going.

"I know what you're going to suggest, Erik, but we've been through that. First of all, it's forbidden, and second, it's too risky, even for us guides, who—"

"As far as I recall, you're retired."

"Oh, come on," Elias says, brushing off the comment with a wave of his hand. "If you'd let me finish. It's far too risky, even for *you* guides who have experience traveling via mirrors. You know, as well as I do, that traveling internally in Urari is far from the same as traveling back and forth between the two worlds. For Shaika's sake, Erik. That's how Crane recruits his people! It drives you insane. We'd risk giving him exactly what he wants—all of Urari in one single blow. Served on a damn silver platter."

"Not necessarily," Starck says, gesturing toward the guest room where Lisa is spending the night. "Look at the girl in there. She faced a mirror in Attica's theater after arriving, and she has recovered pretty well, wouldn't you say?"

Elias empties his glass and coughs, as if the whisky went down the wrong way.

"And she hasn't been here before?"

"No. She has seen glimpses of it in dreams and mirrors, like most of them, but she has never physically set foot here."

"I'll be damned."

"I know. I think there's an explanation, though," Starck says, resting his elbow on the edge of the table and leaning closer to the candle at the center of the table. Its flame reflects in his glasses, framing his field of vision in a translucent ring of fire. "I think it's because they were together. The two of them got here on their own, without using a mirror. They traveled through eye contact."

"Empaths?" Elias exclaims. "Really? No one has even heard of that since . . . since Julian and Leona. To be honest, I never thought we'd see anyone with those abilities again."

All of a sudden, he goes quiet, and the astonishment on his face turns into worry.

"If Crane finds out about this . . ."

He doesn't finish the sentence and doesn't need to. Both of them understand what it could mean for the balance of power if Crane were to get his hands on a couple of empaths. If he no longer needed the mirrors.

Starck rises from the chair and walks over to the window. He stands there for a while, gazing out at the empty street. In the moonlight, the city of columns is a beautiful sight—one he, at this moment, appreciates more than ever. As is often the case with things you suddenly realize you might lose.

"What exactly is it you're suggesting?" he hears Elias say. His voice sounds troubled yet determined.

"My suggestion is that you come with us when we leave for Soto. And that you back me up when we present our plan to the council."

"And what does it sound like?"

"Cattle herding," Starck replies as he turns around and flashes his old friend a cryptic smile. "We gather as many as we can—not just guides, but anyone who has shown talent toward mirror traveling and precognition. We send them out with the message that people need to collect all the mirrors and bring them to central locations in the cities, all the way from the Wastelands to the outer perimeter. Once that's done, we station guards at every single one, making sure to cut off Crane's escape routes. Just like herding cattle."

Elias shakes his head.

"It's not that it's a bad idea, but you're demanding too much from the guards. Even *if* we manage to gather enough people, only a fraction of them will have the psyche to keep him locked in, let alone send him on. The mirrors are gonna break them."

"Not if they break the mirrors first."

"If we smash them, you mean?"

Starck nods, after which he goes back to the table and takes a sip from his glass. Elias stares at him silently for a moment, then shakes his head.

"There are mirrors all over Urari," he says. "We'll never be able to track them all down."

"True, but Crane knows that he risks being trapped in the void if one of the mirrors is destroyed while he is on his way out . . . and if he doesn't know which ones are going to break and when, he'll be forced to use only the mirrors he can be sure are intact. That leaves him with just two options if he tries to escape: the Mansion of Mirrors or the dungeons beneath the council's headquarters in Soto."

Elias can't hide that he's impressed by this unexpected twist in the plan. Still, he ends up shaking his head.

"No, I just don't see it. You'll never get the council on board with it—especially not with Bernard being the current chairman.

Moreover, it's too risky. There just aren't enough people with the strength to pull it off."

"With all due respect, Elias: How many lost souls have we helped safely through Urari in our time as guides?"

"I don't know." Elias shrugs. "Lots. I stopped counting a long time ago."

"And how often did you think along the way that they wouldn't make it?"

Elias hesitates for a long time before answering. Several times he lifts his glass, only to put it back without drinking from it. Finally, he plants his elbows on the table, clasps his hands under his chin, and lets out a sigh.

"I hope you know what you're asking of me."

Starck, who has known the old watchmaker long enough to know that those words mean that Elias is on board, nods and smiles gratefully. Now there is only the hard part left.

Apparently, Elias is able to read this thought on his face, for now his eyes become small and wary.

"What? I already gave you my yes. What more do you want?"

"You won't like it."

"Just spit it out."

"We're going to need *everyone* with special talents."

"Well, yeah, we've already established that. I really don't see what—"

But he suddenly does.

"Sunni? Hell no! There's no way, we're not doing that! He is way too young. Christ, Erik, the kid is *eleven* years old. He's nowhere near ready for something like this!"

"But you yourself said he had the potential to become a guide—and that was years ago. Back then, I had my doubts, but after seeing his paintings today, it's obvious that he has been chosen to take Lisa to the mansion. That also explains why I didn't get any visions of her. That boy—"

"That boy means everything to us!" Elias jumps up so abruptly that his chair slides backward behind him. "If anything were to happen to him...Mary would be devastated. *I* would be devastated! This is insane! This is asking too much! He's *not* ready."

"Yes, he is."

The soft voice that cuts into the conversation makes them both fall silent and turn their gazes toward the kitchen doorway. There Mary stands in her floral nightgown, her arms hanging limply at her sides.

"Yes, he is," she repeats gently. "I don't like it either, but Erik is right. You'll need all the help you can get—and Sunni *is* ready. He sees the most incredible things in his dreams, and he puts them on the canvas down to the smallest detail. If anyone has a chance to get inside Crane's head, it's him. And now that we've met Lisa . . . you heard how she reacted to the paintings."

She walks slowly across the floor and places her hand on her husband's shoulder.

"That boy was made to be a guide," she says. "Those were your own words."

37

While Starck outlines his strategy for Elias, Michael lies on a cot in the guest room, writhing, gasping, and drenched in sweat. The cause is what's playing out behind his closed eyelids. For with the exception of the nightmare that drove him back to work, this is without a doubt the worst one he has had since the accident.

As always, it unfolds in the dark hall he now understands must be the interior of the Mansion of Mirrors. Searching for the plaque with his son's name, he wanders through the endless rows of sheet-covered mirrors. This time, however, he can't find it. Every time he approaches something that, from a distance, looks like Benjamin's name, the letters blur and shift, transforming into another name: Daniel Crane. And when he pulls away the dusty, burgundy sheets, it's the same sight that greets him over and over. A smooth, black surface. No reflection.

Only when he finally gives up, dropping to the floor, does something happen. A voice suddenly breaks the silence, ringing out from the darkness at the far end of the hall. Sharp. Mocking. A voice Michael recognizes instantly.

The officer. The psychotic cop who, in every other dream about the mansion, has kept Benjamin trapped inside a mirror.

"You're not gonna find him here, silly! It's a dream!"

"Who are you?" Michael shouts back. "Why are you doing this to me?"

The voice doesn't answer, but Michael can hear its owner drawing closer. The footsteps grow louder, and it's only a matter of time before the officer will step into the beam of moonlight streaming through the skylight.

"Answer me, asshole! Why are you doing this?"

"Oh, again with the endless search for answers," the voice says. "What is it with you people? What's the meaning of life? Is there a God? I just came from a chatterbox who wanted all the answers. And now you're starting too?"

Now he steps into the light, spreading his arms as though he were the savior himself on the day of redemption. He is dressed in black instead of the usual uniform, yet Michael has no trouble recognizing the policeman's pale face and excited eyes. Especially those damn eyes.

"But fair enough," the man says, straightening the collar of his shirt. "How about we strike a deal. I'll answer your question if you answer mine. Agreed?"

Michael nods.

"Excellent! You asked who I am, and I suppose it's only fair that we introduce ourselves properly." He squats down in front of Michael. "My name is Daniel Crane."

"Where is my son?"

Crane rolls his eyes and gestures indifferently toward the mirrors on the left side of the hall. Then, keeping his index finger extended, he brings his hand back and lets it hover in the air right in front of Michael's face.

"Now, now. Don't forget the deal. One question at a time. It's my turn."

Michael has to restrain himself from grabbing that damned finger and snapping it in half. He wants to hurt this man—more than he ever thought possible—but he also understands that, right now, all of this is happening on Crane's terms. Consequently, he holds himself back and settles for a nod.

When Crane opens his mouth, the question that comes out isn't the one Michael had expected to hear. Nevertheless, it gets to him—both in that moment and in the following days.

"Shouldn't you be picking up the pace?"

"What do you mean?"

"I guess I'm just wondering why Starck insists on taking his sweet time getting you to the mansion. I mean . . . he's a guide, right? So, he is used to traveling through the mirrors, isn't he?"

"The mirrors are dangerous," Michael replies coolly. "They drive you insane."

Crane throws out his pale hands to the sides and nods.

"My point exactly!" he exclaims. "The mirrors *are* dangerous . . . and if your son starts to get bored waiting for you, he might be tempted to pull off a few sheets to see what's hiding underneath."

It takes a moment for the words to sink in properly with Michael—but when they do, it feels as though someone has pumped every vein and artery in his body full of acid. As if all his organs are about to burn up from the inside. Because with the understanding of the words also comes another realization:

Crane isn't talking about a dream version of the Mansion of Mirrors like the one they're in right now. He is talking about the Mansion of Mirrors that they're headed to. The one that exists physically in Urari.

And the flickering spark of malice, now drawing in oxygen

and flaring up in his black pupils, confirms that he isn't talking about a dream version of Benjamin either.

"You're lying!"

"Maybe." Crane's smile widens, and he shrugs casually. "But what if I'm not? What if you can't trust Starck, and he is just using you for his own agenda? Are you really willing to gamble with your son's life like that? I mean, you have to admit, it's pretty strange that he insists on traveling for weeks when you could just use a mirror and jump straight over there."

"I don't believe you," Michael insists, but the tremor in his voice reveals his doubt—both to himself and to Crane, who bursts into laughter.

The pale man's mocking laughter is the last thing Michael hears before his brain decides it's time to cut the connection and pull him out of the nightmare. And as he sits on the edge of the bed, staring at his trembling hands in the dim light, Crane's carefully chosen words burrow deeper and deeper into his mind.

For even though he tells himself that it was just a nightmare and that nurturing the seed of hope that the dream has planted in his soul will do more harm than good, he can't let go of the doubt.

Is it possible that Benjamin could be alive? That he could be here . . . in this terrible place?

38

"Tom!" Crane snaps his fingers and slaps his palm flat against the city map spread out on the coffee table. "Focus, please!"

"Huh? What?" Tom blinks in confusion, forcing his gaze away from his new toy—a snub-nosed Colt Detective—which has a habit of stealing his attention.

He got the revolver from Crane right after he woke up, and ever since, he has grabbed every opportunity to sit and fantasize about the ways he could use it to take out the girl and the old geezer. Truth be told, he has also been daydreaming about putting a hole in the crybaby's forehead, but since that's a definite no-go, he keeps that part to himself.

"They're staying here," Crane says, his finger tracing the map before stopping on a winding side street off the city's main road. "That's where I want you to go. You don't have to do anything except keep an eye on them. I want to know what they're up to. I have a good connection to Michael at night, but I don't know how long that is going to last."

Tom scratches the bruise on his forehead. The swelling has gone down a bit, but it still itches like hell.

"Why don't we just go over there and shoot the fuckers? Wouldn't that be easier?"

Crane responds with a small, dismissive shake of his head.

"You just keep an eye on them for now. They'll need to stock up on supplies before they continue their journey—that's when we strike."

"And if they spot me?" Tom asks, discreetly running the tip of his finger along the metal guard in front of the revolver's trigger.

"They won't," Crane replies, his voice making Tom jerk his hand back as if the metal had suddenly turned scalding hot. For a moment, he doesn't know what to do with either his hand or his gaze. In the end, he places both on the city map.

"Yeah, make sure to study it thoroughly," Crane says. "We can't have you getting lost."

His voice has returned to its calm tone, but the underlying threat is unmistakable: Should Tom get any clever ideas about breaking their deal and running off, there will be consequences.

Tom doesn't plan on running, though. The reward for their working together is far too valuable. Crane has promised to shed light on his past, to tell him who he was before. For that, Tom is willing to do just about anything—despite something deep inside him whispering that he's heading into deep water.

But hell, when it comes down to it, what does he really have to lose?

39

As Lisa walks alongside Michael, Starck, Elias, and Sunni down a small street parallel to the main road in the late morning, many shop owners are still putting up signs and display items on the sidewalks. Most greet them with friendly smiles—and the elderly gentleman who has just waved them over is no exception.

Lisa is also smiling, because she has—all things considered—had a good day so far. Her morning began with the comforting sound of Mary's voice drifting in from the kitchen. She was humming a tune, unfamiliar to Lisa but beautiful, as she prepared breakfast—a meal consisting of small, pancake-like breads that tasted absolutely delicious.

During breakfast, Lisa found out that it had been decided that Sunni and Elias would join them as they continued their journey, which also helped lift her spirits.

The next steps in today's agenda also seem promising. It includes the promised visit to Scruffy and Felicia, as well as a shopping trip to prepare for the rest of the journey.

"A gift for the young lady," says the elderly gentleman who waved them over. He smiles as he extends something toward her.

"It might not look as beautiful as you, but I promise you that it tastes wonderful."

The man owns a small produce stand, which consists of nothing more than three fruit baskets and the awning above them. The object he compares Lisa's beauty to is a purple fruit that he has pulled from one of the baskets.

Aware that all eyes are on her, Lisa tries to come up with a clever response, but the unexpected kindness and compliment have caught her so off guard that it's a hopeless task. In the end, her creativity amounts to nothing more than a blush and a subdued, "Thank you."

"I don't know about the taste," Elias teases. "But I'd say that the color of your cheeks is starting to match the fruit's color very well."

This makes the fruit vendor chuckle. He shapes an invisible gun with his thumb and index finger and fires it at the watchmaker. Then he tucks the weapon safely back into his pocket and turns his attention to his fruit baskets.

After leaving the man's stand, Elias and Sunni lead them down the street and from there to the left onto a small road paved with cobblestones. At the end of it lies their first stop; a white, half-timbered house, which, together with its associated stable building, is framed by an iron fence. The home of Scruffy and Felicia.

Prior to meeting Scruffy and Felicia, Lisa had a clear idea of what it would entail. Her expectation was that Elias would try to make up for the 'Fenris card incident' by showing her some beautiful animal that could rival the wolf-like creatures of the Wastelands. She assumed that Scruffy would be a pet belonging to Felicia.

In a way, she was close. However, it turns out that Felicia is the pet, not Scruffy.

Scruffy—whose given name is Jim—is the city's blacksmith and just about the farthest thing from a pet one could imagine. He is a huge man, dressed in brown work pants and a dark blue apron that looks almost ridiculously small against his massive arms and the red beard jutting out in every direction. One look at that mane, and it's obvious why people call him Scruffy.

When it comes to first impressions, Lisa figures life must have thrown its fair share of challenges at this man. Fortunately, it only takes a few minutes to realize that beneath his intimidating exterior lies a kind and warm-hearted person.

The other thing that takes Lisa by surprise is just how breathtakingly beautiful the pet is. She had expected . . . yeah, well, what had she expected? Certainly not something as unbelievably stunning as Felicia.

"She could very well be the last of her kind," Scruffy declares, his deep voice carrying a mix of pride and sorrow. He grabs the animal's muzzle and presses his face against her cheek. Felicia blinks her crystal-clear blue eyes, lets out a single soft huff, and then leans toward her master.

"Does she like strangers?" Lisa asks.

Scruffy motions for her to come closer.

"As long as you come one at a time."

Lisa moves slowly, taking careful steps until she is right in front of the animal. There, she stops, letting her gaze travel over Felicia as she wonders if it would even be possible to describe a creature like this with words.

From a distance, it might resemble a horse, but then again; a horse would be taller and have a tail. Felicia hasn't got that. Instead, she has what could almost be described as a kind of fan on her back.

A horse would also have hooves and a broader muzzle. But above all, a horse would have hair, fur on its body, and certainly not the mysterious white structure that covers Felicia. It looks like small, pentagonal crystals, but they feel soft under Lisa's fingers as she gathers the courage to stroke them over the animal.

Felicia lets out a low hum and flinches backward at Lisa's touch. However, shortly after, she bends her front legs and leans toward her, just like she did with Scruffy.

"She's beautiful," Lisa says. "What kind of creature is she?"

"We call them seraphs," Scruffy replies. "You know, like the angels."

"No," Lisa says, squinting her eyes. "I don't know . . . but I do now."

She pulls her lips into a smile and so do Sunni and Starck, who stand by the barn gate. Michael, however, positioned to their left, remains stone-faced. He has been like that all morning, distant and withdrawn. Whatever is going on behind those marine-blue eyes is a mystery to her, but one thing is certain—something is weighing heavily on him.

"You say she might be the last," she says, turning back to Scruffy. "Why is that?"

"Shadow hunters."

Lisa looks over at Starck.

"Poachers," he explains. "Seraph hide is to them what ivory and tiger pelts are to poachers in our world."

"Actually, that's how I got her," Scruffy says, running his hand over the animal's neck and down the front of her leg. He stops and points to a mark just above Felicia's knee. "See this? That's the scar from the rifle shot that nearly killed her. I spotted her during a salvage run in the Wastelands. There was only one single tree for miles, and she was lying there, right in front of it. She was completely drained, and no wonder. The ground around the tree was covered in tracks. She had been dragging herself around in circles, following the sun to stay in the shadows. To stay alive. Luckily, I had the flatbed truck with me. It was a hell of a job, getting her up there. We did it, though, didn't we, princess?"

Scruffy gives Felicia a gentle pat and clears his throat before continuing:

"Anyway, all of that was a long time ago, and as you can see, she's back on her feet and doing fine. And I get to boast about being the only one to have ever tamed a seraph—the most beautiful creature in all of Urari."

"Oh, come on, Scruffy, show them already!" exclaims Sunni, who up until now has been sitting on a stool in one of the corners. Apparently, his eleven-year-old patience has reached its limit. "Pull the rope!"

Michael and Lisa exchange puzzled glances and then look to Starck and Elias. Both shrug and offer the same cryptic smile.

"Yeah, I was curious to see how long you'd be able to sit there completely still," Scruffy says with a laugh as he walks over and grabs hold of a rope hanging down along one of the barn's walls. "But alright then, you'll get your wish."

He gives the rope a firm tug, and above them, where the barn's wall meets the roof, a pulley wheel lets out a piercing squeal. Right after, one of the roof panels lifts, allowing a single beam from the midday sun to stream in.

As the light hits the crystal-like structure on Felicia's back, Lisa suddenly understands both the cryptic smiles and Sunni's impatience. The single beam from the roof breaks into hundreds of shimmering rays, forming a web of light that seems to connect the creature to every surface surrounding it.

Felicia lifts her head and lets out a deep, guttural groan while she glances around in confusion, as though she is trying to figure out where the sudden warmth is coming from. When she spots the opening in the roof, she shifts her weight onto her hind legs. Rearing up in a majestic stance, she remains still for a moment —a radiant, snow-white creature, towering above them and shimmering like a living diamond.

Lisa remains still, struck with wonder, unable to think of anything to say. She might not have had any idea that the word *seraph* has to do with angels, but now, she can easily see why these creatures were given that name.

She makes eye contact with Elias and gives him a grateful smile. He winks at her and responds with a nod.

You're welcome.

40

Tom has pulled the revolver from the pocket of his fleece jacket and braced himself to use it. In fact, he was about to disengage the safety when the girl stepped out of the stable and called Michael over to her. Up until that moment, the crybaby had been standing still in front of Tom's hiding spot in the vegetation along the edge of the blacksmith's driveway so long that he was sure he had been spotted.

Lucky for you, he thinks, watching Michael's back as he walks away.

Truth be told, it's probably also lucky for him. He doesn't like to imagine what Crane would do if he disobeyed orders and put a bullet in the whiner's forehead. Still, it would've been satisfying to shut him up. *Jeez, yeah*, it would've been the perfect way to wrap up his little scouting trip.

Tom is pretty satisfied anyway, though. He has gathered some solid intel. He managed to get confirmation that they're heading to Soto, he found out how many people are going, and he learned when they'll be leaving. He also knows which gas station they're planning to stop at right before departure. And as a bonus, he found out what the blacksmith has stashed away inside the stable.

A domesticated seraph, he thinks, his eyes darting indecisively between the stable and the gate leading to the street, where the crybaby's crew is currently heading out. *A fucking domesticated seraph!*

A part of him is tempted to linger for a bit, maybe even get a closer look at the animal if the opportunity arises. But since the blacksmith seemingly has no intention of leaving along with the others, that ship has sailed. He's a bit too big and red-haired for Tom's taste.

So, Tom decides it's time to head home. He has followed them long enough and knows what he needs to know. Besides, the idea of making the mirror man wait longer than he has to doesn't exactly appeal to him.

About fifteen minutes later, Tom jogs up the stairs to the empty apartment he shares with said mirror man . . . only to come to an abrupt halt in the doorway, as if he had walked straight into a glass wall.

"Come on in," Crane says, gesturing with two of his long, crooked fingers toward the only empty chair at the dining table. "Join the party. We've been waiting for you."

Tom hesitates, staring at the empty chair before glancing around at the unfamiliar group of people who have occupied the rest of the seats while he was gone.

The urge to join this gathering isn't exactly overwhelming—especially since Crane's guests seem to have skipped tableware altogether, opting instead to lay out handguns where plates and silverware should have been.

"You invited guests?" Tom stammers as he steps over to the table and puts his hands, slightly tremoring, on the back of the chair.

"Oh my, where are my manners?" Crane exclaims, making a sweeping motion with his arms as if lifting an invisible object and presenting it to the two people on his right. "This is Hain and Petturi."

The two nod in unison, and Tom notices they both wear the same expression of indifference. Beyond that, though, their appearances could hardly be more different. Hain has dark hair, narrow, reptilian eyes, and sharply defined cheekbones, while Petturi's large, protruding eyes sit beneath a broad forehead and a thick, dark unibrow.

Now, Crane turns to the two on the left side of the table, presenting them with the same invisible gift.

"And this is Jack and Anton."

On this side of the table, the reception is a tad warmer. Jack —a lanky guy wearing a worn-out tank top with a faded yellow smiley face printed on its front—gives Tom a two-finger salute, while Anton offers a smile beneath his brown mustache.

Unlike his seatmate, Anton is short and rather overweight, and he seems just as tense about the situation as Tom. At least that's what it looks like by the way his chest rises and falls in short, jagged intervals beneath his shirt.

"Holy fuck, Anton," the man next to him exclaims, pulling out the fabric of his tank top. "Anyone ever told you that this is exactly what you look like when you smile?"

The outburst leaves no doubt that Jack is the youngest member of the group—and that he likes to emphasize this with his rebellious attitude.

He's not completely wrong, though. With his sweaty, glistening forehead and round cheeks, Anton's smile does make him look a lot like the smiling yellow face on Jack's tank top.

"Would you shut up already, Jack?" the big man on Tom's left grumbles.

"Oh, chill, Petturi. I'm just messing with him. And come on, it's true. Hey, Anton. Give us another smile, would you?"

He nudges Anton with his elbow but gets no reaction. The chubby little man just sits there, staring at his folded hands in silence—which makes Jack roll his eyes and throw his hands out to the sides in exasperation.

"You might *think* you're funny," Petturi replies, "but there's only so much crap a person can take in a day—and we've been listening to your bullshit all fucking morning."

Jack lifts a finger as if ready to fire back but lowers it again when he catches the look in Petturi's eyes.

"Yeah, that's what I thought," Petturi says, crossing his arms and flexing his biceps so it makes the bat tattooed on his right arm spread its wings even wider. "Big mouth, no fucking balls."

"You done yet?" Crane asks, sending them a look telling them that they most certainly are. Next, he leans over the table and pushes the city map so it slides over to Tom. "The floor is yours, Tom. Let's hear it. What are Starck and his gang up to?"

"You, um . . . you were right," Tom says. "They plan to go to Soto. And not just the three of them. The watchmaker and the boy are going with them."

"The boy?"

"Yep," Tom says, rubbing his beard, which still holds traces of dried chocolate from yesterday's feast. "He lives with the watchmaker and calls him granddad. That can't be right, though, because the kid's some Chink brat, and the watchmaker and his wife are white as—"

"Did you find out when they're leaving?"

"Tonight. Around seven o'clock," Tom says, smiling to himself as he prepares for the pat on the back that's sure to come. Because now is the perfect time to share the crucial detail that will emphasize his exceptional work. "And they're planning to stop at the Cibus station on the outskirts of town to fill up the car before they leave."

"Excellent," Crane says, looking around the table. "And that means we have a lot to prepare, gentlemen."

Tom lowers his gaze to his hands, feeling a deep sense of relief. Partly because he's received something resembling praise in the form of the word *excellent*, and partly because Crane's attention is no longer focused solely on him. Besides, he's fairly certain that the results of his reconnaissance have earned him a bit of respect from both the boss and his new acquaintances. At least, there's something in their eyes when they look at him—a shared expression he can't quite define, but it feels good, and it looks like acceptance.

Anyone else would have recognized it immediately.

Madness.

41

When Michael, the day before, got the same tour as Lisa of Sunni's studio, he was obviously also fascinated by the boy's talent. However, he didn't get the same feeling of having his inner life exposed.

The paintings stirred emotions in him, no doubt about that, but nothing beyond what one might expect when looking at works created by an eleven-year-old that could rival that of professional artists.

The true understanding of the boy's talent doesn't hit him until they've returned to the watchmaker's home after the visit to Scruffy and Felicia. Because that's when Elias asks them if Sunni remembered to show them *the big one*—and when both Michael and Lisa answer with a shrug, he nearly drags them out into the backyard.

Seeing the painting, Michael immediately realizes that Elias wasn't exaggerating when he described it as *the big one.* It's a large mural, at least ten feet wide, adorning the wall of the workshop on the side facing the backyard. Above it, the watchmaker has installed an improvised awning to protect it from weather damage—a gray-green tarp stretched between the wall and two wooden beams. The bottom corners of the painting are slightly damaged, but otherwise, the awning does its job well. What's most important is the massive architectural structure at the center of the painting, and this remains perfectly intact.

The Mansion of Mirrors. This is what it looks like.

Since he has never been there, except perhaps in his nightmares, and has never seen it, Michael can't possibly be sure. Still, he doesn't feel a shred of doubt.

Intuition? Premonition? Call it whatever you want, but one thing is certain: that, right there, is the Mansion of Mirrors. That's just the way it is.

"May I?" he asks, glancing down at Sunni.

The boy raises his hand in a gesture that says *knock yourself out*.

Michael places his hand flat against the rough surface of the wall. Cold. Without even realizing it, he spreads his fingers, then clenches them tightly again—almost as though he believes the wall is a piece of paper that he could crumple up if only he squeezes hard enough.

However, the ashen mansion beneath his hand remains indifferent. It holds its ground, mocking and defiant, with its mysterious, dark windows and its towers that stretch greedily toward the sky. From them, long shadows spill out, dividing the barren landscape on either side of the wide staircase leading up to the entrance gate.

At the foot of the staircase, two identical statues can be glimpsed in the shadows. Facing each other, they hold the exact same posture—cowering, hands raised protectively in front of their faces, like they're mirroring each other and dreading what they see.

Remembering Starck's description of the mansion, the sight

of those statues sends a chill down Michael's spine, and he feels a strong aversion to the idea of having to go there.

"Michael?" Starck sounds worried. "Everything okay?"

"Yeah. It's just . . . this is the Mansion of Mirrors."

Starck smiles, after which he walks over to him and looks at the picture. His eyes hold a peculiar, dreamy expression—somewhere between compassion, awe, and envy.

"No, it's not," he says. "It's just a wall painting."

While he speaks, Starck glances back at Elias. The watchmaker nods solemnly, then drapes one arm over Sunni's shoulders and uses his free hand to tap Lisa on the arm.

"Why don't the three of us go inside and see what Mary has come up with for dinner?"

Sunni and Lisa glance back and forth between the watchmaker and the librarian, then they nod and follow Elias into the kitchen. A couple of times along the way, though, they pause and glance back over their shoulders—Sunni with curiosity in his eyes, Lisa with concern.

Once they're out of sight, Michael takes a few steps back to get a better view of the scene. Something tells him that he should take his time, absorb as many details as possible. That he is going to need every bit of knowledge he can gather about the large, gray building before the day comes when he must face it.

"Can my son be in there?"

"Your son?" Starck exclaims. However, the surprise in his voice isn't real, Michael hears that right away. There is sympathy and there is concern. No surprise.

"Yes, my son," Michael repeats, pointing toward the painting. "I've had nightmares about that place nonstop since the accident—and every time, they end the same way. I see my son trapped behind the glass in one of those fucking mirrors. And now, I'm here, in a world where the Mansion of Mirrors actually exists. So yeah, as nuts as it sounds, I'm asking you—could my son be here? Could Benjamin be alive . . . trapped in that awful place?"

Maybe he's contemplating a lie, maybe he's just looking for the right words. Whatever the reason, Starck hesitates for a long time before the answer comes.

"Did you see him . . . I mean *his body* after the accident?" he asks. "In the hospital or somewhere else? Because if so, we can rule it out completely."

"No, I, um . . . wasn't allowed to see either Ann or Benjamin," Michael says, his voice trembling. "The policeman said the car caught fire, and that they w-were completely . . ."

He raises his hand to his mouth, fingers spread, and presses against his chin until his knuckles turn white.

"That there was nothing to see," Starck finishes for him. "Well then. In that case, there is a chance your son might have ended up in Urari."

"Oh God," Michael sighs—and immediately, Starck raises his voice.

"But make no mistake," he says. "It's a very small chance. And even if he is here, that doesn't mean he is okay . . . or, for that matter, that he's still alive. You have to prepare yourself for that."

He grips the frame of his glasses on one side and pulls them down slightly, peering at Michael over the lenses.

"Can you do that?"

Both Starck and Michael know he is lying when he answers with a nod. But that's okay. It would be unfair to expect a father to be able to prepare himself for losing his only child a second time.

Even in Urari.

PART SIX
THE GAS STATION

42

"Thanks for everything, Mary," Michael says, holding out his hand.

The chubby little woman stares at his hand with such disapproval that you'd think he was holding out a rattlesnake. Then she waves it away.

"You're not getting off that easy," she says, pulling him in and planting a kiss on his cheek.

"You better watch yourself, young lady," Elias chuckles. "Don't think I haven't noticed the way you look at that young man. The least you could do is wait until your husband looks the other way."

"Easier said than done," she says, letting go of Michael and making her way over to said husband. Once she reaches him, she takes his hands, lifts them to her lips, and kisses them. "My husband is very attentive."

Her lips are smiling, but Michael notices a wet streak on her left cheek.

"Do we have everything?" Lisa asks. She is standing with her hands on her hips, glancing back and forth between the car's open trunk and the door to the watchmaker's shop. Her blonde hair is pulled back into a ponytail that sways in time with the wind.

If he didn't know, Michael would have a hard time believing that this is the same girl as the one they found in front of the mirror inside the theater's restroom just three days ago. Staying with Mary and Elias has done her good.

"Well, there is one more thing," Mary says, slipping her hand into the pocket of her apron. She pulls out a piece of jewelry—the silver bracelet with the clover pendant that Lisa fell in love with when they arrived in Baixa. "Sunni told me you were absolutely smitten with this."

"Is that . . .?" Lisa gasps, bringing her hand to her mouth as she looks over at Michael and then back at Mary. "I don't know what to say."

Mary takes Lisa's hand, turns it over, and lets the gift fall into her palm. Then she gently folds Lisa's fingers around it and gives her hand a soft pat.

"You don't have to say anything, dear. Now, you best get going before I change my mind."

"You stay right there," Elias says twenty minutes later as Starck pulls the dark blue station wagon in under the Cibus gas station's canopy and parks in front of pump number two. "I'll take care of the first fill-up."

Starck nods and then reaches under the dashboard where he pulls the lever that releases the fuel cap.

"The cover can be a bit stubborn but just wiggle it upward a little."

"I'll figure it out," Elias replies as he unbuckles his seatbelt and opens the door to step out. However, he barely gets one foot on the ground before Sunni pokes his head out between the seats.

"Are you going into the store too?"

"Didn't plan to, no. What do you need?"

"Well . . ." Sunni shrugs. "Nothing in particular. Just wanted to take a look."

"Oh, I don't know, Sunni. We spent all day at the market."

From his seat in the back, to the left of the boy, Michael sees disappointment spread across Sunni's face and immediately feels sorry for him.

"You know what?" he says. "You go ahead and fill up the car, Elias. I'll take him inside. I'd like to see what they have too."

He leans forward and throws a questioning glance at Lisa. She hesitates for a moment, then wrinkles her nose and shakes her head.

"Okay, then. Guess it's just you and me, Sunni."

After stepping out himself, Michael stays by the car, holding the door open while Sunni climbs out. Afterward he shuts it and instinctively puts his arm around the boy's shoulders. He regrets it, though. Because Sunni is about the same height as his own son was—and for a fleeting second, the narrow shoulder beneath his arm doesn't belong to Sunni. It belongs to Benjamin.

In an effort to regain control of his thoughts, Michael spends a moment studying the carvings on one of the six marble columns supporting the canopy.

Baixa's trademark clearly hasn't been forgotten during the construction of the gas station. That's understandable, though, given that the station is located right by the city limits—and has a view of a large sign, which on one side bids passing travelers *WELCOME TO THE CITY OF COLUMNS* and on the other side says: *SEE YOU SOON IN THE CITY OF COLUMNS*.

Compared to the grand columns of the canopy, the station's shop seems rather modest. A small, white-brick building, tucked behind advertising posters, fold-out signs, and a pallet of gas canisters. The entrance is on the left side, consisting of two glass doors.

Inside the store, Michael quickly realizes that modern marketing strategies are also used in this other world. At least, there's no doubt that the layout of the Cibus shop has been carefully designed. Everyday essentials—bread, milk, meat, and such—are strategically placed at the far end of the store. To reach them, customers will first have to navigate through a maze of impulse items, ranging anywhere from leather bracelets with skull pendants to decks of intricately decorated Spindle cards.

Despite these overwhelming temptations, Michael and Sunni manage to reach the counter with only two items. They place these on the counter—right in front of the smiling yellow face on the clerk's shirt.

"A water and a bag of Crunchers?" the skinny clerk says, picking up the items and studying them before setting them back on the counter. "That all?"

"Yes," Sunni replies. "How much is it?"

"You sure? We have a deal—two bags for twenty dakra, and we'll throw in a couple of freshly baked dumblers."

"Thanks, but no thanks," Sunni says, shaking his head.

"How about one of these?" The clerk pulls out a small box of what looks like licorice pastilles and shakes it in front of them.

"We'll just take this," Michael says.

"You sure? They're good."

Beneath his cap, the skinny clerk flashes a smile, and his voice carries an unsettling cheerfulness. Either he's unusually persistent, Michael thinks, or he's set on pissing them off.

"Are you absolutely sure? I also got deals on wholegrain bread and pouch milk."

"We're sure," Michael says firmly. This time, he makes no effort to hide his irritation.

"Oh, come on. If you act fast, I'll throw in a pack of biscuits and a couple of challors. They're damned good, if I do say so myself. A fine last meal for the kid. Or how about two cans of beans for just twelve dakra? Probably not a deal my boss would approve of, but hey, I'm in a good mood."

Sunni looks up at Michael, his eyes wide with surprise. Without saying a word, they ask if he also caught what the clerk slipped into his sales pitch—without the slightest change in tone.

Pretend you didn't hear it, Michael answers silently. *I don't think he even realizes what he said, so just ignore it and play along.*

Yeah, but how do you do that when you're faced with a clerk like this? Someone who ignores the customer's obvious reluctance and relentlessly rattles off one outrageous deal after another. A clerk who—whether knowingly or not—just tried to sell Sunni his last meal.

"How about it, folks?"

"Really, we'd just like to pay, please."

"Oh, come on, don't be so glum," the clerk says, grabbing the bottom of his shirt and pulling it out to show off the design. "Keep Smiling. That's my motto."

I doubt it always was, Michael thinks, staring at the clerk's exposed wrists. *You don't get those kinds of scars from falling off a bike.*

When neither Michael nor Sunni says anything and simply continue staring silently at the grinning yellow face on his shirt, the clerk rolls his eyes and taps a small bell on the counter a couple of times.

"Petturi!" he shouts. "You can come in here now. They're boring as shit!"

Moments later, the door to the shop's restroom swings open, and out steps a man whose appearance sends a chill down Michael's spine. He's big—the door behind him must be around six and a half feet tall, and judging by that, Michael estimates him to be about six foot three. And well over 260 pounds.

"What is this?" Michael asks. He tries to sound calm, but it's hard when his throat keeps tightening, making it feel like he is trying to swallow a fistful of sand. "Is there a problem?"

"Nah, I don't have any problems," the clerk says. He turns his face questioningly to the giant by the restroom door. "Petturi?"

The giant shrugs and hooks his thumbs into the wide belt around his waist. Even from at least thirty feet away, Michael can hear the leather creak as he presses down on it.

Instinctively, he steps forward, placing himself between Sunni and the terrifying giant.

Not that it'll make any difference, he thinks. *If it comes to that, he'll walk right over me.*

"What's this about?" he tries once more.

"I already told you!" the clerk exclaims. He looks like someone who's just had a brilliant idea and can't wait to share it. "We have an offer for you guys . . . or well, just for you, really. You come with us without making a fuss . . ."

As he speaks, one of his hands disappears behind the counter. When it reappears, it's holding a revolver.

"And in return, we promise it'll be over quickly for the kid and your friends outside."

∽

The town of Gleamsdale, where Michael grew up, was a well-functioning and peaceful place where there was rarely any trouble—and, unbelievable as it may sound, he has only seen a real firearm three times in his entire life. And that, mind you, includes Starck's rifle . . . which also happens to be the only one of the three he has seen fired.

That doesn't mean he hasn't wondered what he would do if he were ever threatened with a gun. However, in those scenarios, the threat was always a criminal acting out of desperation. Someone robbing a bank to pay off gambling debts or to buy medicine for his dying wife. In other words, someone who could be reasoned with—and never someone like the lunatic standing behind the counter now, chuckling with excitement.

"So, what's it gonna be?" the clerk asks. "Fast or slow? Your choice."

"I don't know what this is about," Michael begins. "But it's pretty clear that I'm the one you're after. So how about you let the others go?"

"Oh, someone catch me, I think I might faint!" The clerk takes off his cap and clutches it to his chest. "Did you hear that, Petturi? The hero wants to sacrifice himself for his friends. That's just hilarious! Although Tom did say you were a bit of a drama queen."

A jolt of surprise ripples through Michael. If he is talking about the same Tom who attacked them in Attica, this can't possibly end well. That madman tried to kill him—not just once, but twice. If these guys are mixed up with him, there's no telling what they might do.

Maybe, if I'm fast enough, I can throw myself over the counter and get the gun away from him, he thinks. *Then I can . . . yeah, what exactly? Even if that were to work, you still got the giant over by the restroom door. He's armed too—and he knows how to use his weapon. You wouldn't even know how to check if the safety is off.*

"Why are you doing this?" he asks, stealing quick glances around him to assess their chances of escape.

"And now he's trying to buy time by chatting," the clerk sighs, after which he leans toward Sunni. "This guy is a walking cliché, isn't he?"

Sunni doesn't answer. Instead, he stands completely still, staring out the window at the black car that just pulled in under the canopy.

"Hey, kid! I'm talking to you!" the clerk snarls, waving his revolver in front of the boy's face—but Sunni just keeps on staring out the window.

What are you doing, Sunni? Answer him. You don't mess around with these guys. They'll kill us if—

No further does Michael get before it dawns on him what the kid is actually doing. Sunni is creating the distraction he needs.

"What the fuck are you staring at, you little rice muncher?"

Still not getting an answer, the clerk follows the boy's gaze out the window. As he sees the black car, his eyes grow wide.

"Oh, fuck! We need to get out of here, Petturi, and it's gotta be the back door. Hain is early."

He turns his gaze back to Sunni and pulls back the hammer on his revolver.

"Sorry, kid. We ain't got room for dead weight."

This is it, Michael thinks as he throws himself forward and grabs the clerk's narrow wrist. *You get one chance. Don't waste it.*

That's his last thought before the revolver goes off right next to his ear with a deafening blast.

Everything is shrouded in a dense, white fog. In front of him, Michael can make out the faint outline of a boy crouching between two shelves. The boy's lips are moving, but all Michael hears is a high-pitched ringing. Now the boy reaches out and grabs his arm, trying to pull him closer—but without success.

On the shelf above the boy's head, something bursts, and the contents of it—small white grains—start to rain down on him. Some cling to his black hair, resembling tiny snowflakes, while the rest scatter across the floor.

A second later, the same invisible force pulls down another object. This time it's a plastic bottle from the shelf to the left of the boy. It arcs through the air, slamming into the wall beneath the store window before landing on the floor. There, it spins around a couple of times, after which it rolls over and comes to a stop next to the boy's right foot.

To Michael, the entire scene seems to unfold in slow motion. Everything feels unreal and distant, like a dream. But then, the boy clenches his fist and slams it into his shoulder—and the impact simultaneously lifts the fog and snaps time back to its normal pace.

"GRAB IT!" Sunni cries, stretching out his arm and pointing at the floor beneath one of the shelves. "YOU GOT IT FROM HIM! IT'S RIGHT THERE! GRAB IT!"

Sure enough, about five feet from where Michael is lying, he sees the revolver's grip sticking out beneath the lowest shelf. He rolls onto his back, shifting his position. From this angle, he can see a shadow moving along the floor behind the last row of shelves. It must be the clerk's companion, the terrifying giant.

Michael casts another longing glance at the revolver. The distance is too great for him to reach it, but if he pushes off with his feet against the counter, he might be able to slide over there before the shadow reaches the corner.

He bends his knees, pulling himself closer to the counter, and plants his feet on either side of the corner where the front panel meets the adjoining wall. However, just as he's about to push off, the giant fires his weapon. The bullet rips through the counter, leaving a hole just to the left of Michael's hip.

"Petturi, you asshole!" the clerk shouts from behind the counter. "Watch it with that thing! You almost hit *me*, for fuck's sake!"

There's a brief silence, and then suddenly, he bursts into laughter.

"You did make a nice hole in the Gaffer Kid back here, though."

The Gaffer Kid? Oh God!

Until now, it hadn't even crossed Michael's mind that the nutcase with the Smiley shirt might not be the store's real clerk. But of course, he isn't. The two psychos must have jumped the store attendant before Michael and Sunni walked in, and 'Keep Smiling' back there must have put on his cap.

How did he not see that from the start? Parallel dimension or not, no one in their right mind would hire someone with sociopathic traits that obvious.

In the wake of that thought comes a terrible realization. If the Gaffer Kid—as Keep Smiling calls him—was hit by that shot, it would indirectly be Michael's fault. He's the one they're after, but in the process, it could cost another person's life. An innocent person.

Two innocent people. What about Sunni? Did you forget him?

The shadow takes a step closer to the corner, and Michael realizes that it's now or never if he's going to make a successful attempt at getting the gun.

With all the strength he can muster, he pushes off. For one terrible second, he's convinced that he has misjudged the distance—then he feels the wooden grip slide into his palm. He spins around, cocks the hammer, and takes aim, the revolver in his right hand steadied by his left.

A second later, the giant rounds the corner and charges straight at him, his boots pounding against the tiles like rolling thunder.

43

What is he doing? Lisa thinks. *Isn't that the wrong side?*

She's sitting with her head resting against the window, staring in bewilderment at the tall, black-clad man who just parked his car at the farthest pump. He got out a moment ago to refuel, but after grabbing the hose, he went to the wrong side of the car. At least, Lisa is pretty sure that the round thing she can see on the right side of the car is the gas cap.

She leans forward and places a hand on the shoulder of Starck, who is rummaging through the glove compartment, searching for something.

"Look at that guy. He's on the wrong side, isn't he?"

"Just a sec," Starck mumbles. "I could've sworn I had a pack of lens wipes in here."

He doesn't sound particularly interested, so Lisa turns to Elias, who is standing outside the window on her left, fueling the car. When she catches his attention, she tries to gesture toward the other vehicle, but he just waves at her and then turns in the opposite direction.

She raises her hand to try again when something on the ground between the two cars catches her eye.

Is that . . . gasoline? she thinks, staring at the large, dark pool that seems to crawl toward them like a living shadow.

She squints her eyes. Oh, yeah, that rainbow-colored sheen on the surface is unmistakable. Definitely gasoline.

What is he doing? she thinks once more, letting her gaze wander in a line from the pool up to the man's face. *What are you up to?*

The man smiles and shrugs as if he has read the question in her mind. Then he raises a finger in a *just a moment* gesture and pulls something out of his pocket.

At first, Lisa can't make out what it is—but then, all of a sudden, it hits her like a punch to the gut.

"We need to get Michael and Sunni out of there. Now!"

In her head, she is shouting, but the sound that comes out is monotonous, almost robotic.

"What?" Starck says.

"We need to get them out, right now!"

"What is it you—"

"DRIVE!" she suddenly screams at the top of her lungs, pounding on the window to warn Elias. "IT'S A LIGHTER! FOR GOD'S SAKE, DRIVE!"

44

Michael had meant to give a warning first, but the moment he sees the bloodthirsty look in the giant's eyes, that thought is instantly pushed aside. There is no mercy, no hesitation in those eyes—only the clear message that the giant wouldn't stop if a meteor hit him.

He hasn't even raised his gun. Why isn't he aiming at me?

Deep down, Michael does know why, though. It wouldn't be enough. A quick death wouldn't give them proper punishment for all the trouble they've caused.

Suddenly, a series of events flashes through his mind like a film reel played at double speed: First, the huge man lifting his foot and kicking the revolver out of his hand, after which he yanks him up and holds him in place. Then Keep Smiling picking up the weapon, pressing it against Sunni's temple, and pulling the trigger—while Michael can do nothing but watch in helpless terror.

With this image on his retinas, he fires the revolver.

The bullet strikes just above the giant's elbow, making his entire upper body—including his right hand—twitch so he loses grip on the revolver. He almost drops it but manages to catch it with his left hand's fingertips.

Stunned, he stares at the gun in his hand, at Michael, then back at the weapon. And then he does something Michael will never forget. He tilts his head, pulls his lips back in a shark-like smile . . . and throws the gun away. It slides across the floor tiles with the sound of fingernails against a blackboard.

"What the hell are you doing, Petturi?" Keep Smiling yells from behind the counter. The maddening enthusiasm in his voice has been replaced with tension.

"Shut the fuck up," the giant growls, folding his hands and making his knuckles crack. "Didn't I already tell you that you've used up your bullshit quota for today?"

"No, I'm serious. We don't have time for your macho shit! Hain is out there, and he ain't gonna wait for us just because you want to act all tough. Get it over with, and get it over with *now*, so we can get the hell out of here!"

He doesn't need to say it twice—the giant is already on the move. Three massive strides, then he leaps toward Michael, roaring like a feral beast.

Michael fires a shot that hits him in the stomach, but it makes no difference. The giant still has enough strength to grab him by the shirt and hurl him backward like a rag doll. Michael tries to regain his footing but ends up tripping over his own feet —only to slam against one of the rear shelves before landing flat on his back.

The collision with the tiled floor knocks the wind out of him, leaving him gasping for air. For a moment, he's sure he's going to pass out, but then his own jagged breathing is drowned out by another half-choked, gurgling sound.

"LET GO OF HIM, YOU MOTHERFUCKER!" he yells before he has even managed to turn around to see what's making that terrible sound. He doesn't need to see it, though. He knows that the sound is coming from Sunni.

"WOULD YOU JUST LET GO OF THE FUCKING KID?" Keep Smiling screams. "IT'S THE OTHER ONE WE NEED. WE HAVE TO GET OUT OF HERE, AND WE NEED HIM WITH US! CRANE IS GONNA LOSE HIS FUCKING MIND IF WE DON'T BRING HIM BACK!"

The giant doesn't react. He just stands there, staring at Sunni, while he chokes him to death with his huge, veiny hands. The boy's feet are kicking out in despair, yet they hit nothing but the empty air in front of the huge man's belt.

How is he able to do that? Michael thinks as he looks around frantically to find out where the revolver ended up. *He just took a bullet to his stomach. How the hell is he able to hold him like that?*

Above the counter, Keep Smiling's head appears. Strands of light-colored hair peek out from under his work cap, damp with sweat and sticking to his freckled cheek. His eyes are wide, darting back and forth between the giant and the window.

"I'M NOT FUCKING AROUND, PETTURI!" he bellows. "JUST LOOK OUT THE FUCKING WINDOW, YOU HALFWIT! HE'S DOING IT NOW! HAIN IS STARTING THE PARTY *RIGHT THIS SECOND!* JUST LOOK OUT THERE, GOD-DAMMIT!"

The giant scoffs but still turns to see what the clerk is rambling about. When he turns his face back toward his partner, the color has completely vanished from his cheeks, and he mouths a silent *fuck*.

Keep Smiling rolls his eyes and nods toward Michael and then toward the back door of the shop. Seemingly, the message gets through to the giant this time. At least, he releases his grip and lets Sunni drop.

The boy lands on his feet but has neither the strength nor the awareness to stay upright. His skinny legs wobble for a moment before giving in to the weight of his upper body and letting him collapse on the floor. There he stays, motionless.

The giant, on the other hand, suddenly bursts into motion. For the second time, he charges forward, his merciless gaze locked onto Michael—who doesn't have a firearm to defend himself with this time around. It would hardly make a difference if Michael could reach the revolver, though, because behind the giant he can see the clerk rounding the corner of the counter. Gun or no gun, he'd never be able to stop them both.

Then, something unexpected happens. A high-pitched, screeching sound emerges from somewhere outside of the shop —tires spinning on asphalt. This is immediately followed by a short, hissing noise and then a powerful blast. So powerful, in fact, that the windows behind the giant bend inward before shattering completely, sending a hail of glass shards down on them.

With the glass comes the flames.

45

At the moment the first gas pump explodes, Starck shouts something to Lisa, but his words are completely drowned out by the deafening blast—and the subsequent ringing in her ears. Nevertheless, his message gets through when she sees him frantically waving his hand up and down between the car seats.

Get down—and stay down!

Without hesitation, Lisa throws herself down on the seat and presses her hands and feet against the doors on both sides, hoping it might save her life if one of the next explosions should be strong enough to tip the car over.

There are eight pumps at the station, and so far, only one has exploded—but it'll only be a matter of time before the others follow.

No sooner has she finished this thought than the next devastating bang comes. Thankfully, the blast wave doesn't topple the car, but it *is* strong enough to send some large object hurtling through the air. As it passes, it scrapes against the top of the car, and Lisa gasps when she looks up and sees that the roof above her has been torn open. It looks as if someone has been standing up there, trying to hack their way through with an axe.

"Michael and Sunni?" she shouts, her voice shrill with fear.

"I can't see them," Starck replies, yanking the wheel so hard that the car skids sideways. "The entrance is black with smoke, but I'm circling around the shop now."

Lisa raises her head just enough to peer out the window. He isn't exaggerating, the entire facade of the shop is hidden behind a dark veil of smoke.

"Oh God, oh God, oh God! What do we do?"

"Lisa, you need to keep a cool head. If we panic now, we're done for. Do you understand what I'm saying?"

Lisa nods, tears streaming down her cheeks.

"Good. Once we get around, I'll pull up in front of the entrance and lay on the horn so they can hear us. And you make sure they get in the car . . . but you stay down. Can you do that?"

"Y-yeah, I can do that."

"I know you can. Now hold on. It's gonna be a sharp turn."

Lisa takes a deep breath and buries her face in the seat.

Beneath the car, a sharp screech fills the air as the tires slide sideways across the asphalt.

46

This is it. Tom smiles to himself. Holy crap, has he been waiting for this moment. Finally, he's gonna get his revenge. Would he have preferred to put a bullet right between that crybaby's eyes as well? Of course. But since that's not an option, this will have to suffice. Besides, it's not like the girl and the old clown with the rifle haven't done plenty to deserve a bullet or two.

The girl, that little bitch, had the nerve to taunt him back at the theater while he was tied up and couldn't do shit about it. And the old guide? If anyone deserves a set of fresh body piercings, it's him—with the condescending way he treated Tom.

That was the warning shot. That's what he said when he strolled into the theater's lobby after shattering the windows with his rifle. *I hope I won't have to take proper aim next time.*

The audacity! Talking like that to an unarmed man! He's gonna regret it, though. Because the tables have turned, and this time, Tom's the one holding the weapon while the old sucker has no idea what's coming. And Tom sure as hell isn't planning on firing any warning shots.

He raises the revolver, aiming at the corner behind the shop. Judging by the sound of screeching tires, they'll round the corner and come into view on his side in just a few seconds.

47

They'll need to act quickly if they are going to escape this alive. The explosion has—for the time being—forced the giant and his deranged sidekick to abandon their plan and flee out the back door. That only solves one of Michael's problems, though, because he doesn't have much time to get Sunni and himself out. The flames are already eating away at the store's interior—and only God knows what will happen once the fire reaches the pallet of gas canisters he saw on the side of the building earlier.

"Sunni!" he moans. "Are you okay?"

No answer.

He squints, trying to focus on the curled-up boy's chest, hoping to see it rise and fall. But the smoke is thick, and it stings his eyes.

"Sunni!" he repeats as he starts to crawl forward across the floor. Shattered glass crunches beneath him, jagged shards dig into his arms. It hurts like hell, and at one point, the pain forces him to stop and pull a couple of them out. "Sunni, wake up! Dammit, wake up!"

Something's happening. The boy doesn't exactly respond, but

he lets out a faint whimper, and his leg twitches slightly. It's not much, but it's a sign of life. Maybe there's still hope for—

WHOOOSH!

Michael's thoughts are mercilessly torn apart by the next explosion, and he lets out a startled scream as something big comes crashing through the shattered window frame to the right of the cash register, breaking a good chunk of the wall beneath it in the process.

When the worst of the dust has settled, he notices a large metal panel jutting out from the shop's shattered counter. The explosion has cracked its paint, but the blue number *two* is still visible, telling him exactly where it came from. He saw it when he got out of the car to enter the shop with Sunni. Back then, the metal panel belonged to the gas pump they had parked at.

Crawling a little farther enables him to see something else as well. Right next to the metal panel, there's a narrow crack in the front of the counter. Behind it, the store's real clerk sits.

The Gaffer Kid. That's what Keep Smiling called him, and now, Michael realizes why. The young man's head is wrapped in at least three layers of duct tape, wound so tightly that his comfort clearly wasn't a concern during the application. In a couple of places, the tape has ripped out chunks of his hair, leaving them to hang in small arcs from his face. Above the tape, his eyes stare into the air, unblinking.

There's nothing you can do for him now, Michael tells himself. Even so, he struggles to tear his gaze away from the body. He feels guilty, ashamed that this innocent young man is dead because of him.

He forces himself to look down and focuses on crawling the rest of the way to Sunni.

"You need to get up, Sunni," he says, grabbing the boy's shoulder and giving it a firm shake. "We have to get out of here."

The boy makes a strained swallowing motion and slowly opens his eyes. For the first few seconds, his gaze is dazed and unsteady, but then the confusion fades. His head turns toward the counter.

"They're gone," Michael says. "They ran out the back. And we need to get out as well, Sunni."

Almost on cue, there is another bang outside—this one not as loud as the previous two. A brief silence follows, then two more explosions in quick succession. It sounds like they're coming from the back of the shop.

"We'll go that way," Michael says, pointing toward the entrance. He hesitates, then places his hand on the boy's shoulder again. "We're gonna make it, okay?"

Sunni doesn't exactly look convinced. Still, he presses his lips together and follows as Michael starts crawling forward.

Together, they make their way toward the entrance, crawling as fast as they can along the floor, where the smoke isn't as thick, and doing their best to avoid the shattered glass and burning groceries scattered in their path.

48

Tom stomps the ground in frustration while his gaze follows the blue station wagon, now driving in a wide semicircle around him.

He would have hit. If it weren't for Jack and Petturi, he damn well *would* have hit. He had the old jerk in his sights when those two halfwits came crashing out the back door and threw off his aim. Now, thanks to them, the bullet is buried in the station wagon's right headlight instead of the driver's forehead. And to top it off, they don't even have the crybaby! For fuck's sake, they were supposed to grab him while he took care of the others!

"NOW LOOK WHAT YOU'VE DONE!" he screams desperately at his accomplices, after which he starts running after the car.

He fires two more shots, but neither comes close to hitting the target. One bullet skims the asphalt a few yards from the left rear tire, then ricochets into a pile of bags on a pallet on the neighboring lot. The other vanishes into the void, apparently hitting nothing at all.

The chances of him catching up to them now are slim, given that his knee is still aching from the kick Michael gave him at the theater. Still, he has to try. No fucking way he's going back to Crane without at least having made an effort. Thus, he follows, limping and cursing, as the car rounds the corner.

By the time he gets there, much to his frustration, he realizes he was nowhere near fast enough. All he can see now are a pair of red taillights disappearing into the dense smoke beneath the canopy.

He slows down and presses a hand to his forehead. What the hell is he supposed to do now? Sprinting toward a bunch of gas pumps surrounded by flames isn't exactly at the top of his wish list.

Unexpectedly, the solution presents itself.

"Oh . . . yeah," he mumbles, shrugging. "That would work."

He has spotted Elias crawling on the ground at the left side of the driveway. Even from a distance, it's clear that the old watchmaker is an easy target. For one, large portions of his body are burned. And for another, he's leaving a long, red trail of blood behind him. He looks like he's in agony.

A state Tom is happy to help him out of.

49

The timing couldn't have been better. Just as Michael and Sunni reach the entrance, the station wagon's rear door comes into view. The car is barely more than a few feet away, but apparently, they can't be seen from inside the vehicle, because Starck leans on the horn while Lisa pushes the door open and calls out to them.

"Here!" Michael shouts, waving at her. "We're down here."

"Get them in here!" he hears Starck roar from inside the vehicle.

Lisa obeys the librarian's order, reaching her hand out toward them. Seeing it, Michael helps Sunni onto his knees so he can go first—then, as soon as the boy is safely inside the car, he follows.

The instant the door slams behind them, Starck puts the car in reverse and starts driving—which causes Lisa to look from side to side in confusion.

"What are you doing? They're back there!"

"They're behind us, yeah," Starck says, slamming the accelerator. "But so is Elias."

All three passengers in the back seat turn around and stare

out the rear window as the car reverses. For the first few yards, the thick smoke obscures everything, but then a figure emerges.

Even with his back turned, Michael instantly recognizes Tom—the dark brown fleece jacket is unmistakable. He also sees the hand gripping the revolver . . . and what the gun is aimed at.

Instinctively, Michael tries to shield Sunni from the sight by covering his eyes with a hand, but he's not fast enough. In the split second before the car slams into Tom's back, the boy sees the man he considers his granddad get shot.

The man who has dedicated his life to taking care of him now lies on the ground, writhing in pain, bleeding and burned.

"Get him in, but be careful," Starck says as he brings the car to a stop.

The timbre of his voice makes Michael exchange an anxious glance with Lisa before they step out. It's the first time they've ever heard the librarian sound like this. He is terrified—and that terrifies them.

"Careful," Starck repeats as they kneel on either side of the wounded watchmaker. "Watch his back."

"We *are* being careful," Michael replies, after which he looks at Lisa, who grabs ahold behind Elias' knee and nods.

"Good. Then we lift."

Michael has braced himself for hearing Elias scream when they lift him—but it doesn't happen. He just keeps breathing in long, heavy gasps, his gaze fixed on the sky. It's not looking good. Even if he hadn't been shot, those burns would be nearly impossible to treat in time.

You know that too, Michael thinks, glancing at Starck. He has a strong feeling that this situation would have played out very differently if it weren't for Sunni's presence.

Once they've gotten Elias into the back seat, Michael climbs into the front—and as the car starts moving, he looks back.

There, he sees Tom crawling across the ground before struggling to his feet against the wall near the back corner of the shop. Keep Smiling and the giant stand a little farther away. All three look exhausted, and none of them make a move to resume the chase. However, Michael is pretty certain that won't last forever.

From their attackers, his gaze shifts to the back seat, where Lisa and Sunni sit staring at Elias with the same blank, uncomprehending look in their eyes. As if their brains simply can't process what they're seeing.

Michael has seen that look on Lisa before. Out in the desert, right when they first arrived. Back then, her fingers were fumbling frantically with the plastic bracelets on her wrists—just like they are now.

"What do we do?" he asks as Starck steers the car onto the main road in front of the gas station.

The librarian bites his lip, thinking, but no answer comes from him. Instead, it comes from Elias in the back seat.

"It's too risky . . . to stay here," he groans, his voice rough and strained, every word taking a toll. "We continue to Soto."

Starck meets his gaze in the rearview mirror, grimaces—and then turns right, heading toward the large sign at the city limits.

"No!" Sunni screams. "We can take him to Francisco. He can help him!"

"Francisco . . . doesn't have the equipment to treat gunshot wounds," Elias says. "But there are doctors in Soto who do."

"No!" Sunni repeats. "It's too far."

"Sunni," Starck says. "You need to—"

"NO, I DON'T! I DON'T NEED TO DO ANYTHING!"

Out of the corner of his eye, Michael sees Lisa reach out to comfort Sunni, but he rejects her, shoving her hand away with a low, almost animalistic growl.

"YOU THINK YOU KNOW BEST JUST BECAUSE I'M A

KID!" he screams. "BUT I CAN SEE HOW BAD IT IS, AND I ALSO KNOW WHAT WILL HAPPEN IF HE DOESN'T GET HELP RIGHT AWAY!"

"Erik knows that too," Elias suddenly says. "But he *also* knows that we have no other choice. We can't stay here. Soto is our best bet."

He pauses, takes a painful breath, and places his hand on Sunni's arm.

"Besides . . . I ain't gone yet, am I?"

Sunni doesn't answer. He just turns his face to the window and sobs as the car moves farther and farther away from his home.

PART SEVEN
THE DEVIL'S GLASS

50

From a balcony, a fair distance away from the burning gas station—safe from explosions and gunfire—Crane watches the blue station wagon as it disappears beyond the horizon.

Standing next to him is Anton. He is breathing heavily while his fingers fumble with one of the buttons on his shirt. Around his little, chubby body hangs a nauseating stench of sweat. Crane knows exactly what's causing it—and it's not the heat. God knows the fat bastard could stand to lose a few pounds, and the desert wind *is* scorching today, but that's not the reason.

No, Anton reeks like a moldy dishcloth for the simple reason that he's terrified of what Crane is going to say and do next. That suits Crane just fine. He has different strategies for keeping his people in line. Some need hope, others need to feel important—but when it comes to the fatty beside him, fear is what works. Hell, Anton would force-feed his own mother cockroaches until she choked if it meant saving his own ass.

"Looks like you'll be going on a little hike," Crane says.

"What, um . . . what do you mean?"

Anton sounds pathetic, almost on the verge of tears. If he

weren't such a coward, he'd probably have jumped off the balcony just to get away.

"Well, if those idiots couldn't handle it, we'll have to bring out the heavy artillery, right?"

At the word *heavy*, Crane lets his gaze drift down to his companion's gut, causing Anton to lower his eyes in embarrassment.

"Can't we just follow them? I mean, they hardly had time to fill up the car."

Crane answers the question by slowly turning his head from side to side, then bares his teeth in a predator's grin.

"Well, if you're not planning to contribute at all, we could always just send you back to where you came from," he says. "I happen to know that there's a big mirror in the interrogation room at the police station in Torremolinos. To be fair, I've never tried traveling through one of those one-way mirrors they use, but hey, there's a first time for everything. I wonder if it's even possible to come back from them. I mean, there must be a reason why they're called *one-way*, right?"

"No, please don't," Anton cries, clasping his chubby fingers together and wincing. "I can't go back there. I'll do it. Whatever you want me to do, I'll do it, I . . ."

He stops mid-sentence, and behind his glasses, the realization dawns in his eyes.

"You want to send me to Soto."

Crane nods, Anton sighs.

"I'm the only one they won't recognize. That's why."

Crane smiles. Anton might be pretty useless when it comes to fistfights and firearms, but he's sharp in other ways—and maybe, just maybe, that's exactly what's needed right now.

"Starck is up to something," he says. "And it's not just getting the newcomers safely to the mansion. If it was just that, he wouldn't have bothered bringing all of them."

As he speaks, Crane pulls a small, oval mirror from his pocket and hands it to Anton. It looks like the kind of small makeup mirror you'd typically find in a woman's purse.

Anton turns it over in his hands, examining it. A few times, the light from the setting sun catches the glass, reflecting sharply into his face. At first it makes him flinch, but then something in the mirror seems to draw him in, gradually sending him into a dreamlike, almost hypnotic state.

"But he did," Crane continues. "Starck brought both the boy and the watchmaker. I want to know why, Anton."

Anton's lips curl into a faint smile beneath his mustache as he nods and, with a nasal hum, signals that the message is understood. Then, without another word, he turns and walks through the doorway into the house, still humming, still staring at the mirror. He is holding on to it with the careful reverence one might show a newborn child.

Once Anton is gone, Crane turns his attention back to the street in front of the burning gas station where four figures are emerging through the smoke. They're moving slowly, two of them limping.

One of the limpers is undoubtedly Petturi. Even hunched over, clutching his stomach, the big brute still stands a head taller than the others.

The second injured person could be Tom, but the wall of smoke behind them makes it hard to tell.

In any case, Crane will be better off waiting until morning to send them after Starck's group. Ordering them out now, the way they're staggering around, would be a recipe for disaster.

Hardly has he finished that thought before the tall figure stumbles and crashes face-first onto the ground. The other three gather around him, gesturing wildly. They stand like that for a while until finally one of them crouches down and leans over the body. A few seconds pass, then the figure gets back up, says something to the others . . . and without further ado, the three move on, leaving Petturi's lifeless body in the middle of the street. A cruel reminder that Crane has overestimated his helpers—and underestimated his old colleague.

You're going to pay for this, Erik, he thinks, shaking his head. *You're going to pay dearly for this.*

51

As they put more distance between themselves and Baixa, the adrenaline in Michael's veins starts to fade, and his pulse gradually steadies. His brain, on the other hand, refuses to rest. It demands answers—and it knows exactly where to get them.

"What the hell was that about?" he asks. "And don't you dare lie to us!"

Starck sighs and glances at the back seat, where Elias is half-sitting, half-lying down, his lips pressed together and his gaze shifting unsteadily. Still, he's awake enough to give the librarian the go-ahead with a faint nod.

"I'm afraid you've unwillingly been caught up in a political conflict," Starck says. "You remember how I told you that guides are supposed to keep people out until they're ready and help them when they are? To protect their minds."

Both Michael and Lisa nod.

"The guides have always been Urari's . . . safety filter," Starck continues. "But over the past few years, things have gotten complicated because one of the guides rebelled, starting a long-running conflict with the council."

"The council? They your superiors or what?"

"The Guide Council is Urari's highest authority," Elias interjects from the back seat, his voice hoarse and raspy. "Our government, if you will."

Starck shoots him a disapproving look, something along the lines of *save your breath, you stubborn mule*, before turning his gaze back to Michael.

"The Guide Council drafts and enforces Urari's laws, and they're also the ones who set the rules that guides operate by. And since overthrowing an institution of that scale is a humongous task, Crane quickly realized he would need allies—and it didn't take him long to figure out that the innocent people drawn here by grief are easy to manipulate once they've fallen victim to the influence of the mirrors. Therefore, he started recruiting among the most vulnerable, meaning newcomers and those who have dared to enter the Mansion of Mirrors before they were ready. And since the two of you not only fall into that first category but also were able to cross over on your own, we have to assume he finds you extra interesting. He has been looking for people with that particular talent for a long time."

"Why did he decide to—" Lisa begins, but before she can finish, Michael cuts her off by raising a finger.

"Wait a minute," he says. "Crane . . . as in Daniel Crane?"

Starck stares at him in surprise. Beneath his silver-gray hair, the weathered skin of his forehead creases, creating small horizontal lines above his eyebrows.

"How do you know his first name?"

"Daniel Crane is the name of the police officer who knocked on my door the day I lost Benjamin and Ann," Michael begins, but as he hears his own trembling voice say the words, he realizes that it's not the real explanation. "No, he didn't give me his name back then. He only did that later . . . in the nightmare I had at Mary and Elias' place."

As a cruel reminder, Michael sees Crane's face before his mind's eye—pale and grinning widely, just as it was that night. With it comes the memory of the words he said.

Shouldn't you be picking up the pace? The mirrors are dangerous . . . and if your son starts to get bored waiting for you, he might be tempted to pull off a few sheets to see what's hiding underneath.

"He's the one in my nightmares about the mansion," Michael continues. "Every time I find Benjamin's mirror and pull the sheet off, it's always him, Crane, keeping my son trapped behind the glass. Are you telling me that he's behind all of this? That he had something to do with what happened to me and Lisa . . . with Benjamin's disappearance? Is *that* what you're saying?"

"I can neither confirm nor deny that," Starck says. "And we'd be wise to keep that in mind. Crane has plenty of terrible things on his conscience, and I can't rule it out—but the most likely explanation is that he is manipulating you. That he's feeding you false hope to get you to enter the Mansion of Mirrors before you're ready."

Starck lets go of the wheel and turns his face so he can make eye contact with Michael.

"And even if he is telling the truth, it won't help anyone— especially not your son—if you let Crane get under your skin and chose to rush headfirst into the mansion. You'd be giving him exactly what he wants."

"That's easy for you to say, isn't it?" Michael says. He struggles to preserve the anger in his voice—because he *wants* to be angry and he *is* angry—but when the words come out, it's the other dominant emotion in his heart, *despair*, that colors them. "You're not the one who just lost your family!"

Starck presses his lips together and nods.

"You're right. I'm not."

52

The long period of silence that follows Starck's apologetic response is spent differently by each of Lisa's four companions.

Starck keeps his gaze fixed firmly on the road ahead, Michael busies himself by picking at a crack in the rubber frame of the side window, and Sunni spends most of his time casting worried glances at his injured granddad every time he breaks into another fit of coughing. During one of these fits, Lisa sees tiny, rust-colored droplets of blood land on the hand Elias holds to his mouth. For Sunni's sake, she keeps that detail to herself.

Her own way of dealing with the awkward silence in the car has been to pull her phone out of her pocket again. She doesn't actually use it, doesn't even turn it on, but there's something comforting about feeling the scratches on the screen's surface beneath the tip of her thumb. Maybe it's because the phone is something she brought from home, making it feel like a link to a life that seems very far away.

At some point, though, it starts to bore her, so she puts it away and shifts her attention to the landscape outside.

Before they arrived in Baixa, what she saw through the window was almost exclusively sandbanks, tumbleweeds, and rocks. Beautiful, silver-glinting rocks, sure—but still just rocks. During the past hour, however, the landscape has undergone several dramatic—and almost surreal—transformations. So many, in fact, that Lisa has the feeling that this other world must be divided into smaller but more intense climate zones. At least, she's fairly certain that the drastic changes in both wildlife and plant life she's observed over such a short span of time would have required a journey of several days in the world she still considers the *normal* one.

Right now, they're making their way across an old, dried-out riverbed in a forested area, where smooth tree trunks stretch high into the sky, their canopies glowing orange—round and almost translucent, like the halos of dandelions.

Between the moss-covered tree trunks scattered across the sandy bottom of the riverbed, a group of small creatures that look like squirrels with large, owl-like eyes dart back and forth. They look adorable—like living versions of the wide-eyed plush toys she and Emma used to collect when they were little.

Deciding that the silence has lasted long enough for the conversation to be resumed in a calmer fashion, Lisa takes the chance to repeat the question that was cut off earlier.

"What was his reason for it?" she asks. "Why did Crane rebel against the council?"

Starck nods as though he has been sitting there just waiting for that exact question to be asked.

"There are two things you need to understand," he says. "One is that Daniel Crane hasn't always been what he is today. He used to be a good man, and during his time as a guide, he has helped many people safely through Urari. Back then, we were colleagues, he and I . . . and we were good friends. Until the day everything fell apart for him."

He pauses to clear his throat, and Lisa notices that there's something almost apologetic in his voice as he continues.

"The second thing you need to understand is that a job like this can take a serious toll on a person. You witness a lot of tragic fates, and at times, it's hard to leave it behind. Having someone to lean on is crucial. Not that you can—or even should—strive for a normal life alongside this job, but it's important to surround yourself with good people. Even if you can't necessarily tell them the truth about what you do. Crane had that. In fact, that was exactly the problem. He managed to do what very few others have been able to—and which actually goes against the unspoken rules of being a guide. He had a family life alongside his work in Urari."

"Like . . . in our world?" says Lisa, half questioning, half stating.

"In your own home state, no less. Crane had a wife and a daughter in Pennsylvania. They were everything to him. They were the reason he could handle the tough experiences of Urari. He used to talk about them all the time."

Starck looks at his passengers.

"I know what you're thinking, and yes, he did lose them. They didn't die, though . . . or rather, no one knows if his daughter actually died. That was the worst part. Isabel, that was her name, just vanished. Seven years old, the most beautiful little girl in the world, and one day, she was simply gone. Crane's wife, Rebecca, was with her at the time. They had stopped at a fast-food restaurant on their way home from a shopping trip, and Isabel was allowed to play on the swings outside while her mom went in to get their food. But when Rebecca came back, her daughter was gone. And no one has seen her since."

At those words, Lisa places a hand on Michael's shoulder and gives it a gentle squeeze. Michael takes her hand but says nothing. His gaze remains fixed on the barren desert landscape rushing past outside the car window.

"Rebecca was never the same again," Starck continues. "She withdrew from the world—and especially from her husband. Crane, on the other hand, accepted the situation fairly quickly. You see, being a cop, he had a tough but rational approach to Isabel's disappearance. You've probably heard that missing persons cases are rarely solved unless there is a solid lead within the first twenty-four hours. That was what Crane focused on, and he tried to get Rebecca to accept it too. Of course, he was only trying to help her through the loss by pushing her to move on. The trouble was that his solution was bringing her to Urari."

"To the Mansion of Mirrors, you mean?" Michael asks, and Starck nods.

"We all warned him against it, but still, he sent her to the mansion before she was ready to confront her demons. And that had serious consequences. One thing was that Rebecca wasn't ready—but Crane himself wasn't ready either."

"Did she go insane?" Lisa asks. "Like the guy in the theater?"

"Had it only been that," Starck says bitterly. "She never even came back. As far as anyone knows, the moment Rebecca stepped through the doors of the mansion was the last time Crane saw his wife."

For some reason, that information makes Lisa feel disappointed and slightly offended.

"So, he just stayed behind? Why didn't he go with her?"

"That's the price of being a guide," Starck says. "We've been given the gift of traveling freely between the two worlds through the mirrors, but the mansion is off-limits to us. There has always been a strict rule against us going in there."

"Yet Crane did it anyway," Michael says.

Lisa looks at Starck, and when he confirms with a nod, her gaze shifts to Michael.

"How did you know that?"

"I'd have done the same."

Starck doesn't comment on it, but it's clear that this remark stirs something in him and changes the way he looks at Michael. Lisa can't quite put her finger on it, but something definitely flickers in his eyes. Maybe it's caution.

"Some say Crane waited outside the mansion for three whole days before he couldn't take it anymore and went in after her," says Elias, who apparently has decided to join the conversation again, even though it's clearly painful for him to speak. "Others claim he tortured himself for weeks without food or water before he finally gave in."

"As is often the case with stories that have no firsthand witnesses," Starck continues, "it tends to grow more dramatic with each retelling. On late nights in taverns of Soto, I've even heard claims that Crane's wait reached the full biblical forty days and nights. No matter the version, they all agree on one thing, though. Crane gave in. He defied the ban and went inside. And when he came back, he was no longer the man we knew and loved. When he returned, madness had taken hold. What he experienced in there, I wouldn't dare to guess. But Crane came out a shattered, bitter man, consumed by hate. Hate against life, hate against himself for failing to save his family, hate against those who still can—and above all, hate against the Guide Council and everything it stands for. He believes it was the council's rules that kept him from saving Rebecca. That he could have changed the outcome if he had gone in with her from the start. That is why he seeks revenge on them."

Starck pauses and gazes thoughtfully out the windshield.

"The problem is that he's not just fighting a group of politicians. He's waging war against the institution itself—and since the council's primary role is to maintain sustainable societal structures in Urari . . . well, the most effective way to fight them is to create chaos. Thus, Crane started building an army, recruiting from the most vulnerable. And judging by the state of Attica, he has gained a lot of followers."

"You think that was him?"

"I'm sure of it. Crane and his supporters follow a certain pattern, waging a kind of guerrilla warfare in the towns close to the Perimeter. They're easy targets since they're rarely densely populated. On top of that, the border towns are prime recruiting grounds because they're where newcomers typically go after arriving in Urari. Those two factors make them ideal targets for Crane. It is, however, troubling that he went for Attica already. Because even though Attica is close to the Perimeter, it's a fairly large town that has a significant population."

"*Had* a significant population," Lisa corrects. "It's in the past tense now, isn't it?"

"Oh . . . yes. Yes, of course. Had."

Starck lingers on the word, as though it hasn't fully sunk in just how empty and abandoned the city truly was. This puts a lump in Lisa's throat. For all she knows, he might have had friends there. However, before she can dwell on it any further, he adjusts his glasses and, in his usual manner, refocuses on the matter at hand.

"Unfortunately, this suggests that Crane has built a far larger following than we previously assumed. Otherwise, Attica would have been too much for him to take on."

"What about the fire?" Michael asks. "If he was only hunting for newcomers, he didn't need to burn it all down like that."

"Burning the cities is a symbolic act on Crane's part," Starck replies. "A message to the council that our world is on the brink of collapse. You see, in Urari, it is customary to cremate the dead rather than bury them, and then scatter their ashes on Mount Heriotza in the Wasteland. And the very last thing that Crane did before permanently turning his back on the guides was to make a promise to the council. He promised that one day he would stand on the top of that mountain and see nothing but ashes. That's what the burned cities are meant to remind us of."

Just under four hours pass before the inevitable occurs—the car runs out of fuel. Four hours that Lisa spends stealing glances between the gas gauge and the wounded watchmaker in the back seat, because it feels like some cruel higher power has set a terrible race in motion. A game of fate, where the question is who will be the first to give up—Elias or the car.

Now that the car has admitted defeat and Starck pulls over to the side of the road roughly five hundred yards from the first of the four mountain passes still lying between them and Soto, things have thankfully quieted down in the back seat. Elias has settled into a steady breathing rhythm, and Sunni has fallen asleep, leaning against him.

Every now and then, Lisa notices the boy shifting restlessly, as if caught in an unsettling dream. Each time it happens Elias gently strokes his cheek until he settles down. However, as soon as it's over, the watchmaker's hand always returns to his own face, carefully tracing a burn scar that starts at his chin and curves into a red crescent along his cheekbone.

Above the scar, his eyes are wet with fever, but his gaze is unbending. He has no intention of giving up without a fight.

"We'll have to camp here," Starck says. "It's not safe to head out on foot after dark in this area, so we'll have to wait until morning to look for fuel."

Lisa catches Michael casting a worried glance at Elias—and so does the watchmaker.

"I'll make it through the night," he grumbles, clearly annoyed. His voice sounds convincing. The color of his face, not so much.

"Sorry, Elias. I didn't mean to—"

"Ignore him," Starck says. "He always gets cranky when things get rough."

Elias responds with a scoff, which makes Starck turn to face him.

"You remember Baldraki?"

The watchmaker lets out a sound somewhere between a cough and a chuckle, then shifts his voice into a high-pitched imitation of a woman.

"If it hadn't been shut . . ."

"We probably wouldn't have even looked in it," Starck chimes in, matching the falsetto. Then he, too, starts laughing—only it's a desperate, chilling chuckle. And when he looks up again, his pupils are wide and misty.

"We've got more memories than good knees," Elias sighs.

"True—and some stories are better left for the quiet hours," Starck says as he opens the door and steps out. "I'm going to see if I can get a fire going before it gets dark."

"What do you say?" Michael asks, looking at Lisa. "Should we give him a hand?"

Lisa doesn't hesitate to nod. Having a simple, concrete task to focus on is exactly what she needs after everything that's happened.

Outside, the air is cool, and twilight slowly spreads over the mountains ahead, their peaks blending into the dark blue sky.

Had it not been for the blanket of stars, it would have been almost impossible to tell where the mountains end and the night sky takes over.

Lisa wonders if there might be snow up there. She also wonders if there could be other things—and before she can stop it, fragments of the conversation she had with Starck after the incident with the Fenris card surface in her mind.

You will encounter . . . unusual things as we venture deeper into Urari. One of those things is the wildlife.

She can still see the spider in her mind, hear the sound of its legs drumming across the floor, like fingers tapping on the edge of a desk.

"It's too exposed out here by the car," Starck says. "I'm thinking we set up camp under that plateau over there, where there's more shelter from the wind."

He points toward a ravine that starts about 200 yards ahead and from there zigzags toward the base of one of the mountains. It looks deep and unnerving in the darkness, but the plateau he is talking about is only six or seven feet down, nestled between some small sandstone cliffs. And it's fairly well lit.

"As long as we don't have to go all the way down into the dark," Lisa says. "That's where I draw the line."

"In an hour, everything will be pitch black anyway."

"Sorry, what?"

Starck doesn't reply. Instead, he turns to Michael.

"Can you grab the green bag and the pot? The tripod and the matches should be in the pot but check just in case. If not, they're with the rope. Oh, and bring the flashlight too."

Michael opens the trunk and starts handing the smaller things to Lisa. Meanwhile, Starck opens the passenger-side door and leans in toward Elias and the sleeping boy.

"You can start waking him up. We're setting up camp by the ravine over there."

"I heard," Elias says, pointing up at the cut in the car's roof made by the front plate from one of the Cibus station's gasoline pumps. "The old girl isn't exactly soundproof anymore."

"Do you think you can walk over there? It's a bit of a distance."

"Might need a shoulder to lean on, but I'll make it."

And he does. For the first part of the walk, he leans on Michael and Starck for support, but the last fifty yards, he insists on walking alone, using Starck's rifle as a cane. He's tough, but it's more than that. He fights his exhaustion with a calm, disciplined determination that Lisa can't help but admire.

Twenty minutes later, all five of them are sitting in a half-circle around the fire, staring impatiently at the lid of the pot as the flames lick its sides.

Every now and then, Starck shifts onto one knee and leans in to adjust the position of the tripod. Each time he does so, the fire sends a cloud of embers into the air. Most die out almost instantly, but a few get caught by the wind and drift down the ravine, casting eerie shadows on the walls.

"When we've eaten, we sleep," the librarian says in the candid manner that is his hallmark. "We'll take turns keeping watch, so the fire doesn't go out. I'll take the first shift, Michael the next, and so on. It's going to get cold out here."

"And tomorrow?" Michael asks.

"Tomorrow, our first priority is getting fuel for the car. There's a town on the other side of the mountains where we might get lucky."

For a moment, Starck looks like he has more to say, but instead, he gets up and walks over to their backpacks, which lie in a pile some distance away from the fire. Standing there, he catches Michael and Lisa's eyes and, with a subtle hand gesture, asks them to join him.

When they get over there, Starck places a hand on each of their shoulders.

"Listen, I realize that you two are the least familiar with Urari," Starck whispers, "but if you're okay with it, I'd like to send you out for gas tomorrow. With the state Elias is in, there's no way he can handle the trip, and Sunni can't be left alone with him if . . . if *it* happens while we're gone. On the other hand, I don't want to take the boy with us and risk him missing the opportunity to be by his granddad's side when it happens."

Starck doesn't elaborate, but he doesn't need to either. All three of them know what he means by *it*. And that *it* is inevitable.

"I wish there was a better way," he continues. "But this is the best I've got."

"It's okay," Michael says, glancing at Lisa, who agrees with a nod.

After the conversation, Lisa walks over and sits down next to Sunni, who is drawing on a stone with a piece of charcoal from the fire. Even now, limited to a primitive tool and a less-than-ideal canvas, he manages to create something beautiful. This time, it's an almost perfect replica of the coat of arms that decorated the backs of the Spindle cards from the night before.

"It's beautiful," Lisa says.

"You think so?" Sunni shrugs and tosses the charcoal back into the flames. "I think it's ugly. Ugly and stupid."

Out of the corner of her eye, Lisa sees Elias take a deep breath and open his mouth, no doubt about to tell the boy to watch his language. However, before he gets a chance to do so, she lifts a hand to stop him. After all, she is well aware that Sunni's outburst isn't really directed at her. It's born from the frustration of having to stand by helplessly while Elias keeps getting worse.

And if his anger, in any way, helps him cope, she sees no reason to take it away from him.

It's the sound that initially catches Lisa's attention and snaps her out of the drowsy haze she drifted into about an hour and a half into her shift. A hoarse, rasping noise that reminds her of the drunken, middle-aged men she often encounters on Sunday mornings when she goes down to pick up bread at the local bakery. They'll stand there, halfway passed out, one elbow resting on the garbage container outside Rosa's Bodega, reeking of booze and loneliness, trying to charm her with a muddled greeting that sounds more like a dying man's final breath than an actual word.

Now the sound is back—a hoarse, intrusive hissing. Where the hell is it coming from? There's something eerily human about it, and yet . . . not quite.

Even though something tells her it's a bad idea, Lisa crawls on her knees over to the bag and pulls out the flashlight. She shines it in the direction the sound seems to be coming from. The beam reveals nothing but a circular indentation in the gravel.

She kicks at the fire. It flares up for a moment, casting an orange-red glow over the rocky ground in a radius of about six feet. Not enough to reveal whatever is lurking in the darkness.

"Michael," she whispers. "Michael, are you awake?"

Michael doesn't respond. He is lying on his stomach, sleeping with his head resting on his crossed arms. She's about to poke him when the sound returns. It's no longer coming from some undefined place in the darkness ahead—it's right behind her.

Lisa spins around, aiming the flashlight at the terrifying source of the sound—and freezes in place.

The terror is a crawling creature, which, judging by its upper body emerging from the ground, must be about a yard long. It's slowly digging its way out of the gravel with long-clawed, hairy paws. Above them—where a face should have been—is a pulsating, ruddy growth, shaped with the symmetry of a starfish. Small spikes cover its surface, circling a slimy hole that must be the creature's mouth. It opens and closes in a slow, rhythmic motion, generating a series of wet *plop* sounds, while its whispering lamentation continues without pause.

Lisa stands completely still—partly because she's paralyzed with fear, and partly because she doesn't know how the creature will react to sudden movements.

Very slowly, she turns her head. The rifle lies on the ground between Starck and Elias.

With a body that feels like she's wading through knee-deep mud, she starts moving backward. She tries to do it silently, but the gravel betrays her, crunching beneath her sneakers.

To her horror, she realizes the creature is mirroring her movements. Every time she takes a step back, it digs its long claws into the ground and makes a clumsy, seal-like lunge forward.

Why aren't they waking up? she thinks, and then, almost as a desperate attempt at telepathy: *Wake up! Wake up and help me!*

Right then, her left heel gets caught on a rock jutting out of the sand. She stumbles, nearly falls, and before she can stop herself, a frustrated yell escapes her lips.

Instinctively, she claps a hand over her mouth—but it's too

late. The canyon walls mock her, echoing the torn remnants of her swear word back from the darkness.

"... uck ... uck!"

The creature responds with a gurgling hiss and lurches forward with another couple of seal-like hops, this time more eagerly. It's close to her now, and there's no longer any doubt that it navigates by sounds. Not that this should surprise her, considering that the beast is best described as a giant mole with an octopus' mouth instead of a face.

Hardly has this thought taken shape in her mind before Michael starts to wake up. He rolls onto his side, stretching his arms and yawning. The sound makes the creature hesitate and then change direction. It shuffles across the ground, positioning itself between his back and Lisa's feet.

"Don't," she whispers as Michael starts to move. "Don't turn around. Whatever you do, don't move. Just ... stay there."

She holds still for a moment, watching his back. No sign of movement. Good—he did hear her.

She steps backward over the rock that nearly tripped her and crouches down. The creature twists its upper body, placing its face mere inches from hers. A foul stench pours from its slimy maw, forcing her to hold her breath. It smells like the clams she and Emma used to find on the beach as kids—the ones with bits of decaying flesh still clinging inside.

Relax, she tells herself. *No sudden moves. Nice and easy.*

She reaches for the rock. It's half-buried in the gravel, and sharp pebbles wedge under her nails as she starts digging, making her fingers ache badly. She keeps going, though, and soon, the rock starts to loosen. Once it's free, she gathers the last of her strength and uses it to lift the rock above her head.

A crunching sound erupts as Lisa brings the rock crashing down on the creature's back. It thrashes wildly beneath the stone, its rear lifting off the ground before slamming back down over and over. It tries to dig itself free but fails—its frantic clawing only shoveling sand and pebbles into its sticky, pink mouth.

"WHAT'S HAPPENING?"

Michael's roar causes the others to jump up, and within seconds, everyone except Elias is on their feet. As always, Starck is lightning-fast, and before the others can even take in the situation, he has got his finger on the trigger, the barrel of his rifle aimed straight at the creature.

"Lisa!" he barks. "Step back! Step back so I can get a clear shot!"

His voice is deep and commanding, but Lisa ignores him. Her focus is on the beast's right shoulder blade as she stomps down and makes it crunch with the sound of dry twigs snapping. She stomps again, and a thick, black liquid spurts out beneath the sole of her sneaker. The creature curls up, writhing in agony. Lisa steps down harder, lifts her foot, and slams it down again . . . and again.

The animal lets out a final, drunken sigh and lifts its claws slightly. They linger a few inches above the ground for a moment, trembling, before finally falling down.

"It's over," Starck says quietly. "You can stop now, Lisa. It's over."

Sobbing and grunting from the effort, Lisa slowly lifts her foot. Beneath the sole of her sneaker, black, glistening strands stretch before snapping and gathering into thick droplets as she pulls her foot away.

"What . . . is . . . that?" she moans.

"A maulwert," Starck replies. "They're . . ."

He says something else, but Lisa has stopped listening. She has already turned away, making her way toward the rock wall.

Once there, she sits down, lights a cigarette, and takes a single drag—after which she turns her head to the side and vomits.

By the time dawn breaks and the sun's first rays paint the sky pink behind the mountain peaks, Lisa is feeling much better. A big reason for that is Michael and Starck's decision, about an hour and a half ago, to get rid of the maulwert's remains. They dragged the carcass behind a large boulder farther down the ravine, leaving behind only a trail in the sand as evidence of the night's struggle. Well, that and the black streaks on the leather of Lisa's right sneaker. But she can live with those—as long as she doesn't have to look at that monster anymore.

"How are you holding up?"

It's Elias. He's sitting by the ashes of last night's fire, a blanket wrapped around him like a shawl.

"Okay," Lisa answers, moving to sit beside him. "What about you?"

"Fantastic."

"You don't look fantastic."

"Gee, thanks."

"Are you still warm?" she asks, placing a hand on his forehead, even though it's obvious that the fever has only gotten worse overnight, transforming Elias' face into a glistening death mask.

"I think it's getting a little better," he lies.

"We're heading out soon to the town Starck mentioned. Maybe we can find something there to bring the fever down."

"Maybe. Who's going?"

"Me and Michael. Starck and Sunni are gonna stay here with you."

"Just you and Michael?" Elias raises one eyebrow. "I'm guessing that was Erik's idea?"

Lisa shrugs her shoulders and nods. That's the closest any of them come to saying outright that a different distribution could entail that Elias would end up leaving the world without the possibility of holding the hand of a loved one.

"Before you leave, there's something I need to talk to you and Sunni about," Elias says. "Something important. Can you get him for me?"

Lisa nods and starts to get up, but immediately, Elias grabs her wrist.

"There's one more thing," he says. "When Sunni comes over here, I want to ask you not to make it harder for him than it needs to be."

Lisa looks at the watchmaker, then down at his hand. It looks the same, but there's no strength left in it. If she wanted to, she could pull free without the slightest effort. And part of her wants to—because even though she has no idea what Elias means, she can hear the weight in his voice, and it scares her.

"I promise," she says.

When Lisa brings Sunni back to the firepit, the first thing the boy does is pick up the water bottle and lift it to his granddad's lips, gently supporting his neck with his other hand. The next thing he does is scold Elias for not drinking enough.

"You're right, Sunni," Elias replies, wiping his mouth. "Thank you very much."

Sunni starts to sit down but then stops halfway through the motion.

"I'll get you something to eat as well."

"No, Sunni," Elias says. "Stay. There is something we need to talk about. Something about you and Lisa."

For a moment, Sunni stays frozen in the same position, half-standing, half-sitting. His eyes are uncertain—like an animal's eyes in that split second before choosing between fight or flight. Then he exhales softly and lowers himself to the ground.

"It's because of my paintings, isn't it? Because the things I paint are . . . Lisa's stuff."

Elias nods, and Lisa feels her stomach tighten as she suddenly starts to realize where the conversation is headed.

"Sunni, how much do you know about what I used to do?"

"I know you were a guide, like Erik." Sunni squints his eyes. "I know that you helped new people who came here, and that you traveled with them to the Mansion of Mirrors, just like Erik is doing now with Michael and Lisa."

"Do you also know how guides find out who they're supposed to help?"

Sunni shakes his head.

"They dream about them," Elias says. "Before Michael got here, Erik had already dreamed that it would happen—before it actually did. He dreamed about Michael . . . but he didn't dream about Lisa."

Beneath the tousled, black bangs, understanding begins to dawn in Sunni's eyes, and he lets out a nervous, half-choked laugh.

"We believe you're meant to lead Lisa to the mansion," Elias continues. "That you've been chosen to be her guide."

Lisa and Sunni stare at each other, the same uneasiness reflected in both their eyes. Then, almost in unison, they let out a deep sigh and look up at the sky, where a bird of prey patrols the air with slow, heavy wingbeats.

A vulture, of course it has to be a vulture. As if they need such a harsh reminder of Elias' condition.

"I've talked to Erik about it," Elias says. "He'll take care of your training, and he'll do everything in his power to make sure you are ready for it."

The voice Elias is using is new to Lisa, but she imagines it must be the one he uses when customers in his watch shop try to haggle a little too hard over the price of a piece of jewelry. A firm, authoritative business voice that makes it clear—none of this is up for debate.

"And when you get to Soto, he'll take you to the council, where you can go through the trial and—"

"I don't want to go without you," Sunni suddenly blurts out. His lips tremble, and he fights to hold back tears. "It's not fair."

"Sunni, listen to me. We've had you since you were two years old. I've raised you as my own, and I've seen the incredible things you're capable of."

"I have too," Lisa interjects, remembering the promise she made to Elias. "And even though this is a lot for me as well, I trust you."

"But I don't want to be a guide," Sunni says, burying his face in his hands. "And I don't want to be trained by Erik. If I have to be trained, I want you to do it."

Elias reaches out and gently runs his hand over the boy's head.

"You remember Beaufort?" he asks.

Sunni says nothing, but he lifts his head and stares at his granddad, as though he's afraid that the fever has finally short-circuited his brain.

"Good gods, that dog could drive me crazy sometimes," Elias says. He smiles again, and for a brief moment, the glossy death mask fades, making him look like his old self. "Do you remember how it used to put on a show when Mary made soup?"

"Yeah, it whined," Sunni says.

"*Whined*, you say?" Elias scoffs. "That wasn't whining. It wailed and squawked like a group of sirens at high tide. And it never let up."

"That's not true. Grandma could get it to settle down when she brought out the green blanket."

"Mmm, that's true," Elias admits. "You ever notice that she still puts that blanket out in the mudroom when she makes soup?"

Sunni nods.

"Do you know why she does that?"

The boy wipes his eyes and nods slowly.

"She says she can still hear it howling the moment the soup starts boiling."

"Do you get what I'm trying to tell you?" Elias asks.

Sunni nods again.

53

Right on the other side of the mountains turns out to be a very generous interpretation. It's a long walk, and by the time they reach the town that Starck spoke of, Michael and Lisa are on the brink of total exhaustion. They didn't get much sleep last night, and the midday sun couldn't care less about their water bottles having been empty for nearly two hours.

To make matters worse, the mountains have marked yet another dramatic shift in Urari's ever-changing landscape. This time, it has reverted to a dry, desolate desert, and what few patches of yellowish vegetation are still in sight appear lifeless, caught between rocks and gravel.

The town—another generous description—turns out to be a small, horseshoe-shaped cluster of no more than thirty buildings. The entire area is enclosed by a metal fence, the kind you'd typically see around an outdoor sports court or a military base.

The first building they pass inside the fence is a stable. Next to it is a house that could very well be the farmer's residence, and just beyond that is a long wooden building with a large porch—a tavern from the looks of it. The tables on the porch are covered with tablecloths that were probably once bright and colorful but have since faded under the relentless sun. Every now and then, the wind grabs them, making them flap against the table legs with the sound of flag ropes snapping in the breeze.

There aren't many people on the street. Two older women stand together a couple of houses to the left of the tavern, chatting as they hang up laundry. A stern-looking elderly man watches Michael and Lisa from the steps of a closed barbershop, and half-hidden in the shadows behind an open gate, a group of young boys sits on the ground, rummaging through an old cardboard box.

In many ways, it feels as if time has stood still in this place. If not for the fence and the flatbed truck propped up on a stack of pallets to the right of the barn, this town could be the perfect backdrop for a classic Western movie. Even the obligatory well in the middle of the town square is there—a charming stone structure, covered by a small roof made of weathered wooden planks.

When Michael and Lisa spot the well, they stop in their tracks and exchange a brief glance, as if to confirm with each other that it's not a mirage. Then, almost without him realizing it, Michael's fingers loosen their grip on the gas can, letting it drop to the ground.

"Do you think it works?" Lisa asks, and before Michael can even start to answer, she takes off in a staggering run.

As she grips the handle of the well's winch and starts to turn it, curiosity stirs among the town's residents. The two women set down their laundry and move over to the picket fence in front of the house. The old man on the stairs adjusts his vest, takes a few steps down, and crosses his arms. In the windows behind the tavern's porch, curtains are drawn aside, and a few pale faces emerge from the darkness—floating like disembodied heads.

Are we offending them? Michael thinks. *Should we have asked for permission first?*

Slowly, he walks over to Lisa, while discreetly studying the faces of the townspeople. He doesn't see anything wrong with taking a bit of water from the well, but who knows what the norms are in a place where people go to the trouble of fencing in a town that's smaller than the average FullCart shopping mall? Besides, the town is located in Urari, where *all* the rules are new to them.

Apparently, Lisa is starting to share his concern. At least, she suddenly looks incredibly self-conscious, standing there with the bucket in her hands and water droplets on her chin.

As Michael reaches her, she hesitantly hands him the bucket, both of them stealing glances at the older gentleman on the barbershop stairs.

Whether it's his crossed arms, the unyielding expression, or something else is hard to say, but something gives Michael the sense that this man is the one who calls the shots around here.

After a few long seconds—where the wind seems to howl the way it always does before a shootout in a Western—the man offers them a brief nod. Then, hooking his thumbs into his belt, he strolls toward them.

"The water is free," he says. "But if you're hoping for a meal, you'll have to pay. It's been a tough year for the crops, and it'll be three weeks before the next shipment comes in from Baixa."

"That's alright," Michael replies. "Right now, we're just grateful for a sip of water. But thanks."

"Sure. If you change your minds, head on over to Dolores' place." He nods toward the tavern. "She doesn't take too well to strangers, but if you pay upfront and mind your manners, she'll do the same."

The man's lips curl into a smile, but the chuckle that escapes his lips sounds forced and ominous. Maybe even threatening.

"Water is just fine," Michael repeats. "I'm Michael, by the way, and this is Lisa."

Lisa smiles and extends her hand, but the man just stares at it blankly until she lets it drop back to her side.

Oh, it's like that? Michael thinks. *Seems the tavern lady isn't the only one who doesn't like strangers.*

"Where are you headed?" the man asks.

"Soto."

"On foot? That's a long way."

"We have a car, but we ran out of gas on the other side of the mountains. We were hoping—"

"Are you gonna cause me trouble?"

The question comes out of nowhere, leaving them both dumbstruck.

"Trouble? No, we—"

"You look like trouble," the old man says, eyeing them up and down.

Michael looks down at himself—and suddenly, the man's reluctance doesn't seem strange at all. There are smudges of soot on his jeans, his forearms are scraped and bruised, and his shirt has a long tear on the left side—from when the giant grabbed him and hurled him through the rows of shelves at the gas station. Lisa doesn't look much better, and he considers whether he would invite strangers into his home if they looked like this.

"It's not our fault!" Lisa sounds like she's on the verge of tears. "Ever since we got here, we've been shot at, attacked by psycho animals, and chased by a bunch of lunatics who either want to kidnap us or kill us!"

Michael nods and adds, "We'd be really grateful if you could help us get some fuel—and maybe even some painkillers for our friend, who's badly injured. That's all. No trouble."

"And you're not hiding any mirrors in that thing, are you?" the man asks, his tone so serious you'd think he was accusing them of smuggling weapons.

Except that mirrors are worse than guns, Michael thinks. *In this world, they're far worse.*

"Because if you are—"

"No mirrors."

"Good. The Devil's Glass was banned in Pai two years ago when the war started, and we wanna make sure it stays that way. Especially with the stories going around these days."

"Noted," Michael says, while his mind lingers on the man's choice of words—not *the Devil's Glass*, that part is pretty self-explanatory, but *the war*? Starck described it as a political conflict. Is it actually an all-out war?

Starck is just using you for his own agenda, Crane's voice whispers like a distant echo in the dry desert wind.

"Fuel, you say?" The old man rubs the back of his neck and coughs before gesturing toward the ground, where a wide trail of hoofprints forms a circle around the well. "As you can see, we're more of a four-legged transportation people. Although if you're lucky, there might be some left in the tank of the truck."

He turns around and strolls casually toward the jacked-up flatbed truck they spotted when they entered the town.

"It belonged to an outsider who got stranded out here about six months ago. He said he'd send someone to pick it up, but we haven't seen anyone yet."

They *were* lucky. Not only did the abandoned truck still have fuel in its tank. The old man also found a rubber hose inside the barn that they could use to siphon it into their can.

As for medicine, the goddess of fortune wasn't as generous. The closest they got to a painkiller for Elias is a grainy salve that one of the laundry-hanging women makes herself. That, and a small bottle of liquor.

These items now sit at the bottom of Lisa's bag, along with two full water bottles.

"Looks like we're just about ready," Michael says, nodding toward the full gas can in his hand. "We really appreciate this."

The elderly gentleman stares at them silently for a while, holding the same posture as when they arrived in town—thumbs hooked into his belt, eyes sharp and watchful. Then, for the first time, his lips curl into a genuine smile.

"That should be enough to get you to Soto," he says. "Now you'd best get moving before Dolores catches wind that there are outsiders in town."

Michael smiles and nods after which he and Lisa start walking back the way they came. However, they don't get far before he stops again and turns around.

"One more thing," he says. "The war you mentioned. You said you hear stories?"

"Probably just rumors," the man says. "Often is out here. But word has it that Crane has found himself some empaths he intends to court."

"Empaths?"

"People who carry the Devil's Glass in their eyes. The ones who don't need the mirrors."

Lisa and Michael exchange a nervous glance.

"What does he need them for?"

"I don't know . . . but surely nothing good. It goes without saying that it would be bad for all of us if someone carrying the mirrors' abilities were to join Crane."

"But there's no reason to think that, is there? That the empaths would want to join him, I mean."

"A noble thought," the old man says, offering them a cryptic smile. "Also, a bit naive. Crane chooses his followers, not the other way around—and he can be very persuasive."

He lowers his gaze, pausing in thought. When he looks up again, his eyes are narrowed.

"How are you sleeping at night these days?" he asks.

"What do you mean?"

"You're the ones he's after, aren't you?"

"We really don't know what you—" Lisa starts, but Michael raises his hand, stopping her.

"I should have known," the man mutters, biting his lower lip. "You're headed for the mansion, I reckon."

Michael nods.

"You got help?"

"We have a guide with us."

"Good. That's good."

"We really need to get moving," Lisa says. She clearly doesn't like Michael openly laying their cards on the table like this. But she'll just have to deal with it—because this old man holds knowledge that Michael wants. And unlike Starck, he's willing to share it without withholding details.

"There's one thing I can't make sense of," Michael says. "Not long ago, we were attacked by a group of Crane's men, but it seemed like they were only interested in me. If we're both empaths, wouldn't Lisa be just as important?"

"Divide and conquer," the man says coldly. "That's my guess. Empaths always come in pairs, and they're strongest together. So, I'd wager he's trying to separate you to make things easier for himself. He is known to be a manipulative bastard who stops at nothing to get what he wants."

Michael hears the words and nods, but at the same time, he's surprised to realize that he isn't as outraged by Crane's actions as he probably should be. Because no matter how he looks at it, he shares something with Crane. Both of them have felt the searing pain of losing a child. And though Michael isn't proud of it, he carries some of the same anger. The one that drove Crane to set the world on fire. It's always there, a flickering spark just beneath the surface. He can only pray it'll never get enough air to ignite.

"He, um . . . he claims that my son is trapped in the mansion. My son, who . . . who I thought I lost in a car accident. Crane says he's trapped in the Mansion of Mirrors."

"Your son?" The old man whistles softly, staring at Michael for a long, timeless moment. "And what does your guide say?"

"That the chances are very slim . . . and that I should prepare for the worst."

"I see," the man says, nodding. "But when it comes down to it, that question isn't meant for me or him."

"It's the mirror," Michael sighs. "There's a mirror waiting for me in there . . . a mirror with my son's name on it, isn't there?"

"We've all got one in there. Whether we like it or not."

He makes a gesture in front of his chest, tracing what looks like an invisible circle with a vertical line running through it. What the divided circle is supposed to symbolize, Michael doesn't know, but he guesses it's the equivalent of Christians making the sign of the cross. However, this ritual ends quite differently. Instead of an *amen*, the man closes his eyes and murmurs:

"Fucking Devil's Glass."

"We couldn't agree more," Lisa says, shooting an impatient look at Michael, who answers with a nod.

"Yeah, we better get going. Thanks again for your help."

The old man doesn't reply—he just gives a courteous nod before strolling back toward the stairs where he was standing when they came into town.

Michael has a strong feeling that's where he spends most of his time.

54

Tom is on the verge of exploding with anger. Not only did Crane force them to wait until the next morning to go after the crybaby's crew; Tom also has to put up with sharing the back seat with Jack.

Ever since Petturi kicked the bucket, that snot-nosed brat has been parading around like a self-appointed king just waiting for his coronation. And now, the asshole has outdone himself—spending the last half hour with his upper body poking out of the car's sunroof while he alternates between howling like a wolf and belting out songs to which he doesn't even know the goddamn lyrics.

But that's not even what pisses Tom off the most. What really sends him into a blind rage is the fly. The fly in Jack's pants that he keeps rubbing against Tom's shoulder—while that ridiculous smiley face on his T-shirt laughs at him.

I could take the glass shard out of my pocket, Tom thinks. *I could pull it out right now and cut off his fucking ball sack.*

He stares at the tiny black eyes on Mr. Smiley's yellow face. They're jumping and dancing in random patterns every time

Jack moves.

What do you say? he asks the ever-grinning face in his mind. *You think he'd do better as a castrato singer?*

Now Jack spins around up there, bumping into Tom's shoulder once again—this time with his hip.

Tom's fingers find the glass shard in his pocket, caresses its edges.

One more time, he thinks. *Do it one more fucking time.*

Jack doesn't. He does something much worse. He pulls his head down through the sunroof, glares at Tom, and says:

"Really, man? Give me some space here, alright? I'm flattered and all, but poop pushing isn't really my thing. I'm more into chicks."

And then he pouts his lips, making a duck face.

A fucking duck face.

Tom's fingers grow warm and wet inside his pocket, and his vision is filled with tiny sparks as if someone had lit sparklers at his temples.

Without the slightest thought about the consequences of his actions, he pulls the glass shard from his pocket. He's just about to stab when Hain unexpectedly slams on the brakes, bringing the car to such an abrupt stop that Tom's head smacks into the seat in front of him.

"Jeez!" Tom roars. "What the hell are you doing?"

"Look there!" Hain says, pointing out the windshield. "I think we found them."

"Seriously?" Jack sticks his head back up through the sunroof. "Damn, you're right. It's them!"

Tom leans in between the front seats. This time, he pays no attention to Jack's crotch pressing against his ear.

He narrows his eyes. Yup, no doubt about it. That's Starck's blue station wagon parked up ahead where the road narrows before a mountain pass. And the slim figure standing beside it—definitely the girl. A little farther to the right, the others are making their way toward the vehicle. The little rice muncher is in the lead, followed by the crybaby, and closing the procession are Starck and the watchmaker that Tom shot in the back.

Amazingly, he's still alive, though he doesn't look too well. He's hunched over, a blanket draped over his shoulders, and Starck is holding one of his arms. With his free hand, the watchmaker is leaning on some sort of cane.

"I don't know about you guys," Jack yells from the sunroof, "but I'm gonna enjoy every second of this. There'll be no easy outs for them on my watch."

He underlines his words by smacking his hand against the car's roof and letting out another wolf howl.

Tom smiles. For once, something sensible came out of Jack's mouth . . . and Tom couldn't agree more. No easy outs. He plans to take his sweet time. Especially with the girl. He'll save her for last. Maybe he'll even tie her up, just like they did to him in the theater, and leave her stranded out here in the middle of nowhere. Alone, with nothing to look at but the rotting corpses of her friends.

55

On this hot afternoon in Urari, the wind comes from the south, and when it does that, the many ravines and hollows in the narrow mountain pass make it wail fiercely. Therefore, none of the members of Starck's traveling party hear Jack howling at the sky from the roof of the black car that's speeding toward them while they're busy packing the last of their stuff.

It's been fifteen minutes since Michael and Lisa returned from the strange, timeless western town, and the group has spent that time preparing for the next part of their journey. With Sunni's help, Michael has been carrying their gear from the campsite back to the car, where Lisa carefully packs everything into place in the trunk.

Sunni is a good, but also very quiet, helper. At least, he has been quiet up until now when he suddenly stops midway between the camp and the car and looks up at Michael.

"Grandpa won't make it to Soto," he mumbles, and as soon as the words leave his mouth, his gaze drops to the ground. "He knows it too. He said goodbye to me yesterday. Not directly, but it was a goodbye."

"Sunni, I . . ."

"He also says that I've been chosen to be Lisa's guide."

"Yeah, Lisa told me."

"I don't think I can do that. What if I mess up and I . . . you know, break her?"

Michael glances at Lisa, who is struggling to pack a particularly stubborn bag into the car's trunk. She is moving with quick, methodical motions, and once again, it strikes him just how different the girl he is looking at now is from the fragile soul he met at the library. They're—quite literally—worlds apart.

"I don't think you need to worry," he says. "She's pretty tough."

Almost as if she can hear them talking about her, Lisa waves at them.

"I'm just about done, so you guys might want to hurry up," she yells. "Do you want the blanket in the trunk, Elias?"

"Nah, I think I'll keep it on." Elias glances down at the rifle, which is currently serving as a makeshift cane. "But if there's room for this . . . ?"

"Oh crap, I forgot about that," Lisa says, scratching the back of her neck as she peers into the trunk. Then she leans forward and pulls out one of the bags—but just as she's about to set it down on the ground, she freezes. "We've got company."

At first, Michael doesn't understand what she means. Then he follows her gaze down the road, where a black car comes speeding over the asphalt, dragging a trail of sand behind it.

Over the car's roof, the upper body of the crazed clerk comes into view. His arms are stretched forward, making it almost look like he's steering the vehicle with reins. Except, of course, that this scrawny, T-shirt-wearing version of Ben-Hur hasn't got reins in his hands. He's got guns.

"IT'S THE GUYS FROM THE GAS STATION!" Michael roars, yanking Sunni with him. "WE NEED TO GET OUT OF HERE!"

As they run, he glances back—and realizes that Starck and Elias aren't moving. Elias has placed his hands on Starck's shoulders. They're discussing something.

Michael isn't able to catch the words, but when Starck nods and then heads toward the car without Elias, the pieces fall into place. The watchmaker intends to stay behind to buy them time.

Just as this thought passes through Michael's mind, Elias looks up and meets his gaze. The expression on his fever-flushed face is peculiar, somehow commanding and pleading at the same time—but when he subsequently tilts his head toward Sunni, Michael suddenly understands what those gray eyes are asking of him, and he responds with a solemn nod.

Elias smiles briefly, and then his expression changes. It becomes focused and cold—the way Michael imagines the watchmaker must have looked back when he was still active as a guide.

With his gaze locked on the black car, Elias lets the blanket slip from his shoulders and starts limping across the rocky ground.

When Sunni, running ahead of Michael, hears the sound of Elias disengaging the rifle's safety, he stops dead in his tracks and spins around.

For a moment, he just stands there, eyes wide, staring blankly into space as though his brain has temporarily malfunctioned. Then, without warning, he bolts back toward Elias, screaming at the top of his lungs.

In an attempt to fulfill the unspoken promise he made to the watchmaker only a moment ago, Michael reaches for Sunni, but the boy is too quick and slips past him. However, he doesn't get far—only a few yards—before Starck grabs him and holds him steady.

Behind them, somewhere in the narrow passage of the mountain pass, the wind's wailing rises once more, expressing its sympathy for the boy who struggles fiercely, while he alternates between screaming at Starck to let go and begging Elias to turn around.

But the librarian doesn't let go, and the watchmaker doesn't turn around.

56

"Damn, he's cold!" Jack shouts from the roof. "Look at him! Total badass cowboy!"

Tom leans forward between the seats to get a better look through the windshield and realizes that, for the second time this sunny morning, he agrees with the Smiley kid.

The *badass cowboy* is the watchmaker, who, instead of getting into the car with the others, has taken a stance in the middle of the road. He stands there, legs slightly apart, watching the vehicle hurtling toward him at a solid eighty miles per hour—and he's not budging an inch.

"Take him out!" Tom bellows. "Shoot that motherfucker!"

"Sorry, cowboy," Jack mutters, adjusting his aim toward Elias.

He fires two shots, kicking up a cloud of sand a few yards to the right of the watchmaker—but even that doesn't make him flinch. It's almost like he thinks there's an invisible shield between them and him.

Might as well be, Tom thinks. *With the way that useless punk aims. Jeez!*

Jack fires another shot, and when it's another miss, he glares down at the guns in his hands.

"I swear, there's something wrong with these—" he starts, but before he can finish the sentence, a blast erupts from beneath the car, followed by a loud, metallic screech—and then the entire world flips upside down.

The seconds that follow after the watchmaker retaliates by sending a bullet straight through the left front tire unfold in slow motion for Tom. He watches as the shard of glass falls—*upward?*—from his hand, to then float weightlessly in the air while the vehicle tilts onto its side. Out of the corner of his eye, he sees Jack, still halfway out of the sunroof, reaching desperately for nothing, while the view behind him changes from the clear blue sky to the road's gray asphalt.

The Smiley kid lets out a scream of agony as the car's weight comes down on him the first time, snapping every rib on the right side of his chest.

The vehicle keeps rolling, dragging the still-screaming Jack with it like a limp rag doll. When the right side slams into the road, his screaming stops at once, and he's thrown forward with more force than his spine can handle. There's an appalling *rriitsch*—like the sound of a cardboard box being torn open—and then the lower part of his spine breaks through the skin just above his hip.

Tom watches his own hands as they reach out, grasping for the driver's headrest. To his astonishment, he doesn't feel it when his fingers wrap around the gray fabric. The adrenaline surging through his body has deadened his nerves, leaving his hands completely numb.

The moment the car's roof hits the asphalt for the second time, he squeezes his eyes shut. As a result, he doesn't see the rear window shatter into a shower of tiny glass shards. He can, however, feel them as they crawl from the waistband of his pants down his back, stinging and biting like a swarm of angry insects.

He presses his forehead against the headrest, bracing himself for another spin. But this time, the car doesn't make it past its center of gravity. It rocks from side to side—first in long, heavy swings, then in short, jerky jolts—until it finally comes to a complete stop.

Slowly, the sound of creaking metal fades away, and Tom opens his eyes. The first thing he sees is the Smiley punk's distorted face, staring at him with wide, vacant fish-like eyes. His head is tilted to the side, mouth half-open against the soles of a pair of brown military boots.

When it dawns on Tom that it's Jack's own boots, his arms involuntarily let go of the headrest, and he falls down. He lands on his back, triggering another wave of stinging bites from the tiny glass insects.

"Hain," he groans as he struggles to turn himself around. There isn't a lot of room—given that the roof has been bent so badly that it's touching the headrests. "Hain, are you there?"

No answer—only the faint, creaking sound of glass succeeding Tom's every movement.

"Hain, are you—" he starts, but by now, he has turned enough for the question to answer itself.

Hain *isn't* alive. If he were, it would be nothing short of a miracle, considering the unnatural angle at which his head is twisted.

Tom realizes he can't stay here. He has no idea how much time has passed, and for all he knows, the watchmaker could be on his way to finish what he started.

Tom looks around, trying to decide which way to go. There is really only one option if he wants to avoid crawling across Jack's contorted body—the window on his left. Luckily, that side doesn't seem to be visible from the road.

He starts pushing himself backward through the window, grunting in frustration as his shirt tightens and presses glass shards into the skin on his back.

Now he spots something that makes him forget the pain and move faster. Not far away—thirty feet or so—the watchmaker comes staggering along the side of the road. He looks worn out, like a man ready to lie down and die.

Alas, the rifle he's leaning on looks to be in excellent shape.

Cautiously, making as little noise as possible, Tom struggles on until he's free of the window and can take cover behind the rear of the car. There, he stays put—sore and out of breath—while he listens to the sound of the watchmaker inspecting the wreck. Or rather, he *tries* to listen, but it's gone silent back there.

Tom doesn't like that one bit. So, against his better judgment, he crawls to the corner to take a peek.

And then, just as he's about to poke his head out, a deep sigh breaks the silence. It's followed by a brief sliding noise. Like the sound of a squeegee on bathroom tiles.

Did he just sit down? Christ, I think he did.

Tom narrows his eyes and focuses on listening.

Nothing. Maybe a faint breath.

He hesitates, then leans forward. Sure enough, the watchmaker is sitting on the ground in a half-hearted lotus position, his back resting against the car. His head is tilted, eyes closed, hands resting flat on his thighs. The rifle lies on the ground beside him. On Tom's side, that is.

What a gift, Tom thinks, not stopping to consider how badly things went the last time that exact thought crossed his mind. *Jeez, what a gift!*

He chooses a suitable shard of glass from the shattered side window, pries it free from the rubber frame, and crawls around the corner. He is doing well at first—not making any noise—but then something cracks beneath his foot, and the watchmaker's fever-bright eyes snap open.

For a few seconds, the two men just stare at each other, frozen in place. Then, suddenly, the watchmaker reaches for the rifle. However, before his fingers are fully closed around the stock, Tom has driven the glass shard deep into his wrist.

The watchmaker screams in pain . . . but that doesn't stop the fucker from making another attempt at grabbing the rifle.

Fortunately, Tom is once again faster. Snarling like a wild animal, he lunges forward and hammers his elbow into the old man's neck. Next he plants his knee on the watchmaker's upper arm, pressing down hard, while his hand yanks the glass shard from his wrist.

"Not much of a badass cowboy now, huh?" he snarls, raising his glass knife to the sky like a macabre trophy. The sun's rays shine through the blood-smeared glass, making it sparkle like a ruby in his hands. It's beautiful.

He smiles and brings it down.

PART EIGHT
SOTO

57

The next few days of the group's journey follow a monotonous, uneventful pattern. They spend nearly all their time in the car, only stepping out to eat, sleep, or refuel in the small towns they pass through. It's as if the awareness of Elias' death has cast a shadow over everything they do. They're exhausted, and they're disheartened.

As the hand on Michael's wristwatch ticks over to 8:30 on the morning of the third day after the events at the mountain pass, that very same feeling permeates his body.

He is sitting on a wobbly bench at one end of the clearing that served as their campsite for the night, telling himself that if he weren't so damn tired, he'd clench his sleep-numbed butt cheeks and whip up some breakfast for the others. The problem is, he's not even sure he can muster the energy to walk over to the car and grab the food, let alone cook it.

It has been a *long* shift—longer than usual—because he couldn't bring himself to wake Sunni and Lisa, even though he should have switched with them an hour and a half ago.

God knows they deserve a good night's sleep, he thinks, looking down at the two young people sleeping on the ground beside Starck. *After all the crap they've been through.*

Right now, the fog is still thick, but the morning sun shines brightly through it, painting the tiny world he's in a blinding white. Soon, it'll take proper hold, the temperature will rise, and it will turn into one of those days that, in his old life, was perfect for playing ball in the park, setting up the kiddie pool in the backyard, or going on expeditions to the local creek, hoping to find the undiscovered species that would secure fame for him and Benjamin.

Wonder what the little blond animal lover would have said to all of this. Some of it, he would, of course, have loved—like the seraph, for example. But what about the other creatures? Would they have frightened Benjamin the way they frightened his father? Would he have run off at the sight of the giant spider in the community house and the maulwert—or would he have paused to stare at them in fascination, the way he did when he found a snake in the yard at the vacation home? Yeah, he probably would have done just that.

This thought sends a cold tear sliding down Michael's cheek, and with it comes a new question that makes his stomach tighten. Because it's one thing to wonder what Benjamin would have said to Urari. It's something else entirely to think about what he would have said if he had seen what this place has done to his dad. If he had seen his dad—justified or not—put a bullet in the gut of the giant back at the gas station.

Maybe you'll get the chance to ask him, Crane's voice taunts from the depths of his subconscious. *You might even get the chance to show him that you're no better than me.*

As this thought slowly fades away, something emerges from the white veil of the fog, taking the shape of a plaid shirt. For a moment it seems to float on its own, suspended in the mist, but then, as it moves closer, the face and hands of its owner—a short, chubby man—materialize above and below it.

Starck said we're two hours from the nearest town. Who the hell takes a morning walk this far out in the middle of nowhere?

As the fog's ghostly fingers release their grip and retreat behind the stranger, Michael considers whether he should wake the librarian, just to be on the safe side. He decides against it, moving slightly to the side instead, so he is able to reach the large branch leaning against the end of the bench, should the need arise.

"A bit early for a morning walk," he says, still wondering where in the world this man could have come from.

There's something strikingly off about the man's attire in these surroundings. His gray pants and plaid shirt look like something you'd expect to see on a man sitting behind a desk at an accounting firm or a bank—not on someone standing at a godforsaken rest stop along Urari's main road at the ass crack of dawn.

The man doesn't answer right away. He lifts a hand in a *give me just a second* gesture, then leans forward, pressing both hands against his knees and letting out a loud groan.

Michael scoots to the edge of the bench, partly to be able to defend himself if this turns out to be some kind of trick, and partly to be able to jump in and help if the stocky man keels over. Luckily, that doesn't happen—and when the man straightens up again, he looks a bit better.

"Sorry about that," he stammers, adjusting his glasses and afterward smoothing down the thinning side part that lies flat against his sweaty scalp. "I . . . oh, whew . . . I've been walking pretty far. You wouldn't happen to have any water, would you?"

Michael stares at the man without saying anything, trying to judge whether it would be risky to turn his back on him.

Concluding it won't, he gets up and walks over to the remnants of last night's fire, where Starck's bag lies.

When he comes back, he tosses a half-full plastic bottle to the man, who catches it with his left hand and extends the other toward Michael.

"Thanks. I, um . . . I'm Anton."

"Michael," Michael replies, but he doesn't take the man's hand or return his smile. He's not ready for that yet. "What are you doing all the way out here, Anton?"

"Well, first and foremost, I guess I'm lost," Anton sighs. "And I'm also on the run."

"Oh?"

Anton nods bitterly.

"I'm from Attica. When they attacked us, some people managed to get out in time . . . but my family wasn't so lucky. My wife and daughter, they, um . . . we got separated, and I don't know where they are. Or if they're even alive."

"I'm sorry," Michael says, casting another glance toward Sunni and Lisa. "We've lost people too."

"Because of Crane?" Anton asks, and when Michael nods, he mimics a chokehold by twisting his fists together. "I wish someone would take that bastard out once and for all."

"Couldn't agree more," Michael says with a nod. "Where are you headed, Anton?"

"Soto. I'm . . . or, well, I *was* heading to Soto. My wife and I agreed to meet there if we got separated. But the group I was traveling with got ambushed a few days ago, so now I'm trying to make it there on my own . . . and I could be doing better, I'll admit. What about you guys? Where are you going?"

Seeing Michael hesitate to answer, Anton shakes his head and raises his hands.

"None of my business, of course. Sometimes I'm too curious for my own good."

"It's okay," Michael says. "Actually, we're heading to Soto too."

"What are you going there for?" Anton asks, but he barely finishes the sentence before rubbing his forehead awkwardly. "And there I go snooping again. Real nice."

"No harm done," Michael says, and this time he can't hold back a smile. Whether it's the man's awkward manner, the sad story that mirrors his own, or a bit of both, he isn't sure—but he is warming up to this pudgy wanderer who appeared out of nowhere. "I can always reserve my right not to answer, right?"

"If you're also going to Soto," Anton begins, but then he sighs and looks to the ground. "Nah, that's not . . . forget it."

"You were going to ask if we'd give you a ride?"

Anton shrugs slightly and nods.

"I can't promise anything," Michael says. He tries to sound firm and feels that he more or less pulls it off. "I'll ask the others, but the final say isn't mine."

"Of course," Anton stammers, once again dropping his gaze to the ground. A gaze so submissive and unsure that Michael can't help but feel sorry for the man.

58

If Anton were to evaluate his own performance, he'd say it was well above average. He's pretty sure the story about fleeing from Attica earned him some sympathy from Michael. And from where he's standing now, awaiting the verdict, it looks like it's going to pay off. He can't hear what they're saying, but he can see the others nodding and glancing his way while Michael speaks.

Come on, he thinks. *Get up. Come over here and tell me that they'll let me tag along.*

Until now, Anton hasn't really considered what will happen if they say no. Now, however, it hits him what a negative outcome could mean. He only barely made it all the way out here—and it's not very likely he has the strength to walk the whole way back.

Almost without him realizing it, his fingers find their way to his pants pocket, brushing against the mirror Crane gave him, and he tells himself that Crane would come for him if they were to say no. That's why he gave him the mirror in the first place, right?

It sounds right, but it feels wrong. Because if they say no, he'll have failed his mission—and Crane isn't exactly known for his merciful nature. Besides, Anton is just one of many followers.

Exactly how many supporters Crane has by now, Anton doesn't know—but he has seen them gathered in the square in front of the abandoned train station in Tagoanan when Crane gives his fiery speeches, and there are easily more than 300 people. So Anton could be replaced without a second thought.

Suddenly, panic grips him, and all the positive things he read on their lips moments ago now seems like indisputable evidence that Michael's group is about to flat-out reject him.

That fat fuck? their lips seem to say. *You wanna bring him? You've got to be kidding! He's so fat even his clothes have stretch marks. He'll stink up the fucking car!*

Now they're getting up, and Anton holds his breath in anticipation as Michael starts walking toward him.

"I talked it over with the others. We've decided you can come with us to Soto. There's room for one more in the car, and honestly, we're . . ."

Michael keeps talking, but his words are drowned out by the wave of relief surging through Anton's body.

"Thank you," he says, clasping his hands like in prayer. "I promise I'll keep a low profile and stay out of your business."

"You don't have to promise anything," Michael says. "As long as you're okay with sharing what we've got—and understand that you're on your own once we get to Soto."

"Of course," Anton says with a grateful smile. "You just saved my life."

Actually, he believes that to be true.

Anton takes his promise to keep a low profile quite seriously, and as the day progresses, he can sense that the others are starting to trust him more. They still aren't discussing their plans when he is near, but they're getting more careless, and they're bound to slip up sooner or later.

With any luck, that'll be now—when he has snuck after Lisa and Sunni as they headed out to gather wood for tonight's campfire.

From his spot in the shadows, he watches them walk along the banks of the Abhainn River, which begins at a spring near the northern perimeter and gradually widens until it reaches Soto, where it's channeled into the spiderweb-like network of canals the city is known for.

And they must be getting close to Soto. Even though it's hard to judge distances in this twilight, when the moonlight hasn't yet touched the surface of the water, Anton estimates the width from bank to bank to be about fifty yards. That's roughly how wide the river is when it flows under the large bridge in Soto. So, assuming that they'll reach the city's gates around midday tomorrow isn't unreasonable.

"These are way too damp. You finding anything we can actually use, Sunni?"

The sound of Lisa's voice startles Anton and makes him take a step backward, thus planting his heel in a cushion of moss. It collapses with a soft, moaning sound—and a second later, a bird takes off behind him, flying out over the water before vanishing between the pine trees on the far side of the river.

Unsure whether they heard the noise, Anton freezes and listens, tension coiling in him.

"I think we need to look under the trees," he hears the boy say, and only then does he dare to breathe again. "The ground's too wet this close to the water."

"It's pretty dark in there."

The girl sounds nervous—maybe even scared—and for a moment, Anton feels sorry for her. He can't help it, even though he knows it would be stupid to let them get under his skin.

"But it'll be okay," she continues. "I've got you to watch out for me. That's your job now, right?"

Something about that sentence sets off a bell in the back of Anton's mind . . . but why? What does she—

"Not yet. I've gotta pass the trial first, remember?"

All at once, everything snap into place in Anton's mind, and he has to bite his lip to keep the thrill of his discovery from slipping out in a verbal outburst.

Of course. *That's* why they brought the kid along, and *that's* why they kept moving without the watchmaker. The boy has been chosen to be her guide, and once they reach Soto, he's going to go through the trial.

Eager to pass this crucial discovery on to Crane, Anton starts scanning the area for a secluded place he can use.

He spots a rocky outcrop with a small recess at the bottom—just big enough for him to sit undisturbed. The ground around it is covered in pebbles and small twigs, which is perfect. If anyone comes near while he's there, he'll be able to hear their footsteps.

He starts walking, careful with every step, but doesn't get far before he freezes again. This time, it's not because of something he hears. It's because he sees what the boy and the girl are about to do.

He didn't notice it earlier when Sunni suggested that they move in under the trees, but now that they're heading in that direction, he sees it. One of the bushes in there is a falseberry bush—and they're walking straight toward it.

That's their own problem, he tries to tell himself, but before the thought is even fully formed, his mouth betrays him—and the warning slips out.

"Watch out!"

Sunni and Lisa spin around, startled, and stare at him.

"Don't touch that," Anton says, pointing. "The purple bush. It's falseberries. The leaves are very poisonous."

Both pairs of eyes keep staring at him in confusion for a moment, but then Lisa's expression starts to change—in a way Anton doesn't like. She looks suspicious, and suspicion could easily lead to questions. And if she starts pressing him about what he's doing out here and how long he has been listening in on their conversation, he's not sure he can improvise his way out of it.

Luckily, it's the boy who opens his mouth first.

"Grandma told me about falseberries before," he says, his eyes shifting between Anton and Lisa. "She also said they're poisonous."

"Right," Anton quickly adds, still watching the girl's reaction. "You'll get blisters all over if you touch them. Stings like hell."

The suspicion lingers in Lisa's green eyes for a moment, but then it fades, and she grimaces in response to their description of the plant's effects.

"This place is the worst," she groans. "But thanks for the heads-up, Anton."

Her final words come with a smile that looks genuine, and Anton feels a wave of relief—tinged with a hint of guilt—wash over him.

"You're welcome."

As he speaks, he sneaks a glance toward the rocky outcrop where he had planned to report to Crane. It's too risky to go there now, with the two of them out here, aware of him. He'll have to slip down there later.

∽

When the moment feels right, Anton clears his throat and gets up from his spot by the fire, while he delivers the line that's been lingering on the tip of his tongue for the past half hour.

"Well, I'm afraid nature's calling. Thanks for dinner and excellent company."

He really *has* been in excellent company, and that bothers him a little. He has enjoyed himself in a way he's not used to. For one thing, no one has made fun of his weight, the way Jack and Hain always do. Even when he dropped a spoonful of beans on his shirt, no one laughed at him. Instead, Lisa brought him a tissue and offered to wash the stain out by the river in the morning. That would *never* have happened with Jack around. Jack would have kicked off a full stand-up show at Anton's expense, packed with fatty jokes.

"Make sure to watch your step. It's dark in there."

It's Michael. He's sitting on the other side of the fire.

"Will do," Anton replies with a smile, after which he starts walking toward the trees. Yet, he only gets to take a few steps before someone calls out after him again.

"Hang on a sec, Anton!"

The sound of Starck's voice makes Anton flinch, and as he turns around, he's certain the guide has finally seen through him.

"Oh, sorry," Starck says, holding up a flashlight. "Didn't mean to scare you. Just thought you might want to bring this."

Anton exhales in relief and takes the flashlight from him.

A little while later, once he's made it down to the rocky outcrop, he sits down on the ground and pulls out the mirror.

Before flipping open its lid, he sits for a few minutes, staring at the moon's shimmering reflection on the surface of the river. Somewhere deep inside of him, there's a small, independent part that desires to toss the cursed mirror into the river. Hurl it out there and just watch as it's swallowed by the dark water—and afterward he could go back to the others. Tell them everything, and ask for their forgiveness.

He might even get it. That's almost the worst part. If he turned his back on Crane now and came clean to them, they might actually forgive his lies. Maybe, in time, they'd even let him become a *real* part of their group and look out for him the way they look out for each other.

The problem is that it would achieve nothing. Because Anton has a debt to pay. Crane saved him by pulling him into Urari before his trial started. A trial where Anton would almost certainly have been convicted for processing the paperwork and funneling money—which was supposed to go to schools in Morocco—into the pockets of the ringleaders of a fake NGO. And into his own pocket too, mind you.

So, whether he likes it or not, Anton owes Crane—and if the debt isn't paid, the pale man will find a way to collect it. No matter how many new friends Anton makes.

There's a soft click as his thumb pushes the lid open, revealing the mirror's glass.

For a moment, nothing happens. Then the image in the small, round frame begins to shift. It starts as a reflection of the night sky, scattered with stars. However, those stars are slowly drawn inward toward the center of the glass, and it feels as though they're pulling the surrounding sounds with them. As if the hum of mosquitoes and the gentle trickle of the water are, somehow, drawn into the glass as well.

As the stars converge in the center, a flash of white light spreads outward—and when it fades, Anton finds himself standing in a large, dark . . . room?

Not a room. A void. I'm inside the void between the mirrors. This is what it looks like.

Now, Crane emerges from the darkness. He moves with his distinctive, swaying manner toward Anton and stops a few feet away from him. There he stays; military posture, hands clasped behind his back.

"You better have something good for me," he says. His cracked lips are pulled into a smile, but the tone of his voice is more threatening than cheerful. "Tom came crawling back yesterday and told me that the pathetic, half-dead watchmaker was too much for two of my best men."

"H-he's a guide," Anton stammers.

"I *know* Elias was a guide," Crane snaps. "I was working with that self-righteous bastard before you even learned how to spell tax fraud and child labor."

The words are practically spat at him, and Anton instinctively takes a step back. This is *not* how he'd pictured the conversation going. He had been so eager to tell Crane about his discovery—but the verbal assault has knocked the wind out of him, and now he's completely at a loss for words.

"What *I* want to know," Crane continues, "is why my connection to the girl is still so weak, even *after* Tom killed her guide."

"It's the boy."

The words slipped out before Anton could think it through, and now he frantically slaps a hand over his mouth as if that might somehow pull them back in.

As a rule, interrupting Crane is a bad idea. Interrupting him when he's already fuming is downright dangerous.

"What was that?" Crane's pupils dilate, turning his eyes into gleaming black holes in his pale face. "What do you mean, it's *the boy*?"

"He's the girl's guide," Anton mumbles, his eyes darting around, desperate to avoid the pale man's gaze. "He hasn't faced the trial yet, but . . . they believe he's the one who's supposed to take her to the mansion."

"What a load of—" Crane begins, but then he pauses. The black holes in his face narrow into two sharp slits. "Are you telling me that little punk has been chosen?"

Anton nods.

"Just like that?"

Anton nods again.

"Well, isn't that just brilliant!" Crane says, bursting into theatrical laughter that sends a chill down Anton's spine. "The kid is still waiting on his first pubic hair, and instead he gets handed the role of a guide. Isn't the universe just wonderful?"

Unsure whether Crane actually expects an answer to that question, Anton shrugs.

"What does the timetable look like?" Crane asks. "When are you expecting to reach Soto?"

"Sometime after noon tomorrow."

"And they're still not on to you?"

"I don't think so."

"What about that mirror you're lugging around? Starck hasn't sensed anything?"

Anton shakes his head.

"Good. I'd like it to stay that way. I've got big plans for that mirror."

He pauses, perhaps to make sure the words have time to really sink in.

"Have you ever been inside the Guide Council's headquarters?" he then asks.

"No, I've seen it from the square outside, but I've never been past the gates."

"So, you wouldn't know how to get down to the chamber where the guide trial takes place?"

Anton looks down at the ground and shakes his head.

"Alright," Crane says. "Then you better listen closely now."

Anton does.

59

The bridge that will allow them to cross the waters of the river Abhainn and reach the massive wall surrounding Soto is both mesmerizing and intimidating. It looks like a bizarre fusion between a steel bridge in the style of New York's Brooklyn Bridge and a suspension bridge made from rope and wood—the kind you'd expect to see in an *Indiana Jones* movie.

The load-bearing elements are four towers, built from metal beams woven together in the crisscrossing pattern often seen in radio masts. Lisa's never been great at estimating distances or heights, but she estimates those towers to be about a hundred feet tall. At the top of them, guards are standing on platforms, scanning the landscape. They're all dressed in the same red and yellow uniforms, clearly inspired by the coat of arms displayed on the large banners flanking the city gate.

"Can we even *drive* on that thing?" Lisa asks, pointing down at the bridge's crossing path. It's made up of a series of horizontal beams stretched between two railings of braided steel cables.

She glances at Starck and catches the faintest hint of a smile at the corner of his mouth.

"Not a fan of heights, huh?" he says.

"I just don't think it looks very stable, and I'm not exactly eager to end up in the water while sitting in a car."

"Just don't look down," Sunni says from the back seat.

"Thank you so much, oh wise sage, for your brilliant advice," she says. "I'll make sure not to look down when we plunge to our deaths. I feel much better now."

She actually does feel a bit better. This is one of the only times since the mountain pass that Sunni, by his own initiative, has taken part in a conversation, and it gives her hope that he might be starting to feel a bit better.

Through the windshield, she sees two guards approaching the car. Since these two are closer than the ones stationed in the towers, she can make out a lot more details in their uniforms—and doing so stirs a sharp, aching sense of homesickness in her gut. They're impressive and fit the surroundings well—that's not the issue. It's just that they're *so* strange, so extremely different from the world she knows. Back home, outfits like that would belong at a Renaissance fair.

Shoulder plates.

Chainmail armor.

Helmets.

Costumes, she thinks. *The kind Andy wears when he heads into the woods with his role-playing buddies.*

The image of a bunch of nerdy boys running around the woods whacking each other with latex swords stirs a deep, and honestly unexpected, wave of longing. For the first time, she finds herself missing the school and her classmates even though she never really felt like she was part of the group.

And that, she tells herself, is one thing that's going to change when she gets back home. She's gonna be a part—a real part—of the group. Someone who gets secret notes from a friend slipped into her hand during class.

"Greetings!" a deep voice booms through the side window—and without even giving Starck a chance to respond, the guard it belongs to adds, "Errand and reason for entry in Soto?"

"We are here to request an audience with the Council of Guides," Starck replies in a solemn tone that makes Lisa and Michael exchange a surprised glance.

"And the reason?"

"We bring news from Attica, near the northern perimeter."

As he speaks, Starck slips his hand down behind the collar of his shirt. When it reappears, he's holding the pendant of a necklace, which he turns toward the guard.

After studying it for a moment, the guard mutters a word Lisa doesn't understand. To her, it sounds like a magic spell straight out of a nursery rhyme.

"Salamin," Starck confirms.

"Passage granted," the guard says. After that, he takes a few steps back and turns to face the other guards in the towers. Then he raises his arm and gives a wordless signal.

Lisa feels her stomach tighten as she follows his gaze and sees the guards lowering their rifles.

"Oh my," Anton says. "They really stepped up security, huh?"

He sounds nervous, and for a brief moment, it runs through the back of Lisa's mind that maybe he sounds *too* nervous. However, she lets the thought pass, telling herself it's only natural to be a bit on edge after having been at the center of a handful of rifle sights.

60

For obvious reasons, Starck parks the car along the curb on a small side street once they've passed through the city wall. The uneven cobblestone streets aren't suited for motor vehicles, and even if they were, getting around on foot would still be faster, since every street and alley is packed with people.

That Soto is a central trading city would immediately be clear to anyone, and the intricate network of canals that channels the waters of Abhainn through it means that the dominant trade commodity is fish. This fact is underscored by the countless stalls they pass as they make their way through the streets. Nearly every vendor has at least one salt tub filled with various kinds of seafood.

It's also a large city—much larger than it seemed from the other side of the wall. It's made up of clusters of timber-framed houses built closely together on a series of small islands, all separated by the canal network. To move between them, you have to cross one of the many stone bridges that connect the islands, completing the spiderweb-like pattern you'd see if you observed Soto from the mountains to the west.

"They completed the entire foundation first," Starck says, answering the question Michael was about to ask. "Otherwise, it would've been impossible to create such precise symmetry."

"How old is the city?"

"Well, as you know, time is a somewhat relative concept in Urari—you'll understand all of that better when you get back to your own world—but it roughly lines up with the 13th century in your way of measuring things."

"I swear, I'm never going to get used to how different it all is," Lisa says.

"Yeah, about that," Starck says, shaking his head slightly at the fourth fish vendor trying to wave them over. "There are a few things we need to talk about before we talk to the council. As you probably noticed when we crossed the bridge, there's a certain code of conduct you have to follow when dealing with the aristocratic leadership here in Soto. A sort of *etiquette*, you might say."

"Salamin."

Starck raises his eyebrow and stares at Lisa, then gives her an approving nod.

"I'll be the first to admit it feels old-fashioned and awkward. Nonetheless, it is what's expected."

"So, what you're trying to say is that you'd like us to keep a low profile and let you do the talking," Michael finishes for him.

Starck shrugs and runs his gaze across their faces, making sure everyone's on the same page. Once he has gotten a nod from each of them, he turns to Sunni.

"You ready to show them what you got?"

"I think so."

"I believe in you." He places a hand on the boy's shoulder. "And so did Elias."

Those are weighty words, and Michael wouldn't have been

surprised if they had made the boy break down in tears—but Sunni holds it together, answering with a solemn nod.

After letting go of the boy's shoulder, Starck moves over to Anton, who has been walking some distance behind the rest of the group.

"And you're aware that we'll be going our separate ways soon? We can take you to the council's headquarters, where they'll probably house you with the other refugees from Attica. But after that, you're on your own."

"Of course," Anton says, fiddling with a loose button on his shirt. "That was the deal. I almost can't tell you how grateful I am that you chose to bring me along."

"We'll keep our fingers crossed that you'll find your family," Michael says.

"Certainly," Starck agrees. "But who knows—maybe we'll get the chance to meet them. If things go the way I'm hoping and the council is open to my proposal, we'll need help from the refugees. In that case, this might not be the last time we see each other."

61

Stepping into the huge, covered passage that serves as the entrance hall to the Council of Guides' headquarters feels, in many ways, like entering a cathedral. Just moments ago, they were bombarded by the noise of street vendors and had to raise their voices just to be able to talk to each other. Now, as they walk along the wide river of light cast onto the marble floor by the overhead windows, even the sound of their footsteps echoes loudly through the space.

Beyond the sudden shift in acoustics, the Gothic architecture of the passage also calls to mind churches and cathedrals. It's lined with towering arches, ribbed vaults, and columns. Marble and gold.

"We're heading for the second floor," Starck says, pointing toward a wide staircase that leads to a landing before splitting into two separate flights.

"It's, um . . . really fancy in here," Lisa says, glancing toward a fountain on the right side of the passage. Standing beside it are two men, deep in conversation. Both are dressed in formal suits, wearing them with the kind of solemn air that often comes with such attire.

As one of them catches Lisa looking at them, he shoots her a disapproving look that makes her glance down at herself, suddenly feeling very self-aware.

Starck must have picked up on this, because at the same moment he moves to her side, gently grabbing her elbow.

"Don't even for a second think that you don't belong here," he says. "I'd like to see one of those snobs handle even a fraction of what you've been through."

Lisa feels her cheeks flush. Not just because of the words, but because Starck is speaking to her with something that resembles fatherly pride. That's something she hasn't experienced in the past year—and, well, to be honest, not really before that either. Robert Swann was a lumberjack all his adult life, and when it came to expressing emotions, he was about as gifted as the trees he cut down. And on the rare occasions when he did show some warmth, it was always Emma who was on the receiving end. She was the one who got his attention, who went on fishing trips with him. She was his favorite daughter, while Lisa was just . . . there.

There is no jealousy, no bitterness in this thought. Maybe there ought to be, but for Lisa, it's just a fact. Something to observe and acknowledge—nothing more.

"We turn here."

She looks up and is surprised to realize that they've already reached the landing where the staircase splits in two directions. They take the path to the right, which leads up through a narrow corridor with small, open windows overlooking yet another street lined with market stalls.

When they reach the top, they step into a room that, for a

brief moment, takes Lisa back to the foyer of Attica's theater. The floor is covered in the same deep burgundy carpet as the theater, and in front of a reception desk in the center of the room are three metal posts topped with gold knobs. Strung between them is a velvet rope—just like the one they used to tie up Tom.

Behind the desk sits an older gentleman, writing in a small notebook. His writing tool, a fountain pen, dances back and forth across the paper, guided by skilled fingers. Every now and then, a wisp of silver hair slips down in front of his glasses and lingers there until he juts out his lower lip and blows it away.

The man is so deeply focused that he doesn't even notice their presence—at least not until Starck puts his hand on the silver bell sitting on the countertop. The sharp ring jolts the man upright with a start, causing him to drop his fountain pen to the floor.

"Oh, would you look at that," he mutters to himself, starting to bend down to retrieve the pen. However, he freezes halfway through the motion when he realizes who the rebellious bell-ringer is.

"Erik? I thought you'd retired."

"Honestly, I kind of wish I had."

"Yes, things haven't exactly cooled down," the man says, his gaze drifting over Starck's companions. "Something tells me that's not news to you."

"Actually, that's what brings us here." Starck nods toward the large brass door behind the desk. "Is Bernard in?"

The man adjusts his glasses, pulling them down to the tip of his nose as he looks at Starck.

"He just got back from a meeting. But he is not in a good mood."

"What else is new?"

The man pulls his lips into a smile, revealing a crooked set of tobacco-stained teeth.

"Shall I let him know you're requesting a meeting?"

"Actually, I was hoping for a meeting with the full council. The sooner, the better."

"The full council?" the man exclaims, his eyes resting on Starck for a moment before drifting back to Michael and Lisa. "Are they who I think they are?"

Starck nods.

"I'll ask Bernard to assemble the council," the man says, getting up from his chair. "Hopefully, he won't bite my head off. He's rarely very thrilled about short-notice meetings."

"I owe you one," Starck says. "There's one more thing before you go, though."

"I'm listening."

"Can you help our friend here?" Starck asks, gesturing toward Anton. "We picked him up on the way here. He fled Attica when Crane attacked, and he's hoping to request asylum, but he doesn't know where to do it."

"I most certainly can."

The man turns to Anton, his expression shifting into something more formal—and when he speaks, it's clear he's now using his professional tone.

"It's located in a separate building a few streets from here. I can have someone escort you there, if you'd like."

"No, that isn't necessary," Anton replies, shaking his head.

"Are you sure? It really isn't a problem."

"Yeah, if you, um . . . if you just tell me where it is, I'll find it. I've taken up enough of your time already."

"As you wish."

The man bends down and disappears behind his desk for a

moment. When he reemerges, he's holding the fountain pen he dropped when Starck rang the bell.

"Would you at least allow me to sketch out the route for you?"

Anton smiles and gives a small nod.

62

It's almost a shame. The chairman's secretary put real effort into drawing the route on the sheet of paper he tore from his notebook—and the first thing Anton did once the door closed behind him was crumple it up and toss it out the window. Now he is standing in the narrow stairwell, feeling a slight pang of guilt as he watches the paper ball float along the canal that runs parallel to the street outside. It manages to drift about thirty feet before slipping under a stream of water from a drainpipe and sinking to the bottom.

But Anton really has no use for that piece of paper. He knows exactly where he's going—and it certainly isn't the refugee camp for those who fled Attica. Christ, he was partly responsible for sending them running in the first place, so his welcome probably wouldn't be a warm one. Besides, the idea of facing them—and by extension, his own deeds—isn't very appealing. After all, he's not exactly proud of having played for the team that burns cities to the ground and tears families apart.

So no, Anton isn't going to the refugee camp. He's going downstairs. He's going to find the room they use for the Guide Trials, and once he's there, he's going to do the thing that Crane asked him to do.

With that simple agenda in mind, he steps away from the window and heads down to the landing where he can get a better view of the passage that runs between the council's buildings.

Standing there with both hands on the railing and an innocent expression on his face, he squints and scans the area. The light streaming in through the skylights reflects off the marble floor, casting a bronze-gold road down the center of the passage. It's a stunning sight, but it also makes it hard for him to tell the doors on the opposite building apart.

From the corridor behind him, he hears muffled laughter, and it makes beads of sweat break out on his forehead. Starck and the others stayed behind with the secretary after he left, but they could come walking this way at any moment—and if they see Anton standing here, they're bound to start asking questions. Moreover, he has about as much desire to face them right now as he has to join the refugees from Attica.

Anton has barely finished this thought before his eyes finally land on what he's been looking for. A small, gilded door knocker shaped like a lion on the third door from the right. That's the one Crane told him to look for.

He lets go of the railing and starts down the stairs, while, in his head, going through the next steps in the instructions Crane gave him.

In fact, he's so focused on this that he doesn't even notice the guard by the fountain, whose eyes are tracking him with growing curiosity.

The basement beneath the Council of Guides' buildings is, just as Crane had warned him, a maze-like tangle of narrow corridors. The only sources of light are a series of oil lamps mounted on the walls at roughly thirty-foot intervals. From them come a strong smell of kerosene that tightens Anton's throat and intensifies the claustrophobia he's lived with for as long as he can remember. The fact that the hallways seem to grow narrower the closer he gets to his destination doesn't exactly help either.

Almost there, he tells himself. *If you haven't screwed up, the trial room should be at the end of the hallway behind that corner up ahead.*

Somewhere behind him, he hears something that makes him twitch. It's a faint sound, barely audible—but it's enough to tell him he's not alone down here in the gloomy maze.

He glances back over his shoulder. There's no one in sight; but then again, the flickering light from the oil lamps is very weak, so he can't be totally sure. Besides, his imagination insists that the massive shadow-pyramids cast on the walls between the lamps could be hiding all kinds of horrors.

With the hairs on the back of his neck standing on end—and with a very strong urge to run—he rounds the corner and covers the final stretch to the door.

In, do what you gotta do, and get out of this tomb as fast as possible, he thinks, pressing down the handle and pushing the door open. *The sooner the better.*

The room is much smaller than he expected. And worse, there's far less stuff in it than he had imagined. He pictured a chamber filled with mysterious artifacts—scepters, altars, and whatever else might be part of the secret rituals of the guides. However, there's nothing of the sort here. In the center is a round stone table with two matching chairs, and to the right of the door, there is a shelf built into the wall. A narrow, reddish-brown rug stretches across the floor in front of it, running from wall to wall. That's all he has to work with. The shelf is even empty.

Where am I supposed to hide it? he thinks, frustrated, as he pulls the small mirror from his pocket. It feels heavy in his hand —much heavier than it should. *There's nowhere in here they won't find it.*

He steps over to the table and bends down to check if he might hide the mirror underneath, but it's no use. The table has a single cylindrical leg that merges seamlessly with the tabletop —all of it one smooth, unbroken surface with no cracks or crevices to conceal the mirror.

The same goes for the built-in shelf. All three recesses in the wall that make up its shelves are clearly visible, no matter where you stand in the room—and that just won't cut it.

The awareness that he might actually fail his mission sends a wave of cold panic surging through Anton—and with it comes the fear of what Crane will do to punish him for his incompetence. Will he send one of his enforcers after him? Or will he, just this once, get his own hands dirty?

And in that case . . . will his punishment involve a mirror?

In an attempt to stop his panic from turning into a full-blown anxiety attack, Anton stomps his foot on the floor. Halfway through the motion—too late to stop—he realizes that whoever else might be out there in the corridors might hear it.

To his relief, the sound is brief and muffled as his shoe hits the floor, kicking up a small, gray puff of dust from the crumbling filling between the tiles.

He stares down at the tiny specks of dust swirling like snowflakes in the air around his foot, and slowly, an idea starts taking shape in his mind.

If that one is loose . . . he thinks, glancing around the four corners of the room to figure out which one is the darkest.

Twenty minutes later, Anton is wiping sweat from his forehead as he admires the result of his work.

All in all, he's pretty happy with it. Sure, if you know what you're looking for, you can tell that a couple of the corner tiles are uneven, but he doesn't think it'll be an issue. Especially not once the carpet is laid back in place.

Now he can only hope that loosening the surrounding tiles within a three-foot radius around the one hiding the mirror was enough. Crane hasn't said outright what the mirror is for, but Anton assumes it's meant to transport one or more people over here—and there should be room for that now.

With that thought in mind, he drags the carpet back in place and turns away from the corner.

Before leaving the scene of his crime, Anton cracks the door open and peers through the narrow gap. The hallway looks just as dark and unnerving as before, and the tight corridor immediately stirs up his claustrophobia again. Still, he can't find a good reason for not stepping out there. Because there's no one in sight, and no noises suggesting he's not alone in the maze.

You might actually get away with this, he tells himself as he rounds the first corner. With every step, this feeling grows stronger, and by the time he reaches the third corner, it's turned into a conviction.

But then he rounds the next corner . . . and comes face-to-face with the guard.

63

Organizing the meeting takes surprisingly little time. Just forty-five minutes after Starck made his request, Bernard's secretary has already managed to gather all the members of the Guide Council.

Starck has spent the time leading up to the meeting preparing for the questions and counterarguments he might face when he steps into the large conference hall to present his strategy. In many ways, it feels like getting ready for an exam—and his palms are indeed sweaty as he pulls out a chair and takes his seat at the table in the meeting room.

There are nineteen members on the Guide Council, all of whom are watching him with solemn expressions at this moment. On paper, that means there are nineteen people he needs to convince, yet Starck knows perfectly well that isn't the reality.

When it comes down to it, there's one vote that carries far more weight than the rest. Bernard, the current chairman of the Guide Council, is the one who needs convincing. If he agrees with Starck's proposal, the others will fall in line.

Unfortunately, Bernard is as cautious in his politics as he is charismatic in his demeanor.

Just as this thought leaves Starck's head, the chairman in question gets up from his seat on the opposite side of the table and lifts the wine glass that he—as the only one—has in front of him.

To an outsider, it might seem odd that only one seat in such a beautifully decorated room has a glass, but for the council, there is nothing unnatural about it. The wine glass is their version of a moderator's gavel—and when Bernard dips his fingertip into the liquid and runs it along the rim of the glass, everyone understands that the meeting has started.

"Fellow council members," he begins, his lips curled into a smile so forced it makes the hairs on the back of Starck's neck stand up. "You've been called to this emergency meeting because Erik Starck, whom you all know, has requested a hearing. On that note, I do apologize for the lack of a pre-distributed agenda, but there simply wasn't time. Nevertheless, I'm confident Erik will brief us thoroughly, so we have a solid basis to work from. I'm told he intends to present a proposal on how we might deal with the situation concerning Crane . . . and apparently, he has also brought us a couple of empaths."

Although that last bit of information can't possibly come as a surprise to anyone in the room, a unanimous gasp ripples through the assembly, and every face turns toward Starck.

He smiles and nods, though, on the inside, he curses Bernard for bringing up the empaths so soon.

"With the chairman's permission, there's another matter I'd like to present to the council first."

"Certainly," Bernard replies with a faint note of irritation in his voice. "Our time is your time."

Before he starts to speak, Starck casts a glance at the inscription on the chandelier hanging above the table.

SALAMIN NADIA SEA TRUSTEA.

The words are from the old language, which, according to legend, died out as a spoken tongue when the portals between Urari and the five other worlds were opened. No one speaks it anymore; only fragments and phrases have survived, mainly because Soto's aristocratic leadership has preserved them in their rituals. One of these phrases is the inscription on the chandelier —which, as he read it now, rings more true to Starck's ears than ever before.

You would do well to remember that. No one should put their trust in a mirror.

"I know your time is valuable," he says. "So, I won't waste it with banalities. Instead, I'll get straight to the point. I'm requesting the council's approval to have one of my traveling companions undergo the trial to become a guide. The candidate is Sung Jung—"

"And just to be clear," Bernard interrupts. He rises halfway from his seat and places his hands on the edge of the table, glancing around at the council members. "We're talking about the boy here. Elias' grandson. Remind me, Erik, how old is he? Eleven?"

Pointing out the boy's young age like that is an obvious provocation on the chairman's part. Starck doesn't take the bait, though. He simply nods and waits patiently for Bernard to sit back down.

"It's true," he says. "As Bernard points out, Sunni is just a boy. If he passes the trial, he'll be the youngest guide Urari has ever had . . . but I have no doubt he'll also be one of the best. I'm convinced that he's been chosen to lead the young girl we've brought with us to the mansion. The premonitions that brought me here were solely about Michael Bendixen—never about her."

"Yet the girl arrived together with him," Bernard adds, casting a dramatic glance at the other council members. "Without the use of mirrors."

Starck nods and suppresses the urge to roll his eyes as yet another unanimous gasp sweeps through the room. Just the mention of empaths is enough to stir up this crowd.

"That's correct," he says. "At first, I didn't understand why that was, and why I had no visions of her. However, when we reached Baixa and I saw the boy's paintings, everything suddenly made sense. Most of what he has painted are moments from her life."

"Have you been able to determine what brought them to Urari?"

"Michael lost his wife and son in a car accident, and I have no reason to doubt that's why the mansion is calling to him. My main concern regarding him is that Crane may have been pulling his strings from the very beginning. At the very least, he has been paying him visits during the nights, trying to manipulate him into going there before he's ready."

"Can't say I'm surprised," Bernard says. "And the girl?"

"She lost her father and her sister, and I believe her presence in Urari is connected to that. However, it happened over a year ago, and I sense there's something deeper at play than just her grief. She has proven to be very strong, though. In Attica, she was confronted with a mirror and walked away unscathed."

"So, you're theory is that what actually brought her to Urari might still be buried in her subconscious?"

Sure, that's the detail you chose to focus on, Starck thinks, but what he says out loud is, "I'm confident Sunni will be able to uncover it during the trial."

"I see. And you understand the consequences if the boy fails?"

"He won't."

"But if he does . . ." Bernard's hands once again find the edge of the table, and he leans forward. "*If* he fails, we risk sending the girl—a possible empath—into the mansion unprepared. Perhaps an experienced guide would be a better alternative."

"Sunni won't fail," Starck repeats. "Besides, you know perfectly well that it won't help to give her an experienced guide if the boy is the one who has been chosen."

Even a man as silver-tongued as Bernard will have a hard time countering that argument, and—not surprisingly—he decides to change the subject.

"Alright," he says, getting up and once again silencing the assembly with the wine glass. "If there are no objections, I suggest we set the decision about the boy's trial aside for now and move on to the next item."

He glances around the room, and when no one objects, his focus returns to Starck, who nods and clears his throat.

"Well, yes. As Bernard mentioned earlier, I think it's high time that we take action to put an end to Crane's campaign of vengeance. Especially after seeing firsthand how bad things were in Attica, it's become clear to me that we need to act before it's too late. Crane has clearly been busy recruiting new followers, and if he keeps it up at this pace, he'll soon be strong enough to target larger cities. Cities like Baixa . . . or Soto."

"A tad dramatic, perhaps," Bernard says with a shrug. "I don't think we're quite there yet."

"There might be something to what Erik is saying," says Reinar—an old man who's been on the council for as long as Starck can remember, always occupying the same spot during meetings; three seats to the left of the chairman. "Attica isn't that small. And if anyone doubts that, they only need to look at the number of refugees we've received from there over the past week. It's a lot."

"A sad truth," Starck says, nodding. "Although, there might be a silver lining."

"A silver lining?"

"The numbers. If my proposal is approved, we'll need to expand Soto's army. In that case, we'd have to recruit volunteers—and where better to do that than among the refugees who have suffered under Crane's rampage?"

Bernard narrows his eyes.

"And what do you intend to use these *volunteers* for? What's your plan, exactly?"

"My plan is to send them out in groups, along with the army, to as many towns as possible and have them gather all the mirrors together. Once that's done, I'd station guards at the mirrors so Crane can't use them."

"You won't find many with the mental strength necessary to keep him contained. Besides, there are mirrors everywhere in Urari. We'd never be able to find them all."

Starck has met this argument before—and his answer is the same one he gave Elias that night.

"We won't have to," he says. "My plan is to initiate a systematic shutdown of the mirrors in a single, well-coordinated strike."

"A shutdown? You mean you want to destroy them?"

Starck nods.

"Not all of them. Just enough for Crane to feel it and understand the message. Enough for him to realize that using the mirrors is no longer safe. That he risks getting trapped in the void if one of them is shattered while he's passing through. My aim is to take away his strongest weapon and make him realize that there is only one place left that's safe for him to travel to by mirror—if he tries to run when we come for him."

"The dungeons here in Soto," Bernard finishes for him, and though he tries to hide it, Starck can see that the plan has impressed him.

He has barely finished this thought when a hand shoots up on the right side of the table. It belongs to Shane, one of the Guide Council's newly elected members.

"Yes, Shane?"

"How do we know that Crane won't choose to flee to the mansion and hide there? He has been there before."

"A fair point," Starck replies. "And you're right—we can't be sure, even if it's highly unlikely. But even if he should choose to do that—and somehow, against all odds, he managed to get back out—we'd still have taken his most important weapon from him."

"Yeah, I can see that," Shane admits. "But perhaps . . . and I know I'm walking on thin ice here . . . perhaps it's time we stop Crane for real. I mean, most of us would agree that what we're dealing with now is basically a war—and in a war, sometimes you have to eliminate your enemy. Shouldn't we at least consider that option?"

"We can't afford to see it in such black-and-white terms," Starck says. "Yes, Crane broke the law and entered the mansion . . . but we all know the reason for his actions. And how many of us can honestly claim we wouldn't have done the same in his place?"

The words hang in the air for a moment, with no one speaking up to challenge him—and as Starck uses the pause to glance around the room, he's pleased to see fewer defiant faces than when the meeting began. Maybe—just maybe—there's still a chance he'll walk out of here with the council's support.

However, there's something about the way Bernard keeps smiling that Starck doesn't like. The big, bad chairman doesn't look like a man about to back down. In fact, he looks more like a chess player who's just figured out how to corner his opponent's king.

"Your intentions are good, Erik," he says, slowly turning the wine glass in his hands so the reflection from the chandelier's light flickers in it, making it look like a little ball of fire. "There's one detail you've overlooked, though."

"And what would that be?"

"Crane's hideout. Since we don't know where he's hiding his army, we have no real idea what we're up against. We don't know how many followers he's gathered or how large an arsenal of mirrors he has."

Bernard ends his speech with a patronizing shrug that makes Starck's temples throb. The chairman has a knack for making him feel like a little boy. Could be that it's unintentional—but that doesn't make it any easier to put up with.

"As long as we don't have that information, it's simply too much of a risk," Bernard continues, his tone growing more and more triumphant. "If we did have it, I'd support you without hesitation, but as things stand now . . ."

The chairman bites his lower lip and shakes his head slowly from side to side.

Starck has a sarcastic reply on the tip of his tongue but swallows it after a brief internal struggle. As much as he despises Bernard's 'smarter-than-thou' attitude, there's truth in what he's saying.

"Maybe we could get that information," Starck says instead. "Crane's advantage mainly comes from the fact that he doesn't hesitate to use the mirrors within Urari. If we did the same, we might be able to gather the intel we're missing."

The moment the words cross his lips, silence falls around the table, and Starck realizes he has lost. Besides, any doubt would have been erased by the faint trace of a smile tugging at the corners of the chairman's mouth.

"Let's just get this straight . . ." This time around, Bernard doesn't even bother to conceal the triumphant edge in his voice. "You're proposing we jeopardize our own sanity and use the mirrors to track down Crane?"

"And I stand by it," Starck replies, even though his thoughts are already revolving around how he is going to tell the others that his proposal was rejected. And that he might have to tell Sunni that Elias died for nothing.

As if he's read that very thought and wants to say, *should've thought of that a little earlier, buddy*, Bernard smiles and offers Starck another patronizing shrug.

On the right side of the table, the youngest member of the council raises his hand once more—this time slower and more hesitant.

"Yes, Shane?"

"What about the empaths?"

"What about them?"

"Well, um . . ." Shane adjusts his shirt collar and glances awkwardly around the room. "I'm too young to have met any empaths, like some of you have. But I *have* heard stories, and if they're true, then empaths have the ability to travel directly to a place—or a person—just by focusing their mind on it. Could we maybe use that to find out where Crane is hiding?"

Starck glances at Shane, then at Bernard—and can't quite decide which of the two is ticking him off the most at the moment.

"With all due respect," he says, "we're talking about a schoolteacher and a seventeen-year-old girl, both emotionally unstable because they're grieving. Yes, they did cross over via eye contact, but more than anything that was by accident—and they don't have control over their abilities. Besides, neither of them has been to the Mansion of Mirrors yet."

After this monologue, another silence falls over the room, no one saying a word. However, Starck can see from the expressions on the other council members' faces that Shane's suggestion didn't land well with them either.

"I believe it's time to begin the vote," Bernard says as he, for the third time, lifts the wine glass from the table, wets his fingertip, and runs it along the rim.

The tone is jarring to Starck's ears—especially because it feels like the symbolic signal of his defeat.

On the positive side, the sound is short-lived, as Bernard's finger only completes two circles on the glass before he's interrupted by a knock at the door to the meeting hall. A second later, the door creaks open in a slow, hesitant motion, and a lanky man with a hooked nose and hair like artificial cobwebs appears in the doorway.

"I'm sorry to interrupt, but I bring news from the guard station that the chairman needs to hear."

"Can it wait? We're just about done."

"I'm afraid it can't," the messenger says. "We have standing orders to report immediately to the highest authority when something like this happens."

"Something like what?"

"That we've got one of Crane's followers in custody."

The confident smile on Bernard's lips vanishes in an instant. It's as if someone has flipped a switch inside his mind, and for the first time in his entire tenure as chairman, he looks utterly speechless.

"How did, um . . .?" he manages to stammer, though the

words, when they come out, sound more like half-choked dog barks than actual human speech. "How did we manage that?"

"One of our guards arrested him. Caught him sneaking around the lower corridors. He is to be taken to the interrogation room as soon as the chairman gives the order."

"Well, that's, um . . . excellent news," Bernard says, and though he tries to maintain his composure, it's clear he's shaken by this unexpected turn. "Guess there's still hope for your plan after all, Erik."

Starck can't help but smile—partly because there's renewed hope of gaining the council's support, and partly because he takes a quiet satisfaction in the bitter realization flickering in the chairman's eyes.

That's right. There are nineteen people in this room, and every single one of them heard you promise me your full support if we had Crane's hideout. And now, one of his followers is on his way to the interrogation room.

"Considering this new information, I would like to request the chairman's permission to lead the interrogation," he says—fully aware that, at this point, it would be impossible for the chairman to deny the request.

"Permission granted," Bernard says, with more than just a hint of irritation in his voice. "Would you like to adjourn the meeting and go down there right away?"

Starck thinks about it—and decides it's probably wiser to take advantage of the momentum he has right now.

"No," he says. "Not yet. If the council allows it, I would prefer that we reach a decision regarding Sunni's Guide Trial first. The sooner he can get started, the better."

"Very well." Bernard lifts the glass and looks around the assembly. "If there are no objections, I'll begin the vote. You all know the drill: when your name is called, you state your position and place one hand on the table. Right hand for yes, left for no."

He pauses as the council members lower their hands to their laps in a synchronized *da-dum* that sounds like the finishing steps of a military march. After that, he clears his throat and says:

"Voting has started. The question at hand is whether we will allow the boy to take the Guide Trial despite his young age. We begin with you, Nikolas."

Nikolas, seated to the chairman's right, clears his throat and places his left hand on the table.

"Against."

"Very well . . . Robert?"

"For."

"Reinar?"

"For."

"And you, Shane?"

"Against."

This continues around the table, until every council member except the chairman has placed a hand on the table. Now, everyone waits in anticipation to see what Bernard will do. It's not that his vote is decisive—Starck already has the council's support, with ten in favor and eight against—but the chairman's vote will still determine how smoothly things go when it's time to put Starck's plan into action.

"The council has spoken," Bernard says. He raises his right hand and lets it hover in the air for a moment before placing it on the table. "And because I trust their judgment, you have my support as well, Erik."

∽

The feeling of hope and confidence that washed over Starck when the messenger interrupted the meeting, announcing that they had captured one of Crane's men, vanishes just as quickly as it came once he steps into the interrogation room and sees who the prisoner is.

"Is this supposed to be some kind of joke?" he blurts out, not even sure who the question is meant for. It could be Anton, sitting at the table and staring at him with anxious eyes, but it could just as easily be the guard standing in one corner, or the court reporter at the desk in the other, jotting in a logbook.

"You know him?" Starck hears Bernard ask, his tone making it clear he already knows full well that Starck doesn't just know the prisoner—he is the one who gave him a ride to Soto. All of a sudden, it's clear to Starck why the chairman insisted on walking him down here, even though he isn't going to be part of the interrogation. Bernard didn't want to miss this moment.

"You know I do," Starck mutters.

Bernard doesn't answer that. He just turns around and leaves the room, probably laughing on the inside. Meanwhile, Starck walks over to the table, pulls out a chair, and sits down across from Anton.

"They told me they found you in the basement, Anton. What were you doing down there?"

"I took the wrong door." Anton's voice is tired and slurred. "I got lost, and somehow I ended up down there."

Out of the corner of his eye, Starck notices the guard's gaze shoot to the ceiling. The poor guy must've heard that lazy excuse more than a few times.

"I must admit, it's a bit of a shock finding you in here."

"Imagine how I feel," Anton replies dryly. He glances nervously at the guard, then leans in and adds in a whisper, "This is a total misunderstanding. You've got to get me out of here."

"If it really *is* a misunderstanding, we'll find out soon enough, and you've got nothing to worry about."

With those words, Starck reaches into his shirt pocket, pulls out an object, and places it on the table between them.

"You know what this is?"

Anton stares at the small, leather-bound object with the uncertain look of a man who's just noticed a broken pane in a terrarium at a pet store.

"It's a mirror," he mutters.

"Not just any mirror," Starck adds, turning it with his index finger so the letters etched into the leather face the right way for Anton. "Notice the inscription? It's a guide's mirror. My mirror, to be exact. Do you know what that means?"

Anton doesn't answer with words, but his eyes speak on his behalf. They narrow and become full of resentment. Beneath them, his round cheeks flush. Whether it's deliberate or not is hard to tell, but in this moment, the prisoner shows his true colors and gives himself away.

"It means it's my *personal* mirror," Starck continues, leaning over the table as he starts to undo the thin strap that holds the cover's edges together. "It's the mirror I use to travel between worlds. I got it after my Guide Trial, and that means I'm the only one who decides who it opens for. In other words, Crane has no access to it."

"What are you gonna do with it?" Anton asks, his voice thick with tension.

"I'm just going to ask you a few questions," Starck replies. "And the mirror is here to make sure you're telling the truth when you answer."

For a while, Anton sits there, stubbornly scanning the room as if everything *but* the mirror is the most fascinating thing he's ever seen. But then, slowly, his gaze starts to linger a bit longer each time it sweeps past the mirror's glass. At first, just briefly—then, finally, it stops there.

"Fascinating, isn't it?" Starck asks, and when Anton responds with a dazed nod, he adds, "You can pick it up and take a closer look if you want. I won't mind."

Anton gives a faint smile, nods again, and picks up the mirror.

Once he concludes that the trance is deep enough, Starck gives a subtle signal to the guard in the corner, who nods and moves over behind Anton's chair. Standing there, he gently places two fingers against the chubby man's neck.

"How is the rhythm?"

"Fine," the guard replies. "Slow, but steady."

He speaks softly, clearly nervous about disrupting the hypnotic state the mirror has induced in Anton. That suits Starck just fine. He'd pick an overly cautious assistant over one who underestimates the risks of mirror hypnosis any day of the week. Unlike regular hypnotherapy, this can, in the worst case, trigger a catatonic state.

"Good," he says. "I'll start now, and if it spikes, then . . ."

"I'll let you know right away," the guard finishes for him. "Don't worry."

Starck nods, then turns his attention back to Anton, who's still hunched over, gazing absentmindedly into the mirror. His round face hangs slack, mouth slightly open. A faint hiss escapes with each breath he takes.

"Anton?" Starck says, his voice pitched lower than usual. "Anton, can you hear me?"

"Huh?" Anton's glazed eyes cross for a moment, then seemingly focus—as if he's just spotted something new and fascinating deep within the glass of the mirror.

"I'd like to talk to you about a man named Daniel Crane. Do you know who that is?"

There's no verbal response, but behind Anton, the guard nods, signaling that the mention of Crane's name caused a spike in his heart rate.

"You can speak, Anton. Do you know him? Do you know a man named Daniel Crane?"

"I know him," Anton mumbles, but at the same time, his head starts swaying slowly from side to side. As if his body is trying, all on its own, to deny what he just said.

"That's good, Anton," Starck says, glancing up at the guard, who responds with a raised thumb from his free hand. "Then maybe you can tell me where Crane and his buddies are staying? You see, I need to—"

"Tagoanan," Anton says flatly, tilting his head like he's trying to gauge the size of some mysterious object behind the mirror's glass. "But they're not his friends. They're . . . afraid of him."

"How about you, Anton? Are you afraid of him too?"

Behind Anton's back, the guard grimaces, then raises his hand and tilts it from side to side.

"You don't need to answer that, Anton," Starck says. "Forget it. Let's go with another question instead. How many are there? How many followers has Crane gathered by now? Do you know?"

"I think . . ." Anton begins, but then he suddenly jerks backward, as though the mirror in his hands has sent an electric shock up through his arms. "I don't want to talk anymore."

Starck turns his gaze back to the guard, who shakes his head this time and raises one finger. *One more question, and that's it.*

"Anton, you're doing very well. I've only got one more question. Do you think you can handle that?"

Anton grunts, falls silent for a moment, and then nods.

"Good. I want to ask you why you were down in the basement corridors earlier today. What were you doing down there?"

"Crane wanted me to plaa—"

That's as far as Anton gets before his body finally rejects the hypnosis. His lips keep moving, yet nothing comes out but a choked gurgle, while his shoulders jerk in spasmodic fits, the mirror flailing wildly in his hands.

"His pulse is off the charts!" the guard blurts out, no longer bothering to lower his voice. "He's going into shock. You need to wake him up!"

"Anton!" Starck says. "You need to close your eyes. You hear me? Close your eyes and let go of it!"

No response. Anton keeps staring into the glass, and the shaking spreads, so it's no longer just his shoulders, but his entire body that writhes in spasms. A small red bubble forms in one nostril. It swells, bursts, and turns into a thin line of blood trickling down into the corner of his quivering mouth.

"Close your eyes, and I'll take away the mirror!"

Something's happening now. Anton's body gradually relaxes, and he slips back into the slumped, lethargic state.

"That's good," Starck says as he leans over the table and gently grips the top edge of the mirror. "You did good, and when you feel ready, you can close your eyes and let go of the mirror."

After a moment of stubbornly holding on, Anton lets go—and the instant his fingers lose contact with the glass, his eyes close and he slumps forward. Behind him, the guard lets out a deep sigh and fixes a questioning gaze on Starck.

We're done now, right?

Starck nods. He didn't get all the information he'd hoped for, but that's okay. They've got Crane's location, and that's what matters most, given that it's the key to securing the council's support.

Besides, a team of guards already searched the basement after Anton's visit down there, and they found no signs of anything being wrong. So, it looks like he was apprehended in time.

64

The room where the other members of Starck's travel party have been allowed to wait while he is at the meeting is known as *the Hunter's Lounge*—a fitting name, given that the paneled walls are decorated with nature paintings and animal skulls.

Scattered across the room are lounge islands with dark-colored couches and tables. It's in one of these couches Lisa sits while they wait for the librarian to return. She has a blanket on her lap. On it, Sunni lies, breathing heavily. She isn't sure if he is sleeping, but if not, he is close. And that's perfectly fine. A bit of rest will do him good.

The same could be said about Michael, but he clearly doesn't want to sleep. He is sitting on a barstool at the other end of the room, and every time he starts to nod off, he shakes his head and straightens his back. He does it now too as the door creaks open.

"You've been gone a long time," Lisa says as she makes eye contact with Starck. "How did it go?"

"It went well," he says. "I got support from the council on both matters."

"Then why do you look so sad?"

"Well, yeah, why do I?" Starck repeats with a sigh. "There were . . . complications."

"What do you mean?"

"Turns out Anton is working for Crane."

"Anton?" Lisa exclaims, staring at him with an uncertain smile. "As in *our* Anton?"

Starck nods, then slowly walks over and takes a seat on the couch across from her.

"Turns out he is a spy for Crane. He was caught sneaking around the basement corridors, not long after we parted ways with him."

"What was he doing down there?" Michael asks.

"We don't know. Most likely, he was looking for the archive. There must be some information down there that Crane wants. Luckily, it seems Anton lost his bearings and failed to retrieve it."

"Him hitching a ride with us was no coincidence, was it?"

"No, we have to assume it wasn't. The only upside is that we were careful not to talk too openly about our plans, so I don't think he learned much by tagging along with us. Even so, we need to be extra careful from now on."

"And what exactly happens *from now on*?" Michael asks as he gets up from the barstool and walks over to stand behind Starck, arms crossed. "What's the next step?"

You're asking about the next step, Lisa thinks. *But what you really want to know is how soon you can get to the Mansion of Mirrors.*

It's not the first time a similar thought has crossed her mind. In fact, Michael's eagerness to get to the mansion is starting to worry her quite a bit. Especially after their conversation with the man in Pai, when she realized that Michael—at least on some level—is hoping he'll get to see his son again when they get there.

No, she corrects herself. *It was before that. It started back when he saw the big painting in Elias and Mary's backyard.*

It's not that she doesn't get it—you'd have to be pretty cold-hearted not to—but unlike him, she has stood in front of a mirror in Urari. She has felt the fear of getting trapped inside the Devil's Glass with nothing but her own demons to keep her company. Briefly, sure, but she felt it. She understands the gravity of Starck's words when he says you have to be ready before stepping into the Mansion of Mirrors.

"The next step is for each of us to prepare for our tasks," Starck says. "Sunni and Lisa need to get ready for the trial. It's in three days, so the two of you will be spending a lot of time together over the next couple of days. During the trial, Sunni will attempt to access your mind through a mirror, Lisa. The fewer obstacles he has to navigate around in that process, the better the chances of success. That's why it's important for you to spend time together, get to know each other's strengths and weaknesses—and work to prevent any mistrust that could become a problem during the trial."

"And what about us?" Michael asks, barely hiding the impatience in his voice. "What are we doing while they get ready?"

"That depends on you," Starck says. "During Anton's interrogation, we learned that Crane's army is based in Tagoanan, and the council has given the green light for us to go on the offensive for once and make the first move. To me, this seems like the perfect chance to stop him once and for all—one we might never get again."

Those last words hang in the air between them for a moment as Starck stares down at his hands folded in his lap.

"There's a catch, though," he says. "Doing so would mean delaying the trip to the mansion."

Lisa, convinced that Michael is about to explode, shifts

uneasily and is already searching for words to calm him down. But Michael surprises her. He shows no sign of anger. He just stands there, arms still crossed and a thoughtful look on his face.

"What kind of delay are we talking?" he asks. "Days . . . or weeks?"

"Days," Starck says. "If all goes well, it'll take three to four days to get word out to all the towns to start gathering the mirrors. That should give the troops enough time to assemble and be ready to invade Tagoanan once all confirmations are received."

"And what if Crane actually *has* kidnapped Benjamin? Would we be putting him in more danger?"

"No," Starck says, and this time his gaze doesn't waver—not down at his hands, not anywhere else. It stays fixed on Michael's face. "If Crane took your son, then he's in the mansion."

But what if Crane escapes and decides to go there? Lisa thinks, but before she has opened her mouth, Michael beats her to it.

"From what I understand, your plan will leave Crane with only two possible escape routes," he says. "And one of them is the mansion, right?"

"That's correct," Starck admits. "However, that doesn't mean he's stupid enough to go back in there. And even if he did, he wouldn't be able to harm your son. If your son—"

"Benjamin."

"Benjamin, yes," Starck repeats, nodding apologetically. "If Benjamin is there, he'll be trapped in a mirror, and Crane won't be able to reach him anymore. The mirrors in the mansion aren't like the ones out here."

For what feels like an eternity to Lisa, Michael remains still, standing behind the cross of his arms without saying a word, just watching Starck. The look in his blue eyes is stern, bordering on threatening. So is his voice when he finally speaks.

"Four days. And then I have your word that you'll take me straight to the mansion afterward?"

Starck nods.

"You have my word."

"No matter what happens?"

"Four days," Starck repeats. "No matter what."

65

That night, Michael sleeps miserably. He and Starck have been given a room on the top floor of the council's headquarters, while Sunni and Lisa are sharing a room farther down the hall.

As such, it's a decent sleeping arrangement. The room is warm, its thick walls block out most of the sounds from Soto's nightlife, and Starck is silent in his bed. Nonetheless, Michael sleeps like crap. He is caught in an endless cycle of intrusive thoughts and nightmares.

When he's not sleeping, his thoughts revolve around Benjamin. He is worried that the four-day delay will turn out to be a fatal decision—that it might be exactly what makes the difference between life and death for his son. And he's also worried that Starck might know this.

Then, when he actually does manage to drift off, those worries carry him into a recurring nightmare—one that, in many ways, is an echo of the one that drove him back to work after the accident.

In the dream, he once again finds himself wandering through the mansion's endless rows of sheet-covered mirrors, and as always, the sound of whispering voices leads him to the mirror with Benjamin's name on it. However, in this version of the dream, just as he reaches out to pull the sheet away, his fingers barely touch the fabric before he hears a sound behind him and freezes.

It's the sound of someone mimicking a ticking clock by clicking their tongue.

No words follow, and turning around, Michael sees nothing but the pale beam of moonlight streaming down from the skylight in the large hall. Still, he has no doubt that the sound is coming from a person. Just as he has no doubt about who it is.

"What do you want, Crane?"

For a few seconds, silence. Then the answer comes—this time from a different place out in the darkness among the mirrors.

"I merely want to help you get your son back. I mean, someone has to, seeing as your guide can't get his act together. The clock is ticking, isn't it?"

"You don't have my son," Michael replies, though he doesn't feel nearly as confident as he tries to sound. "If you did, you'd have given him back to me already."

"Now, as far as I recall, I never claimed that I took your son. What I said was that your son is in the Mansion of Mirrors. But just for the heck of it, let's assume I did take him. Why would you think I'd have given him back to you?"

"Because you're a dad too. You know what it means to lose a child."

"Oh, I see. Starck told you about Rebecca and Isabel. Did he also tell you that I could have saved them, if it hadn't been for him?"

"He told me you defied the orders of the council and followed your wife into the mansion."

"Oh yes, the great council that has your dear Starck bending over backwards. But did he also mention that he was the one who talked me out of going to the mansion right away? That it was his advice to wait that kept me from saving her? That I might still be holding my wife in my arms today if it weren't for him. Did he tell you *that*?"

Don't listen to him, Michael says to himself, but it's hard, because there's something in Crane's voice that wasn't there in the previous nightmares. A frailty that must be a remnant of the man Crane once was. A man who loved and lost. Just like him.

"I trusted Starck, let the clock run out, and waited too long," Crane repeats. "The same mistake you're about to make. And you know what I found when I finally went in there? Do you want to know?"

"What did you find?"

"I found her. I found Rebecca. My wife, lying on the floor in front of a shattered mirror that bore my daughter's name. She was lying there, lifeless on the ground, among the shards of glass she had used to open the artery in her arm."

After those words follows a long, unpleasant silence, and even though Michael opens his mouth to try and break it, he can't. Every time he tries, his throat tightens, keeping any words from escaping.

Because no matter how much he despises Crane, he can't help but ask himself what he would have done in the same situation. And the answer isn't as clear-cut as he'd like.

Now, almost as if he has read the thought in Michael's mind, Crane steps into the light, revealing his face. His pale, wide-grinning face, with eyes that gleam in their sockets like two black marbles.

"You do understand my concern, don't you?" he says. "It's just that I'd hate for you to end up in the same situation as me."

"I'll *never* end up like you," Michael retorts, although the doubt is still stirring in the back of his mind. "I'd never have done the things you've done. True, I lost my family too. And it hurts like fucking hell. But I'd *never* use that pain as an excuse to start a war that hurts innocent people. Because I know that's not what they would've wanted."

Crane doesn't say anything, but he doesn't need to either. The crooked smile on his lips speaks volumes.

We'll see about that, my friend. Just you wait.

"I can't imagine it is what Rebecca and Isabel would've wanted either," Michael finishes, hoping the words will be powerful enough to break through to Crane. That they'll reach the broken man still hiding somewhere behind those black eyes and let him accept the hand being offered. But then the smile returns, and Michael realizes it's pointless.

"Maybe you're right," Crane says with a shrug. "Maybe I'm just the villain in this little drama, and maybe it's a big, fat lie that your son is in the mansion."

He pauses for effect, taking a deep breath and looking down at his folded hands. Whether it's deliberate, Michael doesn't know—but the gesture sends a chill down his spine. It's the exact same motion Crane made right before delivering the news on the day Michael's world fell apart.

"The question is whether you're willing to take that chance," Crane finishes. "Are you ready to blindly trust your guide and let him take his sweet time . . . knowing that by the time you finally reach the mansion, it might already be too late?"

On this, their first night in Soto, it's those same words that wake Michael from the nightmare each time, sending him back into his half-waking speculations.

Are you willing to take that chance? The wording may differ, but the essence is the same as the question Crane asked him in a nightmare when they stayed at Mary and Elias' house: *What if you can't trust Starck, and he's just using you for his own agenda? Are you really willing to gamble with your son's life like that?*

Back then—as well as he does now—Michael tried to tell himself not to let the words get under his skin. Still, something gnaws at him as he lies in bed, analyzing this night's version of the dream. Maybe it's because his background in psychology drives him to search for subconscious messages in dreams.

Maybe it's just that.

But maybe—just maybe—it's because his roommate sleeps like a baby the entire night.

66

As the sun rises the next morning, Tom Cerveau is sitting hundreds of miles from Soto, gathering the courage for the conversation he's been planning to have with Crane. With everything he has contributed by now, he feels it's high time the mirror man holds up his end of the deal—especially considering Tom's role in the plans Crane has for the mirror that Anton planted in the Guide Council's headquarters.

And he is gonna keep his promise, Tom thinks as he folds his hands behind his head and leans back into the soft armchair. *He's gonna help me remember.*

It's been a long time since he has sat this comfortably, and for a moment, he is tempted to complete the experience by kicking his feet up on the table. He quickly changes his mind, though—and for good reason. The courthouse in Tagoanan, where he's currently located, serves as Crane's base, while most of his followers have settled in the other buildings of the abandoned city.

In other words, the courthouse is the closest thing to Crane's home, so he probably wouldn't be thrilled if Tom planted his boots on the table. Especially not with that reddish-brown layer stuck to the soles—a lumpy mix of the watchmaker's blood and desert sand.

Sitting there, comfortably sunken into the chair's soft cushions, Tom can see the glass door of a cabinet standing against the wall across from him. In the glass is his own reflection—and above it, he sees the door behind him slowly creak open, gradually revealing Crane's pale face.

"I wanna talk to you about something," Tom says as he turns around and puts on what he hopes comes off as a confident expression.

Crane raises one eyebrow and tilts his head to the side.

"You promised you'd tell me about my past," Tom continues.

A moment of silence, then Crane lets out a dry, rasping laugh.

"Is that all?" He walks around to the other side of the table, drops into the room's other chair, and kicks his feet up on the edge of the table. "You sounded so serious. I was starting to get all nervous."

Bullshit, Tom thinks. There are plenty of things Crane could be accused of, but getting nervous isn't one of them. Tom, on the other hand, has to work hard to keep his own unease from showing.

"I'm tired of being played for a fool," he says. "And if you want me to kill the boy, I want something in return. You gotta tell me who I was!"

The mirror man stares at him, the wrinkles in his corpse-pale face shifting until they finally settle into a smile—one that, in many ways, is worse than the laughter.

"You're sure?" he asks. "You're absolutely sure you want to know?"

Tom nods.

"Very well."

Crane gets up and walks over to a painting hanging on the wall next to the cabinet with the glass door. It's a small painting depicting a sunset over Mount Heriotza. Without saying a word, he takes the picture from the wall and places it on the table.

"What am I supposed to do with that?" Tom asks. He is struggling to see how an oil painting of Urari's only graveyard is going to help him remember his past. He has heard the story of Crane's promise to the council—that one day he'll stand at the top of that mountain and see nothing but ash—so he gets why the mirror man has it on the wall . . . but what good it's gonna do him, he has no idea.

"Turn it over."

Tom does as Crane asks and discovers that the cracked wooden frame encloses more than just the painting of Heriotza.

"A mirror?"

"Of course," Crane replies. "I'd be a pretty lousy leader if I didn't make sure my people had an emergency exit in case the shit hits the fan . . . or if they need a reminder of who's in charge."

Those are the last words Tom catches before the mirror lights up and reaches out for him with its merciless, invisible hands. It pulls him into the darkness and leaves him there, as his memories start to pour down over him.

At first like soft raindrops, then like icy hail.

Tom looks up just as the first drop falls from the black void above him. A small, white bead of water trailing a streak of blue light through the darkness, until it hits his forehead and, with the jolt of an electric shock, sends the first image flashing through his mind.

Stairs. A hand on a railing. A painting of a hot air balloon on the wall.

I'm . . . home? he thinks, and instantly, another jolt shoots through his body as the next drop falls, hitting the back of his neck.

Golden hair. A girl sitting with her knees pulled up on a bus seat, buried in a book. The world outside rushes past.

Michelle Roux. That's the girl I'm going to marry.

Another drop, another jolt, and his nostrils fill with the scent of rain-soaked asphalt and sunshine.

Same girl, now a woman. Tom sees her from below. She's smiling, proudly holding out her hand. A small silver ring glints in the sunlight.

Tom tries to hold on to this image, but the rain grows heavier, and new drops shatter it.

The sound of a scream. Of pain. The sterile smell of a hospital. The feeling of helplessness turns into the feeling of joy.

From now on, you'll always come first, he thinks, as two new jolts surge through him. One shows a nightlight above a crib, the other a name—*Elliot*—spelled out in red and blue letter blocks on a floor. *I'll always protect you.*

An intense pain, like a divine reprimand, shoots through Tom as another raindrop lands in his hair, and he knows it's a lie. He is back on the staircase, heading down to the living room where she is waiting—and he *won't* always protect his son.

The rain stops, and he remains trapped in this memory for a while, against his will. It's like watching a disturbing movie while wearing a torture device that forces his eyelids open.

On the movie screen, his hand reaches out and opens the door. There she is, the same girl, the same woman, but no smile and no pride. Defiance and an edginess he doesn't understand are all that remain in her green eyes. She's sitting on the edge of the couch, legs tucked beneath her just like she had on the bus seat back when he realized she was the one. However, there's no book in her hands now. They're clasped together, and they're trembling.

"Did you get him to sleep?"

Tom nods to the woman on the screen and twitches as a drop slides down from the hair on the back of his neck and runs along his spine.

"Good," she replies, looking down at her hands. "There's something I need to talk to you about, and I have to do it before I lose my nerve."

Tom opens his mouth, but then feels his throat tighten as he follows her gaze down to her hands. The small movement she makes with her left hand is barely noticeable. She opens and closes it, only for a fraction of a second—but it's enough for Tom to catch sight of the silver object resting in her palm.

The little ring.

The storm begins simultaneously inside him and in the black void above. An overwhelming swirl of confusing sensations and memories crashes down in the form of tiny, stinging hailstones.

Electric shocks blast through his body, and memories flicker past his eyes, rapidly and out of order. Like poker cards being shuffled.

His hand touching her cheek. Her grimacing and turning away. A dog barking at the neighbor's. Elliot opening his eyes and stiffening. A hand on the stair railing. Two signatures on a piece of paper—his in blue, hers in black. A mattress on the floor in an empty apartment. Green leaves turning brown. Her new, stylish haircut. Loneliness and betrayal. A streetlamp in moonlight. *Two* silhouettes in a window. A knife block. Canned laughter from a TV show in the background. A scream. Red stains on a carpet. Stairway. The door to a kid's room. A man's shadow on a child's blanket. Two breaths, one fast and one slow. A triangular patch of light shuddering on a wall, then shooting downward in a single, swift motion.

After that, nothing.

67

"Are you nervous about tomorrow?"

Sunni's question catches Lisa completely off guard, and she doesn't really know how to answer.

Two days have passed since they got the green light from the council, and during that time, she has asked him that same question more than once. The focus has been so heavily on him and his young age that she hasn't even considered whether *she* might be nervous about the trial.

"Why do you ask that?" she says as her gaze drifts to a stone bridge up ahead, connecting the street they're walking on with the one on the other side. "Do I look nervous?"

"I don't know," Sunni says with a shrug. "I guess you don't, but I mean . . . maybe you should be?"

They were given the details of the Guide Trial the night before, and in light of those, there probably is reason to be a bit nervous. They were told that they'll be placed in a room where Sunni must try to paint his way to the reason for her being in Urari. That he'd be given painting supplies and a Guide Mirror which—if he truly *is* chosen—will grant him access to her subconscious. She, on the other hand, just has to be present and try not to shut him out.

Mental brain surgery, she thinks, and suddenly, she does feel a flutter of nerves in her stomach. After all, he is about to go poking around in her mind. And who knows what he'll find in there?

"I don't know, Sunni," she says, lacking a better answer. "I'll probably be super nervous tomorrow, but right now I'm actually just enjoying walking around here with you. It's a nice city."

As if to underline that observation, she nods toward the other side of the canal where a bunch of boys and old men are fishing with lines. Behind them, a group of women sit on benches, chatting as they mend fishing nets and sails.

"Hey, look!" Sunni exclaims, squinting. "I think he's got a bite."

Lisa follows his gaze, and sure enough, there's a boy standing at the edge with a fishing rod bent so sharply it looks like it might snap.

She opens her mouth to ask Sunni if he wants to go over there, but he's already gone, sprinting toward the bridge. His excitement brings a smile to her lips. She's happy for him. Happy that there are still moments when he gets to be the boy he was.

However, this feeling vanishes promptly when he, instead of running across the bridge, stops halfway and leans over the railing, staring down at the water. His face is pale and confused. Whatever he sees down there is definitely something that upsets him.

"What is it, Sunni?" Lisa yells as she picks up the pace. "What's going on?"

"What does it mean?" he says, his voice high-pitched and shaky.

"What does what mean? What is it you're looking at?"

Now she sees it too. In the shadows beneath the bridge; a newspaper boat cutting through the surface of the water like a small, pale gray shark fin.

Everything crumbles, Lisa thinks, feeling a chill run down her spine as the boat turns and reveals that very headline printed along the top edge of its sail.

It's the boat she saw in the last painting in Sunni's studio. That boat, and those words.

Everything crumbles.

68

Some things are too painful to live with. This simple fact is simultaneously Crane's greatest weakness and his strongest weapon. It's the driving force behind his quest for revenge. His hatred for the guides is what keeps his inner demons at bay and pushes his own trauma into the background. Even so, he wouldn't have hesitated to accept if someone had offered him what he is about to offer Tom after the encounter with his past.

And looking at Tom, sniffling in front of the mirror, hands buried in his hair and drool dangling from his beard, Crane knows the same is true for him. He won't hesitate to accept.

"Tom?" he whispers, his voice softer than ever. "Tom, look at me."

"I killed them," Tom sobs, not even noticing the hand now resting on his shoulder. "I killed Elliot!"

"I know, Tom, but you—"

"DID YOU HEAR WHAT I SAID?" Tom screams, lifting his head. His eyes are wild and full of shame. "I KILLED MY OWN SON!"

"It wasn't your fault," Crane says calmly. "You didn't have a choice. She drove you to it."

"But s-she . . . why did you let me see it?"

"You asked for it," Crane says.

"But I . . . didn't know that . . ."

"Of course you didn't." Crane gently strokes his shoulder again before suddenly tightening his grip. "But it was necessary, Tom. Letting you remember your past was the only way to make you understand why the guides need to have their power taken away."

Tom blinks and bites his trembling lower lip as he waits for Crane to go on.

"They let you down, Tom. The guides failed you."

Crane lays it on thick, coats his words in disgust to stir up Tom's thirst for revenge. And judging by the way the vagabond's pupils contract, it seems to be working.

"They could have helped you," he continues. "They *should* have guided you to the mansion. That's their duty, their responsibility. Instead, they let you wander alone in the Wasteland until you lost all sense of who you were."

With each word, the intensity in Crane's voice rises, reaching the fervor of a revival preacher—and the more sermon-like it becomes, the harder Tom nods.

Crane smiles on the inside. Everything is going according to plan. Before long he'll have a perfect ally. One who shares his contempt for the Council of Guides and therefore won't ever question the tasks he's given.

"Let me hear you say it," he says.

"They . . . deserve it."

"Louder, Tom!"

"THEY DESERVE IT!"

Now Crane can't contain it any longer. He throws his head back and bursts into laughter, pounding the table.

Tom watches him warily, then slowly joins in. His laughter sounds thin and hollow, but that doesn't bother Crane. The unbeatable offer still waits like the ultimate carrot on a string—and that will undoubtedly add some depth to Tom's laughter.

"There's one more thing," he says as their laughter fades. "Once we've wiped out the council, I can take you to the mansion and make you forget all of it again . . . if you'd like that?"

After a moment of consideration, Tom gives a firm nod.

"I want that. I want to forget."

"Good. Then, would you be so kind as to remind me what your next task is?"

"The boy?"

"In detail, please."

"I have to wait by the mirror until the boy's Guide Trial starts."

"And when that happens?"

"Then I travel over there . . . and kill him."

69

"And you're absolutely sure?"

"One hundred percent."

"It couldn't have been a coincidence?"

Lisa lets out a deep sigh. This is the third time Starck has asked, and although his wording changes, the core of the question is always the same: Was the paper boat and the text on its sail just something they imagined?

"It *wasn't* a coincidence," she says. "Unless Sunni once saw a paper boat *exactly* like it with *exactly* the same text on the sail, then no. It's not a coincidence. We saw—on the river *today*—the paper boat that Sunni has a drawing of in his studio. But what does it mean? Is he able see the future now too?"

Starck shakes his head and glances around at the eyeless skulls on the walls of the hunter's lodge, where the group has once again gathered around a table.

"We're *not* making it up," Sunni insists. He's sitting on the couch across from Starck, staring at him with a serious look that makes him appear much older than he is.

"It's not that I don't believe you," Starck says. "I'm just tired from all the preparations. The time for the invasion of Tagoanan is drawing closer, and there are still four cities that haven't responded yet. And now this."

He shrugs, looking back and forth between Sunni and Lisa.

"So, no. I don't know what it means. Or if it even means anything at all."

"We've talked about something," Lisa says. "If Sunni is able to paint the future—which I believe is what happened—then maybe he can do more than that."

Starck's bushy eyebrows lift above the rim of his glasses. His brown eyes contain an expression she can't quite read. It might be curiosity—but it could just as easily be skepticism.

"Maybe he can't just *paint* the future," she continues, faltering slightly at her own words. They sound way more stupid now than they did when she and Sunni talked about it on the way here. "Maybe he can change it too."

Sunni nods encouragingly, but Michael is staring at her with a look that makes her feel like a schoolgirl called up to the blackboard just after discovering a rip in the seat of her jeans. It almost makes her give up and tell them to just forget it—but then Starck nods and adjusts his glasses the way he always does when he is about to say something important.

"That might not be so improbable," he says. "It could be that the combination of your unique minds allows for a kind of precognition that goes beyond the normal limits of dream sources."

"Is there, um . . . a version for dummies?" Lisa asks, waving a hand in front of her face to show that she is completely lost.

"I'll try," Starck says, shifting to the edge of his seat. "I think it's a case of time displacement. You see, there are more worlds than just Urari and the one you know—and each of them moves through time at its own pace. Just like time in your own world moves much slower than here."

He pauses to think, then nods to himself and continues.

"And since you're an empath, Lisa, you have the ability to cross dimensions, just like the mirrors. Yes, that's one side of it. The other is Sunni's paintings of your life. They show that the two of you are closely connected. Normally, the dreams of guides are vague and ambiguous, but Sunni's dreams have been detailed . . . and they cover your *entire* life. Not just the event that brought you here."

The enthusiasm in his voice grows as he speaks. It's clear that the idea is starting to evolve into something that makes sense to him.

"So," he says, "my theory is that, unconsciously, you opened a portal at one of the moments when Sunni was dreaming about you. By doing that, you may have pulled him with you, and the time displacement between worlds then made it possible for him to catch a glimpse of your future. It's pretty convoluted, I'll admit . . . but it actually makes sense."

"Maybe it does," Lisa admits. "But you still haven't answered my question. If Sunni is able to see my future—can he also change it?"

"In theory, perhaps. But that would require him to be connected to you while your channels are open, so to speak. And at the same time, he'd need enough control to recognize the moments that can be altered."

"Could we try the dummy version again?"

"Yes, of course. If we use the paper boat as an example, he would not be able to stop it from being made or set afloat. He could, however, have kept you from noticing it. In theory, that is."

"Because someone else made the boat?"

Starck nods, after which he glances down at his wristwatch and grimaces.

"I find all of this really interesting," he says. "And I'd like to help you make sense of it, but I've got a meeting with Bernard in ten minutes, as well as a bunch of other stuff. So, it'll have to wait until tomorrow, after you've been through the trial."

70

Fortunately, Starck's fears about not hearing back from the remaining cities within the timeframe he had promised Michael were misplaced as the last pending confirmations came in earlier this morning with a group of riders from Ciotar.

At this moment, these men—along with hundreds of others—are gathered in the passage between the council's buildings. They're standing in straight, orderly columns, helmets gleaming in the sunlight coming in from the skylight above them. Their faces are turned toward the elevated platform, from which Bernard is giving his speech.

And he's doing very well. Whatever else Starck might think of the council chairman, he has great respect for Bernard's ability to rally a crowd. On his pedestal, that man is like the conductor of a symphony orchestra. He guides them steadily with his hands and his voice, making sure their silence and their sighs fall at just the right moments. He has that rare sense for a crowd's shared rhythm that marks a great leader.

Starck is watching the show from a spot by the railing on the third floor where he has a clear view of the entire passage below.

Michael is right next to him, listening to the speech with the same absorbed expression as the men below.

Sunni and Lisa aren't there with them. They decided to stay up in their room to prepare for Sunni's trial later in the day.

They can probably still hear him, Starck thinks, smiling to himself as Bernard raises his voice even more, prompting the entire hall—including Michael—to nod eagerly.

"He's good, isn't he?"

Michael blinks once, affirming, then lets his gaze drift down over the passage. When it returns to Starck, his eyes are narrow and serious.

"Will it be enough?" he says. "Do we have enough people?"

"Hard to say," Starck admits. "We still don't know how many followers Crane has . . . but I think it will. You have to remember, our goal isn't to fight Crane's army. We just need to scare him enough to make him try to use the mirrors to escape. Besides, we've got more people on our side than the ones you see here."

"You mean the refugees?"

"Yeah. Most of the people who fled from the perimeter towns ended up here in Soto. With them on our side, we can form a closed ring around Tagoanan."

"And that'll work? What if he's not intimidated that easily? What if he decides to fight instead?"

On the platform, Bernard is wrapping up his speech, ending it by giving the crowd a shared mantra. *Crane's tyranny ends today* are the words, and he repeats them over and over until they echo through the entire passage.

"Whether there's a fight or not," Starck says once they're able to hear themselves again, "it won't last long. Crane won't stick around if things start to get messy. That's not his style. I think you know that."

"What do you mean?"

"That Crane doesn't usually get his own hands dirty."

"He sends people like Tom," Michael says, turning his gaze up toward the skylight. After a moment, he adds, "I want to go with them. I want to do my part."

"Your part is getting to the mansion. That's the only thing you need to worry about."

"Just like your part is to take me there?"

For a moment, this unexpected and cynical response leaves Starck feeling paralyzed. There is something in it—something more than just Michael's frustration about not being allowed to join the fight. Something that sounds like genuine distrust.

However, before he has the chance to respond, the passage fills with noise once again. The speech is over, and the soldiers—Bernard's mantra still on their lips—are heading out to put an end to Crane's tyranny.

In truth, Starck is relieved by the interruption, because it's hard to argue with what Michael said. After all, leading him to the mansion is his primary responsibility—and it's a responsibility he has pushed to the background more than once at this point.

PART NINE
THE TRIAL

71

This is a day of change in Urari, and everyone can feel it. For the people in the many towns visited by the council's envoys, it's a mixture of anticipation and uncertainty. They've watched as the envoys gathered the mirrors in the town squares, where they now stand, waiting to be destroyed once the order comes. No one in these towns has protested, because even though Urari's mirrors don't pose a direct threat to the locals, everyone understands they're dangerous weapons in the wrong hands. And many have quietly prayed for this day to come. Still, there's a lingering sense of insecurity at the thought of the unknown future once the mirrors are gone.

For others—like the people of the town by the mountain passage, who long ago banned the Devil's Glass—the plans to invade Tagoanan aren't cause for much concern. No riders arrived in their towns with a mandate to collect mirrors or call for volunteers.

Even so, there is a sense in these towns too that something is on the way. It hangs in the air like an electric charge, making the hairs on the back of their necks stand up. And though no one speaks of it openly, it's clear that everyone feels something.

Something that makes them shutter their windows and stay indoors.

Within Starck's group in Soto, the feeling is also strong—that a lot will have changed by the end of this day. Starck is busy with the final preparations for the invasion, and Michael is preparing for the last, and hardest, part of the journey to the mansion once the war is over. In theory, so could Lisa, but for her, it's not the thought of reaching the final destination that weighs. It's the Guide Trial. The prospect of opening her mind and laying bare her inner thoughts to a boy that's six years younger than her.

For Crane, who is standing at the window of Tagoanan's abandoned town hall, gazing at the mountains on the horizon, it's a tingling sense of exhilaration. He is convinced this will be the day when the balance conclusively tips in his favor. If Tom does his part tonight, Starck's group will be left vulnerable. Lisa will have lost her guide—and with a bit of luck, Starck will be so crushed by the boy's death that the same will go for Michael. Their defenses will fall, and the empaths will be open to his influence. And once they're on his side, the council's days are numbered.

This will truly be a day of change.

72

As the day progresses and the trial draws closer, the tension in Sunni's body builds. It gathers into a knot in his gut that feels like it could tear his stomach apart every time he looks at Lisa. He is so scared of failing that he, more than once, has considered backing out and running away. Therefore, it's almost a relief when they, by late afternoon, are finally led down to the room where his Guide Trial will take place.

The small room, which had seemed bare and cold the first time they saw it, feels completely different now. In fact, it's almost cozy. Candles have been placed on the round stone table at the center of the room, and on the three shelves built into the wall, there are stacks of parchment and oil pastels.

It's the sight of these that finally settles Sunni's stomach. Painting has always been his source of comfort, and the materials on the shelves make him feel at home.

"Hey, are you even listening, Sunni?"

"Huh? What? No, sorry."

"I said, you and Lisa will sit here," Starck says, patting the edge of the table. "Then, once the trial begins, the door will be shut. And it stays shut until the trial is over and you open it."

"And how do we know when the trial is over?" asks Lisa, who is still standing in the doorway.

"You'll know," Starck just says, after which he gestures toward the painting supplies on the shelf. "Is everything you need here, Sunni?"

Sunni walks over to the shelf and lets his fingers trail across the surface of the parchment. Not that he really needs to—even standing in the doorway, he could tell that the materials are high quality.

"Yeah, it's great," he says. "But what about the mirror? Wasn't there supposed to be a mirror in here too?"

"There's a guard bringing it. I'd expect him to be here any moment. After Anton's visit to the basement, the council insisted that we didn't put it out. It shouldn't really make a difference, since it's a Guide Mirror made specifically for you . . . but still, it's—"

"Better to play it safe," Lisa says, flashing Sunni a crooked smile. "You'll remember that, too, when you're poking around in my head, okay?"

This comment makes the knot in Sunni's stomach tighten again, but he manages to give her a smile that he hopes doesn't look too forced.

"Someone's coming," Lisa whispers. "I can hear footsteps in the hallway."

Sunni hears it too; short, hasty footsteps drawing steadily closer—and sure enough, a second later, two uniformed guards enter the room. After them follows an older man Sunni hasn't seen before but who looks like he is important.

The older man pauses briefly in the doorway and gives them a nod before walking over to the table where he places the leather-bound object he's been carrying. Next, he turns around and clears his throat.

"We're ready to commence the trial," he says. "If you'll take your seats . . ."

Lisa walks over to the table, but Sunni stays put, his eyes fixed on the doorway where Starck gives him a last, reassuring wink before turning around and walking out.

The older man clears his throat once again—while casting an impatient glance at the guard to his left.

"Young sir?" he says. "Would you take your seat?"

"Yeah, I . . . I'm coming," Sunni says, but he still doesn't move until Starck's back has disappeared completely from view.

Only then does he feel ready to take his seat at the table.

73

For quite a while after the door has been closed behind them, nothing happens for Sunni and Lisa. They just sit there, staring at each other from opposite sides of the table. Now and then, one of them will tap their fingers on the tabletop or hum a few bars of a tune, the way people do when they don't know what to say—but aside from that, the silence is awkward and heavy.

More than once, the thought crosses Lisa's mind that this all might be a huge mistake. That Starck saw something in them that isn't really there, and that neither she nor Sunni is anything special after all. However, every time that thought arises, she recalls Sunni's studio—and that pushes the doubt away. She remembers how dumbfounded she felt, seeing how accurately he had captured her life in his paintings.

In fact, it's the memory of those that spurs her to ask the question that finally breaks the awkward silence between them.

"Why is it always things?"

Sunni, who has been staring at the blank sheet in front of him, lifts his head and looks at her.

"What do you mean?"

"The popcorn bowl, the tree in front of my school, the paper boat," Lisa explains. "It's all dead things. Objects. There aren't any pictures of people in your room. So, I'm asking, why do you always paint things?"

She can't figure out why, but something about that question clearly unsettles the boy. His gaze flickers from side to side, then shifts to the stack of oil pastels, as if he's hoping to pass the question on to them.

"I . . . don't know," he says. "I guess that's just how I see it, I think."

"Then I've got an idea," Lisa says, sitting up straighter. "Why don't you try painting me?"

"I'm not sure I can," Sunni says. "You're so beautiful, and I'm afraid I won't be able to do it right."

He says it so plainly, so matter-of-factly, that he might as well have said *The earth is round* or *This table wobbles*, and Lisa isn't even sure he notices how the comment makes her cheeks flush.

"Would you try anyway? For me?"

Sunni stares silently at her for a while before he finally nods and reaches toward the pile of oil pastels. He picks up a bronze-colored stick and holds it up in front of his face as he glances back and forth between it and her hair. Then he puts it back and picks up another. He repeats this motion several times before he finds the right shade—and begins to paint.

He starts off slowly, sketching a few lines, lifting his head to study her features, adding a few more, then looking up again. Next, he sets the bronze pastel aside and picks up a pale yellow one. After that, a brown, then a red. With each change, the pace of his movements quickens.

Due to the mirror standing on the table between them, Lisa can't see the paper, but she can sense—and quite literally *hear*—the image taking shape. There's a musical rhythm to the way he shades, a cadence in the strokes that makes the tiny hairs on the back of her neck stand on end.

This is how a real artist works, she thinks. *He's practically in a trance.*

Without pausing, Sunni swaps the red pastel for a black one, and it strikes her that the idea of a trance might not be far off. He doesn't even glance at the stack anymore when picking a new color. His hand moves to it automatically, as if by instinct, while his eyes never leave the paper.

She is tempted to sneak a peek—or at least ask how it's going—but she's afraid it'll break his flow. Maybe a short interruption wouldn't matter, but what does she know? Her biggest artistic achievements are a few stick figures and maybe the first nine notes of *Für Elise* on piano, so her understanding of the creative zone is pretty limited.

Just as that thought passes through her mind, Sunni stops. He stares down at the paper in confusion, then up at her.

"What's wrong?"

"It's your eyes," he says, tilting his head. "I can't get them right."

"Will this help?"

Lisa leans as far across the table as she can without touching the mirror between them. Sunni mirrors her movement, leaning in too, until there's only a hand's width between her green eyes and his brown.

Except they're not entirely brown anymore. There's something white glinting in his pupils—and it's . . . growing?

With that observation, Lisa feels a familiar drop in her stomach, and she realizes that the Guide Trial has begun for real. Her fate now officially lies in the hands of an eleven-year-old boy.

74

The wait is over, and this time Tom doesn't need Crane to tell him. What before was a tangle of glowing jellyfish-like threads behind the glass is now a pulsating darkness speckled with tiny spots of light. Like stars in the night sky. He recognizes those spots from his journeys through the mirrors with Crane, and he knows what they mean. The gate is open.

As though he has somehow read Tom's thoughts from a distance, Crane comes bursting in through the door. He glances at the mirror, then at Tom.

"It's time," he says. His black eyes gleam in his pale face. It's obvious that he shares Tom's excitement at finally getting started.

Under different circumstances, Tom might have wondered why the hell he had to sit here like some idiot, staring at that mirror for hours if Crane could sense the change from all the way downstairs. Right now, though, he is so keyed up he just smiles and nods.

"Do you have a . . . tool?" Crane asks.

Tom nods and raises his right hand, displaying the shard of glass he's holding.

"You wouldn't rather have a real knife?"

Tom shakes his head. The glass shard worked like a charm on the watchmaker, and he sees no reason to fix something that isn't broken. Also, there's a certain poetry in using the weapon that spilled Elias' blood on his successor.

With that thought in mind, Tom locks his gaze on the mirror.

75

After having spent only a brief time inside Lisa's mind, Sunni realizes he has a choice. He can take the memory she has been suppressing and bring it back with him. He can paint it for her. He can let her see it—and in doing so, allow the idea of reaching the mansion to take hold of her soul the way it has taken hold of Michael's. And Tom's. And Crane's.

It would be easy, because he's holding it in his hand—a small, framed photograph of her father and her sister.

On the surface, there's nothing wrong with the image. It's an innocent photo, taken on the day of Emma's ninth birthday, and there's nothing troubling about a father with his arm around his daughter beneath a string of balloons. Not to the unknowing eye, at least.

Yet somehow, Sunni understands that, to Lisa, this photo is the symbol of everything that was wrong. All she would need to do to spark her memory is to look at the hand—her *dad's* hand—that holds on just a little *too* tight, has too firm a grip on his daughter's shoulder.

Sunni could show her. It's within his power to paint it and let her remember the answer to the question that has haunted her for the past thirteen months. He could show her the real reason behind what happened that fateful night. He could reveal that the true killer was never Lisa's sister. That it wasn't Emma who took their father's life that night. That, in fact, it was him who took hers by pushing a girl—already mentally fragile—all the way over the edge. The murder weapon wasn't a knife. It was a hand. A hand with too tight a grip.

All of this, Sunni could show Lisa if he just painted the photograph that her mother threw away when they came home after the funeral. But, by now, he understands that's not his task. His task is to save Lisa, yes . . . but he's no longer so sure that the Mansion of Mirrors is the solution for every lost soul.

Therefore, he brings the photo with him as he moves through the next rooms of her mind. He is looking for a place to hide it; somewhere it will never be found.

He finds the answer when he remembers one of his own paintings—the great oak tree outside the school. It would be perfect. It's the tree she sat beneath the day she traveled to Urari, and it's the last thing he painted before he actually met her. On the bench, beneath that tree, she has been sitting, wondering if things would ever get better—and now he's going to do his part to make sure they do.

He closes his eyes, focusing on recalling the details of the painting, and when he opens them again, he finds himself standing in the shade of the great oak. There, he crouches down and starts digging in the dirt with his bare hands.

Once the hole is deep enough, he gently places the photo at the bottom and covers it up. As he does this, his thoughts drift back to the paper boat—and slowly, an idea begins to take shape in his mind.

I'm ready, Lisa, he thinks, closing his eyes. *I'm ready to paint your picture now.*

When he opens his eyes, he is back at the stone table in the council's basement. Lisa is sitting across from him. Her eyes are open, but she doesn't react—not when he says her name, nor when he waves a hand in front of her face. She is somewhere else. Maybe that's for the best. There's a faint trace of a smile on her lips, and she doesn't look like she's uncomfortable.

Sunni grabs a fresh sheet of paper and starts drawing. The image is crystal clear in his mind, maybe clearer than anything has ever been, and as the oil pastel dances across the page under his skilled hands, the young artist once again slips into a trance-like state.

Because of this, he doesn't notice the sharp flash of light coming from the corner behind him. He also doesn't hear the grating sound of the rug and tiles shifting aside to make room for the uninvited guest.

It's only when a shadow appears on the table beside him that Sunni realizes he and Lisa are no longer alone in the room. A shadow that slowly grows larger—not stopping, until both Sunni's hands and the paper beneath them are covered in darkness.

And then comes the voice. A hoarse, rasping voice Sunni has never heard before, but which instantly tells him that its owner has bad intentions.

"Jeez, kid. You've got some serious talent!"

76

Lisa's first confused thought is that the maulwert isn't dead after all. That somehow it survived being trampled to pieces and has followed her underground, all the way from the mountain pass to Soto.

It's the hole that plants that idea in her head. The hole in the corner, where it looks like the tiles have been pushed up from underneath.

It wasn't made by the maulwert, though. It was made by Tom—and when that realization hits her, she almost wishes it *had* been the terrifying mole-like monster. Its stinking squid-maw would, in many ways, be preferable to the smile on the face of the man standing in the corner with one foot resting on the back of Sunni's neck.

"Oh, you're awake?" he says. "Good. I was afraid you were gonna miss out on all the fun."

He stares at her expectantly, clearly hoping his words will provoke a reaction. However, Lisa—for the moment—is immune to that kind of bait. Her focus is entirely on Sunni's limp body, which still hasn't shown any sign of life.

"What did you do to him?" she snarls, her voice sounding foreign even to her own ears. "What did you do to him, you psycho?"

Tom lifts his foot and glances down at the boy beneath it, regarding him with the disgust of a man who has stepped in gum or dog shit.

What he failed to achieve with his comment earlier, he gets now. Lisa is struck by a fury so intense that it pounds in her temples and makes her vision blur.

In a single, fluid motion, she leaps up from her chair, grabs the mirror off the table, and smashes it against the edge hard enough to crack it. Then she yanks a shard free from the frame.

Tom's eyes light up with excitement, and she realizes she has given him exactly what he was hoping for. But so what? She has no intention of running. That psycho is going down now—and he's not getting back up.

For what feels like an eternity, they stand there, each with a glass knife in hand, measuring each other. Both blades are gripped so tightly that blood runs in thin red lines down the hands that hold them.

"You might as well drop it," Tom hisses, waving his shard through the air in front of him. "You don't stand a chance."

Despite the constant throbbing in her temples, Lisa has enough clarity to realize that she needs him to make the first move if she's going to stand a chance. So, she plays along.

"And why's that?"

"Your eyes," Tom says, still with that damned glass knife dancing in front of him like the head of a snake about to strike. "You don't have it in you. Me, on the other hand, I won't hesitate!"

"I know," Lisa says. "You're way too deranged for that."

There is a slight, almost imperceptible shift in Tom's face

when she says that word. A shadow passes over it, tightening his features and making him look like a child forced to eat something it doesn't like. Or like someone mentally unstable who doesn't appreciate being called *deranged*.

"I'm not crazy!"

"Trust me," she replies. "You're completely unhinged. And I should know—my sister was mentally ill. So much so that she took her own life . . . but hey, compared to you, she was hardly—"

That's the tipping point for Tom. He roars and lunges at her, glass knife raised, teeth bared.

For a terrible second, Lisa is sure her body won't obey her as she tries to hurl herself over the table—but then her feet leave the ground. She jumps up and slides across the tabletop, balancing on her hip and the hand clutching the glass shard. With her free hand, she throws the stack of papers into the air.

The parchments whirl upward. Most of them glide over Tom's head, but two sheets hit him. One—Sunni's portrait of her—flutters across his chest. The other strikes him just above the eyes. It doesn't blind him, but it throws off his balance just enough to make him crash into the table.

He screams—more in anger than pain—and starts to spin around, but now, it's Lisa's turn to make her move. And where Tom charged from the front, she has the advantage of coming at him from behind. She sprints toward him and puts all her strength into the kick that lands at the back of his knee.

"YOU CRAZY BITCH!" he roars as his legs buckle beneath him.

Lisa, no longer capable of forming coherent thoughts, also screams as she lunges once more, hammering her knee into his cheek. The blow lands cleanly, releasing two teeth from his mouth in a spray of blood as he crashes to the floor.

He lets out a rattling gasp as he lands on his stomach, his right hand pinned beneath him. Surprisingly, he stays there, one side of his face pressed flat against the floor, while his left hand stretches forward, grasping aimlessly at the air in front of Lisa's foot.

Beneath his hip, a dark pool of blood begins to spread.

Lisa raises her weapon—but then hesitates when she sees the look of despair in the vagabond's eyes. They're wide and confused. Clearly, he hasn't completely grasped that he has landed on his own weapon.

Lisa feels no urge to solve that final mystery for him. She's perfectly fine with the psychopath's last conscious thought being an unanswered question.

So, she lets him stay in the dark, while she slowly lowers her hand and drops the shard of glass that should've been part of Sunni's Guide Mirror on the floor. Next, she turns and staggers over to the boy, still lying in the same twisted position Tom left him in.

"Sunni?" she hears herself say as she drops to her knees and grabs the boy's shoulders to turn him over. "Sunni, are you—"

The sight of the boy's face closes her vocal chords, leaving her unable to finish the sentence.

77

Starck's plan for the invasion of Tagoanan is simple. There is, however, one crucial factor, and that's the timing. If the invading force and the guards stationed by the mirrors in the towns don't act at exactly the right moment, everything could fall apart. Should the army begin to close the ring around Tagoanan too early, it will give Crane and his followers a chance to escape. On the other hand, Crane's connection to the mirrors will alert him if the guards start destroying them too soon. In that case, he could slip away during the thirty-minute window between 8:30 p.m.—when the army is ordered to start sealing off Tagoanan—and 9:00 p.m., when all the mirrors gathered in the town squares are to be destroyed.

All of this lingers in the back of Starck's mind when he stops halfway up the stairs, because he hears his name being shouted from the far end of the passage. At first, he doesn't recognize the voice. For one, it's unusually high-pitched, and secondly, it's the first time its owner has ever used his first name.

"ERIK! ERIK, WAIT UP!"

Starck glances at his wristwatch. Whatever this person wants, it has to be quick. The second phase of the plan launches in less than half an hour, and he promised to stop by Bernard's office before then.

He turns to say it's a bad time—but the words die in his throat when he sees who it is that comes running across the marble tiles of the passage.

"Erik, you need to come with me!" Michael's face is pale, his eyes wide-open and panicked. "It's Sunni, he . . ."

"What happened to Sunni?" Starck hears himself say, his voice hollow, almost to the point where he doesn't recognize it. "Michael, what happened to him?"

Michael's shoulders and arms drop limply, as if his body has suddenly decided to shut down. The only part of him still moving is his hands. They open and close, open and close.

"Crane planted a mirror down there. He sent Tom in during the trial, and he attacked them. Sunni, he . . . he didn't make it."

The final words hit Starck like a physical blow, and he has to grab the railing of the stairs to keep from collapsing.

"Maybe you should—" Michael begins, but before he can finish, Starck has already pushed past him. He stomps down the stairs and out onto the polished marble tiles of the passage . . . which right now feel like the slick deck of a ship in a rainstorm.

78

Is it enough? If this is all I can hope to achieve by reaching the mansion . . . will it be enough?

Michael's own thought leaves a bitter taste in his mouth, but as he stands there watching Starck cradle Sunni's lifeless body in his arms, he can't shake it. Ever since that day in front of the mural in Elias' backyard, when it first dawned on him that he might get the chance to hold Benjamin again, he has longed for it to happen—no matter what condition he might find him in. Yet now, seeing Starck pull his lips back in a silent scream, he's no longer so sure.

The grief over losing Sunni will hit himself soon enough—his background in psychology assures him of that. But right now, he's paralyzed by the shock. The only thing he can think about is Benjamin.

Something gently touches his clenched hand. He half-opens it, letting Lisa's fingers slip into the space between his thumb and forefinger. She has moved up beside him without him noticing, and now she rests her head against his shoulder.

"It's my fault," Starck mutters, gazing up at them from his

spot on the floor. His face looks ancient and desolate. It pains Michael's heart, yet he has no idea what to do about it.

The echo of Starck's words hang in the air for a while as his tormented gaze shifts back and forth between the boy's face and the hole in the corner. It's like he still can't grasp how the two are connected. Then, suddenly, his expression turns grave.

"We're taking his ashes with us to Heriotza when we continue our journey," he says. "It's what Elias would have wanted."

He pauses again, his gaze drifting once more to the hole in the corner where Anton's mirror still lies, glinting like a small pool of mercury.

"And we *will* continue the journey," he says at last. "I swear I'll keep my promise and do everything in my power to make sure you both reach the mansion."

"We know," Michael says.

Starck nods and lowers his gaze to his folded hands as if observing a moment of silence for Sunni. Afterward he leans down, kisses the boy's forehead, and gently runs a hand down over his face. When he looks up again, his eyes are small, wet—and chillingly cold.

"Can you . . . give me a moment?"

"Of course," Michael says, giving Lisa's hand a gentle squeeze to catch her attention. Once he has it, he nods toward the door, signaling for her to come with him. Lisa follows without protest, and without words.

After stepping out into the hallway and closing the door behind them, Michael and Lisa sit down next to each other on the floor—both with their backs pressed against the icy stone wall and both with their faces buried in their hands.

And then, all of a sudden, the last of Lisa's inner resolve seems to crumble. She curls up, clutching Michael's arm so tightly it hurts.

"It's not fair," she sobs into his shoulder, her voice so weak and muddy he can barely make out the words. "Sunni never did anything to them."

"I know," he says, pulling her closer. But once again, he is ashamed to discover that it's not Sunni's unjust fate he's thinking about. It's Benjamin's.

"And Starck, he . . . oh God, did you see him?"

Michael takes a deep breath and nods. He knows exactly what she means. The shock and grief twisted Starck's face almost beyond recognition . . . but it was more than that. The look he gave them was deeply unsettling. Not only was it stripped of the stoic calm that has defined the librarian so far—it was dangerously close to the irrational, hateful stare that was in the eyes of the man who is now lying lifeless on the floor in there.

Somewhere above them—maybe in the main passage of the council headquarters—a sound breaks out, making them both flinch; a sharp, vibrating tone that reverberates through the narrow basement corridor. The unmistakable sound of a brass instrument.

"They're about to close the ring," Michael says, turning his wrist so Lisa can see the time on his watch. "Nine o'clock. They're beginning the invasion of Tagoanan now."

"Should we tell him?"

Michael looks over at the door, then shakes his head.

"In the state he's in, I don't think it's a good idea to—"

No further does he get before a distressing premonition rolls through him, urging him to jump to his feet.

"What's the matter?" Lisa exclaims, but Michael has already ripped the door open and dashed into the room to find Starck.

Except that Starck—as expected—isn't there anymore.

"Where is he?"

"Tagoanan," Michael says, slamming his hand down on the stone table. "He went after Crane without us. That's why he sent us out. Fuck!"

The table takes another blow—this one so hard that the air pressure pushes a few of the parchment sheets onto the floor. One of them flutters in an uneven arc through the air and lands just a few inches from the hole where Anton's mirror still lies. Michael follows it; first with his eyes, then with his feet.

"What are you doing?" Lisa asks.

"Going after him," Michael says as he bends down to pick up the mirror. However, he barely brushes the edge of the frame before Lisa grabs his forearm and yanks him backward.

"No," she says, her voice just as shrill and panicked as it was the night the maulwert paid them a visit. "Not the mirror."

"But we have to—"

"I know, and I'm with you. Just . . . not the mirror, Michael. Anything but the mirror!"

Michael pulls his arm back and turns to ask what she suggests they do instead—but the question is redundant.

For the answer is given once his eyes meet hers.

They've started to glow.

79

Did you screw it up, Tom? Crane thinks as he returns to the mirror on his desk for the fourth time. *Was a little boy and a teenage girl too much for you to handle?*

It's been over two hours since the jabbering vagabond left, and still—nothing. Every time Crane comes in here, he's greeted by his own pale reflection in the mirror's glass. No Tom.

Sure, he could take a quick trip over there and see for himself —but that would be playing with fire. As unlikely as it seems, it's not impossible that one of the mindless amoebas on the council's payroll has found the mirror. They might even—in a rare moment of elevated thought—have set a trap for him. And he has no intention of walking into that if he can avoid it.

So once again, Crane has to pound the desk and swallow his frustration while the town hall bells of Tagoanan add insult to injury with their chiming from the tower above. They remind him that time keeps merrily ticking on while he trudges up here every half hour to stare at his own damned face—which looks more and more infuriated with each visit.

Nine chimes ring out, and as the echoes fade, he rises from

the desk to head toward the window. However, he only makes it a few steps before a sudden, intense migraine hits him, darkening his vision.

They can't be serious, he thinks, staggering over and bracing himself against the window frame. *They wouldn't dare!*

Even though this particular stabbing in his temples is a sensation he has never felt before, Crane has no doubt what it means. The mirrors are being shut down, and they're screaming at him, their voices painting a picture of children trapped in a burning building.

He has a terrible premonition, and as he lifts his gaze to the window, it's instantly confirmed. In the street below, he sees people—his own people—running toward the town hall, arms flailing wildly. Beyond them, far past the town limits, a wide, dark shape emerges. It stretches like a belt across the sandy plain that separates the city from the mountains on the horizon. A belt of people, tightening slowly but surely.

Beads of sweat break across his brow, and the blue veins in his temples pulse like ticking clocks as his fingernails dig into the rubber lining beneath the windowpane. Oh, how he has underestimated Starck—and now the council has brought the war to *him*.

Somewhere below, the sound of a door being thrown open is followed by footsteps and frantic voices as the first cluster of people from the street bursts into the entry hall. It sounds like someone let loose a flock of squawking hens down there.

He spins around sharply and strides toward the door, his mind already crafting the speech he's going to give them. He plans to pour everything he has into igniting their hatred. And once it's burning at full force in their veins, he'll send them out to fight. Most likely, they won't stand a chance against the council's army—but at least it'll buy him time to get off the sinking ship.

With this plan in mind, Crane places his hand on the door handle. He presses it halfway down—but then stops, realizing he just caught something out of the corner of his eye as he passed the desk.

A flash of light. From the mirror.

"Hello, Dan," sounds behind him—and though Crane hasn't heard his old colleague's voice in many years, he recognizes it instantly.

"Hello, Erik."

80

When Michael comes out the other side, it takes time for him to gather himself. His world is silent and wrapped in a dizzying white haze, while Starck scolds Lisa for following him. He also misses it when the librarian turns his attention back to Crane to tell him it's over—that there's nowhere left to run.

The first thing Michael really registers is Crane's sharp, mocking laughter when Lisa tells him he should have left Sunni alone. That laughter cuts through the fog—and Crane's next words clear it away completely.

"That's where you're wrong, girl," he says. "*You* should have kept the boy out of it. You're the ones who dragged that poor kid into this!"

Michael looks—first at Starck and Lisa to gauge their reactions, then around the room to get a sense of his surroundings.

It's a large room, an office judging by the furniture—and with rooftops visible through the window, they must be on the second or third floor. There's noise below them—the sound of panic and chaos. That's a good sign. It likely means they're in Tagoanan, and that the invasion is going according to plan.

Another good sign is the look in Crane's eyes. Mocking grin or not, those black eyes dart anxiously from side to side. He's cornered, and he knows it. Even though they're at least ten feet away from him, and he's closest to the door, there's three of them while he is alone. Not good odds.

"I'll offer you a choice," Starck says, his voice—much to Michael's relief—far more controlled than it was when he held Sunni's lifeless body in his arms. "You've felt it, haven't you? Your escape routes being cut off?"

"There was a little something tapping at the back of my head earlier, yes," Crane admits. He keeps smiling—but only with his mouth.

"With the mirrors out of the picture, you've got nowhere left to run. But this doesn't have to get any worse. Surrender now and let us take you to the council. Face your punishment—and your people won't have to suffer needlessly."

"*My* punishment?" Crane snarls through clenched teeth. "You *dare* talk to me about *my* punishment? I've served mine—but what about you, Erik? What about *your* punishment, huh? What about the guides punishment? Who is gonna judge *you*?"

"You killed a boy!" Lisa growls, but Starck silences her with a motion of his hand.

"He is right," he says, his gaze shifting from Lisa to Crane. "You're right, Dan. We carry our share of the blame for what happened to Rebecca. If we had stopped her from entering the mansion, maybe things would have turned out differently."

At the sound of his wife's name, Michael notices a shift in Crane's face. His expression hardens, and his eyes go dark.

"We carry our share of blame," Starck repeats. "For Rebecca's disappearance—and for yours. We should have stopped her from entering the mansion before she was ready, and we should have stopped you. But you're wrong if you think we haven't been punished. Everything that's happened since—that's our punishment. All the innocent people who have suffered during your vendetta. What you're feeling right now—the mirrors being shut down—that's part of our punishment too."

"Well, would you look at that," Crane hisses. "Guess the council was right after all. You really *did* lose your fucking mind when you traveled through that mirror."

He glares at Starck with eyes burning with hatred. Above them, a vein writhes like a worm beneath the pale skin of his forehead.

"I've said it before, and I'll say it again!" he continues. "Your punishment isn't served until the day I stand at the peak of Heriotza and see nothing but ashes. You're whining about the fate of the boys? Hell, I'd sacrifice a hundred more for this cause!"

It takes a few seconds for the word to fully register in Michael's mind—but when it does, it hits him like a punch to the gut.

Crane said *the fate of the boys*. Not *the boy*. *The boys*. Plural.

It doesn't have to mean anything, he tries to tell himself. Crane's crusade could easily have affected many innocent boys over the years.

But then there was the look. The knowing look Crane gave him as he said the word. The one that said: *Yup, we're talking about your son too.*

What happens in the seconds after that realization hits Michael disappears into a blackout. It's like blinking and finding himself somewhere else. One second, he's standing in the middle of the room, some distance from Crane—and the next, he's gripping the pale man's collar, shoving him up against the door.

"WHERE IS MY SON?" he hears himself roar through the

thunder of his pulse pounding in his ears. "WHAT DID YOU DO TO HIM?"

"This is the guy you're hoping to get ready for the mansion?" Crane gasps, rising on his toes to catch Starck's eye over Michael's shoulder. "Good luck. You'll need it."

Standing there, Michael is struck by a sense of disbelief. Even now—disarmed, with no way out—there's not a trace of surrender in Crane's eyes. They're still filled with the same inappropriate glee that was glowing in them the day he showed up at Michael's door wearing a police uniform.

That was the first time they stood face-to-face—and Michael remembers thinking the same thing then as he does now:

He is enjoying this. He takes pleasure in watching me suffer.

As if to underline this thought, the excitement in Crane's eyes spreads to the rest of his face as he leans in close to Michael's ear.

"It's not too late," he whispers. "You can still make it. Search your heart, and you know I'm right."

"Shut the fuck up."

"All you have to do is help me get out of here."

A sharp crack fills the room as Michael drives his fist into Crane's chin—and for a second, there's silence. Then the pale man slowly lifts his head, blood trickling from the corner of his mouth—but he's still sporting that fucking smile.

"In return, I can get you to the mansion in a split second," he says. "Get you some answers."

Michael glances toward the window and feels an overwhelming urge to drag the pale man over there and hurl him through the glass, so the pavement below will shut his mouth once and for all. And kill the temptation to listen to his words.

"Don't listen to him," Starck says, after which he turns to Crane. "Maybe you should save your voice and start thinking about whether *you're* ready for what's waiting when we send you to Soto."

As he speaks, Starck takes a step to the side, widening the gap between himself and Lisa, clearing a path to the mirror on the desk. Subsequently, with a calm, sweeping motion, he gestures toward it with his hand.

"You're offering me the front seat?" Crane's smile doesn't fade, but there's a flicker of uncertainty in his voice. "Why?"

"Irony of fate, isn't it?" Starck says with a shrug. "The only safe mirror left is the one *you* planted in the basement beneath the council's headquarters . . . which, right now, happens to be the most heavily guarded place in all of Urari."

What are you doing, Starck? Michael thinks. *There weren't any guards there when we left—and you know that. If we give him a head start, he'll use it.*

He glances at Lisa, who clearly shares his concern. She keeps shifting her weight nervously from foot to foot as if she wants to say something—but when she finally draws a breath and looks at Starck, her gaze immediately drops to the floor. Something in his expression ordered her to keep the question to herself.

Turning his head and receiving the same look, Michael realizes it wasn't an order. It was a question, written so clearly in the librarian's brown eyes that it almost feels like telepathy.

Do you trust me?

Michael feels paralyzed. The wording is different, but at its core, it's the same question Crane has asked him over and over again.

What if you can't trust him?

As if to remind him that he doesn't have all day to dwell on it, he hears the sound of footsteps and voices approaching. Crane's people are looking for him—and if they're not on this floor already, they will be soon.

What if he's just using you for his own agenda? Are you really willing to gamble with your son's life like that?

Since the nightmare at Elias and Mary's house, those words have resurfaced in Michael's mind several times—and back when Starck suggested postponing their journey, Michael found himself seriously wondering whether Starck was really there for Benjamin's sake. But now, when it's time to make the choice, he realizes it's the wrong question. Starck isn't here for Benjamin . . . but that was never his job.

He is here for me. He is here to take me to the Mansion of Mirrors. That's his task, and it's all he ever promised me.

With that in mind, Michael slowly releases his grip on Crane's collar and takes a step back.

"Really?" Crane says, rubbing his neck and wincing. "It's a one-time offer. You won't get another chance."

Michael doesn't answer. He simply lowers his gaze to the floor.

Crane shrugs, then edges past him and walks to the desk, where Starck pulls the chair out for him.

Before taking his seat, Crane bends forward in a mock bow, as if thanking them. When that gets no real reaction, he shrugs, sits down, and locks his gaze on the mirror.

Moments later, a sharp flash of white light bursts from the mirror. When it fades, the only trace of Crane is a silvery afterglow hovering above the empty chair—like specks of dust in a beam of sunlight.

And while that, too, fades, Starck turns to face Michael.

"How did you do it? How did you find me?"

Michael shrugs and glances over at Lisa, silently passing the question to her.

"I . . . I don't really know," she says. "I just *thought* about you, I guess. That we wanted to find you, and then . . . then, all of a sudden, we were here. And if you're about to yell at us again for following you, I'm not even gonna—"

"I'm not going to yell at you," Starck says with a sigh. "But you need to be careful. You got lucky this time, but you could just as easily have ended up somewhere entirely different."

At those last words, Starck's gaze drifts down to the mirror where it lingers for a while. His eyes are heavy with sadness and exhaustion. Part of it is because of Sunni, Michael thinks, but not all of it.

"He didn't go to Soto, did he?" Lisa asks.

Starck shakes his head.

"He went to the mansion," Michael says. "That's why you let him go first."

Starck looks up at him and nods.

"He thinks it's the easy way out, because it's the one place he's sure I won't follow him. But . . . he'll smarten up real soon."

Starck doesn't offer any further explanation—but he doesn't need to either. For even though much about this mysterious other world still escapes Michael and Lisa, they've come to understand one thing:

There is no easy path to the Mansion of Mirrors—and if your mind isn't ready, the demons of the Devil's Glass will punish you severely.

PART TEN
THE WASTELAND

81

When Michael, Lisa, and Starck come back to Soto the next morning, they also come back to the pain of Sunni's unjust death. They handle it in different ways, but what they all share is that they do it in silence.

Lisa copes with her grief by channeling it into physical work —specifically by working like a madman to clean the room where the Guide Trial took place.

Systematically, and with an almost manic look in her eyes, she gathers parchment, oil pastels, and pieces of Sunni's Guide Mirror from the floor, stacks them neatly and returns them to the built-in shelf in the wall. Later, she gets some of the guards to remove Tom's body and bring her a towel and a bucket of soapy water, which she uses to scrub the bloodstain off the floor.

When there's no more blood left to scrub, she finds a new project at the hole in the corner. She kneels down and starts putting the tiles back in place. It's as though she believes that covering the hole will somehow turn back time, making it so that Tom never came through it.

At first, Michael helped her—but before long, it became too much for him, and he left the room. Since then, he has been spending the morning and early afternoon walking the streets of Soto while a steady current of grief, worry, and guilt flows through his mind in time with the waters of the city's canal network.

As for Starck, his actions are guided by one all-consuming thought. He wants to make sure Sunni gets the burial Elias and Mary would have wanted for him. Therefore, he spends the early morning hours sitting in a chair beside the bed where Sunni now lies, covered by a blanket. And then, as soon as the clock strikes eight—the hour when the crematorium opens its doors—he gets up and gently lifts the boy.

With Sunni's lifeless body wrapped in a blanket in his arms, he walks all the way from the council buildings to Avenida Negra in the southern part of Soto, where the crematorium is located. The heaviest steps he has taken in his life.

When he arrives, he is greeted by an older gentleman in a suit who, for a brief moment, stiffens at the sight of the boy in Starck's arms—but then regains his composure and adopts a professional, respectful expression.

The exchange between the two men is minimal. The undertaker asks the questions he has to ask, and Starck gives the answers he has to give.

Once Starck has pressed his lips to Sunni's cold forehead one final time and whispered his last goodbye into his ear, the undertaker gently lays the boy's body on a wheeled stretcher and covers him with a blanket.

Before rolling the stretcher down to the basement furnace, the undertaker tells Starck he'll send word when it's done. Starck shakes his head and says that he'd rather wait there.

The undertaker considers this for a moment, then finally nods and motions toward an armchair in one of the corners.

Surrounded by urns and coffins, and wrapped in remorse, Starck sits on the edge of that chair, asking himself if he did the right thing. If Elias' and Sunni's lives were too steep a price to pay for the victory over Crane. If he could have done it differently and kept them out of it. And whether Sunni might still be alive if it had been *him*, and not Elias, who stepped out to refuel the car at the gas station. Would the outcome have been the same if *he* had been the one injured, the one to sacrifice his life for theirs? And if so, would Elias have refused to bring Anton along—thus stopping the chain of events that ultimately led to Sunni's death?

An eternity later, the undertaker returns from the basement.

"My condolences," he says as he hands the urn containing Sunni's ashes to Starck. "He was too young."

Starck looks down at the urn and nods. He's not able to answer with words. It's as if the cold from the urn's silver base is crawling up through his body, tightening his airways and stealing his breath.

He starts to turn away, but the undertaker gently grabs his arm.

"Just one more thing before you go."

"Oh right, the payment," Starck says. "I'm so sorry. In all the confusion, I forgot."

"Yes, there's that too," the undertaker says with a shrug. "But it's not what I meant."

He rummages through the pocket of his vest and pulls out a small, crumpled ball of paper, which he hands to Starck.

"I found this in the boy's hand and thought that you might want it."

Starck takes the ball, turns it slowly between his fingers, and then unfolds it.

"I'm guessing the boy made that," the undertaker says, and before Starck can reply, he adds, "He was very talented."

Starck looks down at the paper and nods.

"If you only knew."

82

In light of Sunni's death, Michael would have forgiven Starck if he had broken his promise and delayed the journey another day or two. In fact, he even thought about suggesting it himself, because he knows how much the boy meant to Starck.

However, now that they're back on the road, he's glad he didn't say anything—because in many ways, it's a relief to say goodbye to Soto, where they were caught in a strange gray area between grieving Sunni's death and being treated like royalty by the people of the city.

The invasion of Tagoanan was a success, and naturally, Soto's citizens wanted to celebrate them for it. In their eyes, they're heroes, and everywhere they went, they were met with grateful smiles. The only problem was that they were hardly able to return those smiles.

They meant well, Lisa said as they crossed the southern bridge, leaving the city walls behind—and Michael and Starck agreed that it was a very diplomatic way to put it.

Four hours and many silent miles have passed since she said that. In that time, their shared focus has gradually turned toward the huge, dark-gray silhouette of Mount Heriotza, rising high above the southeastern horizon.

Since it's where Sunni's ashes are to be scattered, that mountain will be their next stop, but it's also where their journey to the mansion truly begins. For Mount Heriotza sits on the edge of the Wasteland—and once they pass it, there will be no more roads to drive on. From there, the rest of the journey must be made on foot.

As he sits in the front seat, listening to the constant hum of the car's heater, it strikes Michael that he's been staring at the mountain for quite a while now—without it seeming to get any closer.

"Will we get there before sunset?" he asks.

Starck, who has sunk into a trance-like state, blinks and shakes his head.

"I'm hoping we'll be able to make camp before nightfall, but it might be a bit optimistic."

"Do we have to go all the way to the top?" Lisa asks from the back seat. "I mean . . . I'm fine with it, if we are. I'm just—"

"I know what you mean," Starck says, offering her a tired smile. "And no, we're not going *all* the way up—just a few hundred yards. There is a memorial site on a ledge where people write the name of the deceased and maybe a few words, before scattering the ashes."

"I hate funerals," Lisa says.

Michael nods and turns his face toward the side window while he thinks back on how powerless he felt as Benjamin's tiny coffin was lowered into the ground. The only thing he can think of that surpasses that feeling is the despair he feels now.

Now that he is no longer sure it was even his son in that coffin.

83

The landscape surrounding Heriotza has a particular, rough beauty that the three travelers don't really see until they open their eyes the next morning. The sun had set by the time they made camp at the mountain's base the night before, and the faint light from their campfire didn't do much justice to the surroundings.

Now, however, they've reached the end of the trail leading up to the memorial site, and there's no longer any doubt as to why Heriotza was chosen as the final resting place for Urari's dead. The view is breathtaking, offering a contrast in the divided landscape that seems to capture the fragile balance between life and death.

To their left, several miles away, is the shimmering surface of a river. Birds circle above it in large flocks, and every so often, one folds its wings and dives—no doubt hunting for fish. Farther ahead, the river winds through a lush, green forest. There's *life* in that direction—untouched nature and vibrant wildlife.

However, turning one's gaze to the right is an entirely different experience. On that side of the mountain, the landscape is a parched, rocky expanse that seems to stretch endlessly. It is broken only by a few patches of withered vegetation, swaying alone and lifeless in the desert wind.

That same wind tousles Starck's silver hair as he steps onto the cliff ledge at the end of the trail. He is the first to set foot on the memorial site, and he does so with a reverence that makes the hairs on the back of Lisa's neck stand on end.

How many times has he done this before? she wonders. *How many of the names on that wall belonged to his friends?*

That wall is the rear face of the ledge. It serves as a sort of memorial tablet for the dead. A massive tombstone with not only one, but hundreds of faceless names.

As Lisa stands there, letting her gaze drift across the wall, Starck gently reaches a hand into her line of sight. In it, he holds a stick of oil pastel. She looks down at it—and freezes as she realizes what it is.

"I can't," she whispers . . . yet she still takes the pastel and walks over to the wall. Once there, she finds an empty space in a small, crescent-shaped recess. There, she writes the boy's name in the neatest handwriting her trembling hand can manage. Afterward, she glances back at Starck, who nods his approval.

The sight of him makes her heart sink. He's standing at the edge of the cliff, the eyes in his weathered face brimming with tears. His hands are clutching the urn with Sunni's ashes to his chest as if it were an infant.

At his side, Michael stands, silently staring out at the parched desert landscape to the west. Somewhere out there, a crow lets out a hoarse cry.

Without a word, Lisa walks over and joins them. Standing there, she quietly slips her hand into Michael's. The other hand she places gently on Starck's back. Beneath the rough fabric of his shirt, she can feel the muscles around his shoulder blades tremble as he loosens the urn's lid.

Once the lid is off, he lets out a deep sigh and closes his eyes. Then he tilts the urn, letting the wind carry away the ashes.

"I got something from the undertaker," Starck says once the silent ritual is over. "Something that I believe is meant for you, Lisa."

As he speaks, he slips his fingers into the breast pocket of his shirt and pulls out a crumpled piece of parchment. He looks at it with sad eyes, then hands it to Lisa.

"I've been waiting for the right moment. I think this is it."

"Is this . . .?" Lisa looks down at the paper and swallows hard.

"It's Sunni's last picture," Starck replies. "It was in his hand. I think he was protecting it, so you could have it."

Slowly, Lisa unfolds the paper. It feels so brittle, as if the slightest wrong touch might turn it to dust in the wind.

"I don't know what it means," Starck says as the image comes into view. "But something tells me you might."

The drawing shows the slanted surface of a podium, seen from the speaker's perspective. At the edge of the panel, a small black microphone is mounted—one that, for some reason, feels eerily intimidating to Lisa. Part of the reason lies in the image's upper section being unfinished, leaving the crowd seated in front of the podium faceless. Another part lies in the fact that Lisa— even though she's never stood there herself—knows exactly where that podium is.

"It's the auditorium at my school," she says, confused. "Why did he paint that?"

She tilts the paper from side to side, hoping that it might reveal some hidden message. When that doesn't work, she passes the paper to Michael.

"This *is* from Oakwood, right?"

Michael studies the paper with narrowed eyes for a moment, then nods.

"I'd say so, yeah."

"Why would he paint that?"

"Beats me," Michael says, handing it back to her.

"Give it time," Starck says. "It'll probably come to you on its own. Are you coming?"

Lisa turns around—and nearly drops her jaw when she spots the librarian.

He has made his way back to the trail they came in on. There, he is standing, hands on his hips, one foot resting on a large rock. The backpack is back on his shoulders. His eyes are still wet, but aside from that, the broken man they've traveled with for the last twenty-four hours seems to have vanished along with the ashes on the wind.

What amount of willpower it must take to set aside one's grief like that, Lisa can't even begin to fathom.

She glances at Michael, who looks just as stunned as she feels. Then they both get to their feet and sling their own backpacks over their shoulders.

"Yeah, we . . . we're coming."

84

It's no wonder the area south of Heriotza is called the Wasteland. They're walking through the overgrown remains of a long-dead forest; a barren zone of toppled trees and wild, tangled shrubs that claw at their ankles, trying to tear their shoes off.

On top of that, the terrain is constantly rising, and when Michael looks back toward the base of Heriotza, the withered forest vanishes downward in shadowed layers, making it resemble a giant staircase.

"Why do you keep doing that?" Lisa asks him as they stop for a sip of water.

"Doing what?"

"Looking down there," she says, tipping the half-empty water bottle in her hands to point down toward the mountain.

"I'm just wondering about it," Michael replies with a shrug. "Feels like we've been walking forever, but the mountain doesn't seem to be getting any smaller."

"Well, it's not getting any smaller with you two standing there chit-chatting, that's for sure," Starck's voice says from farther ahead. "At the pace you're setting, we'll be making camp in this crap!"

To emphasize just how crappy the crap is, he stomps on a thorny branch that has latched on to the cuff of his pants—but the only thing that brilliant move accomplishes is that it drags three more of its kind with it. They whip up and grab hold just above his knee.

Grimacing and swearing, he yanks them free with a sharp tug.

"Maybe you could learn a thing or two from our pace," Lisa calls back. "Doesn't look like your strategy's working out too well."

"Oh, zip it," Starck grumbles. "Just get a move on, will ya?"

Michael turns to tell Lisa she might want to ease up on the teasing—but she's no longer beside him. She has slung her backpack over her shoulder and is marching uphill toward Starck.

Her pace has quickened, eyes locked on the ground, and when she glances back, he sees that the smile on her lips has been replaced by a tormented expression. At first, he figures it must've been Starck's threat about spending the night in this eerie, dead forest that wiped it away—but then it hits him what the real reason must be.

"Lisa!" he calls out, trudging after her. "Lisa, wait up!"

Even though she must have heard him, she doesn't answer . . . which only confirms his suspicion and makes him walk faster.

As he catches up to her, he reaches out and grabs her arm—not hard, but firmly enough to make her stop.

She stares at him, and the look in her eyes makes him pull his hand back, as if he'd touched something hot.

"It doesn't make you a bad person," he says. "You know that, right?"

"What do you mean?"

"You, smiling just now," he says. "That you smiled and made a joke, even though we just said goodbye to Sunni. It doesn't mean that you're a bad person."

"How did you . . .?" she begins, but then her lips start to quiver, and her gaze drops back to the ground.

"I knew because it's a completely normal reaction," Michael says. "And because I've felt that way too."

Lisa stares at him, her mouth trembling. She says nothing, but her eyes speak for her—and Michael has no trouble understanding the question they're asking.

"I think the key is to stay focused on the goal," he says. "And I think yours must be to figure out what Sunni was trying to tell you with that drawing. If you're meant to enter the mansion, then that has to be the key to making it out safely."

Lisa's thin eyebrows draw together, and for a while, she says nothing. Her face holds a strange, thoughtful expression that slowly shifts into the faintest hint of a smile.

"Focus on the goal, huh?" she says.

"Focus on the goal," Michael repeats, nodding.

"Three years of psychology at university, and *focus on the goal* is the best you've got?"

"Five years, actually," Michael replies, reaching his hand out to her.

She stares at it for a moment, then nods and takes it.

85

He doesn't know, but Michael's words linger in Lisa's mind for the rest of the afternoon and evening. Not the part about staying focused on the goal, though that did make sense to her. But no, the words she can't stop thinking about are the ones he said right after.

If you're meant to enter the mansion, then Sunni's drawing has to be the key to making it out safely.

She is, of course, aware that the intended message was in the second half of the sentence—but it's the first half that keeps haunting her.

If you're meant to enter to the mansion.

Right from the start, Starck has been under the assumption that her destination is the Mansion of Mirrors, and she has had no reason to question it. Thrown into something she didn't understand, his focused approach gave her something solid to cling to. It has saved her more than once—and for that, she owes him her gratitude. Nevertheless, the more she thinks about it, the more she begins to doubt that the mansion is the right answer for her.

Several times throughout the day, she has been on the verge of sharing this thought with the others, but each time, she has changed her mind at the last second.

She has tried to convince herself it's the fear of their reaction that makes her postpone it. That she couldn't bear it if they were disappointed—or maybe even got angry—if she chooses to back out now, after everything they've been through.

She's especially afraid that Michael will feel abandoned if she doesn't follow him all the way to the mansion. Starck has already made it clear that guides can't go inside—and if she opts out now, it'll mean that Michael won't just be alone when he steps through the gates. He'll be alone with whatever he finds in there too. And that thought weighs heavily on her conscience.

On the surface, that's how Lisa justifies it to herself each time she builds up the courage to inform the others—only to tuck her tail between her legs before the words ever cross her lips. Yet, in her heart, she knows there's another reason too. She might not be able to put it into words, but deep down she realizes that something else is making her postpone it. Something external. Something tied to the strong urge to see the mansion that she has felt ever since they crossed into the Wasteland. An urge that grows more insistent with every step she takes.

Michael feels it too. She has seen it gleaming in his eyes all day—and she sees it now too as he sits across from her on the other side of the fire, legs crossed.

Except that, for him, it's more than just an urge. It has become an obsession. He'd sooner die than give up the mansion . . . and if she doesn't make her decision soon, she's afraid she might start to share that mindset.

"Oh, you're still awake? You were both so quiet, I almost thought you'd fallen asleep."

It's Starck. He left the campsite about fifteen minutes ago and now returns with a fresh stack of firewood, which he tosses onto the fire.

"We're awake," Michael says. "Just barely, though."

Starck plants his hands on his hips and gives them a smile that, with the light and shadows from the fire dancing across his face, looks more unnerving than friendly.

"That's understandable," he says. "We've been making good time. Honestly, I didn't think we'd reach this clearing before sunset."

"Clearing?" Michael says, glancing around. "That's a pretty generous word. Except for the trees, it looks to me like the same thorny shit we've been trudging through all day."

The trees he's referring to are a line of thin-trunked Joshua trees standing in a rough semicircle to their left, toward the east —all of which carry a sickly gray hue that makes them look just as lifeless as the rest of the toppled trees in the dead zone.

"Is the whole trip going to be like this?" Lisa asks, holding up her forearm where a particularly nasty thorn has left a long scratch from elbow to wrist.

Starck shrugs and gives her a smile she's not entirely thrilled about.

"The first few days might leave you with a few scrapes here and there," he says. "But hopefully that's all."

He looks at her for a moment as if he has something more to add—but then leans back in silence.

That's fine, Lisa thinks, catching a brief mental image of the Spindle card with the yellow-eyed Fenris wolf. *If this is just the gentle start, then I don't need you to go into more details right now.*

"At the risk of sounding like an impatient kid," Michael says. "When will we get there?"

Starck, who doesn't seem the least bit surprised by the question, nods and rubs his cheek.

"Yeah, I was wondering when you'd work up to asking outright," he says. "The answer is that if we keep a steady pace, we'll get to the mansion in about a week. That doesn't mean we'll have reached the finish line, though."

"You don't need to say it again. I think we got the message," Michael sighs, shooting Lisa a look as his lips silently mouth the words: *You have to be ready.*

Lisa, who finds this behavior childish, and rather unbecoming, pretends not to see it and keeps staring indifferently into the flames. She doesn't like the defiant tone in Michael's voice—and she especially doesn't like what she believes she hears in it.

You say you got the message, she thinks. *But to me, it sounds like the only part you're hearing is that we'll reach the mansion in about a week.*

86

Three days later, the travelers—hot, sweaty, and exhausted—push their way through the particularly vicious tangle of shrubs and saplings that mark the end of the dead forest.

Beneath them, the forest's gray soil has given way to a moss-like undergrowth, and the terrain is starting to slope down into a valley that runs like a rocky trough between two grassy hillsides.

To the south, beyond the valley, the land swells into a series of bleak ridges and rocky outcrops which would dishearten most trekkers. Still, for now, there's good reason to be hopeful, because between the rocks on the valley floor, a stream of water trickles—and water means wildlife.

With a bit of luck, we'll be eating a lot better tonight, Starck thinks as his fingers drift up to the leather strap holding the weapon on his shoulder. He would have preferred his old rifle, but he is thankful that the council let him pick a new one from the armory. Even if it's a smaller caliber than the one he gave to Elias. *A good meal would do wonders for the morale.*

The air is cleaner here, and before he leads them onward, he takes a deep breath, clearing both his lungs and his thoughts.

He is worried about his companions. He has seen that distant, feverish look in other eyes before—the look that Michael now carries—and it's rarely a good sign. The mansion has infected the young man's mind, and Starck can only hope there's enough willpower and reason left in there to keep it in check.

Lisa is burdened by something too. Most of the time, she walks by herself some distance behind the others, speaking only when spoken to. Obviously, the draining effect of the mansion is part of it, but Starck doesn't believe it's the main cause. Something is going on behind those tired, green eyes. She is struggling with something. What, he doesn't know. He can only hope she'll open up and share it before he is forced to ask.

"Look up there," he whispers, pointing to the sky where a flock of birds circles over the valley. "If we move slowly and don't make too much noise, we might have something other than canned food on the menu tonight."

"As long as it doesn't put us behind schedule," Michael grumbles.

"It won't," Lisa quickly says, thus saving Starck from delivering a snide remark he might later regret. "We're running out of canned food anyway, and then we'll have to start foraging . . . and I don't think there are many places out there with better odds than here."

To clarify what she means by *out there*, she points toward the rough terrain on the far side of the valley.

Michael's eyes flicker, first in the direction she's pointing, then back to her. The aggravation in his gaze is obvious, but Lisa doesn't back down. Her arm stays raised, and it doesn't lower until he finally gives in and nods.

Starck watches this brief, wordless exchange, thinking—not without admiration—that the girl can be awfully stubborn when she wants to be.

With her victory in hand and Michael trailing behind her, Lisa starts moving again. As they descend the slope, Starck begins scanning for a hunting blind. The open terrain limits their options, but he does spot a place beneath the gnarled roots of an old pine tree that leans out over a hollow at the far end of the valley.

87

You can't seriously be surprised, Lisa tells herself as the first members of the flock land on the opposite bank of the rocky stream. *With everything you've learned about this place, you didn't seriously expect them to be ordinary birds, did you?*

From their makeshift hunting blind beneath the gnarled roots of the pine, they have been watching these grayish-brown creatures for quite a while now—and in Lisa's defense, they actually did look like ordinary birds when they were circling the sky, backlit by the sun.

Up close, though, that illusion shatters—because these birds are massive. Far larger than any bird Lisa has ever seen. Their wingspans must stretch eight, maybe nine feet. They kind of look like oversized vultures, with hooked predator beaks and that same cowardly, hopping gait she has seen in nature documentaries about the hunched scavengers.

Like vultures, they wear a scruffy collar of white feathers around their necks—but on their chests, just below the collar, is a bare, heart-shaped patch of scaly skin, more reminiscent of reptiles than birds of prey.

She flinches when one of the winged nightmare-creatures suddenly stretches its long neck toward the sky and lets out an atonal screech that burrows into her teeth as well as her ears.

The shriek is followed by chattering from above and then the dry flap of wings as the rest of the flock joins the frontrunners. A few land on the large rocks in the middle of the stream, but the majority settles in the grass along the bank. There they sit in an uneven line, squealing and twitching their narrow heads as though having a secret conversation.

"They wouldn't like . . . attack us, would they?" Lisa whispers as Starck raises the rifle to his shoulder and takes aim.

He turns his eyes toward her, looking over the rifle's stock with a gaze that leaves no room for misunderstanding.

"Oh, sorry," she whispers, holding her hands up in front of her. "I'll be quiet."

At that very moment, one of the birds starts slamming its wings against the ground, letting out a series of sharp, nasal cries. Others join in, and soon the entire valley echoes with the flock's panicked shrieking.

Lisa's first thought is that her voice startled them. Then she sees the real reason. Something has been hiding in the heather-like brush at the far end of the rocky trough. Something that now leaps out and charges across the landscape at astounding speed —straight toward the birds.

The flock's members see the wolf-like creature coming and take off almost simultaneously, but in their blind panic, several of them crash into each other and tumble back to the ground.

For one of the birds, this mistake is fatal. It lands on its back, one wing folded underneath it—and before it gets a chance to right itself, the wolf-creature has sunk a terrifying set of teeth into its throat.

It has to be her imagination, but Lisa is certain that through the screeching and flapping, she hears the sound of its neck snapping. Loud and clear in her head; the sound of a dry branch being broken in two.

The beast shakes the bird's limp body from side to side, making sure it's finished, then drops it on the ground. Next, it rises onto its hind legs in an unsettlingly human posture, its yellow eyes darting back and forth among the surviving birds as if to warn them not to get any ideas.

As it stands there, hunched over its prey, Lisa recognizes the wolf-like creature. It's not quite as tall as she had imagined, but there's no mistaking its features. Half-human, half-wolf. Just like the one she saw on the Spindle card back at Mary and Elias' house.

Fenris.

A scream builds inside her, and she instinctively clamps her hands over her mouth, trying to smother it. But it wants out. There is nothing she can do to stop it—and when it does come, the valley falls eerily silent. The dry, flapping sound of bird wings dies out. Even the wind that has been making the grass whisper all afternoon seems to fade.

The wolf is quiet too. It's standing there with its pointy ears flattened against its head as it sniffs the air.

"It knows we're here," Starck whispers. "Whatever you do, stay still. If it decides we're not a threat, it might—"

Before he can finish his sentence, the beast bares its teeth and turns its glowing eyes directly toward their hiding spot beneath the gnarled roots of the old pine tree.

Then it charges.

The blast from Starck's rifle is deafening in the cramped space beneath the pine, and for a long while, after the first shot has been fired, Lisa isn't able to hear anything. Her eyes, on the other hand, work just fine. They're telling her that the librarian missed his first chance—and that the wolf isn't intimidated by loud noises. It's still coming . . . while Starck is struggling to reload.

His fingers are trembling, and she feels an urge to scream at him to pull himself together—however pointless that would be. The shot has probably flooded his head with the same shrill ringing that's blaring in hers.

He's not gonna make it, she thinks, but at that exact moment, the round slides into place. Now, Starck lifts the barrel and takes aim—just as the wolf lunges toward him.

The gaping jaws are less than three feet from his face when a flash of light bursts from the muzzle, forcing Lisa to shut her eyes. Deafened and blinded, she throws her hands up in front of her face and flings herself backward, bracing for the coming pain.

In the darkness behind her eyelids, she pictures the wolf's sharp teeth sinking into her forearms, twisting them apart to expose her throat.

And then she feels it, tugging at her, trying to pull her arms apart just as she imagined, but . . . the pain never comes?

She opens her eyes and finds Michael's face staring down at her. He is kneeling in front of her, his hands gripping her wrists. Behind him, Starck lies on his back with the wolf's lifeless body draped halfway over his legs like some macabre blanket. Its snout is slick with foam, its vacant gaze fixed on her. It no longer moves, but still, the sight of those yellow eyes sends a shiver through her.

"Lisa?" Michael's voice is muffled and low, like he's speaking with his face buried in a pillow. "Lisa, look at me."

She doesn't catch all the words he says next, but the look of relief on his face tells her everything she needs to know.

That night, they eat well. The wolf's kill becomes theirs, and it turns out that the foul, vulture-like birds taste absolutely fantastic.

After the meal, they stay gathered around the fire, sharing stories as dusk settles over the valley. Whether it's due to the full stomachs or the excitement of still being alive after the encounter with the wolf is hard to say, but the mood is definitely lighter than it has been in a long time. And because of that, Lisa decides the moment has come to tell the others about her decision.

"There's something I'd like to talk to you about," she says, rummaging through her pocket and pulling out the crumpled paper with Sunni's drawing. "I think I've figured out what this means."

Michael says nothing, but Starck—who has just taken a sip of water—puts the bottle down and swallows with an audible click.

"I'm glad to hear that," he says, wiping his lips with the back of his hand. "Do tell."

"Maybe it's stupid," she says. "But I'm starting to think I'm not supposed to go to the mansion at all. I know it's probably not what you want to hear, but I can't keep putting it off. I'm afraid that if I do, it'll end up being too late."

"Listen, Lisa," Michael says. "I get why you're nervous, but we've been through so much, and we're *so* close now."

"Believe me," she replies, "I'm well aware that we're close to the mansion now, and you're right—it *does* make me nervous. I can . . . it sounds crazy, but I can feel it calling to me. It's been like that ever since we stepped into that forest, and it's driving me nuts. Part of me really wants to follow you in there. Heck, I'm pretty sure I wouldn't be able to turn back if I actually laid eyes on it."

She sighs and looks down at the crumpled paper in her hands. For a brief moment, she considers whether she should tell them that the microphone mounted on the podium at the center of the picture frightens her just as much as the mansion. Especially now, when the flickering light from the campfire dances across the paper's creases, making it resemble the head of a snake.

"I've been thinking about it. A lot. I think the problem is that, deep down, I know the mansion's pull is a lie. It's my brain trying to keep me running, just like I have been for the past thirteen months. It's not the idea of being saved, or finding closure for Emma's death, that draws me to the mansion. I know I'd lose my mind if I went in there—and *that's* the tempting part. The idea that I could just go crazy like Tom and never again have to deal with a reality that hurts. So, if there is a path home that doesn't go through the Mansion of Mirrors, I think that's the one I need to take . . . and I think that's what Sunni was trying to tell me with that drawing."

In the silence that follows, Lisa realizes she has been giving a monologue, and that makes her feel embarrassed. She closes her eyes and lets her head drop forward, bracing herself for when the two men, both far more experienced in life than her, will start picking apart her logic, lining up the flaws. Maybe they'll even laugh at her naivety and chalk it up to her age.

Nothing of the sort happens. Starck does ask her a question, but there's nothing condescending or accusatory in his voice.

"How sure are you?" he asks.

There's something eerily definitive about the words, and Lisa searches her heart before lifting her head to meet his gaze.

"Pretty. No. I'm *completely* sure. If there *is* another way home, then that's the one I need to take."

"But there *isn't*," Michael interjects. "If there were, don't you think we'd have taken it a long time ago?"

Lisa responds with a nod, but her gaze never drifts toward him. It remains fixed on Starck's shirt pocket—where she suspects another answer might be hidden. One bound in leather and bearing his initials.

Starck stares at her for a long time through the flames of the fire reflected in the lenses of his glasses.

"There *is* a way," he finally says. "But it's not one I would recommend. Nonetheless, I have to admit and respect that, in the end, I wasn't the one chosen to guide you."

Despite the answer being more or less what she had expected, Lisa still feels a flash of indignation at hearing him say it outright. Hearing him admit that the Guide Mirror he has been carrying in his pocket right from the start could have opened a portal back to their own world at any time. However, she also knows that's the wrong way to look at it.

"Wait a second," Michael says, pointing a finger at Starck. "Are you telling us that you could've sent us home whenever you felt like it? That all the shit we've been dragged through was just . . . what? For the heck of it?"

"That's not what I'm saying."

"Then explain it to me," Michael snaps, kicking at the ground at the edge of the fire, sending a cloud of embers swirling into the air. "Explain why the *fuck* we're only hearing about this now!"

He spits the last words out in a tone and rhythm that immediately make Lisa's stomach tighten. He sounds an awful lot like Tom. And the way he's glaring at Starck—with the same manic look she has seen in the psychopath's eyes more than once—doesn't help.

"Would you have taken it?" Starck asks. "Knowing what you know now, would you have taken it?"

"Would I . . . what? Oh, cut the cryptic bullshit! What the hell are you talking about?"

"I didn't offer you the way out," Starck continues, "because it never truly existed. And because I was afraid that you'd try to take it anyway. But tell me now: Would you have taken it? Looking back—with the knowledge you possess now—would you have accepted the mirror if I'd handed it to you?"

Lisa, fearing that these words might push Michael over the edge and drive him to actually take a swing at Starck, opens her mouth to suggest that they all take a deep breath. However, she doesn't get a single word out before Michael raises his hand and stops her.

"What the fuck is wrong with you, Starck?" he growls. "What kind of ridiculous question is that? That's not even the point. The point is we trusted you—and now we find out you've been lying to us from the start. And you know I'd walk across all of Urari a thousand times over if there's even the slightest chance that Benjamin is in the mansion. But what about Lisa, huh? Why did she have to be dragged through all of this crap? Explain to me why she had to—"

"BECAUSE YOU HAVE TO BE READY!"

Her own outburst takes Lisa so much by surprise that she instinctively claps a hand over her mouth. But it worked—the shock silences Michael and buys her the time to say what's on her mind.

"Because you have to be ready," she repeats more gently. "Starck said the Mansion of Mirrors is the way home, yes. But he also said it's just as much about being ready. Meaning ready to face the mirror when you go home."

She pauses for a moment—partly to find the right words, and partly to summon the courage to speak them.

"And that's what I am now. I'm ready to go home. No—I *have* to go home now. Even though I feel terrible about leaving you like this, I have to . . . and I hope you can find it in your heart to forgive me."

For a long time, Michael says nothing, but the tale of his inner conflict is clearly told through his eyes. He is fighting to suppress the anger in his gaze so that Lisa doesn't think it's aimed at her—while at the same time holding onto just enough of it to let Starck know that it's still there.

"There's nothing to forgive," he says. "I understand your decision, of course I do, and it's not you I'm angry with. You know that, right?"

Hearing his voice return to a more measured tone—even if it might only be for a moment—sends a wave of relief washing over Lisa. And when he puts a hand on her shoulder afterward, she can barely hold back her tears.

"When will you leave?" he asks. "Do we get a chance to let it sink in?"

"I'll go with you as far as I can, but if the mansion keeps gnawing at my brain, then . . ." She makes a circling motion with her finger in front of her temple. "I definitely need to be out of here before we can actually see it."

Michael nods and shifts his gaze back to Starck.

The content of the wordless exchange that plays out between the two men over the next couple of seconds is something Lisa will likely never get to know. Still, she feels fairly certain what Michael's eyes are saying—and why it prompts a solemn nod from Starck.

If you ever lie to us like that again . . .

When Michael finally lowers his gaze and instead turns to stare into the fire, Starck sits in silence for a moment. Then he lifts his hand to his shirt pocket, slips two fingers inside, and pulls out his Guide Mirror. He turns it slowly in his hands a couple of times before clearing his throat and looking at Lisa.

"Because I respect Sunni's decision as your guide, I'll give you my blessing to use my mirror. As long as you understand that there's no easy way back if you change your mind."

"I do," Lisa says. "And I accept that."

In the early hours of the third day after their conversation by the fire, Lisa opens her eyes and admires the growing dawn. She watches the daylight creeping in, adding a delicate pink glow to the white morning mist. And then, but a moment later, the mist is completely gone. It vanishes in the blink of an eye, leaving no visible trace behind. Had she not seen it, it would be as though it had never been there.

Thinking this, she realizes that something similar might soon be said about her, and that makes her feel a bit sad. God knows she is looking forward to going home, as her stay in Urari undoubtedly has brought some of the worst experiences of her life. It has, however, also saved her, in a way. That's not an unfair way of looking at it, because despite Sunni, despite Elias, and despite everything else, she is grateful. She has met Michael. Whether it's because they're empaths—which apparently is all the hype in Urari—she doesn't know, but what she does know is that he has understood and listened to her story in a way no one else ever has.

He has looked her in the eyes.

That thought still fresh in her mind, she turns over and looks at him. The sight that greets her feels so far from the prominent figure she had in her head that it makes her gasp. His half-open eyes are bloodshot and feverish. The face around them looks like a furrowed skull.

"Good morning," she says. "You don't look so good."

"You don't exactly look like a bubble bath either," Michael replies dryly as he looks around. "Where's Starck?"

"Finding something to eat, I think. Supplies are running low."

"And?" Michael shrugs. "Does it matter? He said we'll reach the mansion before sunset today. We can manage that, right?"

"Yeah, I . . . I guess. Are you still mad at him?"

"Why are you asking?"

"You've barely said a word to him since that night by the fire."

Michael turns his face toward her and raises one eyebrow. He doesn't argue, though.

"He didn't really lie to us," she goes on. "Not really. You know that, right? The mirror would've screwed with our heads, made us like Tom, if we'd tried to go home."

"That's what he says, yeah."

Neither the words nor the shrug that accompanies them seem particularly convincing, and Lisa realizes she will have to dig up something she'd rather not revisit if she wants to convince him.

"I never really told you what happened to me in the bathroom at the theater, did I?"

"No. I know it had something to do with the mirror, but beyond that . . ."

"It was the mirror, yeah. I was . . . trapped in it. It took me back to the night Emma killed my dad and let me relive it all. Left me standing on the bedroom floor between my dad on the bed, full of stab wounds, and my sister, who was sitting against the closet with, um . . . with blood running down her wrist because she took her own life with a kitchen knife."

"Holy fuck, Lisa, I . . . I don't know what to say."

Lisa shakes her head.

"I'm not telling you this to make you feel sorry for me. I'm telling you because I think it's important that you understand what the mirrors are capable of. If you guys hadn't been there back then, I don't think I would've made it out, and I think . . . no, I'm *sure* the same thing would've happened to us if we tried to go home using Starck's mirror. That's why I'm saying he didn't lie to us. And I also think it's important that you don't hold it against him when you move on without me. That you . . . have each other's backs, you know?"

Michael looks up at the sky for a moment, then takes a long breath, and releases it in a sigh.

"I hear what you're saying," he says.

As his gaze drops back down and meets hers, Lisa is relieved to see that it looks like he means it.

She leans forward to place a hand on his shoulder and thank him for listening to her but stops short as a sharp jolt of pain shoots through her left thigh.

Michael sees her wince and starts to get up, but she shakes her head.

"Don't worry," she groans, pressing her thumbs into the sore muscles. "It's just a cramp. My thighs aren't too happy about this hike."

That's the understatement of the year. Six days of hiking through the Wasteland's uneven terrain have turned her thigh muscles rock-hard, and it feels like she's trying to massage a lamppost. Her veins are swollen. She can feel them through the fabric of her jeans—like strands of spaghetti slipping away beneath her fingertips when she touches them.

Now, by chance, she feels something else beneath the fabric. Something she had forgotten all about.

She slips her hand into her pocket and pulls out a small silver chain. It's the bracelet Mary gave her when they left Baixa—the one with the clover charm that she fell in love with the moment she saw it in the shop window.

As she sits there, staring at it, it doesn't feel like it was a coincidence. It feels like this bracelet was always meant to be hers.

"Maybe it's time for a change of style," Michael suggests, pointing at the yellow and purple plastic rings around her wrist.

"They were my sister's."

"I know."

Lisa lets her gaze drop to her hand and realizes he's right. Thirteen months she has been wearing those colorful plastic rings around her wrist. Thirteen months without seeing them for what they really are.

Handcuffs.

Handcuffs that keep her chained to the past.

This realization gives her the strength to do what needs to be done—and determined to get it over with before her courage slips away, she places her hands on the ground and pushes herself up.

Fresh waves of pain flare up in her thighs with the first few steps, but she grits her teeth and pushes through, making her way on unsteady legs to the remnants of yesterday's fire. Once there, she starts taking off the rings. One by one, she pulls them from her wrist, and when she has freed them all, she extends her hand and holds them still in the air above the ashes for a moment.

Then she lets go.

When the time comes for Lisa's farewell, the three traveling companions find themselves in a gray, rocky landscape about ten miles south of the campsite. Even though Starck's wristwatch claims the afternoon has only just begun, the sky above them carries a dark, unsettling gray hue. The air almost crackles with electric tension. If you didn't know better, you would think a storm was brewing.

Lisa does know better. She knows the sudden change in the weather means that they've just crossed the border into what Starck calls the inner perimeter—the innermost of the circles surrounding the Mansion of Mirrors.

In just a few more miles, its outline will start to show on the horizon.

And this is where she has to say goodbye.

Maybe Starck has reached the same conclusion. At least, she can tell by the sound of his footsteps that he's picked up his pace to catch up with her.

"You're in a hurry," Lisa says as he reaches her. "Scared I was gonna run off?"

She intended this to be an innocent remark to lighten an otherwise tense mood—but when she sees the librarian's face, she wishes she'd kept it to herself.

That's exactly what he was afraid of, she thinks, shuddering as her gaze drifts past his shoulder and lands on Michael. *That I'd ignore him and just march on like some brain-dead zombie is exactly what he feared. And with good reason.*

"I feel it," she says. "It's still pulling at me, and it's getting worse. It's like . . ."

She hesitates, searching for the right word. When she finds it, a faint smile appears at the corner of her mouth.

"It's like my brain is caught on a fishhook. But don't worry. I've made my decision."

Starck stares at her solemnly and then takes her hand.

"Lisa Swann," he says. "When you get back home, you'll find that very little has changed in the world you left behind. As you know, time works differently in Urari, and although you've spent a long time here, it's likely only been a day or two for them. It can be difficult to wrap your head around at first, but I promise it gets easier. Just remember—you've fought hard for the life you're going back to . . . and you've earned it."

Slowly—and with a gravity that brings a lump to Lisa's throat—he opens her hand and places his mirror in her palm.

"When we see each other again, I hope it's about a problem with your library card." He smiles and shrugs. "What the heck, I could even live with it being about a book returned too late."

She takes a step forward and lets him embrace her. Resting her head against his chest, she breathes in a bittersweet scent of pine needles and dirt that reminds her of her grandfather.

Almost as if he's read this parallel in her thoughts, Starck gently kisses her hair—just like her grandpa used to do when she was little.

Now Michael joins them. He waits patiently in the background as Starck gives her one final nod and steps aside. Then he approaches her.

"Is it time?"

Lisa nods. It's all she's able to do.

"I'm going to miss you," he says. "I wish you didn't have to go."

And I wish you'd forget all about that damned mansion, Lisa thinks as she wraps her arms around his back. *Tom was right when he told you it's a dangerous place.*

That's what she thinks, but the words never make it past her lips—and as she feels him turning his head to glance toward the south during their embrace, she understands that it would've been a lost battle anyway.

"Thank you for everything, Michael," she whispers as she pulls away. "I hope you find Benjamin."

She feels his gaze searching for hers, but she turns her face away. Now, more than ever, she's afraid of making eye contact. Afraid of where those deep, marine-blue eyes might take her to if she dared to meet them.

"Goodbye, gentlemen," she says, staring down at the mirror, where the familiar glowing threads are already emerging behind the glass. "I can honestly say you have put my prejudices about boring librarians and schoolteachers to shame."

This makes them both smile—and their smiles are the last thing Lisa sees before the blinding white light rises from the center of the mirror and pulls her away from Urari.

88

For a while, they stand there in silence, watching as Lisa's translucent, ghost-like silhouette fades away. Starck's thumbs are hooked behind his belt. He looks like a man who could stand there just like that well into the next age.

But then, as soon as the last afterglow is gone, he steps forward, bends down, and picks up his mirror. Once he has tucked it back into his pocket, he tightens the strap on his backpack and turns his gaze south.

He doesn't start walking, though—and when Michael does, he grabs his arm and stops him.

"Do we need to clear the air before we move on?"

Michael, caught a bit off guard by the question, stares at him for a long moment before shaking his head.

"No. But no more secrets. If there's anything I need to know, you tell me now. Understood?"

This time, it's Starck's turn to think before answering. And when he does answer, Michael feels the hairs on the back of his neck stand up.

"You'll get your ending," Starck says. "But I can't promise you it'll be a happy one. That's the only truth left to tell."

Michael nods and shifts his pack from his left shoulder to his right. The backpack is nearly empty by now, but even so, its weight makes him groan and wince.

"That's all?"

"That's all. I promise."

With those words, the two travelers resume their harsh pilgrimage. The first few miles are tough, making Michael's spine feel like it's been wrapped in barbed wire, but after a couple of hours on the move, the worst of the stiffness has left his body. He starts to walk faster—and when the outline of the mansion begins to take shape in the distance, he no longer walks. He jogs.

It's straight ahead; a misty constellation of towers and spires, floating like an optical illusion above the bleak, sprawling horizon. Slowly, it takes shape and becomes the gray-black structure he first saw depicted in a mural on a wall in Elias and Mary's backyard.

And the resemblance *is* striking. Everything about the shadowy mansion seems to match Sunni's painting perfectly.

The tall, dark towers rise above the structure, casting long shadows across the landscape on either side of the staircase leading up to the entrance gate, just as they did in Sunni's picture. The two statues stand at the foot of the stairs in the same pose they had in the mural; crouched, with their hands held up in front of their faces, as if they're mirroring each other and fearing what they see.

There is, however, one detail the young artist didn't fully capture in his version—though there was a hint of it. Back when Michael stood with his hand on the mural in the backyard, he felt a reluctance toward visiting the mansion. It was something he wouldn't have been able to explain at the time.

He is now.

The Mansion of Mirrors is alive. It's as simple as that. It's alive, and he can feel its awareness reaching out from the black eye sockets of its windows. All at once, knowing that he has to step inside overwhelms him with terror.

He looks over at Starck, their eyes meet, and they understand each other.

"Do you see it now?"

Michael nods. It has taken a journey to another world, a war, the death of two new friends, and six grueling days of trekking through the Wasteland—but yes, he thinks he gets it now.

No one can promise him a happy ending, and *no one* can guarantee he'll get to see his son again.

As they stand there in the barren, lead-gray landscape, where nothing moves, Starck sets down his backpack and reaches out his hand. Michael looks down at his own dirty palm, wipes it on his shirt, and then takes it.

"This is your stop?"

"I'm afraid so."

"But you'll wait out here, right?"

"I'll make camp here and wait for you as long as I can, yes." Starck hesitates, then adds, "I wish it didn't have to be this way, but . . ."

"You're a guide," Michael finishes for him. "And guides have no business going into the mansion. You don't need to explain. I already met one former guide who'd been in there. One of Crane's kind is enough. Besides, you kept your promise. You brought me here."

"Guess that's true," Starck replies. "Then I just hope that damned mansion gives you what you're looking for."

"It always does . . . isn't that what you say?"

A faint smile crosses the librarian's lips, but behind the lenses of his glasses, the seriousness, as always, remains. More than ever in this moment.

"Well, would you look at that," he says. "Seems you were paying attention after all."

"More than you think . . . and I *am* ready now."

Starck stares at him for a long moment, then nods.

"Guess you'd better get going before the last of the daylight disappears."

Michael smiles as he slowly begins to loosen his grip on Starck's hand.

"Thank you for everything, Erik."

"You're welcome, Michael. Hold on to yourself in there."

"I will."

Such is their farewell, and once it's said, Starck remains where he stands beneath the pale, tattered sky, while Michael begins his walk toward the uncertain fate that awaits him behind the dark windows of the Mansion of Mirrors.

PART ELEVEN
YOU'LL GET YOUR ENDING

THE MIRROR

Hinges screech, and thin flakes of rust fall from their cylinders as Michael wraps his fingers around the door handle and pushes open the massive oak door to the Mansion of Mirrors.

In front of him, a long, shadowy corridor stretches. A few torches cast a dim glow on the sloping ceiling, but it's only just enough to outline the contours of the space.

The air in here is nauseatingly heavy. He can feel its damp caress against his cheeks as it brushes past his face. It carries with it a smell that, for a moment, takes him back to the flooded cellar at his grandparents' farm, filling his nostrils with the stench of rotting beams and stale water.

Beneath that smell lies another. Warm, claustrophobic, and earthy . . . the scent of an animal's den.

Reluctantly, yet with a strangely calm acceptance of the inevitable, he steps across the threshold and listens for what he knows will come. And it does. Slowly, it rises from the darkness; a low, grating hum of voices chanting in a forgotten tongue.

They're the voices of the mirrors, and despite countless nightmares having prepared him for them, they still make his heart pound madly against his ribs. There's something in those voices that no nightmare could have prepared him for. A threat so primal that reason cannot grasp it, and instinct can only barely sense its raw, unforgiving nature.

As he approaches the end of the corridor, the door that must be the entrance to the hall of mirrors comes into view. It's slightly ajar, and from the narrow gap between the door and its frame spills a beam of dusty, bluish light.

Once he has reached the door, he stops and concentrates on listening.

The voices are louder now. There's no doubt that who—or what—they're coming from is somewhere in there.

He braces himself and pushes the door with the tip of his shoe. Slowly, it swings open, revealing the inside of the Mansion of Mirrors.

Just like in his dreams, the dark hall is lit by a single beam of moonlight. It's pouring down through a skylight, casting an eerie, ghostlike glow over the endless rows of sheet-covered mirrors.

He stands still for a moment, studying the first row of small bronze plaques hanging between the furniture legs beneath the sheets. None of them bear the name that now escapes his lips—halfway as a sob, halfway as a whisper.

"Benjamin?"

The hall accepts the name and answers with a few seconds of deep silence. Out of that silence grows a new sound. A high-pitched chirping that could almost be a child's laughter—if it wasn't for the ominous, dissonant undertone. In many ways, it's the kind of sound you'd expect to hear behind the barred windows of an asylum.

With fear crawling through his nervous system on spider legs, Michael follows the sound and steps into one of the narrow aisles between the mirrors. Cautious steps carry him from one row to the next, and as he reaches the nineteenth, he finally locates the source of the unsettling giggling.

The dark figure is kneeling, eyes fixed on the floor. The shoulders—thankfully, a man's shoulders, not a child's—hang limply on either side of his bowed head. On the ground in front of him lie hundreds of tiny shards of shattered glass, glinting in the moonlight like freshly fallen snow.

Michael gasps as his gaze drifts up to the empty mirror frame at the figure's right side. Engraved on the small bronze plaque beneath the frame are six letters:

Isabel.

As though he has heard his daughter's name in Michael's thoughts, the hollow shell of what was once Crane lifts his head, allowing the moonlight to chase the shadows from his face. He stares at Michael with eyes full of helpless confusion. There's no sign of recognition in his gaze, no trace of the excitement that once lit up those dark pupils.

A part of Michael understands that the mansion has extinguished that spark forever. Still, he takes a step forward. Then another.

A sharp crack sounds as one of the shards gives way beneath his shoe and breaks under the pressure. He wants Crane to hear it. He wants to provoke a reaction . . . a confrontation.

It's in vain. The pale man simply continues to study his intrusive guest with a look of mild curiosity. Shortly after, he loses interest and turns his attention back to the shattered mirror on the floor.

And then—as if to tell Michael that there are more important things to attend to—the low, grating murmur of the voices returns.

Despite each individual voice in the chorus barely being

louder than a breath, he is able to sense a movement in the sound. It's like listening to an invisible crowd of people passing him by on their way toward the center of the hall.

Haunted by the same slow-building dread that has plagued his dreams of the mansion, he turns his back on Crane and begins walking toward the voices. The sound of glass shards breaking beneath his soles accompanies his first few steps, but he doesn't look back to see if it makes an impression this time.

Row upon row of burgundy shadows glide past the edges of his vision as he makes his way through the narrow aisles between the mirrors. Every so often, the worn fabric of the sheets brushes against his elbows, and each time it makes him flinch. Fear still has its grip on him, and only the clear sense that the voices will lead him to the right mirror allows him to keep it in check.

And they're still there. Though the sound of the chorus has softened to a low, drowsy hum—like that of a high-voltage cable—it's constant, and each step brings him closer to the place it's coming from.

You'll get your ending, Starck's voice whispers like a distant echo in the back of his mind as he steps into the cold glow of the moonlight and catches his first glimpse of the mirror he has been searching for, for so long. *But I can't promise it'll be a happy one.*

Twelve, maybe thirteen rows farther ahead it stands. One among hundreds of identical mirrors, all covered with dusty, burgundy sheets—and yet, he knows instinctively that this is the one.

The sense of déjà vu is overwhelming as he walks the final stretch to the mirror, where the plaque bearing Benjamin's name emerges from the shadows between the furniture legs.

Very slowly, he lifts his hand and reaches toward the sheet. As he grips the soft fabric and pulls, a cloud of tiny white dust particles swirls into the air, enveloping him in a glittering, frost-white world.

It's through this he sees them.

Benjamin's deep, blue eyes.

Like an old-fashioned photograph emerging in a tray of developer, they appear behind the dust's deceptive veil—and for a moment, the sight of them has Michael hoping for the happy ending that Starck didn't dare promise him.

In a just world, it would have ended there. In a just world, this moment—this merciful split second, if you will—would have been the last, and the story would have found its ending while the portrait being painted behind the glass was still incomplete.

But.

The world isn't always just, and the portrait *is* completed. It ends in a close-up of the boy's face and then slowly transforms into a cinematic scene, in which the camera zooms out to reveal that the boy is sitting in the back seat of a vehicle.

In the rear window behind him, gray posts of a guardrail blur past. Something about them feels both familiar and disquieting to Michael. However, before he has time to dwell on it, a woman's voice emerges inside his head.

"What was going on with Jane?" the voice asks as the camera behind the mirror's glass shifts to the hands on the steering wheel, revealing that both the voice and the point of view belong to the woman driving the car.

The landscape flickering past outside the vehicle suddenly makes everything click into place for Michael—and now the cold hands of panic start to close around his throat.

The vehicle is on the Haywood Bridge. The voice belongs to Ann, the boy is Benjamin, and they—*oh God*—they're on the bridge. If this is what he fears it is, then, in less than five minutes, he's going to witness the traffic accident that took everything from him.

"Thomas broke her hairband," the boy replies, and before his mom can respond, he adds, "And it wasn't an accident, Mom. He's always picking on her. It really sucks."

The camera shifts focus to the boy's face in the rearview mirror. He looks sad.

"I'll have a word with Kirsten about it tomorrow," the woman's voice says. "Then she'll have to talk to him again, and if that doesn't work—"

"The school will talk to his parents," the boy finishes for her. "I know!"

On the other side of the windshield, something red and white dances past. It's the windsock that marks the end of the bridge . . . which means they're nearing the forest where the accident will happen.

Michael never actually saw the wreckage—it had already been cleared by the time he got there—but he did see the tree that they hit. He saw the way the bark was ripped apart, and he saw the scorched grass in front of the tree where the car had come to rest.

"Can I play when we get home?" the boy asks, apparently deciding that the conversation about the school bully has run its course.

"Depends. Homework?"

Ever since Benjamin got his PlayStation, that conversation was a daily ritual. And when the boy in the mirror—as always—responds by rolling his eyes and letting out an exasperated sigh, the ache of missing him cuts so deep in Michael's heart that it nearly breaks him.

He doesn't get the chance to dwell on the pain, though, because over the hills ahead, the first dark-green treetops start to appear. At the speed they're going, that means the car will reach its final destination in less than a minute.

Since there were no witnesses to the accident, Michael can't know for sure, but he always imagined that they were forced off the road by an animal that had accidentally wandered onto the highway. So, he holds his breath and focuses on watching the road, silently willing his wife to do the same.

But Ann doesn't watch the road. Instead, she grabs the rearview mirror and turns it toward herself.

As the pupils of her green eyes come into focus behind the glass, Michael is struck by a strange, trembling sensation. He just —and only just—has time to realize it's the same feeling he had in the library office when his eyes met Lisa's, before the world explodes in a dazzling bloom of silent, white light.

The next thing he sees behind the mirror's glass is a rapid stream of fragmented images flashing past. It's as if the invisible force within the mirror has decided to fast-forward the film. He sees the front of the car veering right, despite the hands on the wheel fighting to pull it left. He sees the hood crumple against the tree trunk, while the camera appears to be flung into the windshield. It cracks the glass and then slams down onto the dashboard, where it stays. Now, there's nothing left to see in the mirror's surface but the textured gray plastic of the dashboard and the lower edge of the passenger-side window.

From the small slats in the air vent, a thick, dark gray smoke starts to seep out. It takes on an eerie orange-red glow as the engine catches fire with a sharp hiss.

From the back seat, another sound: a short, croaking cough.
He is alive.

Despair crashes over Michael, so sudden and so overwhelming that his legs nearly buckle beneath him.

He is alive! Ann, for God's sake, help him! Benjamin is alive!

He tries to scream, tries to force the words out so they can cross time and space and reach his wife in time, but his throat tightens as if he's the one trapped in the car, choking on the smoke. Meanwhile, precious seconds turn into life-or-death minutes while the camera doesn't move an inch.

Why are you showing me this? What is it you want from me?

Even though part of him already knows the answer to that question—and, in a way, has known it since the moment they crossed the border into the Wasteland—Michael still jolts when he feels the touch of the entity that lives inside the mirror. It's inside his head in a split-second, and it's strong. He can feel its presence, its invisible claws scratching and tearing at the frayed seams holding his sanity together.

And as the threads begin to break, the mirror does the same. Tiny cracks shoot out and spread across the glass like the root system of a massive tree.

A second later, the first shard of glass breaks free from the mirror's frame. It hits the floor with a crack that seems to echo through the entire hall. More shards follow, and before long, the mirror's entire pane lies scattered across the floor at his feet.

That's the only answer he gets. It's wordless, but it doesn't matter. Michael has met Tom, he has seen Crane, and he fully understands what the mansion is offering him.

And a part of him wants to accept it. A part of him wants to forget.

You can't ask that of me. It's not fair.

His gaze is fixed on the shattered glass on the floor, but it's no longer the mirror he is speaking to. This time, the words—as they often are when people in despair hurl such accusations—are directed at God. Directed at the almighty father figure whose existence he has spent most of his adult life trying to disprove in the name of psychology.

Because there isn't supposed to be a choice. The mansion is supposed to either give him back his son or take away his sanity. That's how it has always played out in his mind when he imagined the final act of this drama—and that's how it should be. Free will isn't supposed to be part of the equation.

Only now, as he hears them again, does Michael realize that the voices in the hall have been silent ever since he uncovered the mirror. Now, the choir is back, and a chill runs down his spine when he notices that the eerie chanting has changed.

It's no longer a jumble of incoherent whispers from different voices. They've merged into a single voice. One unified chorus, all repeating the fateful question Crane asked him when they first met:

"Are you Michael Bendixen?"

At his feet, the glass shards start to glow with a faint, pulsing light, rising and falling in sync with the rhythm of the chorus. In a way, there's something calming about it. It's like watching the sound of a heartbeat.

"Married to Ann Bendixen?"

In a slow, hesitant motion, Michael sinks to his knees. Somewhere on the edge of his awareness, he feels a sharp pain shoot through his thighs as they take on the full weight of his exhausted body, but it feels distant, irrelevant.

"Father of Benjamin Bendixen?"

With fingers that seem to have lost all feeling, he reaches out and picks up one of the nearest shards of glass. It rests facedown in his hands. He holds it like that for a long, quiet moment before turning it over—and for the first time since arriving in Urari, he's confronted with the reflection of his own face.

He looks like something out of a nightmare. His hair hangs in matted clumps over his forehead where grief and exhaustion have carved a web of deep, furrowed lines. Grime clings to the stubble on his cheeks, and dark brown stains—very possibly dried blood—mark his neck and the collar of his shirt.

In the cold glow of the moonlight, all these details tell the story of his unraveling with haunting clarity. Yet nothing frightens him more than the one thing that remains unchanged behind the glass.

The eyes. They look so much like Benjamin's, and it's in them that he finally sees—and grasps—the full meaning of the words Tom said to him back in the theater.

For the rambling vagabond was right. The real hell isn't a land of fire beneath the ground. The real hell is a hall full of mirrors. Except in Michael's case, it won't be a hall—it'll be a *life* full of mirrors. A life where he'll be haunted by his son's deep blue eyes every single time he is face-to-face with his own reflection.

In that realization lies the deepest sorrow he has ever known. But it's also what suddenly makes everything crystal clear to him.

He knows what he has to do.

With great care, he returns the glass shard to the floor. This time, he places it face-up, and before turning away, he steals one last glance at the eyes behind the glass. The stubbornly pulsing glow has gathered around them now, and he allows himself only a brief moment to look at them. He knows that he'd be unable to tear his gaze away otherwise . . . and then, the choice would be made for him after all.

The sheet lies crumpled in the shadows next to the empty mirror frame. As he grabs its corners and starts to pull it over the mirror, part of him is terrified that the light will flare up again or that he'll hear panic in the voices.

That doesn't happen. On the contrary, both the light and the voices seem to fade away as he covers the mirror—and when it's done, the hall is completely silent.

He stays there for a few minutes with his hands clenched between his thighs, waiting for his emotions to settle. Then, feeling a bit calmer, he stands up and starts to walk back.

As he makes his way through the narrow paths between the mirrors, he once again passes the spot where Crane sits. This time, he also pauses and takes a few steps closer—but when he does, he is surprised to find he no longer desires a confrontation. His anger, his hatred, and his thirst for revenge all seem to have vanished along with the whispering voices. Looking at the pale man with the empty stare now only makes him feel sorry for him.

"Crane?"

Nothing.

"Crane?"

Still nothing.

Maybe the third time would have been the charm, and maybe Michael would have reached out his hand if Crane had answered, or even just reacted to the sound of his name. Maybe he would've helped him up and told him that it's over now—for both of them. That the dead deserve to rest in peace. Maybe he'd even have dragged him out if he refused to let go of his impossible jigsaw puzzle on the floor.

Maybe he would.

Maybe.

In the end, though, there is no third time, and there is no response from Crane, so, Michael leaves the hall alone, hearing nothing but the sound of his own heavy footsteps.

How much time he has actually spent inside the mansion doesn't dawn on Michael until he steps back out into the corridor that brought him there.

At the far end, the large oak door is still open, and through it he can see the morning sun casting a blinding, violet glow over the rocky landscape where he and Starck said their goodbyes.

And the librarian is still there. He is crouching in front of a campfire that looks like it's just about to go out. When he spots Michael, he stands up, waves, and starts walking toward him.

As the two men draw closer to each other, it becomes harder and harder for Michael to keep himself together—and when only a few feet remain between them, the tears can no longer be held back.

He tries to wipe them away with his torn sleeve, but they stream down his cheeks in an unstoppable flow. Tired, hopeless tears that break the world into prisms and make him stumble forward helplessly.

Starck catches him and pulls him into a tight embrace.

"I know," he whispers. "I know."

PART TWELVE
THE GIRL ON THE BENCH

EPILOGUE

In the yard outside Oakwood High School, a massive oak tree stands as a majestic centerpiece. On a bench in front of that tree, Lisa Swann sits. She's the same girl one might have seen sitting there six months earlier . . . and yet, she's not. A lot has changed.

Her hair is different. It's freshly cut and no longer hangs like a half-drawn theater curtain hiding her face from the world. The heavy black eyeliner is gone too. It has been replaced by a soft blush on her cheeks that brings out her smile. The colorful yellow and purple plastic bracelets that used to sit on her left wrist are also gone. In their place hangs a silver chain with a small clover charm that glints in the sunlight.

Behind the blonde girl, a window opens with a metallic scrape. She turns and smiles when she sees her history teacher's face behind the glass.

"You're up in just a moment," says the gray-haired woman behind the window, her voice carrying the melodic tone her students have come to recognize as her trademark. "It's getting pretty crowded in there."

"Thanks, Bridget," Lisa says, placing her hands on the cracked surface of the wooden bench and pushing herself up.

She starts walking toward the door leading into the school auditorium but then hesitates when she realizes that the face behind the window is still there.

"I think what you're doing is really brave," the teacher says as their eyes meet. "Just thought you should know that."

Lisa feels the warmth rise in her cheeks—but she doesn't lower her gaze as she says thank you.

She also doesn't lower it a few minutes later when she steps up to the podium set up for today's school assembly.

She is tempted. The crowd—which on the crumpled paper in her pocket is faceless—stares at her in a challenging silence, and part of her wants to look away before they do.

Yet she doesn't. She meets their eyes—and that's where the biggest contrast between the new Lisa and the old one lies. The new Lisa doesn't flinch from their gaze. And to her relief, she finds that they don't flinch from hers either.

That's how she wants it. She wants their eye contact, and she wants their attention. Because she has something to say. She has a job to do.

The microphone crackles as she taps it like they do in the movies, and aside from a bit of whispering in the far corner, the sounds in the auditorium fade away.

"Yeah, um . . . hi," she says, clearing her throat. "I'm Lisa Swann. Some of you know me already, but to a lot of you, I'm probably just that annoying girl who cut in line and grabbed the last piece of the lasagna that Ursula and the cafeteria girls served last Wednesday. For that, I apologize."

She practiced that opening, and she's pleased to see several faces in the audience light up with a smile. One of them actually belongs to Ursula from the cafeteria.

"I'm not up here to talk about lasagna, though. I'm here to talk about something much more serious. I'm here to talk about death."

A murmur spreads through the rows, but that was to be expected, and it doesn't throw her off. At the very least, she has their attention now.

"It sounds a bit harsh when you say it that directly, I know. But I also know it's a problem that death is such a taboo. That's why I want to talk about the group that me and some of my friends have been working on the past few months. You've probably seen the posters. We've plastered them all over the bulletin boards."

She points, guiding the audience's attention down to the large bulletin board next to the glass doors at the far end of the room. On it hangs the poster she wants them to see. It's too far away for her to read the text herself, but she hears someone in the front row whisper the headline: *Look Death in the Eyes*.

"The Empaths—that's what we call us—is a group of young people who all have one thing in common. We've lost someone close to us. We also have in common that we've felt the wall of silence that starts to build around you when you've been touched by death. We know it's never because of ill intent that the friends you used to talk to about everything suddenly can't meet your eyes anymore. Still doesn't make it hurt any less, though. That's why we're hoping that by starting this support group, we can help break the taboo around death while also creating a safe space where people can show up and talk to others who have been in the same boat."

Out of the corner of her eye, Lisa notices a figure quietly tiptoeing up to the edge of the stage and placing something on the floor next to the podium.

The silent delivery is a bottle of water. It's accompanied by a wink from a pair of deep, marine-blue eyes and a smile—one that Lisa takes the time to return before shifting her attention back to the audience and saying:

"The time after a loss is already hard to get through. And if you don't have anyone to talk to about it, it can easily end with you giving up and shutting yourself off from the world. That's what happened to me. For a long time after I lost my dad and my sister, I felt completely cut off from everything around me. It wasn't until about six months ago, when I met someone who actually listened to my story, that I started to feel better. He was grieving too. At first, I thought that was what made it easier for me to open up . . . but I'm not so sure anymore. I think what really made the difference was that I finally pulled myself together and let go of the fear. Looking people in the eye when you're grieving is insanely hard—because in a lot of ways, it's like staring into a mirror that only reflects all the things that hurt the most. But that's only how it feels at first. With every time you do it, it slowly starts to get easier."

This is an important point, so Lisa lets it linger in the air for a moment while she picks up the water bottle from the floor and takes a few sips. The water is cold and refreshing, but it also makes her realize just how dry her throat is. The moment is approaching, fast, and she can feel the nerves starting to settle in.

"It gets easier," she repeats. "That's the claim I want to prove, and it's why I agreed to stand up here today. I'm here to tell my story. It's not an easy story to listen to, and it's still not an easy story for me to tell, but I want to show everyone—those of you who've experienced loss firsthand as well as those watching from the sidelines, seeing a friend in pain—that there *is* a path leading to the other side of even the worst tragedies. What that path looks like, and how hard it is to walk it, obviously varies. But I truly believe that it always starts in the same place. It starts with eye contact . . . and so, I hope you'll give me yours today."

Her pulse quickens, and a wave of anxiety rolls over her as she realizes that this last sentence was the cue. She tries to spot Ursula from the cafeteria again, but the real trial has already begun, and all the faces are vanishing behind a blurry, white fog.

This is it, she thinks, once again fighting the impulse to lower her gaze. *This is the moment Sunni wanted to prepare you for.*

Her heart pounds against her ribs like a desperate bird, her throat feels like sandpaper, and for a terrifying moment, she is not sure that she is able to go through with what she came here to do.

But then she sees her.

The dark-haired girl sits on the floor beneath the window on the left side of the auditorium. Her back is against the radiator, ankles crossed in front of her. There's no one around her. In a room full of people, she is completely alone. Everything about her—her clothes, her hair, the crossed arms, the lowered gaze—claims that her solitude is by choice. Yet Lisa knows it's a lie.

And that's where she finds the strength to go on.

THE END

Other Novels by Per Jacobsen

Strung (2021)

Strung II: The Valley of Death (2022)

Strung III: The Last Drop (2022)

The Rude Awakening of Theodor Moody (2023)

Dry (2023)

Rose's Story (2024)

25 Days (2024)

Printed in Dunstable, United Kingdom